STUPID BOY
The Beginning

A Stupid Boy Story

G YOUNGER

Stupid Boy: The Beginning

A Stupid Boy Story

First edition. December 1, 2017

ISBN-13: 9781973441298

Author: Greg Younger

Chief Editor: Bud Ugly

Editors: Chipster82 and BlackIrish

Table of Contents:

Chapter 1 – Change Does a Body Good

Monday August 26

I woke to the sound of my bedroom window rattling. Was someone breaking in? A flash of lightning almost blinded me as it lit up my room. I waited several seconds and then the rumble of thunder rolled in. Rain began to pelt the roof and the wind started to gust as a black wall of clouds moved in to blot out the morning sun. The weather fit my mood: I felt depressed. It didn't help that my head was pounding. I always seemed to get a headache when a cold front came through due to the change in barometric pressure.

I looked at the clock by my bed and the neon-blue numbers said it was 6:59. I knew I had something important to do today, but for a moment I couldn't get the fog out of my mind. I wasn't a morning person, but something told me I needed to get up. I heard my mom holler at my brother and me.

"Get your butts out of bed, you have school today."

There was another flash of lightning and much quicker rumble. The storm was getting closer. My first day of high school and I was going to get drenched running to the bus.

I heard my older brother get to the bathroom before I did. Great, he was worse than having a sister. He would hog the bathroom until it was time to go. We shared a bathroom between our two rooms. To heck with it, I had to pee. When I heard the shower start, I walked into a wall of steam that escaped from the shower. My brother Greg jerked the shower curtain back. His dark brown hair was plastered to his head and I saw his blue-gray eyes communicate my impending doom.

"You flush it and you die."

My evil grin made him nervous. The plumbing in our home was terrible. We live in an old Victorian-style house, circa 1925. Our neighborhood had been the upscale section of town back in the day. Over the years, many of these large homes had gone into disrepair.

In the mid-2000s a revival came when the housing boom occurred. These old Victorians had a lot of square footage and natural wood floors under layers of carpet and padding. It became very profitable to buy and flip them. My mom, being in real estate, saw the potential and talked Dad into buying this one. For the past ten years, we had worked on this home to bring it back to its former glory. The plumbing was from a renovation in the 1960s. Obviously, they hadn't done a very good job. If you flushed the toilet, the shower would go scalding hot.

"What are you going to do for me if I don't?" I challenged my big brother.

"I'll make this easy for you: I won't beat your butt!"

Well now, he thought he was a tough guy today. I loved pulling his chain, but I needed a favor. I was in no mood for the bus, so I got a serious look.

"The last time we wrestled, I won. I'm not really all that scared. You'll have to make me a better offer."

Since mid-spring, I had hit my growth spurt. I grew a little over six inches and put on thirty pounds. I was now over six feet tall and 185 pounds. My brother was three years older, five-ten and 175 pounds. On Saturday, I caught him unaware and tackled him from behind. It was a game that we'd played since we were little boys. To our mother's bewilderment we had fallen right back into it when I came home. I'd reached for his wrist to try to put him into a submission hold. Luckily, I had grabbed his thumb. As I bent it back, he squealed like a little girl. I held on for dear life, knowing if he broke free, I was dead. To my surprise, he surrendered. This was my first clear victory in almost a year. I felt it necessary to gloat.

Greg started to step out of the shower and I decided to try another strategy.

"Hang on. I don't want to have to wrestle you into submission, especially with you all wet and *naked!*"

The naked comment slowed him down. He knew I would kick him in the balls if it looked like I would get my ass kicked.

"Why don't you just agree to give me a ride to school today, since it's raining?"

Greg knew that Mom would make him take me anyway, so he smirked and said, "Okay."

I'd just gotten home from my summer of internment the previous Friday. It felt good to fall back into my relationship with Greg. I'd missed him.

Two weeks before summer vacation started, I talked some friends into a party. I'd started to hang out with a wilder crowd and drifted away from my friends. I found an empty house. Actually, I used my mom's realtor website to find a foreclosure. If they ever found out, she could get into serious trouble. I jimmied the lock on the back door to break in. This house didn't have any neighbors, which made it perfect for our needs. I turned on the water and power so we'd be comfortable.

I wasn't sure why, but I was out of control. Here I was in middle school, and I'd broken into a home so my crew could have a party. Just a few months ago, this would have been unthinkable. I had good friends and a stable family life. However, I found myself depressed. When I got stoned and drunk it made me numb so I wouldn't have to face my inner demons.

There were rumors that mental illness ran on my mom's side of the family. I sometimes wonder if I might have similar issues. Mom was a great example. She seemed to have no filters. Whatever was on her mind, she'd say. I know it bothered her when she hurt someone's feelings, but she did make life interesting. When I started to drink, I wasn't sure if it was because something was wrong, or just normal teenage angst.

On the night in question, one of the girls, Lily Harris, was drunk and passed out. She was a cute little pixie. Because of her size, she had a hard time keeping up when we all started to drink hard, so I wasn't too concerned when I saw her drooling in a corner. I did check every now and then to make sure no one molested her. There were a few people at the party I didn't trust. Then one of the girls screamed. I looked over and Lily's lips were a pale blue. All the color had drained from her face and she looked dead. There was bedlam as teens scattered.

My dad was in charge of Parks and Recreation for our town and had taught my brother and me CPR. The training kicked in. I checked her and found she wasn't breathing. I detected a pulse so I worked to clear her airway, and found vomit had blocked it. I turned her on her side and slid two fingers into her mouth to clean the worst of it out. I gagged and almost puked on her. I have a hair-trigger gag reflex when I either saw or smelled puke. I breathed through my mouth so I couldn't smell it. She still wasn't breathing after I cleared her throat. That meant that she had it in her lungs. I turned her on her side and with the flat of my hand, I beat on her back between her ribs.

"You're hurting her!" Sharon Riley yelled.

I felt her try to pull me off Lily. After the fifth time I hit her on the back, Lily coughed and I heard her suck in a huge breath. I made sure she was breathing before I rolled her back into my lap. The color returned to her face and her lips went back to being pink. I started to cry and rock her in my arms. Bill Rogers pulled Sharon out the door. He gave me a look that said, 'Keep your mouth shut!'

When the police arrived, Lily seemed to come to for a moment. The cops decided I was up to no good, so they cuffed me. They had me sit Indian style while the paramedics rushed in. I told them what I'd done to clear her airway, and that she'd stopped breathing. They put an oxygen mask on her, loaded her on a gurney, and rushed her out.

I probably would have gotten out of any trouble but I refused to tell the cops who all had been at the party and how we got in. Luckily, I was smart enough to keep my mouth shut. It was my idea and I'd broken into the house. The detective was persuasive when he pointed out that they'd all abandoned Lily and me.

All I thought about was the last image of Lily strapped to the gurney as the ambulance door closed. The 'what ifs' about killed me. What if I hadn't wanted to have a party? What if I'd paid more attention? My mind went in circles with one conclusion: my actions had injured a 14-year-old girl. Hell, Lily might be dead by now.

The good boy in me wanted to tell the police everything. The smart boy, the one in charge of self-preservation, kept me quiet. It wasn't because I was scared what the other kids would think. It wasn't even that I was scared of Bill. Truth was... he did scare me. I kept quiet because I knew if all the facts came out, my mom would catch some of the flak. If it were just me, I would have told them.

Since the police didn't know I was the instigator, they only charged me with underage drinking. I was positive they went light on me once they confirmed I assisted in helping Lily. The district attorney dropped the charges a week later. It turned out Lily was fine. She had a minor case of alcohol poisoning and they kept her in the hospital overnight, mostly for observation. When I learned that, I showed no emotions. Later that night I cried myself to sleep with relief.

Of course, my parents got involved and Mom flipped out. She said I was no longer the son she thought she knew. She wasn't sure she wanted me to come home. My heart broke; it was the darkest time in my short life. I was sure I would end up out on the streets.

It was obvious I'd ruined every significant relationship in my life. My best friend wouldn't talk to me. My old friends kept their distance. My new crew was afraid I would rat them out. My family was ready to disown me. At that point, Dad stepped in and decided I would go to my uncle's farm for the summer. My uncle needed some help, and Dad figured if I was stuck 10 miles from the nearest town I wouldn't have a chance to get into any further mischief.

What I didn't know was my Uncle John had a degree in child psychology. I just thought he was a farmer. With a combination of hard work and long talks, I began to pull my life back together. We put in new fences around several pastures. I used a posthole digger for the duration of the summer. At the end of each ten-hour day, I was exhausted. I was sure there were child labor laws, but who was I going to tell? In the first two weeks, I decided he wanted to kill me. I had never been so sore in all my life. Each night I would force myself to eat dinner and shortly thereafter, I would collapse in my bed.

The funny thing was the last week before I came home I'd looked for something in the barn. I found an attachment to the tractor for drilling postholes! When I got my uncle and showed him, he just laughed at me. At the time, I didn't think it was funny.

Uncle John helped me get back on track. He made me realize I had turned into someone I didn't really like. He treated me like a new colt. His gentle, assured approach seemed to calm me. I was full of hate and self-loathing. My first reaction was to blame everyone but myself. It took me nearly a week before Uncle John and I said ten words to each other. Suddenly the dam broke and I spent a day crying and telling him everything. Once I realized I didn't like myself, it was easy to figure out I wanted to change. Uncle John spent the rest of the summer helping me work towards those changes. I was still trying to figure out who I was going to be, but I was now confident I could become a better person. I owed that man my life.

The other good thing was between my growth spurt and my sadistic uncle working me ten hours a day, I had turned all my baby fat into muscle. My body had undergone a transformation. Uncle John called it a metamorphosis. Just as a tadpole transforms into a frog, I was changing. I was no longer a short, slightly pudgy nerd. I was now very lean with a narrow waist, but my chest, shoulders, biceps and thighs had gotten noticeably bigger. A posthole digger works your whole body. My frame had a nice V-shape.

The transformation wasn't only my outward physical appearance; I had grown a lot emotionally. Uncle John helped give me the tools to cope. I no longer felt the need for alcohol or drugs. He also taught me a lot about personal responsibility. Did I still have a touch of depression now and then? Yes, of course, but Uncle John gave me the tools to get myself out of my funk.

When I got home the thing that helped the most was Greg. He acted as if I'd never left. We spent Saturday and Sunday just hanging out. This was kind of a big deal. When Greg dated someone, we rarely saw him. Dad let me know Greg was seeing Cindy Lewis. She was smoking hot. He'd sacrificed time with his girlfriend to be with me.

I darted back to my room and got dressed. I ran down the stairs two steps at a time, and this got my mother to yell at me.

"Slow down in the house!"

I slid on the kitchen floor and hopped up on the bar stool at the counter. The sameness of everything reassured me. It was almost as if I'd been home for the past three months. Mom made me a bowl of my favorite cereal and I dove in. She had sworn I would eat them out of house and home. But hey, I was a growing boy, and growing boys eat a *lot!*

Mom and I hadn't talked much. She was, I don't know, cordial. It was weird. She kept an eye on me, and waited for me to do something stupid. I didn't expect her to fully trust me yet, but we needed to come to an understanding. The subtle message was if I messed up, it was back to my Uncle John's farm. In the last two days I'd caught her with a strange expression, but I intended to get back into her good graces.

"Where's your brother?" she asked with a scowl on her face.

Mom wasn't the easiest person to live with. She had a sharp tongue that could shred you.

"He was taking a shower. He should be down in a minute."

I needed to clear the air.

"Mom?" I asked, and she just looked at me. "We need to talk."

She got a sad look on her face and it looked like she made a decision.

"David, we don't have time right now. Let's talk after dinner."

"Okay, Mom, but I want you to know I love you."

She seemed to weigh my words and see if I meant them.

"I love you, too."

It sounded forced. Before I could overthink the situation, Greg came down the stairs. He grabbed some toast.

"Come on, we don't want to be late," he said

I ran out first and came to a dead stop when I went through the back door. Greg about knocked me down.

"What the heck, dork?" he asked.

Standing by the car was Tami Glade. Tami and I had been best friends and neighbors since we were five. I wasn't the only one who'd grown up over the summer. Tami had curves. She looked good wearing her usual red

Phillies baseball cap with her long silky brown hair in a ponytail sticking out of the back of the cap.

Tami wasn't a classic beauty, because the end of her nose was a little too big, but she had a healthy girl-next-door look. I'd never thought of her as sexy until just now. I saw she'd started to mature. The hint of a flare in her hips was a real turn-on for a teenage boy. It probably also had to do with being stuck on a farm for the last three months with little female contact.

I was jarred back to reality as I remembered the last time we'd talked. About a month before the party, Tami had screamed at me that she never wanted to see my loser butt again. She was the last person I expected to see.

Tami was always a tomboy. She loved to play baseball, and we had been on the same Little League team. Tami played second base to my shortstop. For a girl, she had a cannon for an arm. She gunned down more than one boy who tried to test her. She was now five-eight, and with her budding body she no longer really fit her tomboy image.

When she saw me, her eyes got wide. I saw her face go through several emotions in rapid succession. I could tell she was still mad at me, but the final emotion was relief. I saw she was going to say something but I never gave her a chance. I rushed up and pulled her into a hug.

"I'm sorry. I missed you so much," I choked out.

I felt her relax in my arms and I heard her sob. Tears ran down my face. I had missed my best friend. I looked over at Greg and he had a goofy grin on his face. I did the math and realized that he set this up. I mouthed, 'Thank You!'

She leaned back.

"When did you get back?"

"Friday," I said as I fell into the pools of her brown eyes.

"How come you didn't come see me?"

I gave a little chuckle.

"Did you want to see me?"

She at least blushed and shook her head 'no' as I released her from my embrace.

"I let a lot of people down. Over the summer, I changed. I'm not the same guy you remember. I'm no longer the 'stupid boy' you knew." 'Stupid Boy' was her nickname for me. "I'm also not the jerk I was in the spring. I'm clean and sober and I intend to stay that way. I'm hoping you'll give me a chance and we can be friends again."

Tami looked like she was going to cry again.

"I missed you. Why didn't you call me over the summer?"

How could I explain how messed up I was?

"I wasn't ready. I had to fix me before I could come back, but I'm back now. Look, will you give me a chance to make it up to you?"

She took a deep breath and nodded her head 'yes.'

"Let me get a look at you," she said.

She looked me up and down and did a little twirl with her finger to indicate she wanted me to do a spin. If Tami wanted to check out my butt, who was I to argue? I did a little spin for her and I heard her make a little gasp.

"When did you get such a hot body? I mean, you were always cute, but dang, boy, you're going to have to beat the girls off with a stick."

I was glad to hear her tease me. I didn't know where the 'cute' thing came from; I guess in my mind's eye I was still the slightly chubby nerd of four months ago. I never had the best body image of myself, so it was hard to imagine being cute.

"Look who's talking. You actually look like a woman now. Someone grew up over the summer, and I have to say you're filling out your jeans nicely."

"You pig!"

Greg laughed at the two of us and told us to get in the car. Tami beat me to the front seat, so I jumped in the back. She could have shotgun the rest of her life as long as I was with her. High school was going to be okay.

✧✧✧

On the ride to school, I took the time to look at the old neighborhood. It had once been the place where people with money lived. Then things aged and it began to run down. Ten years ago, the neighborhood had started to come back. These big houses were on half-acre lots. It was perfect place if you had children because of the big backyards. Now there was a mix of older people, who had lived here forever, and families like ours.

The neighborhood had an easy rhythm about it that made you feel at home. It was the type of neighborhood you would only find in a small town. No one locked their doors. We all were friendly and looked out for each other. Part of the charm was the giant oak and maple trees that lined the streets and created a canopy. It was a great place to grow up.

Greg laid down the rules before we were in the high school parking lot.

"This is the first year we'll both be in the same school since grade school. You will not embarrass me and act like a dork in front of my friends."

"I'm not a dork," I said, letting him know he'd hurt my feelings.

Tami didn't help, she giggled. I gave her a mock scowl and got her laughing even more.

"Settle down, David. I know you're not a dork, just don't act like one."

Greg and I were actually very close for brothers with a three-year age difference. He was a senior and one of the Big Men on Campus. I would start as a lowly freshman. Greg never tore me down in public like a lot of brothers do to their siblings. Mom and Dad taught us that you didn't embarrass each other outside the home. Believe me, break that rule and Mom and Dad could be much more embarrassing.

"After school I'm meeting Cindy to, ah, study. Do you think you can find your way home?"

My older brother was a legend when it came to girls. All my friends gave him rock-star status. The funny thing was, my brother wasn't the best-looking dude in school. If the rumors were true, he'd slept with half the cheerleading squad and most of the other hot girls. He had a long list of cutest girls going out with him since he was a freshman. His current girlfriend was Cindy Lewis.

Every man rates a girl in the first three seconds of meeting her. Yes, we would never admit this to a girl, but we do. For Cindy the rating went like this. First, she's definitely a 9 to 9.5 on looks alone. I think I subconsciously deducted a half point because she was dating someone. If I were to judge her as a total stranger, and not knowing about her going out with my brother, she would be a solid 9.5.

Second, her breasts were sized somewhere between grapefruits and melons. I would give them a solid 9. Now her butt is another story. I *love* a fine bottom. Cindy had one of the top five butts in our school. Her butt rated a 10.

Finally, of course, is 'Would you bang her?' This goes from, 'Right here in front of everyone!' all the way down to, 'Not even with my worst enemy's willy!'

Overall, I would rate Cindy a solid 9 out of 10. She'd always been the type to go out with the current Ken-doll jock type. I would say she was odds-on favorite for Homecoming Queen this year. When she agreed to go out with my brother, everyone was shocked. The strange thing was, if the rumors were true, my brother had stopped dating other girls. It looked like this was his first serious girlfriend. His almost three-year streak of a new girl each month had ended.

If you had told me that my brother was off the market, I would have laughed. It wasn't that he went out with multiple girls. He actually had a couple of firm rules. The first was never go out with a girl who's in a relationship. The second was while you were with someone, you didn't cheat. By some unspoken agreement, girls seemed to go out with Greg for 3 to 6 weeks, and then they moved on.

What always amazed me was you never heard a bad thing about Greg. It seemed everyone he dated truly liked him, even after they stopped seeing him. Somehow they set expectations where what they were doing was for fun. Because no one expected the relationship to get serious, no one was disappointed.

The best thing about being Greg's brother was hot older girls flirted with me. They went out of their way to stop and talk to me. I knew they weren't interested in me. The conversation always turned to questions about my big brother. What it did was make me comfortable talking to them. Most guys my age became a quivering mess; I just took it in stride.

My friends were a different matter. If they saw a varsity cheerleader saunter up to me and give me a hip-check, they would just about pee themselves. Junior and senior girls didn't talk to guys our age.

When we pulled into the parking lot, the rain had stopped. The sky was still angry, and you could see the spider web of lightning flashes in the distance. The humidity would be killer today, with the temperature expected to be in the low 90s.

Greg spotted Cindy waiting by her car. She melted into his arms when they met. Cindy wore a white button-up blouse and a plaid pleated skirt. She looked like the porn-star version of a Catholic schoolgirl. She had long, straight, dark brown hair that came down to the middle of her back. I thought her best features, besides the obvious ones, were her pale blue eyes and her pouty lips. Whenever you saw her, you could just imagine falling into those eyes and kissing her. She looked exceptional today. I adjusted her rating to a solid 10. The deciding factor was I would do her in the parking lot in front of Greg.

She spun Greg so his back was to the car and pressed her body into his. He reached down, slid his hand up the back of her legs and pulled her skirt up as he groped her. Holy cow, she was wearing a thong! I had an instant physical reaction and she jumped to an 11. Okay, 11's aren't allowed, but she was perfect. Her skin was flawless, and the shape of her bottom would fit into your palms perfectly. I wanted to drop to my knees and worship at the altar of her butt. I decided this would be my new religion. I zoned out as I admired Cindy. Her perfect teenage butt would be masturbatory material for the next few weeks. On further inspection, it was obvious her summer had included tanning nude.

Tami broke my concentration.

"Pick your tongue up off the ground," she said as she smacked me in the back of the head.

I gave her a wink.

"I think my brother's in love."

Tami nodded.

"I think you have the hots for your brother's girl."

I hated it when she could read me. I didn't even bother to respond because we both knew it was true.

They broke their kiss and Cindy looked over at me and smiled.

"Looks like both the Dawson boys are happy to see me. David, you got big over the summer!" she said, as she stared at my obvious problem.

I about died as I headed to the front door. I could hear Cindy giggle as I hurried off. Tami just shook her head and followed my hasty retreat.

✦✦✦

Constructed in the late '50s, Lincoln High was built to accommodate the baby boomers. Beyond the change of seasons, there never seemed to be any difference to the campus. Whenever they added a new building, it always looked old before it was half completed. The sameness to the place was somehow soothing. I approached the school and took in its old façade. I was full of hope for the coming year.

My friends Jeff Rigger and Alan Douglas met me at the front door. Jeff was a tall, dorky kid who currently had on a butterfly t-shirt. Seriously, you wear a butterfly t-shirt for your first day of high school? I just shook my head—not that I was cool by any stretch of the imagination, but just wow!

Alan still hadn't hit his growth spurt. What was the best way to describe Alan? Alan had, let's say, *unfortunate* hair. His hair was curly, and not in a nice way. It reminded people of a shaggy poodle. He was also slightly overweight, so his pudgy face combined with the hair made him the target of a lot of teasing. To top it off, he was both hyperactive and bossy. The combination was just too funny. Jeff and I cracked up when he started to tell everyone what to do.

When my friends saw me walk up, they both stiffened. I must have been a bigger jerk last year than I realized. I definitely had some fences to mend. Luckily, they saw Tami with me and I caught her giving them a nod. I could see them visibly relax. My best friend was going to make starting freshman year go better than I deserved.

As I walked up Alan laughed.

"Got some wood this morning, David? What set you off?"

I dropped my book bag in front of me so it hid my current state. Tami just smiled and let me twist in the wind; some friend she was. One thing I'd learned from Greg was you never kiss and tell. I figured it wasn't my place to tell everyone Cindy and Greg's business, so I just smirked.

"If you haven't noticed, there's a stiff wind out there today," I explained.

Jeff chuckled.

"I know what you mean. I get one of those every time I turn around. This morning it was looking at the bus driver, and she's like 50 or something. But man, she has big tits."

Go figure, a teenage boy and hormones.

It started to rain again. We all hurried inside. As soon as I went through the front door, the skies opened up. I glanced out the door and I saw Peggy Pratt run up the sidewalk. She looked like a drowned rat. I had swimming for PE this semester and I had a towel in my backpack. I hate the feel of the ones they handed out in gym. I pulled it out and held the door with it draped over my arm as she ran in.

"For you, madam," I said.

Peggy was a junior and one of Greg's ex-girlfriends. I really liked her. No, that wasn't right, I *really* liked her. I struggled to understand why people didn't love the things I loved. For instance: I once went to a piano bar with my dad and there was this woman singing. I loved her. I couldn't figure out why there were only 30 or so people at this bar. She should have been a top 40 artist! Who wouldn't love this? Me, I loved natural redheads. I adored alabaster skin, freckles and green eyes, the whole redhead fantasy girl.

Peggy was my dream girl. She wasn't stuck-up like some of the other girls Greg went out with. I could understand how some of his exes would be aloof. They must get hit on all the time. Peggy was fun and outgoing. Everyone loved her. She was gorgeous and didn't seem to notice how fine she was.

Her long curly red hair was a mess. She looked at me and winked as she took the towel. She gave me her best southern belle.

"I do declare, a gentleman has come to my rescue."

Miss Peggy took notice of me, gave me the once-over and smiled even bigger.

"I see you grew up over the summer. I think I like what I'm seeing," she teased me.

I just smirked, and she got a chuckle out of Alan and Jeff. Tami just rolled her eyes. They were reminded of my ease when talking to good-looking older girls. Where I had problems was with girls my own age. I guess I figure there was no chance with the older girls, so I didn't seem to get nervous. Tami hauled Jeff and Alan off to class, which gave me some privacy with Peggy. Tami would get some kind of reward later for being a good wingman.

It was apparent Peggy hadn't worn a bra today. She looked like a hot wet-t-shirt babe. You could clearly see her nice breasts; in my inexperienced opinion, a B cup. Her alabaster breasts were highlighted by her pink nipples, standing proud, a shade of pink found only in true redheads. I reached into my bag and handed her my gym t-shirt.

"Madam may wish to change before class," I said, hamming it up.

She leaned over and gave me a kiss on the cheek.

"Thanks, David, you're a good friend."

She left to go to the ladies' room to change. I watched her walk away, and seeing her wet clinging jeans made me wish we were more than friends. I was sure nothing would top that for the day. I had seen Cindy's, the likely Homecoming Queen's, butt and now Peggy's, my long time crush, perfect breasts. I might have to go to the restroom and take care of something before I went to class.

When Peggy came out, she looked much better. Well, maybe not *better* to a teenage boy's eyes, but more presentable to the public. I walked her to her class and she gave me directions to mine. We quickly looked at our schedules and agreed to meet at the cafeteria for lunch at noon. She gave me another peck on the cheek and went in with a happy smile and a bounce to her step that had people watching her as she passed. I watched her until she sat down and looked at me, and then I grinned and left.

✧✧✧

I rushed to my first period class to find the door starting to close. I squeezed in.

"Sorry."

I found myself staring at a pretty teacher who was in her mid-twenties. She arched her eyebrows and I scurried to an open seat. Unfortunately, the only seats available were in the front row. I looked around and many of the students had laptops open on their desks. I would have to remember to bring my tablet to take notes.

"Good morning. This is Algebra II and I will be your instructor for the semester, Mrs. Sinclair. This being first period, this also is your homeroom. So when I call your name please raise your hand.

"Mindy…"

When roll call was over, she continued with announcements.

"Today at lunch there will be club sign-ups. Please note that having some clubs on your transcript may be beneficial for college applications. I will make a personal pitch for Math Club."

She then handed out a class syllabus. I zoned out for the lecture that covered what we had learned last year. I pulled out my schedule. After Algebra, I had World History, Biology, Lunch, PE, and English, and then Study Hall rounded out the day. I was glad when the bell finally rang.

✧✧✧

Before lunch, I met Tami at my locker. In middle school, we'd always made a point to go to lunch together. It was nice to see things hadn't changed. I had just closed my locker when I heard a girl scream.

"David! David!"

Out of the corner of my eye, I saw Tami take a step back. I began to turn when I was tackled and I bounced off my locker. I ended up on my ass with a wiggling bundle of blond energy who straddled me. She wrapped her arms around my neck and pulled me into a fierce kiss.

"Hrmmph."

I moaned, trying to catch my breath.

"Lily, you might want to let the 'stupid boy' breathe," Tami said.

"Mwuaaa," Lily broke the kiss and looked expectantly into my eyes.

I grinned from ear to ear.

"You seem happy to see me."

"Yes, I am. I've been looking for you all day."

I heard Tami snort and I saw her grin as she took in my predicament. I stared into Lily's light brown eyes and I could feel the warmth of her feelings for me pour out of them. I'd never had a girl look at me like that. I felt little butterflies flutter in my stomach as I started to become nervous.

Tami cleared her throat to get my attention. Lily and I had started to attract a crowd. Her expression became more intense.

"I need to talk to you."

"Okay, but you're going to have to let me up."

With a happy giggle she bounced up and latched herself to my arm. Tami's eyebrows arched and I could tell she was asking, 'What is this was all about?' I gave her a shrug; I was clueless when it came to women.

We made it safely to the cafeteria and got in line with our orange cafeteria trays. Great, it was mystery meat day.

We made it through the line without saying a word. I scanned the cafeteria, found an empty corner table and guided Lily to it. About that time, I saw Alan and Jeff. I nodded to Tami and she saw them. She grabbed the guys before they could join us and steered them to another table.

Once we were settled, Lily began to talk.

"I just wanted to thank you. You saved my life."

"About that…" I began.

She would not be deterred.

"David, you're a hero. I've been trying to get in touch with you all summer so I could thank you. I'm not really sure what I can do, but just name it."

As she said this, she moved closer and closer to me. I started to react to her as she invaded my personal space.

"Ah, Lily," I tried again.

She got a sultry look in her eyes.

"Seriously David, I mean if there's *anything*... I owe you."

Oh, man, being a virgin really sucked. I had some very specific ideas of what I'd like to do, but I wasn't quite sure how to go about it. I suddenly felt a presence behind me. I turned around and Tami stood there. She gave me a headshake and walked away. She's right. I shook my head to clear it.

"I'm just glad I was there. You scared the crap out of me."

I shuddered to think what could have happened.

"The doctor told me if you had been only a little bit slower I'd've suffered brain damage." That was scary. I remembered being scared to death she would die in my arms. It brought back a flood of images. She must have seen the faraway look. I felt her reach over and squeeze my hand.

I gave her a half smile.

"I'm just glad you're okay."

"I'm so sorry you got in so much trouble. I heard they made you go away for the summer," she said as she looked down.

I needed to look at the positives.

"You know what? It was the best thing to happen to me. I was a jerk who was out of control. I look at it as a wake-up call. The summer at my uncle's farm gave me the time to figure out what's important to me. The biggest one is I need to be a better person. Seeing you, uh, I thought you were dead."

"Everyone was surprised when you didn't tell the police who all was there."

"To be honest, I was surprised too. Somehow, I knew I needed to own that night and my role in it. I'm sorry I allowed you to be hurt."

She looked shocked.

"But you *saved* me! You didn't do anything to hurt me," Lily said.

I blinked in surprise. I wasn't sure what I should do about this. Lily and I were never close, even though I had recently started to hang out with the stoner group. She was a cute girl. At the time, I was much more of a nerd, and girls like her didn't give me the time of day. It was obvious this hero worship had built up over the summer. I was sure if she knew me, she could quickly be cured. I'm not the hero kind of guy.

"No, Lily, a better friend would have realized you were too drunk and needed help. All I cared about that night was getting wasted."

She looked at me as if I were nuts.

"Nonsense, I was the one who drank so much I essentially killed myself."

"What?"

"The doctor told me I drank enough to put myself into a coma. No one forced me to drink."

I guess I'd never thought of it that way. I actually felt as if a weight was lifted. I had carried around the responsibility for what happened. She was right: I didn't make her drink. I needed to let it go. I took a deep breath and let it out slowly. I knew if I continued to dwell on this, I would slip back into depression. Uncle John had pointed out numerous times I couldn't take on the responsibility for the actions of others. I thought I could finally forgive myself. Lily could see I was much happier that I knew this.

"Thank you for saying that. I was afraid you'd hate me."

"No. I'm just thankful you were there," Lily said.

"Stop," I said to get her to slow down. "I just happened to be trained in CPR. My training kicked in when I saw you weren't breathing. I'm not anyone special. I saw you were in trouble and I reacted."

"But..." she started.

I interrupted her.

"Okay! Can we agree you're thankful I helped you out? Please, I'm really uncomfortable with the whole hero thing and no, you don't owe me anything. I would *never* expect anything for what I did."

She had a grin from ear to ear.

"Alright, you have a deal. I'll back off with the hero talk and respect your wishes."

She screwed her face up and then turned to look out the window once before taking a deep breath.

"One thing the police never made public is they found Rohypnol in my blood work. The combination was almost fatal."

What the hell? Rohypnol was known as a date-rape drug. No one had ever mentioned Lily was a target. If I'd known, I would have been more cooperative with the police. I was sure they didn't tell me because I was a suspect. How could someone do that? The scary part was we were just kids. I mean, we were all in middle school at the time!

"Do you have any idea who might've slipped it into your drink?"

Her eyes looked dead.

"I've gone over it in my head many times, but the drug must have done something because I honestly can't remember. I've talked to Sharon about the party a few times without telling about the drugs. I'm really embarrassed it happened. I could've easily been raped. That is *not* how I want to lose my virginity."

She suddenly went bright red when she realized what she'd told me. I instinctively pulled her into my embrace. Her head rested on my chest. She began to cry softly. She obviously had held this in for a long time. I became aware we were in the middle of the cafeteria. All conversation had gone quiet around us as everyone tried to figure out what was going on. A crying girl will do that, but I didn't care. I felt her shudder and then stiffen. I think she also realized our surroundings.

"Oh God, David, I'm so sorry I just dumped all that on you."

I saw the fear in her eyes.

"Lily, I'm flattered you felt comfortable enough to tell me that. You have no worries about me talking about this."

I saw her visibly relax. Teenagers could be cruel. I'd seen it before, and it made me a little sick to think people could be so uncaring of other's feelings. I was a nerd and so were most of my friends. We experienced it on numerous occasions.

I needed time to process what she had just told me. I decided to change the course of this conversation.

"Do you see the old gang?"

"Not really. I run into Sharon occasionally. She lives down the street and has invited me to some parties, but after that night I decided to make some changes," she said.

She looked out the window again. Then she smiled.

"Plus I got grounded for the summer. Dad wasn't happy. I think you know what that's like," she said.

I knew what she meant. I just nodded.

"David, I really no longer have any friends," she continued.

"Of course you do."

She looked into my eyes and I just nodded. Lily gave me a hug. I suddenly noticed she felt good in my arms. She had her next class across campus and had to get going. I went over to where my crew was eating and sat down. Tami raised her eyebrows, gave me a pointed look and then indicated with her eyes towards Lily as she walked away. I shrugged.

"Lily just wanted to thank me for helping her out."

Alan couldn't keep quiet.

"What did you do to make her cry? Did you say something stupid to her? I know Tami's always calling you 'stupid boy.' Is she a good kisser?"

Jeff came to my defense.

"Hang on, Sherlock. Even though those are all very good questions, I'm not sure they're really appropriate."

"Why not? We all want to know what's going on. So, David, are you and Lily going out?" Alan asked.

Tami leaned over and whacked Alan on the forehead.

"Ouch, what was that for?"

Tami just smirked.

"Settle down. Let me handle this," she announced.

That got Alan to shut up. Everyone knew Tami was the master at getting people to talk. I waited for the interrogation to begin. She looked at me.

"Are you okay?" she asked.

I felt my eyes begin to water and I just got up and walked out. She caught me off guard. I had tried to tamp down my emotions for Lily's sake. Then I tried to play it cool with the gang all there. I think I could have handled any other question but that one.

"What the heck?" Alan asked, which was followed by the sound of Alan's forehead being smacked.

"Ouch, what was that for?" he complained.

✧✧✧

Chapter 2 – Football?

Monday August 26

Right after lunch, I had PE. By the time I got there, my emotions were back under control.

For first semester, I signed up for swimming with Coach Engels. He was also the freshman football coach. We were lucky to have a swimming pool. A few years back one of the wealthy boosters organized a fundraiser for a swimming complex. We were one of the few schools in our area that had one. I really liked to swim. Dad had gotten me involved in swimming through the park district. Next year I'd be old enough to be a lifeguard. I think that would be a great summer job.

"Dawson, get over here," Coach Engels said.

Crud, what had I done? It was only the first day, after all.

"Coach?" I asked.

I could see several other freshmen watch us. I would shortly be the talk of the school, with a crying girl at lunch and now Coach getting on my case. Little did I know that when I helped Peggy this morning, it would be an even bigger topic of conversation.

Coach turned to the others.

"You guys get in the water and start swimming laps."

He waited until we were alone.

"John called me. He said you're going out for football."

I looked confused. I realized Coach was talking about my uncle. They'd been college roommates. I also knew better than to contradict my Uncle John. For the past few months, he'd been my anchor. If he said I was going out for football, I was going out for football.

"What do I need to do?" I asked.

Coach Engels arched his eyebrows in surprise. He knew I wasn't a jock and had asked out of courtesy to my uncle. When I didn't hesitate, it shocked him. He quickly gathered his wits.

"You've missed the first two weeks of practice, so you'll have to start at the bottom and earn a spot on the team."

"Yes, sir."

"I need you to get your parents to sign a permission slip. I expect to see you at practice after school on Tuesday."

"Yes, sir."

I guess I would go out for football.

✧✧✧

I trudged into the kitchen after a long bus ride. I thought it would have been faster to walk. For some reason I was the last stop. The good news was if I rode the bus in the morning, I'd have a short trip. I went up to my room to unload my backpack. There was no homework yet, but I wanted to get a handle on things. I'd never been strong in the sciences, so I pulled out my Biology book and did the reading suggested in the syllabus.

Normally I was a solid A/B student, without ever cracking a book, but this year I was determined to do better. My parents weren't well off, so if I planned to get into a good school, I would need some financial support. An academic scholarship would go a long way to make that dream happen.

Over the summer, Uncle John worked with me to figure out how I wanted my life to go. One of my goals was financial stability. I didn't necessarily need to be rich, but I wanted to be able to have a comfortable life. Once I had the destination figured out, the path to achieving the goal became clear. A good education suddenly became a priority if I wanted to have financial stability.

Other goals weren't as obvious, like being physically fit. Uncle John made the point that this should be part of my plan when he pulled out his high school yearbook. The previous fall they'd had their reunion. He showed me photos from that event and we compared them to the yearbook photos. He let me draw my own conclusions. It was apparent physical fitness was a worthy goal. I was sure this was why he had talked to Coach Engels about me playing football.

The next thing we talked about was a solid moral foundation, one I could use as a sounding board for decisions I would make. This went beyond a religious aspect, though that was an important part of my life. This had to do more with becoming a man of integrity, a man of my word, a man people could trust.

I remembered the example he gave me.

"Do you think you're a man of your word?"

"Of course I am," I answered.

He arched his eyebrows.

"So, if you say you'll do something, you'll do it?"

I stopped to think for a moment. There had to be a catch in there for him to be looking like that. Then I thought I caught it.

"Yes, with the exception of it causing harm to me or to someone else."

"Interesting, you're using your brain today. So if we take the exception of harm out of the equation, you'd say you're a man of your word?"

"Yes."

"Would you agree being a man of your word is important in how others will perceive and interact with you?"

I looked at him in confusion. There had to be another trap in there. I couldn't find it this time. If someone told me they would do something and then did it, it would be better than not.

"Yes, I would agree."

"Good. Let me give you two examples of your recent behavior, and you tell me if you still think you're a man of your word."

Oh, crap. Here we go.

"Yesterday you told me that you'd dig postholes to finish the dirt road section. But when offered to go out for lunch, you accepted instead."

"Hang on, something better came up. No one would expect me to dig holes over getting off the farm for even an hour," I reasoned.

He waited me out. He was good at that, and sometimes it drove me to distraction. Then it hit me: the men who placed the posts and strung the fence had to dig most of those holes, and my uncle paid for the extra labor. My lunch had cost him an extra $200. I hung my head, and he saw I realized what I'd done. I said I would do the work. I didn't tell him I wasn't done, which caused a problem later.

"David, two things I want to point out. The first is there are times that being a man of your word sucks. Remember three weeks ago when I told you we'd go shopping for work clothes?"

"That was the night we went to dinner with that girl you're sweet on."

"Well, a better opportunity came up. I could've dumped you and gone out with Ann, but I made you a promise. I came to you and asked you if, in addition to getting you some clothes, you wanted to join us. How many guys do you know would've just gone on the date?"

"Almost everyone. I see your point. You kept your word, but when something better came up you worked it out so everyone was happy. So let me ask you: if I said no, would you have gone on the date?"

"No."

"Wow."

"Let me give you some other examples. You like to gossip."

I gave him a look.

"Don't bullshit me, you tell me stuff all the time. If someone tells you something in confidence, is it yours to retell?" he asked.

"No, I guess not."

"But you still do it all the time. Do you really want to be the guy no one can share with because sharing with you means they'll be sharing with everyone else?"

"No, of course not."

"This becomes even more important when you start to date. The time you spend with a woman is not meant to be shared with anyone but that woman. Your partner may choose to share, but I would suggest you not be the one doing the sharing.

"Two things I want you to take away from this. First is before you say you'll do something, think it through. The second is to learn how to say 'no,'" Uncle John said.

The final thing I put on my list was a healthy sex life. Since I currently didn't have one, this was the area I would have to work on the hardest. Uncle John agreed this was important but was unwilling to help me out with it. Go figure.

By the time I'd finished my Biology reading and doing the practice problems, I heard someone downstairs. I bounced down the stairs to find Dad in the kitchen.

"Need any help?" I asked, which startled him.

"Oh, I didn't know anyone was home. What do you want for dinner?"

"Anything, you've no idea how bad a cook Uncle John is. I swear his country-fried steak was made with newspaper," I said.

"Why don't you pull out the frozen bread sticks and we do pasta?"

"Sounds great. Have you talked to Uncle John?" I asked.

"We talked for a little bit on Sunday. Why, what's up?" Dad asked.

"He called Coach Engels and told him I was going out for football," I said, and wondered if Dad knew about this development.

"First I've heard of it. What do you think your mom will think?" Dad asked, as we both knew this could be a sticky topic.

"If it gets me out of the house and out of trouble, I'm sure she'll be okay."

"What time did Greg say he'd be home?" Dad asked.

"He didn't. Want me to text him?"

I grabbed my phone and found him in my contacts.

"Tell him dinner will be ready in 30 minutes," Dad told me.

I sent Greg a text.

'*Get off the Hot GIRL–food in 30*'

'*FU–see you then,*' Greg sent back.

I went to set the table as Dad signed the football permission slip. Mom was out showing houses and would be late. Twenty minutes later Greg came in. We each shared our day over dinner. I talked about my football news. Greg talked about the pre-college courses he was taking and Dad about work. It was nice to be home and spending family time together. I missed everyone, and I think they were both shocked when I hugged them before heading upstairs. After I caught up with my studies, I played some video games and then hit the sack.

✦✦✦

Tuesday August 27

The next morning I walked to school early to see Tami. I wanted to talk to her and see what was going on. I was seated on the front steps when I saw her walk in with Bert Nelson; they were deep in conversation. When they got to the steps, Tami and I just nodded to each other and she and

Bert went into the school. Seeing them together like that about killed me.

I knew Bert from middle school. He was a nice guy, but we never ran in the same circles. I tended to hang out with the nerds, and he was a jock and a rich kid. I had to admit they made a nice-looking couple. No one ever accused Tami of not being good looking. She was just always a tomboy. Dressed like a girl, I could see where Bert would be attracted to her. Her long dark brown hair was no longer in a ponytail; it had been styled to have a little body and framed her cute face.

Before I started to sulk too much, first bell rang and I made my way to homeroom. I wouldn't see Tami until lunch.

Lunch finally came and Tami waited for me at my locker. I launched right in.

"So what's the deal with you and Bert?"

Tami gave me a dirty look and surprised me.

"Drop it. I'm warning you, if you don't, we're talking about you and Lily all through lunch."

I blinked twice; well okay. Something was wrong, and I didn't know where to begin. I shrugged, doing my best to remain calm.

"Okay, we have a deal."

We made it to the cafeteria without saying a word to each other. I could feel the tension build between us. Tami and I didn't keep secrets. That was what made me nervous. She and I had only actually talked a few sentences since we reconnected yesterday. Aside from her reading my mind, we hadn't talked about anything significant. I started to believe there was much more going on than I knew. The only secrets she ever kept from me were things like birthday presents, never anything important.

When we finally made it to our table, I found Alan, Jeff and Lily waiting for us. Alan had grilled Lily, and I could tell by Jeff's shrug that Alan had started to irritate her. Tami walked up to Alan and smacked him on the forehead.

"Ow! What was that for?" Alan asked.

She looked him in the eyes and left no doubt she was serious.

"Do you want David to bring his friends to the table and eat with us?"

He looked a little sheepish.

"Yes," was his one-word answer.

"Then don't pry into their personal business."

She said it loud enough that we started to get noticed.

As a freshman, being noticed in a high school cafeteria wasn't always the best thing. I sat down next to Lily and winked at her. She seemed relieved. Out of the corner of my eye I saw a flash of red hair coming my way. I smiled and jumped up to greet Peggy.

"Hey, Gorgeous."

Peggy beamed and leaned in and gave me a kiss on the cheek. I noticed that half the lunchroom watched us. The funny thing was a vast majority of those who watched were girls. Greg had a huge grin on his face and gave me a wink from across the room as she flirted back.

"Hey, Good-looking. The stuff you loaned me yesterday, I have it at my locker. I want to thank you for being such a gentleman. Most boys would have either leered at me or let me go to class like that."

The whole time she was rubbing her hand on my chest. That was fine except for one little thing. Did I just say little? Well, the little guy—Mr. Happy was his name—had taken notice that the woman of his dreams had caressed me. I arched my eyebrows, and she suddenly noticed what she was doing and jerked her hand away.

"You don't have to stop, I was enjoying that," I said with a stage whisper as I leaned in.

She gave my arm a playful swat.

"I bet you were."

I just leered back and used my best sexy voice.

"I think you enjoyed it too."

She blushed, so I changed the subject.

"Why don't you join us for lunch?"

Peggy thought about it for a moment and just nodded. She went to her table, and you could hear the volume of girl-chatter go up when she gathered her lunch and joined us. Before Peggy made it back to our table, I heard a smack.

"Ow! What was that for?" Alan complained.

Alan and Jeff were in shock all through lunch with Tami and Lily taking up residence on either side of me, and Peggy across from me. Funny how a pretty girl will do that to a guy. I had two of the better-looking freshmen and a smoking-hot junior seated at our lunch table.

Every time I tried to get Tami's attention, she seemed to ignore me. I wasn't going to get anywhere with her at lunch. Towards the end, the subject of football came up. I think Tami was trying to head me off so she wouldn't have to talk to me. "David, what's this I hear you're going out for football?" Tami asked.

The lunch crew all turned and looked at me. I was about to put a bite in my mouth but stopped to answer.

"Yes, I got the permission slip signed and tonight I have a physical. If everything's okay, my first practice is Wednesday."

Lily was enthusiastic.

"You have the body for it."

I groaned as everyone else chuckled. Peggy wasn't to be outdone.

"Lily, you're right, he does look like such a jock now that he's spent the summer on the farm. How did you get so many muscles?"

Tami frowned and added her two cents.

"I don't know, is his new body all show, or does he have real muscles to back it up?"

I made the mistake when I flexed my arms and chest. Lily and Tami took that as an invitation to grope me. I looked at them in mock horror.

"Ladies, careful with the merchandise; you break it, you buy it."

Peggy grinned.

"Keep flexing like that and I might have to check your bod out a little closer."

"You can have the shirt off my back, any time, any place," I said, as I looked her in the eyes.

"Oh, I do declare, I feel faint," Peggy said to tease me.

Lily slugged me in the arm and Tami gave me a disappointed look. I suddenly felt like I may have crossed a line. Everyone burst out laughing at the look on my face.

The bell rang and we headed to our classes. Alan pressed me for details about Peggy in PE next period.

"Well, let me put it to you like this." Alan leaned forward, looked around to see if anyone was listening, and spoke in a lowered voice, "Peggy, that absolutely gorgeous thing you were talking to, is a complete and total slut."

My head snapped around. I guess it was time for another Alan beatdown. Ever since Jeff and I had known him, one or both of us usually ended up smacking him about once every other week. I figured I would give him a little more rope and then let the beating begin.

"Do tell," I said calmly.

He was in his own world or he would have seen the danger signs I gave off.

"Well, first of all, your brother went out with her, and we know he bags every fox in this school."

"Really, Greg never told me any such thing."

"No, he never does talk, but it's common knowledge."

"Where are you getting this 'common knowledge' from?"

I think he caught the edge in my voice and decided to take another tack.

"Never mind, let's take your big brother out of the equation."

"Let's, and before we go much further, Peggy is one of the most popular girls at school and a personal friend."

He looked at me in confusion.

"What does that have to do with anything?"

I took a deep breath.

"Don't you think if she were a slut, the other girls would be trashing her?"

He wasn't to be deterred.

"Well, she must not've slept with any guy that has a girlfriend."

This had gotten interesting. Alan's convoluted logic had me intrigued.

"So she's a slut with a code of ethics then–like the Bro Code?"

The Bro Code said if another guy was into a girl, you backed off until it was obvious he had no shot. Sometimes the 'no shot' portion of the code was blurred, but in general the system seemed to work. You also didn't go after taken girls.

"Yes, that must be it. Anyways, I heard that Jimmy Alton bagged her over the summer."

This was news. I had been out of the loop, but Jimmy Alton was a known liar.

"Are we talking about the same Jimmy Alton who's a bigger dork than we are?"

"Well, yes," Alan admitted.

"The same Jimmy Alton who said you stole his lunch box last year?"

"The F-in' liar!" Alan exclaimed, showing his anger at the false claim.

"Exactly my point."

Alan suddenly got it.

"Well, she's still a slut."

"Alan, I'm about a minute away from smacking you. Peggy's a good friend of mine, and unless you have some proof, I'm going to take offense."

"Sorry."

The rest of the day Alan was subdued. Jeff asked what his deal was and I told him what was up. Jeff just gave me a knowing look and we dropped it. Later that day in the hall, I heard a smack.

"Ow! What was that for?" Alan's voice cracked, making it even funnier.

I just grinned. My avenging angel had just taken care of it.

✧✧✧

Chapter 3 – Makeover

Wednesday August 28

Last night I had my physical and they cleared me for football. I was now officially six feet and a half inch tall and weighed 187 pounds. The doctor confirmed my growth spurt had slowed down; he felt I would end up at six-one or six-two, probably by Christmas.

I found my commitment to read ahead had helped me understand more during my class lectures. After my first two classes, I stopped raising my hand with answers when everyone started to look at me strangely. I didn't want the 'nerd' label to carry over from middle school, but I wasn't going to dumb it down if called upon.

In third period, I received a note that said I should to report to the training room at lunchtime to get my football equipment checked out. I grabbed a sandwich and skipped lunch with the gang. Being a freshman, and the last one to get equipment, I got the worst of the lot.

PE was a surprise. Coach Engels explained that football players were required to do strength and conditioning. So today was the last day of swimming.

✧✧✧

After school, I suited up for football. Coach Engels waited for me on the field.

"Dawson, get over here."

I trotted up. Bert Nelson had just fumbled the ball, and I have to admit it brought a small smirk to my face. The defense high-fived each other and danced over Bert.

"Go in for Bert."

"Sir?"

He jerked my facemask, so we were just inches apart.

"Do I have to repeat myself?"

I just jogged out to the huddle. Mike Herndon was our quarterback. I looked at Mike and he gave me a disgusted look. I didn't blame him. I'd never played organized football and all these guys knew it. I was always the slightly overweight nerd, as far as these guys were concerned. I hated to ask, but I had no idea what position Bert played.

"What's my position and what do you want me to do?"

Mike popped his head out of the huddle and looked at coach as if to say, 'Are you kidding me?'

"Run veer right!" Coach yelled.

At least I knew what the veer option was. I loved watching it. It's a simple concept. The quarterback reads the defense and decides where the ball will go. When done right it's impossible to stop. It was designed for teams who are intelligent and quick. Most times the quarterback would line up under center to take the snap. The fullback and tailback would line up in an I-formation. He would put the ball into the fullback's stomach and ride him down the line to see if the fullback had an opening. If he did, he would release the ball and the fullback would take it from there. If the linebacker filled the gap, then the quarterback would pull the ball and work his way down the line.

The critical block was the tackle. He had to block his player for the veer to work. This left the defensive end to cover two players at the line of scrimmage. The quarterback would read the end, and if he closed on him, he would pitch the ball to the tailback. If the end cheated out to cover the tailback, the quarterback tucked the ball and ran up field. It was like a magic show of where's-the-football.

Mike took pity on me.

"David, you're playing fullback. You'll line up in the I-formation in front of Jake. We're running the veer option. I'll ride you into the hole and I'm going to give you the ball. Your job is to score. On two, BREAK!"

I looked across the line and saw the middle linebacker, Tim Foresee, as he cheated to the right. Hell, the defense had a huge advantage because they knew where the ball was supposed to go. I would be creamed. I suddenly felt sorry for Bert.

"Down! Set! Hut, Hut!"

I exploded out of my stance and Mike slapped the ball into my stomach. Mike saw the wall of defenders come and just let go to save himself, the bastard. I figured 'what the heck' and exploded into Tim. I didn't just hit him, I ran through him. Later I heard that you could hear the crack of pads clear over at the varsity practice. It was beyond the normal crack you heard in a play. It was the kind of noise that made everyone turn to see what had just happened.

Tim bounced off me, stunned, and I just kept churning my legs. I plowed through the grasp of the wall of defenders and broke free. The free safety had me dead-to-rights and I decided to run him over too. I got low and I think he had the same idea. There was another tremendous crack and I just spun off him and trotted into the end zone.

There was stunned silence. I looked back. The safety and Tim were laid out, and the trainer sprinted onto the field to make sure they were okay.

Next thing I knew there was pandemonium. Mike and the rest of the offense sprinted to me, jumped up and down, and slapped my helmet. They all grinned like idiots.

"Holy crap man, that was awesome!" Mike declared.

"I just did what you told me."

Coach Engels decided we were done with scrimmage for the rest of the day. He didn't want to lose any other defenders. He had Mike, Jake and me work on running the veer option. By the end of practice, I started to understand what I was supposed to do.

Then I think Coach thought it was a good idea to kill me. He took me aside and had me run conditioning drills for the rest of practice. It was obvious to everyone that missing two weeks of practice meant you weren't in football shape. When I finally collapsed, everyone else had left and it was just Coach and the trainer.

The trainer was a cute girl just out of college, Ms. Becky Grimes. I was still getting used to my new body and there were times I wasn't very coordinated. Becky stopped me and wanted to check me out. I noticed my shoulder was sore from hitting Tim. It should be; Tim outweighed me by fifteen pounds.

"When you get home put ice on the shoulder, and I want you to drink plenty of fluids to rehydrate and to flush your system. If you don't, you won't be able to walk in the morning."

After that, the trainer headed to the locker room. Coach Engels stopped me to talk.

"I just want you know that you surprised me today."

"You and me both, Coach."

"Look, I stuck my neck out to let you play."

I was shocked. Coach put his hands up to stop me from saying anything.

"I know you had some trouble last spring. That's exactly the kind of trouble I don't need when I'm putting together a football team, but on John's recommendation I'm letting you play. Please don't disappoint either John or myself."

"No, sir. I won't let you down."

"Good. Tomorrow I want you to make time to meet with Ms. Kim. She's going to put together a strength and conditioning plan to help you with your coordination."

I just nodded.

"Now go hit the showers."

✧✧✧

After practice, I was supposed to meet Greg for a ride home. He was picking up Cindy from cheerleading practice, which ended about the same time as I finished. As

I walked out to meet Greg, I felt a hip bump me and I almost stumbled.

"Wake up, Dawson."

I looked over and saw a sexy senior smiling at me. Beth Anderson was the down-to-earth girl-next-door type who happened to be the head cheerleader this year. She was in tight jeans and a baggy t-shit. Beth had a great body, but she didn't flaunt it. Her long brown hair was in a ponytail. I put my arm out and she slid up next to me to get a hug. I leaned down and kissed her cheek.

"Hey cutie, how've you been?" she asked.

"I've been doing well."

"Where have you been?"

"I was at my uncle's all summer helping him on his farm."

"It looks like the fresh air did you some good."

She ran her hands over my chest and smiled at me. I knew she was teasing me, but we were good friends. Our moms have been best friends since high school and her family had a pool. You would find Greg and me as almost permanent fixtures in their back yard most summers. She couldn't help but know where I was all summer, but Beth was polite enough to allow me to tell her.

What amazed me was Greg never went out with her. They'd been friends all their lives. The two of them were the same age, and when they were little they were as close as Tami and I were. I think our families had always assumed they would get together, but they had some kind of disagreement when they were freshmen and seemed to drift apart. This was when Greg began his conquest of the hot women at our high school. They remained friends, but gradually Beth and I became better friends. If it weren't for Tami, I think we may have become best friends.

"So did you like having Greg all to yourself this summer?" I asked.

A flash of disappointment crossed her eyes, but then it was gone.

"No, I never saw him."

"That's too bad. You two would make a cute couple."

That got me a strange look. She just giggled as we walked out to a sunny afternoon. When Beth laughed, it lit up my world. She knew I had a crush on her, but she never teased me about it. It was nice to see her again. The difference between her and Tami was I had no problem thinking of her as a sexual person. Not that Beth dated much or had a reputation.

"How're you and Tami doing?"

Fair question; the last time we talked, I had told her Tami didn't want to see me. She knew this hurt me, but she was honest with me. She pointed out Tami had valid reasons for not wanting to be around me. What I liked most about Beth was she was always straight with me. I knew when she said something, she had my best interest at heart. I found she never offended me with what she said, because of that level of trust.

"We really haven't had a chance to talk. I just got back last week," I said, as she looked concerned. "Beth, she is, was, I don't know, my best friend. I'm going to do everything I can to not lose that."

"She's been mad at you for a long time. Don't push it, or you might lose her. Tami needs to see you're no longer the jerk you were."

I had a mock look of shock.

"Thanks, Beth."

"Well, you were a jerk."

"I know I was. Thanks for caring," I said, and I meant it.

She was one of the rare people I felt safe telling anything, and it was a two-way street. Her sophomore year she had her heart broken by a senior. She had poured her deepest feelings and insecurities out to me. She never told me exactly what happened, but I was there to listen. I think she just needed to talk, and honestly, I was probably too young to explain the private details to anyways.

"Let me give you one piece of advice," she said as I paid rapt attention. "You need to really listen to her. Your meltdown affected her more than you know. It was one thing for you to be around and her mad at you. It was another for you to leave. With you here, she at least was able to see you, even though she didn't want to talk to you. If I remember right, she would text you every now and then. It really hit her hard, you leaving for the summer. When you left, there was zero contact. She was completely cut off from you for the first time in over seven years. Tami needed you."

"What do you mean?"

She seemed to think about my question.

"That isn't my story to tell. I'm just telling you that you need to have an open mind when you talk to her. There are major changes about to happen for Tami, and I'm sure she'll need your support."

What was going on?

"Okay, I promise to listen."

She took a deep breath and I could see her pull herself together.

"Okay, it's time I cheered you up. Why don't you come over a week from Sunday and go swimming? Bring Tami if you can."

This weekend was a holiday weekend and I had to work for my dad. I'd really missed Beth. Even though she was three years older than I was, she always treated me like a friend.

"What time?"

"We get back from church around 11:30. Why don't you come over around noon and I'll have my mom cook you a nice lunch."

I smiled. It felt like old times. I needed that.

"It's a date."

"Good. I'll see you then."

I saw Greg and Cindy as they walked towards us. Greg said something to Cindy and she headed to her car.

"Hey Beth, how are things?"

"Things are good. How come you never came over to see me this summer?"

It was Greg's turn to squirm, but before he could answer, Beth checked her watch and bolted for the parking lot. She waved at us.

"I forgot. I'm late."

As we watched her run away, my brother turned to me.

"Hey, do you have any plans this afternoon?"

"Several of us were going to jump online and play Black Ops. I'm supposed to be online in about 45 minutes," I said as I looked over at my friends.

He looked disappointed.

"Don't suppose you'd do your big brother a favor, would you?"

I could tell this might pay off if I played my cards right.

"What do you want?" I asked.

"Cindy has to babysit the neighbor kids until their mom gets home. I'm hoping you would stand in for her so we could spend some, ah, quality time together," he said, and he at least had the decency to blush. "I'd owe you big, just name your price."

I already owed him big-time and almost just agreed, but something in the back of my mind told me that we needed to get on with our lives, so I played it straight. I knew if I caved right away, I wasn't going to get a favor back.

"I just can't think of anything I want right now. Maybe next time I can help you out."

"Really? Seriously, I'll do anything, within reason," Greg said.

Nice save. I could see my big brother was desperate. He must have told his girlfriend he could deliver. Maybe I could use this to my advantage and get something I really wanted. I thought back to yesterday morning and seeing Peggy's hot body. I knew what I wanted, and my brother had a unique skill I needed to learn. Having a healthy sex life was one of my life goals. This I wanted to get started on ASAP.

"No bullshit, you'll do me a huge favor?" I asked, and stared at him to let him know I was serious.

It was Greg's turn to get nervous. He'd never seen me get this intense. He knew I could come up with wild requests. He got a faraway look and I knew I had him. He was thinking about some personal time with Cindy. Hell, I bet he would give his left nut about right now. He looked me in the eye.

"As long as it doesn't hurt anyone, cost me more than 50 bucks, or mean more than a month's worth of free rides, then the answer is yes."

"Well, I'm not sure how long it'll take, but I want you to teach me something you're very qualified in."

Now I was uneasy. If Greg were a jerk, I would never have trusted him, but he never was cruel, so I decided to ask.

"I have a crush on a junior," I started out slowly and then finished with a rush, "and want your help in learning to be successful with girls so I can ask her out and not blow it."

Greg looked stunned. He thought about it for a while and smiled.

"Ah, grasshopper wishes to learn from the master." His fake Chinese accent wasn't very good.

I nodded to him.

"If you're serious, I would love to train you to be a little stud. But you're going to have to do as I say, and some of the things you're going to fight me on," Greg said.

I looked confused.

"What will I fight you on?"

"That's the point: nothing. If you agree to follow my rules, I'll teach you."

I let out a long breath of relief.

"Agreed!"

"So, who is this junior you have the hots for?"

I started to evade the answer.

"Look dumbass, you want help or not?" he asked.

I sure did.

"Peggy Pratt."

"I guess you either go big or stay home. Peggy would be an excellent choice. I think she even likes you."

"Do you really think so?"

"I know so. She always comments on what a nice guy you are. That's half the battle. I even heard you did her a solid on Monday by giving her your gym shirt."

I remembered her wet-t-shirt look and smiled.

"She needed a change after being caught in the rain," I explained.

"Well, I can tell you the rest of the male population at the school would rather she *not* have gotten the t-shirt, but it was a nice gesture, and her friends were talking about you for the last few days because of it."

That caught my interest.

"What were they saying?"

Greg got an evil grin.

"After all the talk about you saving Peggy, they mostly talked about how much you've grown. I think the phrases 'cute butt' and 'hot bod' were used once or twice."

Greg saw me go completely red and he broke out laughing.

"Greg, are you kidding me?"

"Sorry, dude, no, I'm not."

I was too stunned to continue the conversation. I pulled out my cell and called Jeff.

"Sorry man. Greg needs me to do him a favor so I won't be able to play tonight."

"No problem, I'll let Alan know."

"Thanks. I'll see you at school."

I hung up and decided to give Tami a quick call and invite her to Beth's a week from Sunday.

Tami answered and I just started talking.

"Hey, I have to help Greg until dinner. How about I call you after?"

"I can't tonight, Bert Nelson is coming over."

What the heck, did someone just punch me in the stomach? My chest felt like someone was sitting on it. I didn't have any right to tell Tami who she could go out with, but this was *my* Tami. I leave for the summer and she goes from being a tomboy and my best friend to having boobs and seeing a football player? I felt miserable.

"Will I see you in the morning?" I asked.

"No. I'll see you in school."

Sunday was forgotten at that moment. I just told her goodbye and I let Greg drag me to the car. There was just silence as he waited me out. One of the things I loved about him was he never pushed me. I asked him about it one time, and he said it was his philosophy on life. If you don't know what to do, just shut up and see what happens. The weird thing was our silence was always comfortable. My mind was spinning as I tried to figure out what it would mean if Tami were dating. Why did it hurt so much? Did I have feelings beyond friendship for Tami? The image of her with another guy almost made me physically ill.

✧✧✧

Before I could solve my problems, we were at Cindy's house. She met us at the door.

"David! Thanks for the help. The kids are in the backyard running off some energy. Why don't you go back and meet them."

I knew when I'd been dismissed, so I went out back. There were six screaming kids from the ages of 3 to 11. Needless to say, I earned my stud education that day. I also realized I didn't want to have unprotected sex if this was what it created. I was the happiest guy in the world when their mom showed up about two hours later.

Afterwards, I collapsed on the back porch. The little rugrats had worn me out. I wished I had that much energy. It wasn't that they were bad kids, they were just wound up. Finally, Greg came out about thirty minutes later.

"Come on in."

I followed him into the kitchen. Cindy's family had money and their house showed it. Cindy came into the kitchen in a short silk robe. Her hair was a mess and her nipples were very obviously pressing through the flimsy material. She thanked me for watching the little monsters and I handed her the thirty bucks their mother had given me. She tried to give it back.

"No, Greg and I have a deal and it doesn't involve me taking money from you."

"I told Cindy what we're going to do and she wants to help," Greg said.

I was a little pissed he had told her, but I could use a woman's perspective. I saw some real upside to this. Plus, I looked at her in her robe and imagined her naked underneath. Cindy saw me check her out.

"David, are you a virgin?" she asked.

I turned bright red and made some ums and ahs. Could I blush any more today?

"Look at me," Greg said to get my attention. "Lesson one. We're going to have to work on your self-confidence. I want you to realize most girls your age are as nervous as you are. Why do you think most freshman girls are looking to go out with juniors and seniors?"

To be honest, I'd never thought about it. I assumed they liked the looks of older guys.

"When I was a freshman, I was dating a junior," Cindy said. "It had to do with his confidence. He didn't stammer or beat around the bush. He just asked me out and I said 'yes.' I was happy to have someone take me by the hand and teach me about dating. What do you think Peggy will think if you're stammering?"

I just nodded. Wait! How the heck did she know about my crush on Peggy?

She looked me up and down.

"You filled out nicely over the summer, and most girls like taller guys."

She had me off-balance. She'd laid the Peggy bomb on me and then she had checked me out. I decided to follow Greg's philosophy: just wait and see what was next. I think Greg saw my wheels grinding to a stop, so he bailed me out.

"First we need to find out your experience level. Are you a virgin?"

I knew that Greg was aware I was.

"Yes, I'm a virgin. I went out with a girl in middle school, but the furthest it ever went was some kissing."

I had one brief girlfriend: Jan Duke. Jan was cute and had just broken up with Justin Tune. A couple of weeks after our first date I saw them kissing in the hall at school and never talked to her again. Shortly after she broke my heart, I had gone off the deep end. Three months later was when Lily happened.

"Good job, you didn't hesitate, you just answered. So I can see there're two things that are working against you: one is experience asking a girl out, and the second is experience being with a girl," Greg said.

"Yeah, that about sums it up."

Didn't that sum up most 15-year-old boys?

"Okay, lucky for you we have a girl you can practice on," my brother said to stun me.

I looked at both Greg and Cindy and tried to figure out whom they would get to practice with me, when Cindy burst out laughing.

"David, ask me out."

I went bright red again and looked at my shoes. I guess I wasn't done blushing. I figured that if I didn't die from this, it was going to help get a date. If I ever wanted to go out with Peggy, I'd better man up and ask my brother's girlfriend out.

"Cindy, if you're not doing anything Friday night, we could, ummm..."

Greg bailed me out.

"Stop. First, have a plan. What would you like to do with Cindy on Friday?"

I got an evil grin.

"I think I can guess," Cindy volunteered.

Greg gave me a dirty look that said I'd better straighten up or Cindy wasn't going to be my test partner.

"What would be a good first date?" he asked.

I got serious and thought about it for a minute.

"How about I meet her at the football game?"

Both Cindy and Greg shook their heads 'no.'

"First of all, do you want Jeff and Alan hanging around you? Or better yet, how about her friends?" Greg asked.

"You want the first date to be something where you can get to know each other better. The first date needs to be something that can either be short, if it's not working out, or can be longer if it is," Cindy added.

I looked confused. Thankfully, my brother had a solution.

"This was Cindy and my first date: I asked her to Jerry's Ice Cream after school. It's right next to the park, so if things are going well you can spend time taking a nice walk."

Jerry's was an institution. They have the best ice cream in town.

"I remember that. You kissed me on the bridge and then, well, it was the best first date I've ever had."

"I think I've got it," I said, and then asked her out. "Cindy, would you like to go to Jerry's and get an ice cream after school on Friday?"

"Why, David, yes I would."

"Good job, let's talk about appearance. You need to look like a boy a girl would want to be seen with; no girl wants to be seen kissing some dork. You have to look the part," Greg said.

That one hurt. What was wrong with what my clothes looked like? Greg could see that he hadn't worded that quite right.

"I'm not trying to be mean, I'm trying to help," he said softly.

I just nodded at Greg. Wait a minute, did someone say kissing? If I hadn't caught it, Mr. Happy sure noticed.

Cindy was pragmatic.

"You need a haircut, and your clothes need a makeover. I've only seen you in old jeans and bad t-shirts. No girl wants to be seen with someone who has on an 'I'm with stupid' t-shirt."

Sure enough, it was what I had on, but I didn't want to be some Ken-doll knockoff either.

"Cindy has volunteered to help you in the next few days to get you looking like someone girls would date," Greg said.

I was relieved. I wanted to make a good impression. It looked like 'plan Peggy' was shaping up. Cindy clapped her hands.

"Goody, I always wanted to make a guy over. Now for your reward: c'mere and kiss me."

I wasn't going to pass this up, and I think they were both surprised when I walked up to her and kissed her. The first kiss was gentle and tentative. Okay, give me a break. My brother's girlfriend was hot, and he was within punching distance; but hell, yes, she was in a silk robe. I reached out, put my hands on her hips and gave her a second kiss. This one had more passion in it and lasted much longer. I slightly parted my lips and I found a tongue in my mouth. I was a little taken aback, but I found I enjoyed it. I decided to give as well as receive. When my tongue snaked into her mouth, Cindy moaned. Her hands went from my chest to the back of my neck.

Her fingers ran through my hair. I felt her melt into my arms and her body mold into mine. She just kind of eased onto me. I knew she could feel my desire press into her, but my mind had short-circuited because her silk robe was almost as good as having her nude in my arms. I felt her firm breasts and hard nipples drill into my chest. My hands found their way to her butt as I pulled her tightly against me. I was lost in the moment.

I heard Greg clear his throat.

"Okay, horndog, I think the lesson's over for today."

The best make-out session I've ever had was with my brother's girlfriend while he watched. I prayed he didn't plan to kill me in my sleep. I'd really forgotten where I was and whom I was with. As I disengaged from Cindy, I noticed that her robe had fallen open to her navel. It barely covered her naughty bits. Okay, she was definitely a 10.

As we parted, we were both aroused. Cindy's chest was flushed, and she had a predatory look in her eyes. I felt like a little rabbit that was being stalked by a jungle cat. My heart beat like there was a hummingbird trapped in my chest. I broke eye contact with Cindy and looked Greg in the eye. He was trying not to laugh. All I could say was I was sorry.

Cindy smiled at me and I swear she purred.

"No need to be sorry, you come by your kissing talents naturally. If I decide to dump this lug I'll look you up."

Damn, Greg was a lucky man. Cindy made no move to cover up as she walked over to Greg.

"I think you need some practice too. Your little brother may be a better kisser than you are."

Greg growled at her and put a serious lip-lock on her. He teased her.

"You little skank, you're teasing my poor brother with all your goodies hanging halfway out."

She squealed as he swatted her butt.

"David, do you feel abused?" she asked.

I laughed as she flashed me her breasts. Greg grinned from ear to ear.

"I'm not sure I can trust you with my little brother."

She looked at my jeans.

"I'm not so sure he's little!"

Greg just rolled his eyes. I knew I had nothing to be ashamed of. I wasn't the biggest guy around, but as far as other freshmen were concerned, I had one of the larger sizes, based on what I saw in gym class.

It was time to go home.

"Thanks for today's lesson," I said once we were in the car.

"Okay, here's this week's homework. First, you're going to let Cindy make you over. You do whatever she tells you. And second, you'll ask someone out for Friday night."

"Should I ask Peggy?"

"Before you go to the big leagues and ask her out, let's get you a few training dates," Greg coached me.

"You're the boss."

✧✧✧

When we got home, Dad was making dinner. Mom was out selling a home. Dad, Greg and I had learned to fend for ourselves, so it was no surprise to see Dad cooking, and it smelled wonderful. Greg and I never told Mom that Dad was a better cook.

"Greg, come make a salad. David, you set the table and get us drinks."

We quietly fell into our tasks. After I was done, I walked up behind Dad and peeked over his shoulder to see what he was making. It was Salisbury steak with brown gravy and mashed potatoes. It looked like he'd made the mashed potatoes from scratch. He noticed me, turned and gave me a hug and a kiss.

Dad had always kissed us. When Greg turned eleven, it was decided we would no longer be kissed on the lips. Some of Greg's friends had commented on it. After he hugged me he went over, hugged, and kissed Greg. Dad always made me feel loved. It was just his open, friendly personality. He had a charisma that just seemed to draw people to him, and to like him. Greg had inherited the same thing. I just wished I had half of their charm.

"How was your day at school?" Dad asked me.

Dad and I shared everything, so Greg wasn't surprised with what followed.

"Today was great. I like all my classes except English; that looks like it might be hard. I got reacquainted with all my friends. Jeff and Alan seem great. The other morning Peggy Pratt got caught in the rain, so I gave her a towel and t-shirt out of my gym bag so she wouldn't have to be wet all day."

"I tell you, Dad, David made a lot of enemies yesterday. No one was happy he gave her a dry t-shirt," Greg said with a chuckle.

We all went to the table and started eating. It felt good to be having our family dinner together where we shared our day. Dad had a big smile on his face too, so I continued.

"That may be, but I'm not too worried about the guys at school. I'll be worried if the girls are all mad at me."

"He has nothing to worry about. You should hear what all the girls were saying about him at lunch. 'Little Dawson grew up over the summer. He was so cute! And did you see his nice butt?'"

I threatened to flick mashed potatoes at Greg.

"Settle down, guys," Dad warned us.

"After school Greg asked me to help him and Cindy out by sitting for some neighbor kids. In return they're helping me with my dating skills."

Dad's looked shocked and Greg gave me a look, but that didn't stop me.

"I'm thinking Cindy may be the best dating coach ever. She taught me how to kiss."

Greg shot water out of his nose and Dad burst out laughing. Dad was enjoying this conversation.

"Please tell me about the kiss."

I sat up a little straighter.

"You know I can't talk to you about that. A gentleman never gives details."

"That's sound advice. May I ask two questions?" Dad asked.

"If I can answer them, I will."

"Okay, fair enough. First, was Cindy a willing participant?"

I nodded my head 'yes.'

"Second, is your brother a dumbass?"

"Yes, sir, he is. I would never let my girlfriend kiss another guy like that, even if he was my brother."

That got them both laughing.

"The little shit put a lip-lock on her that I swear weakened her knees. We found out pretty quick he knows how to kiss. He'll have them lining up, once word gets out."

"Oh lord, I thought one Casanova was enough."

Greg stuck his tongue out at Dad. Dinner was done, so I helped clean up. Dad told Greg to go do his homework. I wanted to talk to Dad about some more serious matters, specifically Lily, Tami, and Mom. I didn't really know what to think of Tami and Bert. I could also not figure out why Mom had been so mad at me, and still seemed to be leery.

"You remember the girl I helped in the spring, the one I gave CPR to?"

I could see my dad stiffen, but he just nodded.

"She told me someone spiked her drink with a date-rape drug. How dangerous is that?"

Dad thought for a minute before he answered. I could tell he didn't expect this line of questioning.

"I would suspect if she had a high enough alcohol level, the drug could cause serious problems. Especially if it depresses her system, it could potentially cause problems with her breathing."

Dad had become serious at this point and followed up with a question.

"Are you telling me kids your age have access to date-rape drugs?"

"Yeah, it kind of freaks me out to think something like that was going on. My concern is it'll happen to someone else."

Dad just nodded. I could tell we would talk about this some more, but not now.

"I have a problem with Tami."

That got Dad's attention.

"I thought you were working things out," Dad said.

"She doesn't want me to call her tonight because she's meeting another guy. She also doesn't want a ride tomorrow."

"I think if this other guy was anything serious you'd have heard about it from Jeff or Alan."

My dad had a point. If there were any gossip to be had, Alan would have told me. I just nodded.

"Honestly, David, I would wait and see. This could be a lot of nothing. Something else was on your mind; what is it?"

Dad could read me like a book. There was no hiding anything from him.

"Mom and I are going to talk when she gets home."

My dad got a serious look.

"I think you need to know something before you have your talk. She has her reasons for being as mad as she is about what happened, but not all the reasons have to do with you. You need to talk to her about this and listen. Don't get mad. I want you to listen and try to understand."

I think I got the same advice from Beth just a few hours earlier concerning Tami.

"Can't you tell me what's going on?"

"I love you both and I know you can work this out, but you're going to have to come more than halfway with her or we're going to have some serious problems as a family."

I was now a little scared. Was Dad telling me if I didn't shape up, I was out of here? I'd just gotten home. What was I going to have to do to make amends?

"Okay, Dad."

"Why don't you go to your room, and when your mother's ready, I'll come and get you."

I went up to my room to wait. We lived in an old Victorian three-story home. Greg and I have our rooms on the third floor. The heating system has old ducts that made it possible to hear conversations from the first floor. I could hear Mom and Dad, but it only sounded like a mumble. I was tempted to eavesdrop but thought better of it. A few minutes later, I heard the stairs creak as Dad came up. There was a light knock on the door.

"Your mom's ready for you."

I followed Dad down the stairs. When we got to the second floor, he went into the master bedroom. I found Mom in the kitchen, eating a salad at the breakfast bar. I got onto the stool next to her. She gave me a look I couldn't read. I just assumed the worst and started babbling.

"Mom, I'm sorry if this isn't working out. I'll call Uncle John and see if I can go live with him. I know I've disappointed you and you're not ready for me to be back."

Mom was one of those people who just says whatever is on her mind. There was no filter. I sometimes wonder if what they say about opposites attracting was true. Mom's sharp tongue tended to push people away. Dad jokes if she wasn't so good looking he would never put up with her. The truth of the matter was Mom was stop-traffic good looking. I also knew they loved each other. I had to remember she loved me too.

"You are maybe the stupidest kid I've ever known. Why would you ever think I wanted you to move out?"

It sounds like she's been talking to Tami with the 'stupid' comment.

"Before I went to Uncle John's you said you didn't want me in your home. When I got back you just seemed like you don't want me here."

"Like I said, you're stupid."

Okay, I hadn't listened to my dad. He said listen to my mom. I was doing way too much talking and I now knew my mom thought I was stupid. That was what happened I when I didn't pay attention. To my credit, that wasn't the worst thing she had ever called me, so I figured it was time to shut up.

"David, last spring you broke my heart. You'd become someone I no longer recognized. Even your best friends didn't want anything to do with you. The final straw was when you almost killed that girl."

I could feel all the old emotions come back. I felt my chest get tight and I knew I was about to start to cry. I think Mom saw it in my eyes.

"I've never told you about my dad."

The story we were told was Grandpa had died when Mom was in her early teens. No one ever talked about it much, so I was never curious.

"He was an alcoholic. By the time I was thirteen, Mom kicked him out. When he was sober, I loved him to death, but he was a mean drunk. I won't go into details, but it was the best thing for all of us. When I saw you at the police station all those memories came flooding back. I knew I had to do something."

"Going to Uncle John's was for the best. Will I ever drink again? I have no idea, but I don't intend to go back to that lifestyle. I'll only promise to try and make better decisions."

"I know. I've had several talks with John. He says you did a lot of growing up this summer. David, I love you and you'll always be my baby. I know I'm not the easiest person to live with, but you and I are going to be okay. Just give me some time."

"Okay, Mom. I love you too."

After that, we had a long conversation and caught up on everything that went on since I had been gone. It was nice just to talk to my mom. I really missed her. We both realized it was getting late and we went up to bed. I felt much better about things now that we'd talked.

✧✧✧

Chapter 4 – Health and Human Services

Saturday August 31

Cindy showed up around 10 a.m. Greg had something going on, so it was just the two of us. The plan was to check out my clothes and figure out what would work. We would then go to the mall and pick out some clothes, and I would get a haircut.

I'd cleaned my room like a madman the night before. Mom was suspicious because I hadn't cleaned my room in over six months. The last time she threatened not to let me go to spring break at our church youth camp. Greg told her what Cindy was doing, and Mom just smiled and said it was nice to see me growing up.

Cindy was impressed. She'd seen my room a few times and she commented on the changes.

"You go sit on the bed until I need you."

She was going through my t-shirts and putting most of my best ones into a pile. She found a basic black one.

"Put this on," she ordered.

I hesitated, but I remembered what Greg had said, so I just did it. She watched with a clinical eye, so I wasn't too embarrassed.

"Turn around. Now lift your arms. Not too bad, but a little snug in the shoulders."

I'd grown, so most of my clothes no longer fit. She told me to take it off. She put it into a new pile. She continued to hand me shirts until we had gone through all of them. There were only three she liked. My favorites she put into a garbage bag along with all the ones that didn't fit.

She then went to work on my jeans. When she handed me a pair of jeans to try on, I suddenly realized I was without a shirt and was about to strip down to my underwear. I figured to go for it.

"Stop. Seriously, you're wearing tighty-whities?" Cindy asked before I could pull my jeans up.

She went over to my top drawer and started to put all my underwear into the garbage bag. I had nothing to wear. She went into Greg's room and came back with a pair of boxers.

"Put these on."

I was not going to get naked in front of Cindy. I stepped into the bathroom and changed. Thank God, Cindy didn't make any comments. She just nodded and handed me a pair of jeans to put on. It turned out she only liked one pair of jeans and two pairs of my shoes. I was kind of bumming when she made me haul all my clothes out to her car. She took me to the local church and had me put the clothes into the donation bin. She then took me shopping.

I normally hate shopping, but with Cindy, it was fun. She enjoyed herself so much that it was contagious. I have to admit, I looked good in the clothes she picked out. I've never been into tight pants, but Cindy insisted on skinny jeans.

She seemed at a loss for shirts. My shoulders were much wider than my waist, so she said we had to get more-fitted shirts. I wasn't thrilled, but I was not going to hurt her feelings.

"Cindy, this is fun and all, but I don't have the money to buy all this."

"It's my treat," she assured me.

I grinned at her and gave her a hug and a kiss on the cheek. Cindy was beaming. She then took me to a hair salon. I've always had my dad cut my hair and when the gal saw it, she almost fainted. I got the whole treatment of wash, cut and styling. When we left, I had a bag full of shampoos, conditioners and gels.

I looked into the mirror and was amazed. I looked like a much better version of myself. I thought I looked older; I could probably get into a bar looking like this. They cut my hair short on the sides and styled the top; the top curled loosely and looked like I did nothing to it. The trick to get it to look like that had taken them thirty minutes to teach me. It was a distinctive, cool look.

When I finally came out of the back, I noticed the cute receptionist looking at me with a critical eye. "Was she checking me out?" I asked as soon as we left the salon.

"Of course she was. I'll let you in on a little secret: if a girl sees a guy with another girl, she wants him even more."

"No way that's true."

"Want to bet?"

"Sure, what's the bet and what do I win?"

"Go into the sandwich shop and flirt with any of the girls in there and see how far you get with your new look. If you get digits, that actually work, you win and I'll be your girl toy this afternoon. I'll come in ten minutes later and flirt with you. I'll then leave and give you another five minutes to try to get a phone number. If I win, you're mine for the afternoon."

Of course, I would agree to this bet. It sounded like a sure thing either way.

"Deal!"

There were three girls my age or a little older working. I could see all of them talking and glancing over at me. I had this in the bag. The cute girl with long chestnut hair came over. She looked like she was a little older than I was. She had a very athletic look. When she came to the table, she gave me a smile.

"Can I get you something to drink?"

"Sure, how about a Coke?"

"Sorry, we only have Pepsi."

"I'll have Mountain Dew then."

I hated the taste of Pepsi. I'm a diehard Coke man, but I did like Mountain Dew. It looked like radioactive slurry and had enough caffeine to kick-start any day.

"What can I get you?" she asked when she brought me my drink.

I figured to use the direct approach.

"How about your phone number?"

She smiled at me and wrote down her name and number on a napkin. I was amused, she didn't miss a beat. She must get hit on all the time. "What would you like to eat?" she clarified.

No need to push it, but I was a guy. I decided I'd already won the bet, so I left the 'eat' comment alone. I ordered a sub. Cindy came slinking in. She'd watched and figured it was time for her to pay up.

"How did you do?"

I pulled out the napkin and handed it to her. She pulled out her cell phone, dialed the number, and put it on speaker.

"Health and Human Services," a cheerful voice answered.

She hung up and busted out laughing. What the heck? The waitress had given me the number for the local VD clinic. I had to laugh; it was pretty funny. The waitress came back with my sandwich.

I could see her take Cindy's measure.

"What can I get you?"

Cindy was still laughing.

"You gave him the VD clinic number?"

The waitress smiled.

"Sure. If he's that brazen, I figured he needed the number."

They both lost it and I started to get a little uncomfortable. Cindy smiled at her.

"My boyfriend will split his sandwich with me, but could you get me an iced tea?"

As she was walked away, Cindy gave me a kiss. Well, I liked that. I also noticed the girls had taken note.

"Can you put that into a to-go cup? I have to take off," Cindy said when our waitress came back with her tea.

When she returned with the to-go cup, Cindy leaned into me and ran her hand on the inside of my thigh. I jumped because I knew her hand was mere inches from my package. She gave me a nice kiss. The waitress just gawked as Cindy got up and walked out. I didn't say a word but smiled at the waitress. I pulled out my phone and handed it to her. She put her name and number into my phone and told me to call her. I looked down and saw her name, Robbie King.

I finished my sandwich and went to find Cindy. She just smirked and I knew she knew. I just followed her to the car like a good boy toy.

✧✧✧

When we got home, Mom and Dad were there. Cindy decided she would collect her bet by having me model my clothes for my parents. Everyone seemed to have a good time at my expense.

"If I didn't know you, I'd jump you," Mom said.

Talk about too much information. I thought I would die of embarrassment. Cindy gave me a knowing look and smirked.

"I do know him, and I think might jump him. Greg will just have to find a new girlfriend."

I thought we'd have to give Dad CPR when he choked on his drink. I think Cindy was evil, but in a very good way. Greg was a lucky guy. The more I'd gotten to know her, the more I liked her. I think I might like her jumping me.

✧✧✧

Monday September 2

Labor Day was the busiest day of the season for Dad and his Parks and Recreation staff. The parks would be full and it was the last day they had the public pools open. Greg and I always had to help in some way. For some reason Greg had gotten out of helping this time. He got up early and left for the day. Dad made me help the lifeguards at the main pool. You had to be sixteen to do it for money, so I was an unpaid volunteer, or that was what Dad told me.

By 11:00 the pool was packed. It was a perfect end-of-summer day, with the temperature headed to the low 80s and not a cloud in the sky. For many of the teenage girls it was a chance to even out their tans. For the guys it was a chance to flirt with the many pretty girls.

I was put in charge of gofer duty. Anything the lifeguards or staff needed I was sent to fetch. I'd gotten everyone's lunch orders when I saw Bill Rogers and company show up. They were all scruffy-looking guys, and you could see the crowd keep a watchful eye on them. They made no secret they wanted female company. When they found some prime lounge chairs, they chased off the hapless guys seated in them.

It wasn't going to be long before they pissed someone off, and there'd be a fight or the staff would be forced to get involved. I hadn't seen Bill since the night of the party. I could feel the hair go up on the back of my neck. This guy scared me. He was a complete wild card, and I knew he could become violent at the drop of a hat. I had no idea why I went up to him.

"Hey, Bill, how's it going?"

It took him a minute to realize who I was.

"Dawson, it's good to see you, man. I didn't know you worked here. How was your summer?"

"I was sent away for the summer."

"Oh yeah, I heard that somewhere. Hey, thanks for keeping us out of it."

"No problem. I wanted to ask you a favor."

Bill tipped his head forward so he could look over his sunglasses.

"What kind of favor?"

"You're making our guests nervous. I was wondering if you'd do me a favor and leave."

Bill and my eyes locked. Out of my peripheral vision, I saw two of his goons stand up on either side of me. I knew if I showed any fear, they'd jump me. Bill looked pissed.

"Listen, wuss, do you see all this prime trim that needs my attention?"

He pulled his sunglasses off and made a circular motion to indicate all the women close to them.

"Bill, I understand, but to be honest I'm not seeing anyone who's interested. They seem nervous. Today is supposed to be a fun day for everyone. We both know at some point you or one of your guys is going to cause a confrontation."

He chuckled, and not in a nice way.

"David, you have balls. I think our confrontation's about to begin, with you getting your ass kicked."

"Hang on, Bill. You do owe me a favor, and I'm calling it in now."

He got up in my face. The next thing I knew he slugged me in the gut. I went down to one knee and doubled over. Bill grabbed me by the hair and pulled my head up. His face was a mask of pure evil.

"No one tells me what to do! Do you hear me?"

"Yes," I choked out.

He seemed to make a decision. He jerked my hair back, which caused me to sprawl out on the pool deck. He got down close to my ear and spoke so only I could hear him.

"You're lucky. I normally wouldn't let something like this go, but I do owe you a favor. We're even now, but keep an eye out. I may need to kick your ass just to make an example of you."

He stormed out with his goons in in his wake. I got to my feet and several people gave me appreciative looks. None of them seemed to want to check on me. I think they were embarrassed because they were going to let me take a beating. I went to the office and collected myself. It was never good to get on any bully's radar when you're a nerd, especially a bully like Bill. I would have to be careful at school for the next couple of weeks.

✧✧✧

Tuesday September 3

I came to school with my new haircut and wearing the first outfit Cindy had told me to wear. I had on a fitted black t-shirt and black jeans. The shirt was almost worse than going without one. It showed every bump, curve and ripple. The jeans were tight, and Cindy said they made my butt look cute. After a summer of farm work, I was no longer embarrassed about my body, so I wasn't too worried. Jeff and Alan were out front. They started to give me a hard time. Jeff fired the first shot and nodded to Alan to turn around as I came up.

"Alan, do you know who the new guy is?"

Alan spun around and faced me.

"Hey, GQ, where's the photo shoot? Is it true all models are gay?"

"Yes, we are, and I have to say I'm into nerdy little guys. What are you doing after school today?"

Alan started to back up and Jeff burst out laughing. "So what's with the makeover? Did Tami get her wish and turn you into her little Ken doll?" Jeff asked.

I gave them a scowl.

"No, actually Cindy got her claws into me. Seriously guys, this isn't too gay, is it?"

Talk about walking into it; I thought they'd have a stroke, they laughed so hard. I was ready to head home and change when Peggy came up. My back was to her and she saw my best friends crack up.

"Hey, guys, what's so funny?" she asked.

I heard her gasp. I turned to her and saw she was slowly checking me out. I started to worry something was wrong, because I couldn't read her expression. Her hand came to her mouth and I heard her whisper, "Oh, my."

"Are you okay?" I asked.

She seemed to come back to herself, and she looked me in the eye and blushed. Peggy Pratt, my wet dream, had checked me out and blushed. To hell with what Jeff and Alan thought. If Peggy liked it, I would dress up like a GQ model every day of the week! Thank you, Cindy!

"No, I just never realized, uh, dang, Dawson, you're a hottie."

To their credit, Jeff and Alan shut up when they saw Peggy's reaction. I think Tami had smacked Alan enough in the past few days to slow him down. They looked at me in that weird way they do when an older good-looking girl talks to me and I act like it happens all the time. I leaned in close so only Peggy could hear.

"Not too gay?"

She actually snorted. She seemed fascinated with my new haircut. She reached up and ran her fingers through my curls. Any time Peggy was touching me like this it was a very good thing. She leaned in a little closer.

"No. Seriously, I like the new look."

Then she shocked me.

"A hard man is good to find," she said in a breathy whisper.

My eyebrows went up. I'm sure the guys hadn't heard her because they didn't react. Peggy eyed me, and not as just a friend! Then she jerked as if she realized she'd said it aloud. I just winked at her and put my arm out.

"Madam, may I escort you to your locker?"

"Why sir, it would be my pleasure."

She noticeably relaxed. I'm sure she was glad I hadn't pressed the issue, but I was filing this away for future study. I made a significant step towards getting out of the 'friends' penalty box where so many nice guys find themselves. At least she looked at me with a little heat.

We giggled as we entered the building. Then things got a little weird. As we walked down the hall, the crowd seemed to part as we walked to Peggy's locker. She stood a little taller, pushed her chest out, and put a little wiggle into her walk. I could tell she enjoyed the attention. When we got to her locker, she gave me a peck on the cheek.

"Thank you, kind sir. You can walk me to my locker anytime."

I had a stupid grin on my face all the way to my first class.

✧✧✧

At lunch, I caught a nice-looking brunette checking me out. I remembered her from World History class. She must have been from one of the other middle schools who came to this high school, because I couldn't remember her name. She seemed like someone I would like to go out with, so I walked up to her.

"Hi, my name's David."

"Hi, I'm Tina."

The good news was she hadn't run off screaming. She seemed nervous. Without my brother's coaching, I would have just frozen up. When I saw her fidget, I felt liberated.

"I'd like you to go with me to have ice cream at Jerry's on Friday after school," I said.

Did I just say that? I held my breath as I waited to hear her response. "You mean, with other people?" she asked as she smiled at me.

Did she not want to go with me? Not wanting anyone to overhear, I leaned forward and whispered in her ear.

"No, it'll be just the two of us on a date."

My hot breath on her neck caused her to shiver. Her eyelashes did this cute little flutter thing as she stammered.

"I, I, I would love to."

She obviously hadn't expected me to ask her out. Her eyes darted around to look for her friends. I let out more of my hot breath on her neck. Her head went back just a little, and she closed her eyes for a moment. I glanced down and noticed her nipples were erect. Heck yes! It felt good to be in control. I stepped out of her personal space.

"I'll meet you out front after school on Friday and we can walk over."

The bell rang and I went to class. I noticed she and her friends were all huddled together sharing all the details. I was about to find out girls were bigger gossips than guys were.

Tami corralled me and pointed me in the direction of my next class.

"What was that about?"

It felt nice that for once she didn't know everything that went on with me. She obviously noticed the new look and my confidence. I know this was just the opening question in my interrogation. I had three choices: clam up and let her puzzle it out herself; let the interrogation continue; or just tell her. I decided on the latter.

"I got myself a date for Friday night."

She actually stopped in her tracks and snagged my arm to spin me around to face her. Okay, I didn't actually choose to tell her everything. She did rather scare the crap out of me.

"I asked Greg to help me, ummm, socially. He enlisted the help of Cindy to do me over."

She just nodded.

"They've been coaching me, and my first assignment was to get a date for Friday night. So when I saw Tina checking me out, I decided to give it a try. Normally I get all tongue-tied with a pretty girl, but with Greg and Cindy's coaching, I had a plan. Greg helped by telling me the girl I asked out would probably be more nervous than I was. So when I saw she was nervous, I felt at ease."

I tilted my head to indicate we needed to head to class, and I started to walk. She fell in beside me, but remained silent.

"I asked her out for a date to Jerry's for ice cream, and then a walk in the park. It's low-pressure and gives us a chance to get to know each other."

We reached her class and I was happy to see she just shrugged and went in. It was her subtle way to let me know she approved. She could tell I wasn't being a horndog. I was elated the rest of the day.

✧✧✧

After school, I tried to call Tami again, but got no answer. She was avoiding me. I started to get pissed. It wasn't as if she was mad at me, but something had changed. The only thing I could think of was it must be her dating Bert. I debated if I should send her a text, but decided to take my dad's advice and wait it out before I let my emotions get ahead of themselves.

After I hung up on Tami's voice mail, my phone rang. I looked at the caller ID and saw it was Cindy.

"Hey, Boy Toy, how did it go today? Did the new look have the girls drooling?"

"Yep, I had to beat them off with a stick. Actually, it went pretty well."

"Spill it."

"Well, to start with, I got a kiss on the cheek from Peggy. That made it worthwhile. At lunch I asked a girl out and she said 'yes.'"

I had to pull the phone away from my ear as I heard her squeals of joy. Girls cracked me up when they got that excited. I could imagine her doing a little Snoopy Dance of Joy. I interrupted her little celebration.

"Is Greg there? I want to share this with him."

She calmed down.

"No, I haven't seen him since lunch today."

"Oh, he's not home, I just assumed he was with you."

"Nope, I'm flying solo tonight."

She then spent the next ten minutes telling me what to wear tomorrow. Today went so well I wasn't going to argue with her.

✧✧✧

Greg didn't get home until about six, and I was dying to tell him.

"I have a date for Friday night!"

"Great job man, I knew you could do it. I guess I'm going to have to jam about twelve lessons into one tonight."

We went up to his room. He smelled of sex, and went to take a shower before Mom found out. While he took his shower, I tried to put two and two together to figure out where he'd been. I sure hoped he hadn't cheated on Cindy, but it just didn't make sense. Greg had a strict code of conduct that I had *never* seen him violate. Part of his code was not to cheat when he dated someone. Either he'd hooked up with Cindy in the last hour, or he wasn't dating Cindy. The last one was impossible, so he must have shown up right after she and I got off the phone.

Before I could get too far into trying to solve the mystery, Tami called.

"Hey, David, I see you called."

"Hey, long time no talk. What have you been up to?"

I tried to sound upbeat, even though I was worried inside. I needed my best friend back. I heard her take a deep breath and exhale slowly.

"I've had a lot on my mind. I need to work through some things."

I grimaced. I knew how much we each cared about the other, and yet I was uncertain what to say that wouldn't risk our friendship. In these kinds of situation, I would normally ask Tami, but I couldn't when she was involved. I felt my soul was bared and very helpless.

"Anything you'd like to share?"

I think I let some of my concern bleed through, but I had to know.

"Yeah, I would like to share. You're my best friend, after all. But I can't do it over the phone."

Thank You! She was still my best friend. I had held my breath. I let it out in a whoosh.

"I have an idea. Beth Anderson invited us over to her place on Sunday to go swimming. I haven't had a chance to ask, but would you be willing to go?"

"Perfect. I'll meet you there. I'll get the details from Beth."

She actually sounded like her old self. I felt a huge weight lift from my shoulders. I hadn't appreciated how much this had affected me. I suddenly needed to say something.

"Tami, you do know that I love you?"

"Yes, David, I know. You've never told me before, and it's sweet, but I've always known you love me. And best friend of mine, I love you too."

I heard the phone disconnect and I knew all was right with the world. Tami Glade loved me. We never looked at each other in a sexual manner. We never played doctor, or you-show-me-yours-and-I'll-show-you-mine. Tami was my twin sister. Maybe not biologically, but we're as close as twins. We just made each other better people. I think the most confusing thing was when I saw her with Bert and I thought it could be me. I knew our friendship meant more to me than to risk it. I knew I would just be happy for her. She would feel the same way about anyone I dated.

I was pleased when Greg was done with his shower and he came to my room. I hadn't forgotten he came in and reeked of sex. For some reason I suspected it wasn't with

Cindy, but was it really my business? I loved my brother and I really liked Cindy. They made a great couple.

Greg jumped back into the conversation.

"Okay, who are you going out with?"

"Tina... I just realized I don't know her last name."

"It's probably best you don't know a lot about her. It'll give you something to talk about."

He thought for a moment.

"On your walk to Jerry's, I want you to do a couple of things. The first is to tell her she looks nice. When you tell her that, look at her mouth. If you're looking at her tits, she'll think you're a horndog and just want in her pants. If you stare her in the eye, she'll get nervous. Just glance at her mouth and say it. Then glance away, reach down, and take her hand. Once you have her hand, start walking."

"Really?"

"Yep, it's an early indicator if you're doing well or not. You've basically taken possession of her. You'll see many girls will take notice of this as you walk off the school grounds. This'll pay off in spades later on."

"What do you mean by 'pay off'?"

"Okay, I'm about to sound like a complete ass, but if you want to date someone like Peggy, you have to become someone she can date. She can't have an awkward freshman chasing her. She'll cut you off at the knees. A girl who's a junior will only go out with a freshman if it's socially acceptable."

I smirked.

"You're right, you do sound like a jerk, but I think I understand. I have to become cool enough that I can get out of the 'friends' zone."

"Don't get me wrong. Peggy isn't like that. If she wanted you, she would move heaven and earth to be with you. She's one of the best human beings I know. You'll be the luckiest guy in the world if you date her. But the cold fact is she'll never see you for the great guy I know you are until other girls start to notice."

"Yeah, Cindy was telling me a little about that. She said girls are attracted to men other women want."

"Cindy's a smart girl. You'd do well to listen to her. The goal out front of the school is to get the girls to start buzzing about you as a potential date. Up to this point, it's been about you coming out. You started out by showing up at school all grown up. Then you did a brilliant thing in just being you. You gave Peggy a shirt when she really needed it. You have no idea how that affected the girls at this school. It created a buzz about you being a nice guy. Cindy took all that and put it into a package that had all the girls checking you out. Friday, when they see you with a date, they'll be jealous it's not them on your arm. Next week you'll start having girls approach you."

"Okay, I get what you guys are doing. What do I need to do to make this date a success?"

"It's just human nature that boys try to chase and capture girls. It's a girl's job to run and ward off guys. We need to change that mindset or you'll never get past the first date with this girl. On the walk over, take your time and ask her about herself. Let her feel you care about her. You'll never get into trouble if they're talking about themselves unless you become judgmental or get too personal too soon."

"Got it."

"When you get to Jerry's, find out what she wants to order and then order for her. This shows you're a gentleman and you're taking care of her. You're no longer chasing her; you're taking the initial step in changing the dynamics so she can get to know you. She probably has very little experience and this may put her off a little bit, but it just shows you're confident. This is the type of thing that'll set you apart from all the other guys she's ever gone out with or will ever go out with."

I nodded. He was the master, so I wasn't about to question him.

"If she asks you about yourself, give her a complete answer and then turn the conversation back to her."

I was a little confused.

"What do you mean by giving 'a complete answer'?"

"If you give her a half-assed answer she'll think you're a fake. Take your time and tell her what she wants to know and then turn it back to her. You want the conversation ratio to be about 85% about her."

"But what if she asks me about something that's personal?"

"Good, you're thinking. You can tell her it's personal."

"But won't she think I'm being evasive?"

"Maybe, but you'll get more respect having some boundaries than telling her things you probably shouldn't. Here's a great example: Cindy asked me yesterday if I'd ever dated Peggy. I told her yes I did, my junior year for about six weeks. I felt comfortable telling her because I'm sure she already knew. If not, it was something she could ask Peggy about. Then she asked me if Peggy was a natural redhead. Once again, she already knows she is, but it's not my place to tell Peggy's business. The real question was did we sleep together. That's nobody's business but Peggy's and mine."

I nodded in understanding.

"While talking to her, make sure you're sitting on the edge of your seat facing her. By doing this, your body language is telling her you're interested in what she's saying. Don't stare at her, but be sure you make eye contact. Don't make her think you have anything but her on your mind."

Good to know; I knew I hated it when I was with someone and it seemed as if they'd rather be somewhere else.

"Okay, controversial subjects to stay away from: do not ask her about her ex-boyfriends or her sexual experience. Do not gossip. If you're a big gossip, she'll assume you'll gossip about her. Do not put anyone down. I think you get the idea; keep it positive."

Greg gathered his thoughts.

"After you're done eating, tell her she's going for a walk in the park with you. If she does, then things are still going well. If not, this is her chance to bail, and this is important: I don't care if you're having the worst time in the world, you ask her to go for the walk. The reason is your date will set your reputation. She'll be telling her friends all about it. If you're an ass, you will never get another date."

That made sense. Greg had a great reputation and had dated all types before he and Cindy hooked up.

"The reason I told you to tell her you were going for a walk is because most guys are whiney little beggars. Girls hate that. You hear them say stuff like 'please baby let's do this' or 'can we do that.' As soon as you go there, the girl will have you wrapped around her little finger and they know it. By you taking control, it breaks the whole run, entice and evade cycle. They turn themselves over to a more mature and confident man."

I wrapped my brain around what he said as he continued.

"Head over to the lake area and go to the bridge. When you get there, tell her you're going to kiss her. Most guys make the mistake of asking if they can. If you ask and she's nervous, she'll tell you 'no' nine times out of ten. I take that back, she'll probably kiss *you* because you're a Dawson," he said, and smirked to break the tension. "What it'll do is take your nervousness away. You'll feel more confident knowing she's more nervous than you are. If you tell her, and she doesn't want to be kissed, she'll tell you.

You telling her you're going to kiss her will give her permission to do it."

"Now this is the tricky part. *You will not force her!* If you're going to be in control, you have to take the responsibility of making sure she's a willing participant. If you have any doubt, ask her."

"How do I pull that off?"

"Tell her what you're going to do and then pause. If she looks hesitant, then ask her if it's okay. Let me give you an example. You're going to kiss Tina. Say 'I'm going to kiss you.' Don't just grab her and kiss her. Take your time. Look her deep in her eyes and then kiss her. If you see her hesitate, ask her. 'Tina, is it okay if I kiss you?' If she doesn't answer right away, tell her it's alright to say 'no.' If she says stop, you will stop right now. I mean it David, NO means NO."

"I know."

"David, the one thing that will disappoint me is hearing you're the kind of guy who forces himself on a girl. I can't stress this enough. Don't be that loser."

I'd never seen Greg so intense. At that moment, I never intended to let something like that happen. We'd been raised to respect women. I just nodded.

"I don't think you need any advice on kissing. You seem to have it down, according to Cindy. Do not become an octopus. If you go straight for her ass or breasts, you'll be shut down before you get going. No one wants to be fighting off his or her date all night. She'll revert to the run-and-hide, and you'll get a rep as a guy who can't be trusted. Keep your hands on her waist until she gets into it. Once she's going good, take her by the hand and take her to the picnic area just off to the side of the bridge. It's secluded and you'll have plenty of privacy. That'll give her confidence and you'll get much farther. And finally, be prepared."

"What do you mean?" I asked.

"Okay, not that this date is going to go anywhere, but if it does you need to have condoms. Part of being in charge is the responsibility side. It's *not* the woman's responsibility for birth control. If you aren't protecting her, you're not man enough to be having sex. Going on a date unprepared is setting yourself up to fail. When the time comes, it's very hard to stop in the heat of the moment. Don't put yourself or her in that position."

"Oh."

I looked at him, confused, as he got up and left the room. Where the heck was I going to get condoms? A minute later, my big brother came to my rescue. He tossed two foil packs to me.

"Thanks, man."

"No problem. If you're going to be man enough to have sex, then you're man enough to buy your own condoms. I expect you to get your own supply. I honestly don't think things will go so far you'll need them. I'll leave the sex talk for later. No need for information overload."

After my brother left, I thought I would never get to sleep. I was trying to remember everything he'd told me. How could one date be so complicated?

✧✧✧

Chapter 5 – First Date

Friday September 6

The rest of the week was a blur. I went to class and then football practice until I was exhausted. When I got home, I studied and crashed. Then I got up and did it all again. I was nervous about Friday, but Greg and Cindy kept coaching me throughout the week. By Friday, I was ready to go.

I awoke Friday morning to the sunlight as it peeked around my bedroom curtains. My stomach started to knot up when I thought about today and the anticipated *first date* with Tina. The night before, Cindy had jumped onto video chat and I took my tablet to my closet so she could pick out my clothes.

She then took the time to walk me through how to do my hair. I wasn't used to using hair products and she wasn't happy with how I'd slipped on doing my hair each day. I tried to explain that at least three showers a day meant having to fix my hair each time. She gave me a look and I meekly decided to do as I was told. This morning I was up twenty minutes early to shower and do my hair. If the guys only knew, I would catch it all day long.

Greg gave me a ride to school and Cindy did a visual inspection when we arrived. We arranged to meet right before my date since Cindy knew I had PE and would need to do my hair again. I tried to decide if this was irritating or helpful. The sad truth was Cindy was so hot I enjoyed her fussing over me. It gave me an excuse to be around her.

Alan was a big pest all day because he wanted to know details about my plans for my date with Tina. I actually threatened to punch him if he didn't stop. I guess he had sex on his mind 24/7 like almost every other fifteen-year-old boy. Alan was impressed I had one of our fellow freshmen going out on a date the second week of school. I guess I could see his point. I never dated much in middle school. I was confused as to how Alan knew so much about the date. I didn't give out any details, and I knew Tami, Greg and Cindy wouldn't tell either.

Apparently Tina had talked. I found it hard not to share with Jeff and Alan what Greg had told me. I probably would share with Tami, but we hadn't had our talk yet. The one thing I always admired about Greg was he never shared personal stuff about someone else. With Tina blabbing to all her friends, I could see where Greg's approach was better, and I wanted to follow his example. I noticed several girls had taken an interest in me once word got out. I liked the attention, but Greg cautioned me it wasn't a good idea to do anything about those girls until I was done dating Tina. But I made mental note in case this date didn't work out.

Finally, the end of school came. I dropped my books off at my locker, and went to the front entrance. Cindy found me before I went out.

"David, come here."

She was like a mother hen as she fixed my hair and made sure I was presentable.

"Word is there are thirty freshman girls hanging out front to see you guys off on your date."

Was she kidding me?

"You're joking, right?"

"Nope, and that's a good thing."

"How can that be good?"

"It means they've taken notice."

By 'they,' I assumed she meant the freshman girls. Ah, Greg had warned me, but I hadn't believed him. If there was a crowd, I had to remember not to make a fool out of myself.

"Thanks for warning me."

"Okay, you look ready. Go have fun and don't do anything I wouldn't do," she said, giving me a smug smile that begged for a comeback.

"Someday you'll have to tell me what you wouldn't do."

I arched my eyebrows and her grin got bigger. I decided to beat a hasty retreat. She stuck her tongue out at me and just smiled.

The front entrance area was what made Lincoln High a historic landmark. It was originally designed to look like a park. The manicured green lawns and mature oak trees gave it the feel of serenity. The raised planted beds had nice walls, ideal to kick back and people-watch from. I noticed various freshman girls in groups of threes and fours all hanging around the entrance. Cindy's estimate was a little low. There were at least fifty girls who waited for the show. I'd not seen this many girls in one place since school started. I saw that a couple of junior boys had figured it out and worked the crowd. The gossip network was in overdrive. I started to get a little pissed off. Greg said this part of the date was for show. Didn't these girls have anything better to do?

I saw Tina come towards me. I remembered her mentioning she had math last period, which was across campus. She was accompanied by three of her friends who all checked me out and giggled. Tina scanned the crowd and got a smug look on her face. Well, that confirmed it. She was the one who had bragged about our date.

As she walked up, I noticed she wore a short skirt and a pink cashmere sweater. I appreciated she had shown off her nice legs as opposed to her normal jeans and t-shirt. She obviously was dressed to impress today. She saw me notice and gave me a wink.

When she got about six feet from me, she broke away from her friends. Her big smile reminded me of the cat that ate the canary. I was now officially pissed. I felt fifty-plus pair of eyes bore into my back. If Greg hadn't warned me, I would have let my feelings show. I felt like a piece of meat surrounded by a pack of hungry dogs.

"Hi," Tina greeted me.

I slid my arm around her waist, pulled her into me, and gave her a kiss. All conversation suddenly stopped. In the back of my mind, I was chastising myself for being an idiot, so I just continued to kiss her. At first, I felt her stiffen in surprise, but it wasn't long before she actually kissed me back. Whoa, this girl was starting to turn me on. When our kiss stopped, her eyes fluttered open and I smiled at her.

"Hi. I've wanted to kiss you all day."

I heard her breath catch in surprise. Her eyes were as big as saucers. Before she could respond, I grabbed her hand and started to walk off school grounds. I could hear the gaggle of girls explode into conversation as we walked away. Tina didn't say a word, but she went with me. When we got about halfway down the block, I started to feel bad for her. I'd forgotten the *big* rule: don't force yourself on a girl. The worst part was it was done in front of the biggest gossip network known to man, teenage girls. I pulled up short.

"Tina, I'm sorry I kissed you."

"What?"

She sounded pissed. Oh crud, that did not come out right. I saw a flash in her eyes that scared me.

"Oops, I meant I'm sorry I kissed you without asking your permission."

"Oh."

I could see her face go from 'What the heck are you thinking?' to 'stupid boy.' I can live with 'stupid boy.' I'd been in that personal doghouse many a time with Tami.

"Tina, I want you to know no means no. If at any time you're not comfortable with *anything*, do not hesitate to tell me. I want you to know you're in control of how fast or how slow we go."

"David, can I tell you something?"

I just nodded.

"I asked around about you and I know you're a good guy. Peggy, Lily and Tami have all talked to me. I was a little nervous when you first asked me out, but everyone says you have a good heart. When you kissed me, I just wasn't expecting it. To be honest, if you'd asked I'd've said yes."

Two things hit me. The first was that my female friends had talked to my date. Was that a good thing or not? Second, I felt much better knowing she didn't think I was some guy on the make. It was time to change the subject. Greg said to get your date to talk about things that interest them. I looked at her.

"You look very nice."

This seemed to bring her back.

"Thank you."

I was still worried about how she felt about me laying one on her in front of her peers. It was hard to be a teenage girl, and I figured my little display would be seen in one of two ways. I prayed I hadn't made it hard on her. I needed to feel this out a little and see what she thought.

"I think we gave your friends a little show back there."

She laughed.

"Yes, I guess we did."

At least she didn't seem mad. I could tell something was weighing on her mind.

"I'd bet they're all jealous you're going out today."

"I think so. Several of them didn't believe you asked me on a date."

Teenage girls can be mean. It sounded like she'd fought a gallant battle all week. I could tell I was close to what was bothering her.

"Why's that?" I asked.

She looked down. She was as nervous about this date as I was. I pulled her chin up so she could look me in the eyes. She looked so vulnerable I just wanted to wrap my arms around her and hold her until everything was all right.

"Tina, you're a gorgeous young woman and I wouldn't want to be with anyone else right now," I said.

The scary part was it was true. She was cute and had the right balance of looks and innocence. Was she drop-dead gorgeous like Cindy or Peggy? No, but I could see myself falling for her. I like breasts like every other guy, but this girl had my weakness, a cute butt. Throw in a little vulnerability and the male ego will pull out the old white-knight routine.

I saw her eyes fill with tears and she buried her face in my chest. Great! I pulled her into my arms and felt her shoulders shake. What the heck? Greg didn't tell me what to do when this happened. I should remember to bring a hanky next time. Note to self: be prepared. I wrapped my arms around her and gave her a hug. I'm sure if you make your date cry in the first fifteen minutes it can't be a good thing. One thing I'd learned was it was better to be there for a girl when she was crying than it was to try to talk to her, so I gently rocked her in my arms. I tried to make her feel safe and cared for. When she stopped crying, she looked at me sheepishly.

"I'm sorry for that."

"So why did they think you didn't have a date?" I asked.

"I don't know. I guess they were being mean to me like they always are. I've been the quiet one in the group. I'm always the last one to do anything, so when I told them I had a date they didn't buy it. Then, when they found out it was you, they told me you were out of my league. I don't think they like it that I'm the first one to have a high school date, especially with a guy like you."

I was shocked. I wasn't out of anyone's league. She had just described me. I always had been the wallflower who blended in. I started to like her even more. I gave her a smile.

"Are you ready for some ice cream?"

I could feel her relax in my arms, and it was a remarkable sight as she smiled at me. I could feel her gather her confidence.

"Yes, I would love some."

It was a short walk to the ice cream parlor. When we got to Jerry's we found it was a mistake. There were at least twenty people we knew. Our date was good for business. On a Friday afternoon, at this time, there would normally be three to five customers. I saw Alan and Jeff seated in a booth. The gossip network had disclosed the location of our date. Alan waved at us to try to get our attention. Hell if I was going to spend my first high school date talking to them. Tina stiffened and I turned to her.

"You want to skip this and take a walk in the park?"

She looked relieved.

"Please, I don't think I could face them."

As we turned to leave, I smiled at her.

"Did you let it slip what we were doing tonight?"

She gave me a sheepish grin.

"Yes, I guess I did."

I winked at her.

"Note to self: don't tell them where the date is going to be."

We spent an hour getting to know each other and wandered through the park hand-in-hand. She was very shy at first, but as time went by, she became a little chatterbox. She had two little sisters and a dog. The more I talked to her, the more I got the impression she was a good girl and very much a follower. I would have to be careful not to push her into things she didn't really want to do. I'm not sure she would stand up to me. Once she started to open up, I found she had a sharp wit that caught me off guard. She was a lot of fun. She was smart, and when I caught her smile, I found I had fallen under her spell.

The park was one of our town's highlights. There were ten miles of walking and bike trails. It had different athletic venues ranging from softball and soccer to a public pool. I had grown up in this park, since my dad worked for Parks and Recreation. I enjoyed pointing out landmarks and interesting sections. One of my favorite locations was the duck pond. It was a little off the beaten path. The calm weather made the pond look like a reflecting pool. We both went silent as we took in the sight. I steered her towards the bridge that led to a small island in the middle of the pond. I stopped with the pretense of looking at the ducks. I glanced over and saw that she was happy. I found I wanted to kiss her.

I turned to her.

"I'm going to kiss you again," I said.

I paused and she tilted her head to me. She drew to within scant inches of me and I inhaled the intoxicating scent of her perfume. I took the tilt of her head as permission, leaned in, and gave her a kiss. The first one was a nice tentative one, but she was having none of that. She slid her hand behind my right ear and pulled me into a sizzling kiss. It took me by surprise and my eyes popped wide open and looked at her. She wasn't in Cindy's league, but she made up for her inexperience with enthusiasm. I started to get lost in the moment. I could feel my passion ramp up. She had a decided effect on me. She was a quick study and gave as much as she got. As we kissed, her technique improved. When we parted from each other, she responded by wrapping her arms around my neck as she pulled me back to her lips. I remembered Greg's instructions and my hands found her hips. When I parted my lips and the tip of my tongue caressed her lips, she jerked back.

I figured I would play on her inexperience.

"Don't you like my kisses?"

"No, I mean, yes, I do. You just caught me by surprise again," she said. "I think I like your surprises."

She was flushed and breathing a little harder than normal. I was learning to recognize the signs of desire. I wanted to do more than give her sweet kisses. I pushed those thoughts out of my head and just focused on being in the moment, and kissed her. Without the anticipation of pushing things forward, I found our kiss to be more passionate. In the back of my mind, I knew we were exposed on the bridge. I broke our kiss and she all but panted. There was a fire in her eyes that spoke of a need that surprised me.

"Let's go somewhere more private," I offered.

I took her by the hand and led her down a secluded path to the picnic area. There were large bushes on three sides and the lake on the fourth. The far side of the lake was wooded so we had some privacy. I backed up to the end of one of the tables so my butt was pressed against the table's edge, and I pulled her toward me.

"Kiss me," I ordered.

She seemed to relax now we weren't out in the open, and soon we were French kissing. Her right hand ran over my chest as her left played with my hair and neck. I felt my manhood lengthen down my pant leg and I knew she could feel it as she pressed into me. Over the next several minutes, I was lost in her lips. I felt her legs part and then enclose my thigh. Her vee slowly rubbed into my jeans as her passion escalated. She began to moan into our kiss.

"David," she whispered as I began trailing kisses down her neck. "Oh, David, I've been hoping for this since we first met. I was so afraid you didn't like me."

I probably should have said something to reassure her, but my mind was a blank. I just grunted and I ran my hand down and cupped her rear on the outside of her skirt. She moaned as her lips found my mouth. I took her response as approval and made the move I had seen Greg make by sliding my hand under the hem of her skirt. She had on silk panties that felt cool and slick. I massaged her and she wiggled her tail like a happy puppy.

She broke our kiss.

"I want to memorize every detail of your body," she said in a breathy voice. "I want you to teach me to be a woman. I want to please you in every way, but what I really want first is to feel you in me. Before we do anything else, can we just make love?"

You could have pushed me over with a feather. Sweet, innocent Tina had just asked me to make love to her. Now what? I had a basic idea, since I had sex education in middle school: peg 'A' was inserted into slot 'B.' But in practical terms, I was clueless. That didn't mean I wasn't willing. Someone had to be my first, and Tina had everything I hoped for, and in spades.

"Like I told you, we can do anything you want. You set the pace."

I wasn't really sure how to describe what happened next. Tina gave a sexy moan and then latched her lips onto mine. Her hands were all over me. I started to get nervous that I was in way over my head. She ran her hand up my thigh and startled me, causing to make an embarrassing little squeak as I broke our kiss.

"Tina," I warned her.

I felt her grab my shirt and pull it out of my jeans so she could run her hands over my stomach and up my chest. She gave me another toe-curling kiss. My tight shirt obviously didn't work for her, because she broke our kiss and pulled my shirt up. I got the idea and helped her take it off me.

Was this really going to happen? How did she go from the quiet, shy girl to this? Now I wished Greg had taken the time to tell me what to do for this part. Once my shirt was off, she stepped back and made an 'oohing' noise. She liked what she saw. I felt cornered and not sure what to do next.

"You're gorgeous," she gasped as her hands ran all over my chest and to my shoulders.

My summer of hard labor paid off. The next thing I knew her sweater went flying and then her bra. Her breasts were impressive–not that I had a lot to compare them with. She reached down, grabbed my hands, and put them on her breasts. I wasn't sure what to do, so she covered my hands and showed me what she wanted. When she was sure I had the idea, she closed her eyes and leaned her head back. I took that as an invitation to kiss her at the base of her neck.

"Oh God, that feels so good."

She grasped the back of my head so I wasn't going anywhere. I would hate not to give each side equal time, so I went back and forth between the two. After several minutes of this, I noticed the smell of her arousal. That scent will catch any guy's attention. I wasn't sure what it was, but I felt my arousal start to go through the roof.

As I used my mouth on her, she pulled my hands to her butt. I took her subtle clue and began to knead her tight little buns. I really wanted to feel the real thing, so I snaked both of my hands under the waistband of her panties. She reached under her skirt and slid her panties off her hips until they were halfway down her thighs. She brought her thighs closer together and her underwear was suddenly around her ankles. She stepped out of them and spread her thighs enough so I could cup her from behind.

She guided me to her front. I cupped her and I massaged her core. Suddenly her odor was much more prominent. I rubbed her and she stiffened. I thought I had done something wrong. She shivered and I felt my hand get wet. She must be more worked up than I'd realized.

"Yes! Oh David, you're the best. You make me feel so good. I need you."

She pulled me into a passionate kiss as I toyed with her sex. My manhood was crushed in my tight jeans and I needed to make an adjustment. I'd gotten overstimulated to the point of exploding if we continued.

"Hang on," I said.

I reached into the top of my jeans to make the necessary adjustment. She looked down at my bulge with fascination. Her eyes looked up at me and locked. I'm not sure what she looked for, so I just gazed at her. She gave me a steamy gaze that made me shiver. She grasped my belt and undid it. I then felt the button come undone, followed by my zipper going down.

She hooked her thumbs in the waistband of my jeans and underwear and pushed down. My manhood popped out and stood at attention with my jeans around my knees. She just looked at my member as it swung in the breeze. Before my jeans hit the ground, she had taken me into her warm mouth.

I staggered back until I was against the picnic table. If it hadn't been there, I would have fallen down. Never had a girl so expertly handled me before, and the sensations drove me crazy. I swiftly neared the breaking point. I had no idea how to control myself. I lost control and released. She was surprised and made a gagging noise as she jerked me out of her mouth. I had more left in me and I made a mess on her face. She licked all around her lips. *Damn, that was hot!*

She smiled up at me.

"So that's what it's like? I wasn't expecting that."

Me neither! I had never achieved climax that fast in my life. I sure hoped it didn't happen every time. My knees finally unlocked, and I found myself lying on the ground as I looked up at her smiling at me. She grabbed her panties and cleaned herself off.

She noticed I was still hard. She straddled my waist and rubbed my staff into the opening between her legs, and I panicked.

"Stop!"

She got a startled look on her face. I made a nervous laugh and grabbed my jeans. I rummaged through my pockets and found what I was looking for. I handed her the foil packet. Understanding lit up her face and she leaned down and kissed me.

"Good boy, I'd forgotten about that."

She opened the packet and put the condom on. I was glad she seemed to know how. She must have been paying attention in Sex Ed. She then repositioned me and let her weight slowly fall until she hit bottom. Unfortunately, she sat on my left nut. I know in the past I'd said I would give my left nut to get laid, but I thought that was just a figure of speech. The sharp pain caused a tear to form at the corner of my eye. She must have thought I was having some kind of emotional moment because she just beamed when she saw it. Luckily, this caused her to lean forward and give me a passionate kiss, which freed my little buddy.

I now had two things that worked in my favor. The condom helped deaden the feeling, and the pain in my nut wasn't very sexy, so this time when she started to move I was nowhere near a quick finish. I think I was closer to throwing up from the pain.

"Are you ready?"

"Okay, but slowly," Tina told me.

I took over and began to slide my thick spear in and out of her. I would pull almost all the way out and then steadily thrust forward as I held her hips in place.

"This is nice," I sighed.

We got a good rhythm going and I soon found the once shy little Tina was a moaner. Each time we came together, she moaned.

"Ah, ah, ah, ah, ah."

She started to get into it, and her hips met mine. Tina thrust her beautiful round backside at me in the most animalistic invitation possible. I felt myself on the verge, so I slowed down, reached up to grasp both of her breasts.

“Oh, yeah, David I’m going to, going to…! I’m almost there!”

The extra stimulation sent her over the edge. I felt her insides twitch and grab me. I picked up the pace and thrust hard as our thighs slapped together and made a staccato smack, smack, smack sound. Her breasts jiggled as I pounded her.

"Auggghhhh!" she yelped. "Aaahhhhh! Yes!”

"Oh God, I’m there too!" I exclaimed.

I took a few more strokes, and I then threw my head back as found myself in Heaven. She continued to move and then soon joined me.

We slowly stopped moving. Tina collapsed onto my chest. We were both sucking air as if we’d just finished a race. I caressed her back, which was slightly damp from her sweat. When she finally got her breath back, she rolled off me.

I looked up through the diffused light as it was filtered through the canopy of trees and heard her giggle.

“I *knew* we were going to do this tonight. I knew when you kissed me at school I wanted this. I’m glad you didn’t disappoint me,” Tina said softly. I felt a little sleepy.

“How are you feeling?” I asked.

“I’m just a little sore. This is new.” She saw my look of concern. “Don’t worry, big guy, it’s a good sore. I think I’m going to be walking funny for the next few days. Nobody warned me about that.”

I had a big grin on my face I that might now be permanent.

“I’m sorry. I didn’t mean to hurt you.”

“You didn’t hurt me. It was just my first time. When I get more used to it, I’m sure I won’t be sore. We need to practice, a lot.”

She seemed to enjoy making me uncomfortable. I liked the idea of more practice, though. I’d be willing to help her with that. She grabbed my hand.

"Take me home. I didn't tell my parents we had a date tonight."

That was weird. She just jumped up and got dressed. She seemed full of energy, whereas I was ready for a nap. I figured I'd just follow her lead. I thought there'd be cuddling, and I hoped for a second round. As soon as she was dressed, she grabbed my hand and we walked to her house.

We chatted about school and other things on the way home. She only lived about a half mile from the park, so it didn't take too long to get her home. The comment about not telling her parents sounded weird. I guess not everyone had the same relationship with their parents as I had with mine. When we got to the corner before her house, she stopped me.

"David, my parents don't know I went out on a date this afternoon. They say I can't date until I'm sixteen."

Great, I find a girl who I like and we can't date.

"So what does that mean?"

"Well, most days I have to come straight home to watch my sisters until my mom gets off work, but some days Mom lets me hang out after school and will get them a babysitter. For this afternoon I talked one of my friends into watching my sisters."

I looked hopeful.

"Can your friends help us out?"

"I don't really want them to."

I was crestfallen.

"David, it's not that I don't want to see you. I do, but I respect my parents too much to defy them. I want to do what we did today many more times, and I want to do it with you."

I felt myself start to get hard. Many times sounded very good indeed. She looked like she was about to cry again.

"When do you turn sixteen?" I asked.

"Not for another 8 months."

Crap. Mr. Happy did *not* want to wait that long.

"So, why did you go out with me?"

She looked stricken. That wasn't the best thing to say, but now that it was out, I really wanted an answer. Why go out with me if it was a one-time thing?

"Are you kidding? I wasn't missing my chance, and I have to say I made the right decision to have you be my first. It's killing me, but until I'm sixteen we'll have to wait."

Well frick!

"Okay, on the Friday after your sixteenth birthday we have a date."

She squealed and jumped into my arms and kissed my face all over. I'd made the right decision.

"I was afraid you were going to hate me," she confessed.

"How could I hate you? You gave me your special gift. Am I disappointed we can't see each other for eight months? Yes. Will I push the issue? No. I won't go against your family's wishes, because it's important to you."

She got a serious look.

"David, I know eight months is a long time. I don't expect you to wait for me."

I started to interrupt her and she shushed me.

"If this is a one-time thing, I won't be happy, but I understand. I will always cherish today. You made me feel special, and you were gentle and listened to me. I felt safe, and that made me want this with you. I will cherish today forever."

"I don't know what to say."

"Don't say anything. I want us to be friends, but we can't be anything more until I turn sixteen. Honestly, I'm really torn. I don't want to lose you, but I want you to be happy. I want you to date and have a good time. When I turn sixteen, if you're not attached I'll expect to pick up where we left off."

Wow, she was blowing me away. It was true girls grow up faster than boys do. She gave me a quick kiss and walked to her house.

"I'll see you in school on Monday," I called after her.

She sashayed her cute little butt up the block. When she got about ten feet from me, she turned around and tossed me her underwear.

"Here's a little something for you to remember me by." I caught them and smiled at her. She then stopped and looked back. "Don't be sad. I think some of my friends will be looking you up."

It wasn't until I was halfway home that it hit me: I'd lost my virginity. In just under two weeks, with the help of Greg and Cindy, I'd gone from a hapless nerd to having sex. I was in shock. Before I knew it I was home, and Greg had waited for me. He took one look, and I expect he could smell me, and he ushered me upstairs before Mom or Dad figured out something was up. I'm awful at lying. I would never be a very good poker player. Greg could read me like an open book.

"All right, tell me what's wrong."

"We had sex," I blurted out.

"You mean you actually needed the condoms?" he asked in shock.

He could tell it was true.

"Crap, David, that's wrong on so many levels. Was she willing?"

"Up yours! I am *not* that guy! And it was just sex."

I was pissed.

"Damn, so what's next?"

"Nothing."

"What do you mean, nothing? Are you kidding me? You're showing her *no respect!*"

"Greg, you didn't give me a chance. She doesn't want anything more right now. She went out with me so she could one-up her friends. At some point she decided I was going to be her first. Granted, I didn't fight her, but she was the one that decided to do it. She then told me she snuck out. She's not allowed to date until she's sixteen."

He looked down, and I knew he was sorry for being a jerk.

"Sorry, man, that sucks."

"Greg, this week has been the best of my life. I have you and Cindy to thank for that, but it really does suck we can't see each other. I have to respect her wishes."

My brother just nodded and went to his room. I was supposed to meet the gang at the football game, but I really didn't feel like it, so I went to my room to think about what happened. I wasn't sure this hadn't been a mistake. Tami called my cell, but I let it go to voice mail. I might as well mess that up also. How did the best day of my life turn into such a downer?

✧✧✧

Chapter 6 – First Game

Saturday September 7

Saturday morning I had my first football game. Mom loaded me up and took me to the game. She noticed I wasn't in a very good mood.

"Are you nervous about today?"

I just shrugged.

"Not really, I'll be riding the bench."

We rode the rest of the way to the school in silence. When we got there, I just jumped out and went to the locker room. Coach told me to get into the training room and get my ankles taped. I changed into a t-shirt and shorts and found one of the trainers who'd just finished up with Mike.

"Dawson, you ready to put the hurt on some defenders today?"

During the first week of practice, it had become obvious I was bigger, stronger and faster than Bert was. The two weeks of two-a-days experience was the only reason he would start ahead of me. I was sure once I knew the offense better I would see some playing time. My only real concern was trying to get used to my new body. There were times when my coordination was off. Every so often, I found I would trip over my new big feet. I felt like a dork when I would break into the open then then go sprawling over a blade of grass.

"Dude, I have to get off the bench for that kind of action."

Mike just shook his head.

"Don't worry about it. Coach will get you some playing time after I run up the score."

"Dick, if I know you, you'll keep the game close so all us scrubs have to ride the bench."

"You know it," Mike said as he went to get dressed.

After I was taped, I went and suited up. Tim and Mike were captains and they led us out for warm-ups. After we'd stretched, I got a chance to see who was at the game. I was surprised to see my crew there. They really didn't like sports, but it was nice to see them come out to support me. I waved and Lily pointed out that I had noticed them. They jumped up and shouted.

"Let's go, Dawson!"

I suddenly recognized Tina was seated with Tami. I was sure I didn't like that, but there was nothing I could do about it. Tina had two young girls with her that I assumed were her sisters. Tami amazed me when she talked to every girl I even thought about being friends with or dating. Tami and I had shared everything all my life. There was nothing I couldn't tell her, but that was before I started dating. I needed to think about if I wanted some boundaries. Now was not the time. I needed to focus on the game.

After warm-ups, Tim and Mike took us back to the locker room. Coach Engels was waiting for us. We were sky high.

"Okay ladies, settle down."

This was fun. We all went down to one knee in a semicircle around Coach.

"This is our first game and the Washington Eagles have a fine team this year. They'll test us with their high-powered offense. Tim, I want you watching their halfback. He's the key to their success."

Tim looked fired up as he nodded. We'd seen the scouting report and their halfback wasn't going to be on their freshman team for very long. He had some real talent.

"I want you to know the varsity and JV coaching staff will be evaluating the game. Last night's loss was due to some key injuries. They'll be looking at some JV players later today to see if they can be moved up to varsity. In turn, that will open up some spots on the JV team."

I was the worst teammate right now. I had no idea we lost last night. I decided right then to get my head out of my rear end. If I was part of the team, I had to make it to the games. I actually really liked high school football, and I loved to go to the games. Most of the town turned out, and it was the *only* thing going on Friday nights.

"All right men, let's go win our first game."

Not the most inspired pregame speech, but we didn't need much to get excited. We ran out onto the field to the cheers of a sparse crowd. We got settled on the sidelines and then both team captains met at midfield for the coin toss. We won and decided to defer to the second half. Washington elected to receive.

Our kicker shanked the kickoff out of bounds. Washington would start their first series on their 35 yard line. On the first play, we saw why coach was worried about the Washington halfback. They ran a basic trap to the left and Mike read it beautifully. He scraped off the nose guard and filled the hole when the halfback danced in the hole. Normally that was the kiss of death, but somehow he juked Mike and sprinted to open field. Luckily our secondary caught him before he scored, but he had ripped off a huge chunk of yardage. He was taken down on our 12 yard line.

On the next play, they ran a toss to their star and he outran everyone to the end zone. We were down 6–0 with only 52 seconds played. They shortly thereafter kicked the extra point and we were now down 7–0. If we couldn't shut him down, it would be a long day.

I went up to Mike and he glared at me.

"Mike, just put him down. Ignore his dancing and focus on his waist. His waist will tell you where he's going."

Mike gave me a smile.

"I forgot that. Thanks, David."

On the next kickoff, we were only able to get it out to the 9 yard line. On the first play we ran veer right and Mike handed off to Bert up the middle. Bert got about a yard when he was hit hard by their strong safety. The safety had cheated up to cover the run. Bert fumbled the ball and their middle linebacker fell on it. Less than 30 seconds later and Washington was in our Red Zone again.

Their first play was a repeat of the power toss. This time Mike was able to fight his way through and drop their halfback before he could move up field. Our defense stiffened and held them the next two plays. Their kicker came out and kicked a field goal to make it 10–0.

On the kickoff, we were able to bring it out to the 19 yard line.

"Dawson, you're in for Nelson!" Coach Engels yelled.

I trotted out to the huddle and Mike greeted me with a shit-eating grin.

"You ready to put some of them down?"

"You just tell me what to do and I'll do it."

"Veer left on two, and you score."

"Yes, sir."

I was afraid Washington would have something to say about that. I could see the free safety cheat up to defend the run. I knew if I could get past him, they had no one back there to stop me.

"Down! Set! Hut, HUT!"

I exploded to the hole. Mike slapped the ball into my stomach and I could feel him start to pull it out, because the free safety had me. I clutched the ball and Mike had no choice but to release it into my care. I caught a flash of the middle linebacker as he zeroed in on me at the same time. A split-second later there was a tremendous crack of pads as I exploded into both players. I felt myself rise up from the impact, but I kept churning my legs and I broke free. When the crowd heard the crack, they groaned and went silent as they anticipated the worst. In a freshman game, it normally meant an injury, but when they saw me break free, the place erupted. The only guy who had a shot was a speedy corner, but he had too much ground to cover to catch me. 81 yards later we were now back in this game with a score of 10–7. I must have really hit the two players hard, because they needed help off the field. I was swarmed on the sidelines by the whole team. Mike and I found Bert seated on the bench, and he looked dejected. Mike went up to him.

"What're you pouting about?"

"I just lost my starting spot," Bert complained.

"No, you didn't," Mike said with a laugh.

Now it was my turn to look dejected.

"David's never going to play another down of freshman ball after this game," Mike predicted.

Bert and I were both cheered by that.

Our defense finally stiffened and held their own for the rest of the game. I touched the ball ten times and scored three touchdowns of 60 or more yards. I had 273 yards of rushing, a freshman record for one game. After my third touchdown, the varsity coach came down and talked to our coach, and I suddenly found myself on the bench.

When the final gun sounded, we had won 27–17. The teams lined up to shake hands and their star halfback made a point of introducing himself.

"Ty Wilson."

"David Dawson."

"Hey, where did you come from?"

"What do you mean?"

"We scouted your practice game."

"Oh, I didn't start playing football until school started."

"Seriously?"

"Yeah, I've never played a down of football until this year."

He just shook his head.

"David, you are one scary dude. I dread playing against you the next three years."

When we got back to the locker room, I was met by two coaches I hadn't met before: Coach Diamond, the JV Coach and Coach Lambert, the Varsity Coach. Coach Lambert had a booming voice with a Southern drawl.

"Dawson, that there was a hell of a game, yes, sir. I haven't seen that kind of spunk in a freshman in a long time. I heard some rumblings that there was a new kid that could hit, but I needed to see it with my own eyes."

"Thank you, sir."

I noticed the locker room had gone quiet so they could overhear the conversation.

"No thanks necessary, it was my pleasure to see you play today. Coach Diamond, how many yards did David put on them today?"

He looked at his clipboard.

"273 yards on 10 carries."

Coach Lambert nodded his head.

"What's the freshman record?"

Coach Diamond flipped through some pages until he found what he was looking for.

"184 yards on 22 carries."

"And what happened to that player after that game?"

Coach Diamond thought for a minute, looked at the name next to the record, and then smiled as he realized whom Coach Lambert was talking about.

"He moved to varsity where he's a four-year starter, the first in our history."

"Who was that boy?"

Coach Diamond got a big grin.

"Why that's our very own Luke Herndon."

"Well I'll be. Sounds like we have a new rising star. David, I expect to see you at varsity practice on Monday."

I was about to jump out of my skin, but I played it cool.

"Yes, sir."

After the coaches left, the team swarmed me, giving me high fives. Mike rushed up and gave me a one-armed hug.

"Man, I'm going to miss you."

I just shrugged.

"Mike, you'll be there before you know it. If there hadn't been an injury they wouldn't even be looking at me."

Mike gave me a playful shove.

"Don't bullshit me. After that performance you'd be playing varsity regardless of whether there was an injury."

I did my best Southern drawl.

"Like my pappy always says, if you're going to run with the big dawgs, you'd better get off the porch. I guess this big dawg is going to have to play himself some varsity ball. Awhooooo!"

"Big Dawgs need to stick together, WOOF, WOOF, WOOF!" Tim chimed in.

Girls never understand why guys love football. It gives us a chance to be total dorks and cut up. It allows us to get our natural aggression out and have a good time. It was also a great teaching experience for guys. Ever notice how two guys can get into a big fight and then ten minutes later be laughing it up with each other? I think sports has a lot to do with it. We learn we leave it on the field. We don't hold grudges. We can be free and crazy playing one minute, and once the game is over go back to the real world.

✧✧✧

I showered and went out to meet my mom for my ride home. When I came out, Tami, Lily and Tina had waited with my mom. Lily and Tina rushed up and gave me kisses on the cheek. Tami slugged my arm.

"I'm so glad you guys came today, it means a lot to me," I said.

I looked at Tami. She knew we had things to work out. It felt good to have her smile at me instead of look disappointed. Lily was bouncy today.

"You were awesome. How many yards did you get?" Lily asked.

"273, but the bigger news is I just got promoted to varsity," I announced.

I was a little shocked, but I really was proud of my accomplishment. I hadn't felt this good in a long time. I found I liked the physical aspects of football. It was therapeutic. The adrenalin rush and being able to whack a guy was liberating. To have three very cute girls fawn over you was an added bonus. At that moment, nothing could spoil my good mood.

Tami beat the other two in pulling me into a big hug.

"Great news, David! We were all amazed at how well you did. From what I heard, you were hands down the best player on the field. We sat near Mike's dad and he said you're a much more powerful runner than Luke was when he set the freshman rushing record. He said Luke was probably quicker at your age, but he played halfback and you play fullback. All the parents were a little scared of how hard you hit," Tami said.

"Why's that?"

"Mike's dad said it was like in baseball when you hear that perfect pitch. The pop of the glove is just different. He said when you hit someone, it reminded him of a college game. The pop of your pads when you make contact had a different sound. They were worried you might injure some of the players from Washington. Everyone was happy to see you get pulled in the second half," Tami explained.

I had a sheepish grin. It was good to hear how the parents talked about my game. I needed to call my uncle and tell him about my game today. He would be pleased. I gave Tami a kiss on the cheek and she blushed. I became aware I had my left arm wrapped around her waist as we talked. I let her go and turned my attention to Lily. I smiled and put her in a bear hug.

"How's my number one fan doing?" I asked.

I knew this was a big deal for her to hang around friends outside of school. Her old crew had abandoned her, and we'd had a few conversations about how lonely she'd been. I tried to be a friend to her and I was happy Tami took her under her wing. I thought I would make her day and captured her face in the palms of my hands and kissed her on the lips. It was cute to see her eyes get big, but she didn't pull away. I could see Tina behind her give me a big grin. My guess was she knew Lily had a crush on me. I broke the kiss and stepped back, but Lily was having none of that. She pulled me into a hug.

"Better now. You keep that up and I'll want more of those," Lily said.

I leaned in and whispered in her ear.

"You just say the word."

She just leaned back and you could see true happiness in that moment. In a weird kind of way, we had gone through a lot. Not together, but it all stemmed from that terrible night last spring. I did want to become a good friend to her, and I was sure she felt the same. If I thought about it hard enough, I'm sure we could be more than friends. I broke my embrace and pulled Tina into a serious kiss. About halfway through the kiss I remembered the parental unit who stood behind me. She had to be pleased to have a month's worth of material handed to her on a silver platter. I think Tina realized it also, because she suddenly stiffened up and we parted quickly. It could have also been my erection suddenly pressed into her midsection.

Mom couldn't wait any longer. She walked up and pulled me into an embrace as I had the other girls.

"I'm so proud. My little boy is growing up."

She then got a mock shocked look on her face, looked at the three girls and then separated a little bit to look down.

"Did you girls know he really is growing up?" Mom asked.

Okay, I would need therapy from that one. I was sure I would be scarred for life. When I thought it couldn't get any worse, my best friend stepped into the fray.

"I've heard rumors. Turn him around so we all can see," Tami suggested.

Between my mom and Tami's comments, Mr. Happy decided to go hide. I had never gone soft so fast in all of my life. I think all the blood had rushed from my lower areas to my face. I actually felt the heat coming off my cheeks. By now, all three girls were laughing at me. It must have been obvious I had a dramatic change in condition, because Tami just had to make a comment about it.

"Are you sure? It doesn't look that big to me."

Tina didn't realize what sharks she was around, and the worst part was there was now blood in the water. We were about to see a feeding frenzy. She spread her hands apart to demonstrate.

"No, really, he's very big."

Tina had a very sincere look on her face and looked at Tami and my mom as they lost it. My mom had tears streaming down her face, she laughed so hard.

"Oh shit, she did not just say that?" Mom asked.

All I could think was 'Dear *gawd,* Tina, shut up!' Unlike Tami, who can somehow read my thoughts, Tina was clueless. Of course, she was confused and thought she was standing up for me. I couldn't be mad at her because she really did try to help.

"But he is."

Tina finally comprehended what she had said and to whom. She put her hands in front of her face and started to laugh also. I did my best impression of a mouse surrounded by four cats with very sharp claws. My eyes darted from girl to girl as I waited for that final killing blow. Then, out of left field, Lily joined the fray.

"Early in the week we were all taking bets that Cindy had stuffed his pants with tube socks to get that size of a bulge, but after seeing him get all excited throughout the day we all figured out it's really him. Beth, she's a girl in my math class, thinks he's hung like a horse. I think I'll wait to see before I decide."

My dad had always told me, 'When you see you're defeated, just walk away.' The whole Washington defense couldn't do what these four women had done in less than five minutes. They had me running home with my tail between my legs. I shook my head, looked at my shoes and muttered, 'No, no, no,' as I walked to our car. My mom took pity on me and followed me.

"Bye, David!" Tami yelled.

I just lifted my arm and made a wave back to them without looking up. When we got into the car, I looked over at my mom, and she was happier than I had seen her since I'd gotten back from Uncle John's farm. I gave her a sheepish smile.

"David, there are worse things they could have been saying. At least they aren't calling you 'pencil dick.'"

I burst out laughing. My mom had a sharp tongue, but she does love me. She always knows what to say to get me in a better mood. She was right. At least they were all looking at my supposed *big* dick. After I was able to see the humor in what the girls had said, Mom and I had a good time on the way home.

✧✧✧

When I got home, Mom made a beeline to my dad to share how she'd tormented me. I found Greg in our bathroom. He was shaving, so I stepped in to relieve myself.

"Cindy is asking for you to come over today to further your education."

I was relieved my brother was willing to continue to teach me. I'd been worried he thought things were going a little fast.

"Okay."

"We'll head out around one," my brother said.

I went to my room and opened my tablet. I sent a text to Uncle John to jump onto video chat, and he popped on almost immediately. He was in one of the pastures we'd fenced. I was happy to see cattle lounging under the big oak trees. I put on my best serious face.

"I need your advice: Coach Engels is mad at me. I'm not going to play for him."

He just smirked.

"Sorry, Bucko, not gonna work. I talked to Doug after the game. Was he pulling my leg? 10 carries for 273 yards?"

"I know, it's embarrassing I did that well. I wanted to call and thank you for talking to Coach Engels and getting me on the football team. I never would have gone out if you hadn't called him. Someday I need to thank you for a lot of things, but football has been great so far."

"Doug tells me you hit like a ton of bricks, what's that all about?"

"I think it has to do with you trying to kill me this summer using the posthole digger. I just visualize exploding through the player and I seem to lay a serious hit on them. I'm scared it's not going to work on varsity. They're all so much bigger and stronger than I am."

"David, all I ask is that you try your best. Don't shy away from the contact. If you do, you can get hurt. You're better off doing what you've been doing."

In the background, I could hear the chickens in an uproar. I saw Uncle John jerk his head around.

"Stupid pup! I have to go. I have a dog in among the chickens."

I chuckled as he hung up. It seemed like time stopped after the call. I looked at the clock every thirty seconds and tried to will it to be one o'clock. I was eager to find out what Cindy had planned. Dad found me hanging around the kitchen and made me go mow the yard. At least I was no longer looking at the clock.

✧✧✧

Chapter 7 – Stud in Training

Saturday September 7

I hurried and I went out to Greg's car at one. We drove to Cindy's in silence as he seemed deep in thought. We pulled up to Cindy's and I noticed a cute girl waiting by the front door. I recognized her as one of the varsity cheerleaders, Suzanne Ball.

Suzanne had a unique look: her hair was pure white. It was always messed up, but in a good way. I think she styled it so she had bedroom hair. It was full and wispy, like she just got out of bed but ran her fingers through it to get it back under control. Her pale blue eyes just seemed to bore into your soul when you looked directly into them. Her tiny frame and her complexion made her look like a porcelain doll. At school, her nickname was 'Ice Princess.' Her whole persona was sexy and gorgeous. Her perfection made her seem unattainable. She was the unique girl you wanted to put on a pedestal and worship from afar. You just prayed someday this angel would grace you with a smile.

The sad fact was, because of this, she was rarely asked out on a date. It took a very special kind of guy to get up the nerve. Unfortunately, most of those guys are self-centered douchebags. Truth be known, Suzanne just wanted a regular guy. I had no idea of this at the time. I felt I was being graced by royalty.

She wore a cute tank-top-and-short set. It was obvious she didn't have on a bra. Greg went up to her and gave her a hug.

"How's my Ice Princess today?"

"Just fine, Mr. Gigolo." She turned on me and said, "So, is this your little stud-in-training?"

"Suzanne, you remember my brother David," Greg said, as I turned red.

She shook my hand. The front door swung open and Cindy looked out.

"What are you guys all doing out here? Come in."

We followed Cindy through the house and out to the pool house. It had big French doors that opened to the pool. The center area was set up as a bar and game room. To the right were the changing rooms and showers, and to the left was a king-size bed. Cindy headed left. She turned and gave me a knowing look.

"I hear someone popped their cherry yesterday."

I glanced at Greg and saw his ears go red. He obviously was the one who talked out of school. How was I supposed to learn that the better part of valor was discretion if my own brother couldn't keep his mouth shut? I knew he needed to share things with her to help me, but there had to be boundaries.

"Just like big brother, out collecting notches on his belt," Suzanne teased me.

Cindy went in for the kill.

"So, tell me what all happened, and don't leave anything out."

I gulped. There was no way I would spill my guts.

"Let's just say Tina and I went on a date yesterday and we're good friends."

Suzanne snorted.

"He's as bad as his brother, never any of the juicy details. What is it about you guys, are you in some kind of cult?"

Greg turned on Suzanne.

"Listen closely: we do not kiss and tell. No one will ever know who we did what with." He gave Suzanne a meaningful glance, which had her looking at the floor.

Shit, my brother had bagged the Ice Princess. Way to go, bro. Then I remembered he told Cindy about my date with Tina. My head was spinning, but I forgot all that when Cindy grinned at me.

"You passed the first test of the day. If you'd failed, there would be no further training. There's nothing worse than a guy who brags about his conquests. No girl wants to date that guy, but believe me, I've had many dates that turned out to be just like that."

Suzanne just nodded and gave Greg a sideways glance. Something weird was going on between those two. She kept giving him funny looks when she thought no one was looking.

Cindy looked me in the eyes.

"Suzanne is a good friend of your brother and me. What happens here today is not to get out, is that clear?"

I nodded.

"After what happened yesterday we need to speed up your education. Today you're going to learn how to give a woman pleasure," Greg said.

This sounded like there might be some practical training involved, so I was very eager for this to begin. Before I could overthink it, Greg continued.

"Cindy has agreed to teach you some things. You will do *whatever* she tells you. Remember that Cindy is *my* girlfriend. No funny stuff!"

"I'll remember."

I think it must be obvious I had a huge crush on Cindy. I know it was all fantasy because the freshman/senior relationship was never going to work. Older girls in high school simply would not date guys three years younger.

Greg shocked me.

"I'm going to take off. I'm leaving you in Cindy and Suzanne's capable hands." He headed out to leave me to wonder what was next. As he hit the door, he looked back at the girls. "Don't break him."

Cindy took charge.

"David, I want you to strip down to your boxers while Suzanne and I get ready."

They left me and went into the main house. I did as I was told. I wondered what they could possibly have in mind. After what seemed like forever, I heard them chuckle as they came back. I overheard Cindy.

"Yes, he is cute. This should be fun."

When they entered the pool house, they stunned me. Cindy had on black robe that was short enough that I could see her matching panties just peek out of the bottom. Her long brown hair draped forward off her shoulders and rested on the swell of her breasts. She had an amused expression, which lit up when she saw me take in Suzanne. She had on white silk robe that contrasted with Cindy's outfit. The effect of the two gorgeous women was stunning.

I think I surprised them when I crawled off the bed and stepped over to them. I first slid my hand around Cindy's waist and leaned close to her ear so I could share a private comment.

"Thank you."

I saw her get a smug smile, so I figured I would shake her up a little and I sucked her earlobe into my mouth and gave it a little nip. She stiffened and I could feel her tremble.

Suzanne had lost her confident look and her eyes were big as she took in the scene. I went to her and faced her, and then I bent down and kissed her. I gave her the full treatment. It took her a moment to respond, but I soon found I was woefully inexperienced. Suzanne had called my bluff. We finally broke our kiss. The look on my face must have been one of amazement because Cindy took the opportunity to give me a hard time.

"David, for all your cool moves, it looks like you've met your match."

"Damn, I think you're right."

Suzanne beamed with pride, and she had an evil twinkle in her eyes as she appraised me in my boxers.

"Oh, you're going to be fun. Cindy, is he as innocent as he seems?"

I shivered as she raked her manicured nails down my chest to my navel. She then reached up and ran her fingers through my curls. For some reason, since I had gotten my hair styled girls loved to play with my hair.

"Not quite, but that's why we're here. Suzanne, slow down."

Suzanne winked at her and made a little growling sound. Cindy laughed as I took a step back.

"Down, Tiger, I promised Greg we wouldn't break him. Okay, David, there are some ground rules we have to go over. First, you will *not* be removing your boxers. Even if we beg, you have to promise your package will not be unwrapped. If I say stop, you stop. If Suzanne says stop, ignore her."

Suzanne gave Cindy a smirk and just shrugged. It felt like they'd played together before. I found my eyes ping-ponging back and forth as I tried to watch each girl's expression.

"Princess, please get on the bed and prepare yourself," Cindy ordered.

Suzanne's eyes never left mine as she let her robe slide off her shoulders and let it slowly slide down her flawless skin. She stood in front of me in just a white thong. My breath caught; she was spectacular. Suzanne was five-five and could not weigh more than a hundred and ten pounds. She had small apple-sized breasts with long, thick nipples. Her butt was firm, and all I wanted to do was grab it. This was every teenage boy's wet dream. She climbed onto the bed and scooted to the center.

I saw Suzanne check out my package. I was aroused, so there was a no hiding it. She patted the bed and I crawled up and sat down next to her. She laid out the ground rules.

"You will not touch me unless I ask you to. I will touch you when and wherever I want. If I tell you to do something, you'll do it, understood?" Suzanne asked.

There seemed to be a lot of rules. The good news was that Cindy had told me to basically ignore Suzanne. I waggled my eyebrows at her.

"Yes, but may I just say you're sexy as hell."

She ignored me. I could tell I was getting to her, though. She could play tough, but we'd see who was on top when this was over. I had to stop, because I wondered where that competitiveness was coming from. Who cared? Game on.

"I'm doing this as a favor to Greg. He taught me most of what I'm going to teach you. He's the best lover I've ever had, and it's not because he has a big package; he's about average."

Too much information; I really didn't want to compare size with my brother.

"Your brother is very skilled at making a girl happy. To pay it forward, so to speak, is why I agreed to teach you how to please a woman," Suzanne said.

"Thank you," I gulped.

I felt the bed shift as Cindy joined us. She was on the other side of Suzanne and was seated so she could watch. She gave me a wink, and I focused my attention on Suzanne.

"The first thing to learn is how to kiss a woman. To see where you're at, I want you to kiss me."

I moved forward and we bumped noses.

"Sorry, I guess I'm nervous," I said.

"Tilt your head a little to the right as you lean in. Another thing is don't close your eyes and dive in. Make eye contact first and make sure you're both on the same wavelength. Move in slowly, giving the girl the chance to back off... if she wants to. Smile at her. Let her know you like her. Now let's try this again," Suzanne coached.

I looked into her ice-blue eyes and lost myself. I slowly moved in and smiled. She smiled back and we kissed. She quickly broke the kiss before we went too far.

"Much better, but you need to close your eyes just before you kiss a girl. Leaving them open is a little creepy."

"Sorry, I don't want to be creepy."

She giggled.

"I don't think you have to worry about that, you're not creepy in the least. Now for the next kiss I don't want you to have a stiff pucker. Loosen your lips; you're not kissing your grandma. Now try again."

This time I did better, and as our lips touched, she pushed me away.

"Not so fast, Tiger. Only open your mouth slightly. You don't go for the full open-mouthed kiss at first. Keep your lips just barely parted enough so a tongue could slip between them. There's a fine line between being overaggressive and chaste. Try again."

This time I used featherlight pressure at first, so my lips were just barely grazing over Suzanne's lips. As we kissed more, I gradually ratcheted up the passion. I soon found her kissing me back. The anticipation started to build. I opened my mouth, inviting her to use her tongue, and she obliged. I could tell she was testing me, so I gave her a lip-lock, where her lower lip was between my two lips. Then I lightly ran the tip of my tongue over the lower lip. I did this in one smooth, swift motion so that the contact lasted for a fraction of a second.

She seemed to like that. She started to play tag with my tongue, as we were now full-on French kissing. Then she took in a deep breath and pushed me away.

"Damn, David, who taught you to kiss?"

"I'm a little embarrassed to say the only person besides Tina is Cindy."

"You little slut," Suzanne accused her friend.

Cindy just smirked.

"Hey, he's just a natural. But yeah, he can kiss," Cindy confirmed.

“I think you have the basics down. Each girl is going to be different. Take your time to find out what works. Passion goes a long way. Now I want you to touch me while you kiss me.”

I leaned in and gave her a sizzling kiss while I mauled her breasts.

"Take it easy there, stud,” Cindy said. “Did you ask her how she likes to have her breasts played with? How about it Princess? Do you like rough stuff or a lighter touch?"

Suzanne’s eyes came back into focus.

“You know, no one’s ever asked me. I never thought about the differences. I liked it when David touched me, but he was a little rough."

"I’ll give you the biggest secret to getting girls to have a good time: take your time and learn what they like. Use this foreplay to see where their buttons are, what makes them purr, and don’t be afraid to ask them if they like what you’re doing. Princess, what do you want David to do?"

"I like it when you do it gently. Little light touches tease me and make me get excited. "

"Like this?" Cindy asked as she gently traced her fingers over her friend’s breasts.

I copied the moves as I saw Cindy do them. Suzanne squirmed under our combined assault.

“Yes. I really like that. The teasing is killing me.”

If it got her excited, I was going to learn what it took. I mirrored everything Cindy was doing. She started just around her nipple and circled her breast until she was just under it when Suzanne shuddered. She nodded to me.

“Is that sensitive?” I asked.

“Um huh.”

“Do you like it when we touch you under your breasts?”

“Yes.”

"David, keep track of that. We're finding her erogenous zones, places that make her hot. Once you have her mapped out, you can please her. Each girl is different and every time is different. Taking your time to find out what your lover wants will keep them coming back," Cindy instructed.

"Is this what Greg does?" I asked.

They both perked up with big grins and nodded their heads yes.

I pursued Cindy's fingers with my hand off the other breast and we both ended up slipping across her stomach and then circled back up toward her breasts. We spent several minutes as we explored her torso, and each time I would find a sensitive spot, I would confirm that she liked to be touched there. Besides her nipples and under her breasts, I found she liked to have her jaw stroked, her neck caressed, the inside of her elbow tickled and the outside of her hips touched.

Suzanne was about to go crazy. Sometime during our exploration, we stopped matching each other's movements. Our hands crossed and this time I circled the breast closest to Cindy and she caressed the one closest to me. I planned to switch breasts when Cindy stopped to squeeze Suzanne's nipple. I found my hand resting on hers. She smiled at me and I leaned over and kissed Cindy. While we kissed, our hands were all over Suzanne.

Suzanne started to moan. Then her eyes flew open and she begged.

"Pleeeease!"

I watched Cindy place her hand over one of Suzanne's breasts, and touch it just around the base with her fingertips. I followed her lead and cupped her other tit in the same fashion. She then pulled her fingers together slowly and worked her way up towards her nipple. I did the same and watched in fascination as she reached her nipple and we both squeezed.

Suzanne's body went rigid and I heard a whimper as she lifted her butt off the bed. The tops of her breasts and her neck went flush. I heard her breath come out in a whoosh. She looked at us with a lopsided grin.

"You bastards, you just made me lose it. You've ruined me for all others. I'm so excited I don't want you to stop."

Cindy had a knowing smile.

"David, a woman is not some kind of puzzle that once you've figured it out the same things work every time. So don't get lazy. Each time you make love, take your time and get her aroused. Unlike boys, who are ready to go right away, a woman needs time to get herself ready. Now let's see if she's satisfied. Princess, would you like us to continue?"

"Hell, yes, I'm so horny right now. If you don't help me, I don't know what I'll do."

There was a look of lust I had never seen in a woman before. I would remember that look and strive to achieve it repeatedly. I bent down and took her breast into my mouth. She was the perfect mouthful. I sucked on it and used my tongue to mimic my hand motion.

"Shit, who taught you that?" Suzanne asked as she grabbed the back of my head.

I pulled my head back so I could look her in the eyes.

"Did you like that?"

Suzanne looked pleadingly to Cindy.

"Let me do him... pleeease!"

"No, you know the rules. Plus, Greg would kill us if we ruined him."

"Forget the rules! No one said I was going to be climbing the walls. I need to go further than just touching"

Cindy got firm.

"Princess, if I promise you'll be satisfied to the point that'll make your toes curl, do you think you can hold off on jumping my boy toy?"

"Yes, yes and yes! But I need some relief," Suzanne pleaded.

"David, isn't that what you want to hear from your lover?"

I just nodded. I'd no idea that girls could get like this. I only thought boys felt like crawling up a wall.

"You have the right instinct to use your mouth. We got her excited just by using our fingertips. Our next lesson is how to get her to the finish line using your lips and tongue."

Suzanne just moaned.

"Oh hell, I am in so much trouble," she moaned.

Cindy had us position ourselves so we could both lie between Suzanne's spread legs. Cindy proceeded to give me an anatomy lesson. I was taught how to please Suzanne. I think I learned my lesson well, because when she finally collapsed, she curled up in a quivering, whimpering ball. Cindy smiled and looked at my shocked expression. At that moment I was sure she was the best teacher I'd ever had. I wished my other teachers could motivate me to learn like she did. Then again, it could be the subject matter.

"Now if you can get that response from a few of those freshman girls, you'll be set for the rest of your life."

I had to agree, it looked like she'd enjoyed it. I crawled up next to her ear.

"Are you satisfied? Would you like more?" I whispered.

She shivered and looked at us with a big grin. She uncurled like a big cat.

"Yes, please!"

I looked at Cindy and then asked a question.

"Is there something else you'd like to teach me?"

"Oh, honey, we've only just scratched the surface. Our little Princess is going to be screaming before we're done with her."

I was a little scared. Cindy sounded so confident, and I saw Suzanne shudder in anticipation. What was the old saying? If it doesn't kill you, it makes you stronger. I slowly realized I was on the verge of getting overexcited myself. I glanced down at the front of my boxers and it looked like I had wet myself. I was about to run off and do something about the mess when I looked at Suzanne and saw the lust in her eyes. She needed relief more than I did.

Cindy got things back on track.

"All right, we're going to take this to the next level. I'm going to show you how to use both your hands and mouth," she said as she nudged Suzanne's knees apart.

"Let me see your hands."

She checked my fingers.

"I just wanted to make sure your nails were trimmed. Long nails can damage the walls of her vagina, and neither of us wants that. Now go wash your hands."

I got a puzzled look.

"I don't need her getting a yeast infection from wherever your fingers have been."

That made sense. I jumped up and walked to the bathroom. I heard a wolf whistle.

"Nice tush!"

I nodded agreement.

"Thanks, Suzanne. Yes, it is."

Both girls busted out laughing.

As I was washing my hands, I heard Suzanne ask Cindy a question.

"Is he always this confident? I say 'nice tush' and he just cracks back at me."

"I know. It's funny, one minute he's a typical dorky freshman guy, the next he's mister suave and confident. I asked Greg about it. Of course, he tried to play it off as the Dawson charm." Suzanne scoffed and Cindy giggled. "My thoughts exactly! I pestered him until he told me that

David's been around the girls that he's gone out with. They all take to David, for some reason."

I was done washing my hands, but wanted to listen to this.

"When I went out with Greg we came back to his place to pick up some stuff. He left me in the living room and told David to go keep me company," Suzanne said. "I remember this middle-school kid coming in and introducing himself. The funny thing was he just acted as if we'd known each other for years. I really enjoyed our talk. Thinking back, I have no idea what we talked about. I remember Greg had come back down, but neither one of us noticed at first. Greg was just leaning against the door, watching us with a silly grin on his face. I guess he'd been standing there for like ten minutes.

"It wasn't that he was this great conversationalist. He just got the conversation started, and I found I was talking to him as if he was one of my girlfriends. Greg told me later he didn't want to interrupt us, because I was having too much fun," Suzanne said.

"It's funny, you can tease him and get him to blush like all young guys, but then he surprises you. We were teaching him some stuff. I thought I would tease him and see if he knew how to kiss. He didn't hesitate. He laid one on me that made my toes curl," Cindy said, and then paused to remember the experience. Then something came to her. "One thing I've noticed is that he's completely lost when it comes to girls his own age."

"What do you mean?"

"He acts like your typical freshman when he's around freshman girls."

"Why do think that is?"

I walked back in.

"It's because you beautiful ladies are unattainable; whereas, with girls my age I have something on the line when I talk to them."

They both looked at each other confused, so I filled them in.

"Stop and think about it. What's the youngest either of you would consider dating?"

"To be honest, maybe a year younger, but more than likely my age or older," Suzanne admitted.

"Older or my age," Cindy confirmed.

I grinned as they got it.

Cindy got us back onto the task at hand.

What followed was an education every young man should experience. I learned things like the foreplay-to-actual-sex ratio should be 3 to 1. They explained that it took time to get a woman fully aroused. The example Cindy gave was a woman was like a crockpot. Once you got her hot she would stay that way for a long time, but the buildup was slower than what a guy experienced. I learned woman could have two different orgasms. One was a clitoral and the other was from her G-spot.

Suzanne went into teaching mode.

"A clitoral orgasm is different. I lose control and my toes curl. The G-spot is centralized, and I can feel the orgasm radiate from the center of my womb."

"Is one better than the other?" I asked as I tried to be a good student.

"Let me tell you a little secret. If you can pull it off you'll be the biggest stud in school."

She had my attention. Biggest stud in school sounded like a worthy goal.

"Tell me, please!" I begged.

"Use a combination of both and give your gal multiple orgasms before you worry about yours. Tease and tongue her until she's aroused, then work on her G-spot in combination. You'll have her going off with both kinds of orgasm. It's unbelievable."

"Can we practice?" I asked.

Cindy just laughed and left us to our own devices.

"I thought you'd never ask," Suzanne said with a big grin.

I spent the next hour practicing on Suzanne. I lost count of the number of times she came. When Cindy showed up again, Suzanne begged me to stop.

"Save me, he's a sex machine. *Please make him stop!* He won't listen."

"You told me not to," I said to Cindy, and shrugged.

"Yes, I did, but I think we can stop now."

My jaw ached, but it was worth every minute. I think they say 'no pain, no gain.' Cindy's eyes were huge as she took in her friend's state. When Suzanne recovered, I helped her sit up on the edge of the bed.

"I don't think I can walk. Can someone get me a glass of water? I'm dehydrated."

I went to get the water.

"Are you all right?" Cindy asked.

"I'm okay, but my jaw's a little sore," I answered.

Suzanne slugged me in the arm and Cindy laughed. After Suzanne had finished her water, she looked at the clock.

"Shit, I have to get going. My brother's playing football at three and I promised to go to the game."

She grabbed her clothes, and I was a little bummed our lesson was over. She looked at my disappointment.

"Come with me!"

Cindy gave her a look.

"Suzanne!"

She gave Cindy a look that said 'don't mess with me.' I perked up. I went to the restroom to get cleaned up. When I walked out, she was ready to go. She had pulled her hair back and put it into a ponytail. It helped show off her sexy neck. She was walking sex-on-a-stick.

"You look hot."

Suzanne ran into the bathroom to clean up. While she was gone, I went to Cindy and wrapped her in my arms.

"I want to thank you for today. You're really special to me, and the more I'm around you the more I realize what a lucky guy my brother is. If I was a few years older, and he wasn't my brother, I'd make a serious play for you."

She seemed taken aback.

"Are you serious?"

"You bet. You have no idea what you've done for me. You've turned me from being a complete nerd into what I am now. What that is, I'm not sure, but I'm *so* happy."

"Yeah, sex will do that to you. Can we have a serious conversation for just a moment?"

She looked me in the eyes.

"Sure."

"If you're going to have casual sex with a girl, be very careful about laying it on too thick. We're very emotional and vulnerable after sex. Don't tell a girl you love her unless you mean it, and of course, there is a catch-22. You need to assure them they are sexy and desirable. Just now, even though we didn't have sex, we did something very extraordinary. When you said those things, I felt our connection get stronger. If I'm not careful, I could really fall for you.

"Now you need to be extra careful with our Princess. She's working through some things and doesn't need any complications. Please accept the gift she gave you today and just be her friend. I'm pretty sure she's going to jump your bones," Cindy said.

"Do you want me to tell her no?"

At that moment, if Cindy said no, I knew I wouldn't go with Suzanne.

"No, actually I think she needs this. Please don't reject her. But don't try to make it more than it is."

Suzanne came back from the bathroom.

"Princess, thank you for being our test dummy," Cindy said.

Suzanne gave a mock scowl.

"Are you calling me a dummy?"

Cindy put her hands up.

"No, never," she said.

I decided it was time to separate these two, and I went up and put my arms out to Suzanne. She melted into my arms and gave me a kiss as a reward. My hands traveled down and cupped her rear. Yep, no panties.

"I see someone has gone commando."

She grinned at my comment.

"Go back into that bathroom and bring me your boxers."

Who was I to argue with an older woman? When I got back, she giggled.

"Those jeans leave nothing to the imagination."

I looked down and you could clearly make out my religion. I shrugged and took her hand and led her out of the house; I gave Cindy a wink as we left. Suzanne had a cute little Fiat Spider, a small two-seat Italian sports car. It was bright red with a black interior. She was an aggressive driver. In this subdivision, the streets all wound around and made the ride a lot of fun. She was obviously still aroused. The telltale signs were all there. I looked down and I still had a noticeable wet spot on my jeans.

✧✧✧

It was a gorgeous day for football. There were scattered big fluffy clouds and a slight breeze that helped keep it cool. The parking lot wasn't very full, so I didn't expect a big crowd. Suzanne grabbed my hand and led me into the stadium. She walked in like she owned the place. The ticket taker just nodded. She led me onto the sidelines and introduced me to all the JV Cheerleaders. I could tell they were impressed by me being with the Ice Princess. Three things seemed to impress the girls: the first was that some of them had seen the freshman game and recognized me. The second was I was with one of the social elite;

Suzanne only ran with the best crowds. The last, and probably the one that made the biggest difference, was that she was so happy. She wasn't her normal reserved self. Suzanne was bubbly and all smiles. My social standing had gone up by 200%.

The JV football team came onto the field for warm-ups and Suzanne spotted her brother. She gave him a big smile and wave. He was a big white-haired kid, and obviously a lineman. He was a year older than I was, so I really didn't know him. Once she was sure he'd seen her, she whispered into my ear.

"Let's skip out for a little bit."

She led me to the back of the bleachers, to the equipment shed. It had a combination lock on it and she obviously knew what the combination was. She opened the door and pulled me in. She looped the lock through the inner handles so no one could disturb us. The shed was full of tackling dummies and other equipment for the football team. She went over and moved some of the pads to make a bed.

I'd hoped for a lengthier time for our first time, but we'd been playing much too long at Cindy's for that to happen.

While she was busy, I took my jeans off and put on a condom. She turned around to find me with only a smile on my face. She looked down and saw I had put on some protection.

"Look at our little Boy Scout, he's ready for me."

"Not so little," I growled.

I swept in and kissed her. As we kissed, she pulled her tank top off and dropped her shorts. We found ourselves in a tangle on the pads she had laid out for us. There were no preliminaries. She grabbed my manhood and pulled me down on top of her. I made one steady push until I hit bottom.

"You're right, not so little," she moaned.

The condom was a little bit of a drag. I lost some feeling, but the tradeoff was I lasted much longer. Once I was in her it was as if a switch went off. She humped up to me, I got the message and we had hot monkey sex. She was a wild woman.

When we finished, I lay on top of her as I tried to catch my breath. I saw spots on the edge of my vision, and I was afraid I would pass out. She pushed my chest and I rolled off her.

"Nuffff! Too heavy! You big oaf."

I took in her beauty. There was nothing sexier than Suzanne was in her post orgasmic bliss. I burned the images and how I felt into my brain. I wanted to remember this forever. At this moment, I could fall in love with the Ice Princess, but I'd made a promise to Cindy.

"David, last lesson of the day: I'm going to teach you how make every lover happy."

I felt myself come alert. This would possibly be some more good info to learn.

"Most teen girls either never, or rarely, have an orgasm from intercourse. There are three main reasons. The first is that the boy doesn't get her ready. We take longer to get fully aroused. Most guys use the 'wham bam thank you ma'am' approach to sex. The second is the guy doesn't last long enough, and the third is technique. If you do even a tenth of what we did this afternoon, you have the first problem licked. The second will come with practice. The more you have sex, the more you'll be able to control yourself. It's the final reason that I want to teach you about.

"Take your two fingers and smack the inside of your forearm just above your wrist over and over again," she said.

I did as instructed and you could hear the smack, smack, smack as my fingers made contact with my forearm. This went on for the next few minutes. After a while, my arm began to get red and it hurt. I frowned.

"Okay, you can stop. That was what we just did."

I looked at her with concern.

"I'm sorry."

"Don't be sorry; sometimes a woman just needs that," she explained.

Well, it sure felt good to me, but if I wanted to have girls lining up and coming back for more, I needed to make sure they had a good time and didn't feel abused.

"I'm going to teach you a simple technique your gigolo of a big brother taught me."

The good news was Greg must've done a good job, because she took the time to teach me.

"When you enter a woman, slowly work yourself all the way in. Stop and wait until she's used to you."

I could understand what she was saying. I didn't need to just charge in.

"Then you'll slowly pull all the way out until only the tip is inside her. You'll then take ten shallow strokes with about a third of your member. Then you'll take two deep strokes. Then pull back and do nine short and three long. Get my drift?"

I nodded. Add long strokes and subtract short strokes from the sequence.

"What this little trick does is it varies your stroke length and speed. Pay attention to what's working for her. If she responds more to shallow strokes, then you do that. If she needs it deep and hard, give it to her. Even if you have sex with the same woman the rest of your life, she'll want some variety."

I grinned as I asked.

"Shouldn't we practice?"

"Do you have any more of those condoms?"

"You bet."

Greg had given me a supply for today's lesson. I would have to buy more to replace the ones he'd already given me.

Suzanne lasted until we hit eight deep strokes before she detonated. She arched her back and wrapped herself around me again. I would wake up the next morning with bruises and scratch marks. This was more like making love than what we'd done earlier. I had to say I enjoyed both.

I was sure Mr. Happy was done for the day. As we got dressed, Suzanne explained that this was a one-time thing. I would always be grateful for everything she'd taught me. I won't lie and say I wasn't sad, but I'd made a promise to Cindy and I wasn't about to push it with Suzanne. She led me up into the stands and we watched the second half of the game. After the game, she offered me a ride home, but I needed to be alone and said I would walk. She gave me a slow, lingering kiss goodbye.

✧✧✧

Chapter 8 – Big Man on Campus

Saturday September 7

I watched Suzanne drive away and was ready to walk home when the JV Cheerleaders stopped me. They were some of the best-looking sophomores at Lincoln High. Their ringleader and captain was Tracy Dole. Tracy seemed to be everything I despised about high school. She was the heir apparent for *Queen* of the social elite once the senior class graduated. Despite being a sophomore, it was almost a given that when she moved up to varsity she would be Cheer Captain. This would be an unheard of promotion, since a senior had always held that position.

To Tracy's credit, she didn't seem to be mean spirited. For the most part, she ignored the socially inept like me. The one thing she had going for her was she was drop-dead gorgeous. If I hadn't watched her breasts grow from mere pups to the melons they were now, I would have said she'd had a boob job. On her petite frame, they were spectacular.

"Hey David, I've been remiss in not inviting you to my birthday party this Friday."

I was caught off guard. I'd only talked to Tracy a couple of times and wasn't expecting her to be so friendly. Before I made a complete fool of myself, I pulled it together. I quickly checked my social calendar and that day was free. We had a rare Saturday varsity game this week, which left Friday wide open.

Tracy's birthday party was something everyone wanted to attend. It was invitation-only, and you knew you were part of the 'in' crowd if you were invited. I've only attended one of these coveted parties. It was in second grade, and her mom made her send an invitation to everyone. When I arrived, it was obvious I didn't fit in. In third grade, the same thing happened and I hadn't gone.

"I'd love to come," I replied, thinking 'I need to spread my wings a little.'

It would at least make me more *dateable* if I was seen at Tracy's party. A couple of the girls giggled, and I got the double meaning. Who knew cheerleaders had such dirty minds? Tracy played it as if she didn't get it, but she was sharp and I knew she had.

"Great, we would all love for you to *come*," Tracy said as I raised my eyebrows. "I mean, I would love to have you."

"Tracy, you don't have to try so hard, I'm pretty easy when a girl as pretty as you asks."

That got the group to laugh. I liked this big-breasted girl with the quick wit. What surprised me was I wasn't tongue-tied at all with her and her friends. I guess that in my mind I had no shot, so my nervousness went away. "Since it's your special day, do you think I'll be enough for you, or do you need me to bring a present?" I asked just loud enough for her friends to hear as I moved closer to Tracy.

Tracy Dole actually blushed and giggled. I'm sure she wasn't used to someone who flirted with her so brazenly. She recovered and made a little circular motion with her finger.

"David, give us a little twirl, so I can tell if you'll be enough."

I stepped back a little, raised my arms to shoulder level with my hands raised about ear high, and did a slow turn.

"What do you think? Will I do for your present?" I asked.

I'd forgotten I didn't have any underwear on. I saw several of the girls get a little flushed when they saw I'd gone commando, but Tracy took it all in and checked me out from head to toe. She had a big grin on her face. When I faced away from her, she grabbed my butt. I just looked back and smiled at her. She looked around at the other cheerleaders.

"What do you girls think?"

From the head bobbing, it was apparent I was a hit. She laughed at them and turned to me.

"When did you become so cool?"

I just grinned at her. Did she just say I was cool?

"I guess I have to go along with the squad and say you'll be enough. Do you know where I live?" she asked.

Yep, she lived in one of the nicest subdivisions in town. I played dumb.

"Not exactly, why don't you put your contact info into my phone?"

It was her turn to call bullshit, but she played along, and put her digits and address into my phone. Things were looking up. I just scored the JV's Cheer Captain's phone number. Jeff and Alan would wet themselves when they heard this.

✧✧✧

When I got home, I found Greg in his room resting on his bed with his headphones on as he listened to music. I jumped on his bed and scared him when I gave him a big kiss on the cheek. He tried to push me off.

"Get off me, you little fairy!"

I acted like a six-year-old who got a dirt bike for Christmas.

"Thank you, thank you, thank you!"

He pulled his earbuds out and smiled.

"So, I take it your lesson went well?" he asked.

I could tell he had talked to Cindy.

"Dude, Suzanne is frickin' fantastic! I learned so much. You and Cindy are the best mentors ever!"

"Well, you're welcome, and yes, Suzanne is fantastic."

I suddenly felt really close to him. I told him about Suzanne introducing me to the JV Cheerleading squad and that Tracy Dole had invited me to her birthday party. I didn't share what we'd done in the equipment shed or anything we did at Cindy's. I figured if they wanted to tell him, they would.

Greg got a concerned look on his face and grabbed his phone.

"Hey Princess, David said you were great today."

I could hear Suzanne as she talked to Greg, but I couldn't make out the words on her end.

"No, you're no longer the 'Ice Princess.' From what Cindy said, you thawed today."

I heard her laugh at him.

"Hey, question for you. Tracy Dole's having a birthday party and she invited David to go. Can you tell me what to expect?"

My brother listened to the other end of the conversation for what seemed like hours. In reality, it was probably not more than five minutes. I couldn't get a read on him. He wrapped up the call and shook his head.

"Bro, you're screwed!"

What did that mean?

"Why's that?"

"Apparently, you made quite the impression on Miss Tracy Dole."

I couldn't read Greg.

"And that's bad?"

"No, Tracy's a great girl. The problem is, over the summer Tracy went out with Bill Rogers."

I stiffened. Bill was bad news. I was sorry to say I'd hung out with him when I went through my drug-and-alcohol phase. It was rumored he had stabbed someone over the summer. In addition, he treated girls like shit. I'd been at a party where he coerced one of the girls I didn't know into pulling a train. When I understood what was happening, I felt physically ill when Bill tried to get me to join in. That wasn't how I wanted to lose my virginity.

"It seems Bill doesn't think he's done with her. I would stay far away from that situation until it's resolved," Greg advised.

It was advice I planned to take to heart. I didn't want anything to do with Bill.

✧✧✧

After Greg left, I jumped into a hot shower. I was sore from playing football and I smelled of sex. I let the water pound me as I reflected on the last week.

I hadn't comprehended how tense I was when I heard Bill's name again. He'd played a central role in my corruption last spring by introducing me to drugs as my supplier. I seriously didn't want to run into him again. He had a mean streak I feared could be lethal. I decided I'd call Tracy and make sure he wouldn't show up.

However, I had bigger issues. What was really going on with Cindy and Greg? Whenever I saw them together, they acted like they were a couple. I'd missed something, though. They seemed to be more like friends than each other's soul mate. I've seen Greg with girls he really liked, and it wasn't that he didn't like Cindy, but there wasn't a spark.

I also had trouble reconciling how he had stepped back and allowed Cindy to direct my education on dating. He'd disappeared today. If she were my girlfriend, I would have been there. Brother or not, things could have gotten out of hand. The only thing I could figure was Greg must trust Cindy implicitly. He did know he could trust me. To be honest, most high school kids aren't self-confident enough to have that level of trust in their significant other. I figured it wasn't really my issue, so I would let them work it out, but I didn't want to see either one of them get hurt.

Tami was something that did affect me. I missed my friend. It was as if she was there, but not. I got many knowing looks and subtle help, but we didn't have our normal marathon talks or hang out. I needed to find out what to do to fix that. There were things that I could tell only her, things like my date with Tina. I really needed her input on the strange way the date ended. Tina had revealed she'd snuck out and couldn't date until she was sixteen. Should I wait for Tina, or move on? I also wanted to talk to Tami about what happened over the summer, and not just the big stuff. I missed when we shared all the little things.

This was the longest we'd gone without a serious talk since I was seven and her mom had sent her to summer camp. We were both so upset when she got back, our parents had arranged for us to go together the next year. This time it had been nearly five months. That seemed like a lifetime. Was I being selfish in wanting our friendship fixed? I still remembered being half stoned as I acted like a jerk. She had stormed up to me, with tears streaming down her face, and told me off. Then the words that had almost killed me: "I never want to see you again." I still regretted not chasing after her to fix it right then.

I felt the hot water start to run out. I jumped out and toweled off. I wrapped the towel around my waist, grabbed my cell phone and texted Tracy to jump on to video chat. I fired up my tablet and waited for her to log on. I put the tablet into a stand so I could video chat hands free. Almost instantly she popped up and I could see her grin at me from what must be her bedroom. It looked like a bedroom out of one of those home decorating shows. Tracy had her hair pulled back into a ponytail and wore a Notre Dame t-shirt.

I glanced back and wanted to kick myself. My room was now almost back to its typical mess, with the bed unmade and my stuff everywhere. I also should have gotten dressed; too late now. She started the conversation.

"Took you long enough to call!"

I really did like her sarcastic sense of humor. I decided to play the straight man.

"Trace, what are you talking about?"

"Well, I *am* the Head JV Cheerleader and you *are* the Bemoc. Isn't that what everyone expects?"

I was sure I didn't want to know what this was, but I asked anyways.

"What's a Bemoc?"

"B. M. O. C., Big Man on Campus. At least for the freshman class, you are."

I cringed. She was setting me up to be something I wasn't. I had always been the nerdy nice guy.

"How do you figure?"

"All right, since you're a dumb jock…" she began, but I interrupted.

"Hey, I resemble that remark!"

"Yes, you do. So, since you're a dumb jock, I'll spell it out for you. First, who set the freshman rushing record after only six practices?"

"That would be me," I said stoically.

"Second, who's the only freshman who's currently on the Varsity Football Team?"

"That would be me again."

"Third, who went away for the summer and came back a stud?"

"I have no idea on that one."

"That would be you again. Fourth, who got a complete makeover this week and has all the girls talking?"

"Hmm, me?"

"We especially like your curly locks," she revealed. "Finally, who showed up to the JV game in the company of a *very* happy varsity cheerleader? Who, by the way, usually scares the shit out me with her Ice Princess persona, but somehow shows up all bubbly. If I didn't know any better, I would say she got laid."

"She was just helping me with some things today," I said.

Heck that sounded weak, even to me.

"I'm not going to get into that, because she really does scare me. With all that, you're now officially the freshman Bemoc!"

Let's try to bait-and-switch her.

"What about Mike Herndon? Isn't he our Bemoc?"

"Good point. Normally an all-around good guy who's as good looking as Mike is and who just happens to be the starting freshman quarterback would be a shoo-in for Bemoc. But unfortunately for poor Mike, he doesn't stand a chance with you around."

"Tracy, friend of mine, goddess of the cheer world, sexiest woman I know, if you start calling me Bemoc that's the kind of nickname that'll follow me around for a very long time. What can I do to avoid that?"

"Laying it on a little thick, are we?"

"Maybe. But seriously, please don't do that to me."

That got a big grin out of her. Uh oh, I might be in trouble.

"I'll make you a deal: you accompany me to my birthday party as my date, and I'll make sure that the Bemoc thing goes away."

"So we're talking a little blackmail, are we?" I asked as she gave me a look. "Not that I'm against that kind of thing, mind you. But Tracy, you do know that all you had to do was ask?"

"David, I was just having fun with you, but I'd like for you to be at my side at my party."

It was time to poke the bear and push my luck.

"I guess we should add, who got *asked out* by the hottest sophomore who also happens to be the *Head* JV Cheerleader."

"I wouldn't go there, Buster!"

Holy cow, I was a normal, ordinary, everyday fifteen-year-old boy, who had just been asked out by *Tracy Dole*! There wasn't a guy in our school who wouldn't give his left arm to date her, but the cloud of Bill Rogers loomed. There was something off about that guy. When I was around him, the hairs on the back of my neck would rise. As I looked back, he preyed on my gullibility and need for acceptance to pull me into drug use. Hindsight was a wonderful thing, but I wished I'd had it before I jumped in with his crowd. The good news was I would never go back to that life again.

I made a decision.

"I will if you can assure me that someone won't be there."

Okay, I could tell that she was a little miffed. You have to appreciate that Tracy Dole is the Queen of the Sophomore Class and wasn't used to being questioned.

"Give me their names and I'll make sure they're not welcome."

"Bill Rogers."

I could see her stiffen and get a panicked look on her face. This asshole had done a number on her. She stared at me and tried to figure something out. The tone of the conversation got serious.

"How do you know about that?" she asked.

"Did you forget I know him? I've seen him in action. I just really never want to be around the guy again."

"No, I'm well aware you know him," she said, and took a deep breath. "David, I got in over my head. At first, it was just fun and games when I hung out with his crowd. For some reason I'm attracted to bad boys. Bill is the worst of them all, but once I went out with him I knew it was a mistake. I'm not comfortable talking about what happened, but he scares me. I told him we were done, but he isn't taking 'no' for an answer. Why do you think I'm home on Friday and Saturday nights?"

"Do you expect him to be at your party?"

She looked down and I saw her bottom lip quiver.

"I don't think he'd try anything with witnesses around, but he's just crazy enough. He gets sooo mad and loses control."

Her eyes were almost haunted. This just confirmed my worry about hanging out with Tracy if Bill was stalking her.

"Tracy, you need to tell someone. This is more than you should be taking on yourself."

"David, I just told you."

Now it was my turn to go quiet. If Tami were around, she would know what to do. I would see her tomorrow and ask her.

"I'll stand by you at your party. I'm also honored you asked me out."

"Thank you, David. You don't know how happy that makes me."

I could hear the relief in her voice and she visibly seemed to relax.

"Look, David, I'll talk to you at school."

"Okay, I'll see you Monday."

"Oh, and David?"

Hmmm. Something was up.

"Yes."

"Are you naked?"

I blushed.

"No, I have a towel on. I just got out of the shower and was headed to bed."

"Could you give me a little show?"

This was a girl I could really like. I looked at her in mock horror.

"Tracy Dole! Who knew you would try to take advantage of poor little me? Next thing you know I'll have screen shots of me all over school."

"We could play a little you-show-me-yours-and-I'll-show-you-mine."

Now we're talking!

"Yes, we could, but might I suggest we do that in person? How about you unwrap me as your birthday present?"

She shivered.

"David, I would love to, but I'm not sure I'm ready for you. Make me a promise."

"I will if I can."

"On Friday, don't let things go too far."

Normally it's not a good idea to put the guy in charge of what was too far.

"You can trust me, but don't get me wrong: you push all the right buttons for me. If you ever give me the go-ahead, I'll do everything in my power to rock your world."

Her eyes got big.

"I know you will. But I'm trying to take things slow."

"You set the pace," I assured her.

"Thank you. I'll see you Monday."

"Yeah, bye," I said as I stood up, turned around and dropped my towel to give her a view of my butt.

I heard Tracy burst out laughing as I shut down the link. I crawled into bed exhausted. I was asleep soon after my head hit the pillow.

✧✧✧

Sunday September 8

I woke Sunday morning to my dad shaking my shoulder.

"Get up, you're going to church."

Crap. Don't get me wrong, I believe in God, but I went all summer without going and fell out of the habit. I knew Dad wouldn't go, and it sounded like Greg would get out of it too. That meant I had to go and have some one-on-one time with my mom.

I got up, dressed and found Mom waiting on me. It turned out to be a good experience. We went to the early service and got home around eleven for brunch. Greg and

Dad had made bacon, tomato and Swiss omelets; hash browns; melon wedges; and orange juice. It was nice to have the whole family together for a meal. Of course, it was a chance to talk about everything that was going on.

Mom had some news.

"Your Uncle Jim is going to come live with us for a couple of months. He landed a consulting job and I convinced him to stay here instead of paying for a short-term lease."

Uncle Jim was my mom's younger brother. He lived in Florida with my aunt Tanya and my cousins Julie and Elizabeth. I had a soft spot in my heart for El, as we called her. She was three or four years younger than I was. I always made it a point to include her. Her older sister ignored El at family gatherings, which made me feel sorry for her. I was lucky my older brother didn't do that to me. When she was a little girl, at one of our big Thanksgiving get-togethers, El had once declared that one day we would be married. Everyone had laughed at her announcement, but I had curbed my own amusement, because I could see she was serious. Everyone else's reaction put her into tears. I spent the afternoon comforting her. I told her it was all good, and that even though I hadn't thought about getting married yet, that I wasn't opposed to marrying her.

We had an apartment above the garage that I'd always wanted to move into. Uncle Jim had stayed with us twice before on his consulting gigs. Each time he had said he would come for a month or so, and ended up he stayed twice as long. I knew this irritated my dad. Not that he didn't like Uncle Jim, it just seemed he always overextended his stay. Okay, Uncle Jim was a self-centered jerk. Dad was just too nice to say so.

"I want to move into the apartment over the garage," I blurted out, not thinking it through.

I could see Greg ease back from the table. You never wanted to be caught in the crossfire when a family discussion went south, and this had the earmarks of a bad one. Both my mom and dad zeroed in on me. My Uncle John had taught me over the summer that in a negotiation, the first one to speak usually loses. So I just shut up and waited. Greg started to squirm in his chair, because no one had said anything. I was surprised when my dad was the first one to speak.

"All right, give us your reasons for wanting the apartment."

I smiled because I knew he'd given me the opening I needed.

"There are three reasons that I think you should consider accepting my proposal. The first is you could never allow Greg to move into the apartment, because he's such a slut he would have girls in and out all the time." I turned to Greg and said, "No offense, man."

He just nodded. We all knew he was a slut.

"The second reason is over the summer Uncle John introduced me to meditation to help center myself. I'm finding with all the noise in the house that I can't concentrate. The third reason is that I know money is tight. Greg got a car for his sixteenth birthday. Mine is coming up in July. I'll take the apartment instead of a car." I saw my mom flinch at that one. "The final bonus reason is that if Uncle Jim has to move into my old room and share a bathroom with Greg, he's not extending his stay like he always does. Greg's worse than a girl is in the mornings. Uncle Jim will never make it to work on time."

My mom snorted and my dad broke into a big grin.

"You have some valid points. Let me ask you: is this really something you want?" Mom asked.

"Yes, seriously, I think I need this. I need some space right now, and this is the perfect solution."

My mom and dad looked at each other, my dad nodded yes to my mom, and she smiled.

"Okay."

Greg about jumped out of his seat.

"You little shit. How did you pull that off?"

I grinned at him.

"I asked."

Mom looked me in the eye.

"So, you really think this will keep Jim from overstaying his visit?"

We all burst into laughter.

We had a rule in our house that if you cooked, the rest of the family cleaned up, so this time it fell to Mom and me. I told her I'd take care of it. It was the least I could do. I had a feeling she and I had a new arrangement, and she didn't have to clean up if I was involved.

✧✧✧

When I was done with the kitchen, I looked at the time. It was 12:30. I was late. About that time, I got a text from Beth who wanted to know where I was. I sent her a message back to let her know I'd be there in fifteen minutes. I ran upstairs and put on my swimsuit and a t-shirt. Beth lived two blocks down, so I just walked over.

When I got there, Mrs. Anderson answered the door. She and my mom were best friends. She was in many ways my second mom.

"David, how was your time on the farm with your uncle?"

"You know what, Mrs. A, it was probably the best thing I've ever done. Uncle John helped me get my head on right. I was a little depressed after my classmate almost died at the party I threw. I think I blamed everyone else for my problems. Uncle John helped me see the error of my ways."

She just smiled at me.

"I have to say we all missed you and are glad you're back. Also, I have a surprise for you," Mrs. A said, with a gleam in her eye that caused me to break out into a huge smile. "We got a hot tub."

"Awesome! Football practice has been kicking my butt, and a soak would do me wonders."

"Listen, if you need to use it just swing by."

That's what I loved about Beth's family: they were open and I always felt welcome.

"I'll take you up on that. I think you'll be seeing a lot more of me. Hook up one of those big outdoor TVs and you'll never get rid of me."

She led me through the house and gave me a Mountain Dew before we joined everyone in the back yard. Mr. Anderson was in charge of the grill. There were five other teens either in the pool or sunning themselves: Beth, Mike and Luke Herndon, Bert Nelson, and Tami. Seeing Bert almost put me in a bad mood, but Beth changed that when she ran up and gave me a big hug.

Beth's family had gradually turned their back yard into the ideal entertainment area. Up towards the house they had a large eating area where our families had many a meal. Off to the side they had put in a cooking area complete with a large grill and counters with an under-counter refrigerator. Down the middle of the backyard was a large pool. On one side was an area for sunbathing, and on the other was a pool shed for the equipment and a small pool house so you could change and take a shower. Behind the sunbathing area was a new huge hot tub. I would bet we could get eight people in it easily.

"Hey, Beth, are you happy to see me?"

"Jerk, I thought you were blowing me off."

"No, just went to church with Mom and then we had a family brunch. Time just got away from me." I looked out at the group and said, "I think I know everyone but Luke. Are you guys going out?"

"No, we're just friends. When I told him you were going to be here, he asked to come. He wants to get to know you outside of football since you'll be his new fullback. He said you and Mike were becoming friends, so I had him bring him also."

Luke was a senior and the starting halfback. The starting fullback had blown his knee out in the first game of the season. I was the first freshman since Luke to play varsity ball. If he was anything like his brother Mike, I knew I'd like him.

I needed to dig some to see what was up with Tami. I knew she and Beth talked, and I wanted some intelligence before I put my foot in my mouth. It really chafed me that no one had bothered to mention that my best friend was dating. I thought she didn't really like Bert all that much. In middle school he'd been kind of a jerk to her, so I figured Beth might know what was going on.

"I see Tami brought her new boyfriend."

"You'll have to talk to them about that. I really don't know if they're seeing each other or not."

I gave her a peck on the cheek.

"All right, wish me luck. It's time to find out where Tami and I stand."

Beth gave me a hug. Mike was sitting on the closest lounge chair, so I said hi to him first.

"David, hey, I want you to meet my brother Luke."

I shook his hand and turned to Bert.

"Hey, Bert, how's it going?"

"Good," Bert answered.

I walked over to Tami, she got up, and I pulled her into a hug and kissed her on the cheek. There was an empty lounge chair between Luke and Bert.

"Is Beth sitting here?"

"She was, but she said she needed to help her parents get ready for lunch. I'm sure she doesn't mind you claiming it," Tami said.

"I am sure she doesn't either, but I don't want to be a rude guest."

I went over to the pool shed, pulled out a lawn chair and set it up next to Mike. Beth came back about that time and took her chair. I saw Luke nod to me to confirm I'd made a good decision.

"So, I hear you're on varsity now," Luke said.

"Hey, I want to hear about that too. Why don't you guys come over and help me grill?" Mr. Anderson said.

Luke and I jumped up and went over to where Mr. Anderson was grilling. I went to the cabinet, pulled out a water bottle with a sprayer on it and filled it up. I handed it to Luke.

"You're in charge of putting out fires."

Mr. Anderson gave me a sour look.

"Funny. I haven't burned your steak in months."

"Mr. A, I haven't been here in months. Luke, keep an eye on things."

I went up to Mr. Anderson, gave him a hug and then filled him in.

"It's such a fluke. I practiced on the second team for a few days and then only played less than a half. Heck, Bert has more reps than I do. I just happened to break a long run the first time I touched the ball. Then Washington's defense tried to arm-tackle me the rest of the game. On top of that our starting fullback on varsity hurt his knee."

Mike had joined us.

"Okay, I call bullshit. Dawson, you're so full of it. Mr. A, he hits defenders so hard they wish they hadn't been born. The first play in practice he put down our starting middle linebacker and safety. He crushed Washington's linebacker on his first carry. I bet he still doesn't know his own first name. That's why Washington's defense was scared to tackle him."

Luke looked at Mike.

"What do you think's going to happen when he tangles with Kevin Goode?"

Mike broke into a big smile.

"I'll make a bold prediction: he'll put Kevin on his butt."

Kevin was our school's All-State linebacker. He was a beast at six-four and 210 pounds. I was not looking forward to having him hit me.

Luke looked skeptical.

"No way, I've never seen a back put Kevin on his butt."

I could tell Mike had gotten into this argument with his brother before.

"Ask Dad, he saw him play. Luke, he doesn't just hit people, he crushes them. I can't wait until you hear the difference in the sound of the hit when he does it compared to everyone else. His hits sound like the hits you hear in a pro game. With David playing fullback, you'll get a full ride for college. He's a difference-maker. He'll put the defense on its ears, and with your speed you'll rack up a ton of yards. Your numbers are going to go through the roof."

Luke liked the sound of that.

"David, I think you just became my new best friend."

"Luke, *fire!*" I said when I noticed the burgers were blazing.

Luke was able to get the fire out before too much damage was done. Mr. Anderson glared at me and I just gave him an innocent look.

I noticed that Tami, Bert and Beth were in a heated discussion. Beth wasn't happy. I heard her raise her voice.

"You better tell him!"

She got up and stormed into the kitchen. I turned away before Tami could catch me eavesdropping. Shortly thereafter Bert got up and joined our group, leaving Tami all alone. The guys joked around as we watched Mr. Anderson try to burn the burgers.

I wasn't going to talk to Tami right now. If Beth was pissed with her, then I knew I would be also, so I decided it was in my best interest to ignore the obvious invitation to go talk to her. Even a 'stupid boy' like me could figure out she cleared Bert out so we could have some alone time. She had played some kind of game with me all week and I'd had enough.

Before I could get too deep into things, lunch was served. We had a lot of fun. Luke and Mike were a riot. I never realized they were so funny. The one person who wasn't fitting in was Bert. He had always been such a stuck-up snob that I couldn't imagine Tami would have anything to do with him. After lunch, Mike, Luke and Bert all left. The Andersons made themselves scarce to give Tami and me a chance to talk.

"What did you say to piss off Beth?"

Tami blushed brightly and glared at me.

"You're not going to make this easy, are you?"

I took that as a rhetorical question and just waited her out. She seemed to make up her mind and started in with what was going on.

"David, I have an opportunity to go to a much better school to get me ready for premed: Wesleyan Academy. I'll be leaving at the end of September to start the fourth quarter."

I could tell by her body language she expected me to explode over this, but this really had nothing to do with me. She had always dreamed about being a doctor. This school was extremely well regarded for its academics. I had always known that at some point we would go our separate ways. Her schooling would be intense and take many years. At some point, she had to leave me behind. I guess it was happening sooner rather than later.

"That's great news. I understand it's very expensive. How are you swinging the cost?"

Her head jerked up and I could see tears of joy in her eyes. She jumped out of her chair, tackled me and put me in a bear hug.

"Thank you, thank you, thank you for understanding. I was scared you'd be mad. You've just come back and now I'm leaving you. I should've known I could count on you to understand. I'm so sorry for not putting more faith in you. Our friendship means so much to me. I was afraid I'd lose it."

"Tami, you never have to worry about me like that. I know this is important to you. Does it suck that you're moving several hours away? Yes, but we both knew that at some point we would need to have a long-distance friendship. No matter how far apart we are, we'll always be friends. I'll love you wherever you are."

I looked over at the back door and Beth was smiling. She could tell we were fine. My friendship with Beth had also gotten closer since I got back. Maybe that was a good thing if Tami were to leave me. I needed to be surrounded with friends who had my best interests at heart. Beth, Alan and Jeff were all good friends. My new friendships with Lily and the football guys also looked promising.

Then there were the potentially game-changing friends. Cindy, Suzanne and Tracy could potentially be much more than just friends. The dream girl was Peggy. If I could ever break out of the 'friend zone,' I would be over-the-moon happy.

The one that didn't seem to register was Tina. I'd lost my virginity to her, but the way things ended just made no sense. Looking back, I was a little sad I'd lost my virginity to her. There wasn't a real connection there. I would rather have waited and lost my virginity to Suzanne. Even though she told me that what we did was a one-time thing, I didn't think either one of us believed it. I really had done a lot in a short time to get a nice support team around me.

Not having Tami here every day would be hard because of the nine years of history we had. We hadn't talked for the past five months, but for me this had been good in a strange way. I'd had to learn to stand on my own.

Before, I would always bring my problems to Tami, and she would solve them for me. She'd always been my compass that guided me through life. Not having her around over the summer had been hard for me. Uncle John knew he couldn't allow us to communicate or I would have never grown up. I think the reason I hadn't pushed harder to reconcile with Tami was that deep down I knew our relationship had to change. She couldn't just fix things for me forever.

Would I need her as a sounding board? Hell, yes. The thing I knew was that she had my back 100%. She'd never done anything that wasn't in my best interest. Even when she told me to get lost five months ago, she had done what was best for me. No relationship was ever equal, and I knew Tami had given me more than I had ever been able to give back. She never cared, because she knew I would lay down my life for her.

I knew we would always be best friends. Distance wouldn't change that. With video chats, it would be almost as if she was here. Was it a big deal she was leaving to pursue her dreams? Yes, in the sense that she would finally get what she wanted, but it wouldn't change how I felt about her. I knew deep down I loved her and she loved me. Someday, who knew?

Tami suddenly surprised me when she leaned in and kissed me. In the ten years I'd known her, she had never kissed me. This kiss wasn't about passion. This was about healing our relationship. I pulled her into a hug and we remained lip-locked for what seemed like eternity. It was the perfect symbol of our love and friendship. When we finally broke apart, we both had tears rolling down our faces. My throat was so constricted with emotion I couldn't say a word.

Seemingly, out of nowhere, Beth stepped up and smiled at us.

"I take you guys have made up?"

Tami hopped off my lap and I stood up, pulled Beth into an embrace, and gave her a kiss on the cheek.

"Yes, we've made up, and thank you for being our friend. I love you too."

I really didn't know what had gotten into me being so much more affectionate with Beth. It just felt right, and she didn't seem to object.

"Come on in, guys. Mom made a cake and we have some ice cream. We'd all like to hear about Tami's great opportunity."

Beth led the way. I took Tami's hand and we walked in as if we were a couple. For some reason we needed the contact to assure each other that this was real. We walked into the kitchen, and Tami and I both saw it was German chocolate cake, our favorite. We broke out into big grins when we saw two big glasses of milk waiting for us. When the cake was served, there was a scoop of vanilla ice cream on the side. Mrs. A had really made an effort to impress.

"I've been accepted to Wesleyan Academy starting the fourth quarter. They do things differently there. Their school year is broken into four equal quarters instead of the two-semester system we have. I'll be starting when the October quarter begins."

"What will you be studying?" Mr. Anderson asked.

"Premed. That's always been her dream," I said.

"Yes, they have a fantastic premed curriculum. They have it set up so that by my senior year I'll be taking college-level classes. The plan is this should cut at least a year off the time it will take me to become a doctor. They also have close ties to Stanford, Johns Hopkins and many of the other better medical schools."

"How did you get in? It's my understanding that Wesleyan is very exclusive, many times invitation-only," Mrs. A said.

"Actually, that's a funny story. Over the summer I decided not to play baseball because it just wasn't any fun without David." She squeezed my hand to let me know everything was fine. "I decided to learn to play golf. One of the few people I knew at the country club was Bert. Turns out his dad, Dr. Nelson, is involved with setting up scholarships for deserving students who would benefit from an education at Wesleyan Academy. Last week they had a fundraiser for the scholarships, and I was invited. At the event, it was announced I was the first recipient. As a bonus I discovered Bert's a nice guy and we became friends." She gave me a direct look and then clarified. "I said 'friend,' not 'boyfriend.'"

Everyone laughed when they saw my sheepish look.

"The last two weeks have been very busy getting all the details worked out. I'll continue to go to school here until the end of September." She looked me in the eye and said, "David doesn't know it yet, but he's going to help me get ready to go and spend a ton of quality time with me until I leave."

"I think that sounds like a great idea. Just let me know your plans and what you need me to do," I said.

Tami and I were able to spend some time catching up. It felt like things were as back to normal as having only a few weeks left with your best friend could be. We would make it work.

✧✧✧

When I got home, Mom, Dad and Greg helped me move into the garage apartment. By nine, I was exhausted. I curled up on my bed and slept ten hours straight.

✧✧✧

Chapter 9 – Did I Get You in the Divorce?

Monday September 9

I took a quick shower and did my hair. This doing-the-hair thing was a pain. I went down to the kitchen to grab a bite to eat before school and Greg was there. I just ignored him and ate a bowl of cereal.

"Do you want a ride?" he asked when I was done.

I stopped and looked him in the eye.

"Okay, sounds better than riding the bus."

On the way to school, all I could think about was Tami leaving. It wasn't until I was almost to school that it began to sink in what she'd said. She said she loved me and I had told her I loved her too. Was that even possible? Did I love Tami? There was more to this than I knew. As my uncle taught me, just get through one day at a time and eventually things would work out.

When arrived, it didn't take long for my spirits to lift.

"Hey, David," I heard the sweet voice from behind me say, so I slowed down and let Tracy catch up.

We fell into step and I checked out her tight jeans, which hugged every curve. She was so delightful that her presence burned through my funk of worrying about Tami leaving.

I reached out and took her hand. She leaned in so we wouldn't be overheard.

"You're a bad boy. All I could think about was your cute butt."

"How did you see my butt? I thought the connection dropped."

"Yeah, right. You just wanted to see how horny you could make me."

Horny was good.

"Did it work?" I asked.

"What do you think? I was waiting for you like a stalker when you got to school."

When we got to the hall with my locker, I saw Tina waiting for me.

"Hey, save me a seat at lunch. I need to talk to Tina. We had a date last Friday and it looks like she needs to talk."

"Wow, you're the confident one. Aren't you worried I'll get jealous?"

"Tracy, you're the most gorgeous girl in school. You have nothing to be jealous about. Now, do you want to do a little PDA so your friends have something to talk about?"

I nodded to indicate her fellow cheerleaders who were watching our every move. She actually gave a little schoolgirl giggle as she leaned in to peck me on the cheek. I was having none of that. I turned at the last second and laid a sizzling kiss on her.

"I think that'll hold you until lunch," I said.

As I left, her friends swarmed around her and you could hear the girl-chatter triple in volume. I had a feeling Tracy would get even at some point. I really hoped I would enjoy the revenge.

I walked away as she just stared after me. I walked up to Tina and saw she had a scowl on her face. I wasn't in the mood for any drama, so I put on my best smile.

"Hi, Tina. What's up?"

"What's up with you and Tracy? Did you replace me that quickly?"

I was *really* in no mood for the jealous girlfriend act. She was the one that told me to move on, so I was a little short with her.

"Come again?"

She instantly saw her mistake, because she looked apologetic. I decided to cut her some slack.

"Nothing, I'm the one who broke it off. Sorry for being a bitch, but I did want to talk to you. Some of my friends are interested in going out with you," she said.

That was the last thing I thought she would say. I think she could tell it knocked me a little off-balance because she chuckled at my expression. Did she say friends, plural, as in more than one? Why would they tell her they wanted to go out with me? Then it dawned on me: Tina had talked to them about our date. As soon as I comprehended that, my face was suddenly bright red and Tina was now laughing.

"What did you tell them?"

"From the look on your face, probably more than you wanted me to."

Oh dear God, she surely did not share the sex stuff? How do girls read our minds? She just nodded to my unasked question, and I buried my face in my hands. Someday I'll learn that girls give much more detail than a guy ever would. Two guys would just say something like, 'Did you nail her?' and the conversation would be over. Girls gave each other every shocking detail.

"You're so cute. Don't worry, you came off well. They're all waiting for me to give them the go-ahead. Do you want me to give the all-clear today? Or wait a day or two?"

"Please, don't set them loose on me today. I have too much going on, and I have a, oh I don't know, a date with Tracy on Friday. Can you put them off until I find out what that's all about?"

She could see the desperation in my eyes. I was sure she could have toyed with me, but she took pity.

"Sure. Just remember you promised to take me out once I turn sixteen."

"I'm looking forward to it."

The bell sounded to indicate it was time for our first class. I dumped my book bag, grabbed what I needed and headed to class.

✧✧✧

At lunch, I found Lily had waited for me and she looked concerned. I smiled at her to reassure her.

"Did I get you in the divorce?"

"You sure did," she said, and seemed to brighten at my teasing.

I came up and gave her a hug.

"What's bugging you? You look sad."

"Actually, you're bugging me. How come you didn't ask *me* out?"

That brought me up short. To be honest, I hadn't even thought about asking Lily out. It had nothing to do with how she looked. I would be comfortable having her on my arm. The problem was she was the center of so much of my recent past. I still had days where it was almost too much. I could see she was serious and she deserved a serious answer.

"That date was a practice date," I said, and I could tell that confused her. "My brother's been helping me out. He's getting some help from his girlfriend, Cindy. You might have noticed some changes in me over the last few weeks. This is going to sound bad. They've been helping me become *dateable*."

I waited for her to laugh at me. My eyes drifted to my feet in embarrassment. It did sound bad when I said it aloud.

"Hey, look at me," she said, and made me look her in the eyes. "Tami told me what was going on. I just wanted to know why you didn't ask me. If you haven't figured it out yet, I'd like a chance to be more than friends."

I think my response wasn't what she was looking for.

"How the hell does Tami know what's going on? I never told her, and I'm pretty sure Greg and Cindy aren't talking about this."

She chuckled.

"You'll have to ask her. She scares me sometimes with how she finds things out. All I know is that you, mister, better never have any real secrets, because Tami will know them before you do."

"Lord, isn't that the truth."

"So back to my question: do I have a shot at a date?"

I let out a big sigh.

"Lily, I'm just starting this dating thing. I have no idea what I'm doing. Let me get this figured out before I bring you into this mess. You're too important to me to be just one date. You're the type of person I could get serious with."

"Yeah, right, no idea what you're doing. All Tina can talk about is how big you are and how much pleasure you gave her."

I would have to kill my mom. I knew her little talk with the girls would come back and kick me in the butt. Poor Tina was no help when she went on and on about Mr. Happy. At least Lily had the grace to blush. I decided to change the subject before anyone else had an opinion on my manhood.

"Sorry, no details. Are you ready for the big time?" I asked.

She didn't miss a beat.

"All right, I'll bite."

"We're going to be sitting at the 'cool kids' table. It seems I'm now cool since I played well on Saturday. Are you sure you want to spend time with all those stuck-up people?"

"If you're there, I'll be fine."

She was like a puppy. She only saw the best in me. I just wish I were as good a guy as she thought I was. I needed some unconditional love about now. I pulled her into a hug and kissed her forehead. We had grabbed our trays and picked out what to eat when Lily broached the subject that had weighed on me.

"I heard you and Tami aren't talking. Is there anything I can do?"

Lily really is a sweet girl. She didn't know about our talk on Sunday.

"We talked yesterday and we're good. That was nice of you to ask."

I didn't think she expected that because she kind of snorted and gave me a goofy half-smile. I wiggled my eyebrows at her and she fell into step with me.

When we walked into the lunchroom, I was looking for my new cool group. Lily nudged me and pointed with her chin to where Tracy was seated. When we came up, there was only one seat next to Tracy. Tracy looked at Mona Wingman, they did that girl thing where they read each other's mind, and Mona got up to make room for Lily and me. Tracy was a gracious hostess.

"David, Lily, I'm glad you guys could join us," Tracy said, shocking Lily because she didn't know Tracy even knew who she was. "I want to make sure everyone knows each other. This is Sammie Goudy, Kim Sun, Mona Wingman, Mike Herndon, Tim Foresee and Jake Holcombe. Gang, this is David Dawson and Lily Harris."

Mike gave me a big grin.

"Hey Bemoc, glad you could make it."

I gave Tracy a dirty look and she shook her head that she didn't put him up to it, so I just grinned.

"Let me guess. First week of school Tracy tagged you with the nickname?"

"How did you know? I'm hoping to pass it along."

Tim came to my rescue.

"Sorry, man. You can't give your mantle away. Plus, I shudder to think what your new nickname will be once Tracy gets done with you."

Mike looked aghast.

"I hadn't thought of that."

We had a good time until Tracy asked Lily how she knew me.

"David saved my life."

"Seriously?" Mona asked.

"Oh, yes. I was at a party where someone gave me a spiked drink. I passed out and almost choked to death on my own vomit, when this guy saved me. I guess when I was turning blue everyone else bailed on the party and left me to die. David even took the fall for the party to keep everyone else out of trouble."

✧✧✧

A couple of things changed when I joined the varsity football team. The first was in PE. I was given a trainer who monitored my conditioning and weight lifting. I met Jill Kim after lunch. The first day was mainly getting a baseline as to where I was physically. We then went outside and she had me run some drills. She pointed out I was having the typical problem boys have when their growth spurt sets in: I had coordination issues.

We both agreed I needed to bulk up some to take the pounding at the varsity level. She proposed I work on conditioning in the mornings Sunday through Thursday. She would assign me a running partner who would meet me at my home the following morning. I would alternate days between lifting and working on improving my speed. I would lift Sunday, Tuesday and Thursday. I would do speed training Monday and Wednesday.

The only strange thing she had me scheduled to do was Pilates. There was a Saturday class with the park district I had to sign up and pay for. She explained Pilates was the fastest way I could build flexibility, muscle strength, and endurance. The emphasis was on developing a strong core or center, and improving coordination and balance. We had a game Saturday, so I'd start next week.

The second was I was assigned a tutor. In middle school, I was an A/B-average student without cracking any books, so I wasn't too worried about my grades. I made a commitment to improve my grades this year. Our school counselor insisted I have a tutor. She explained that if I wanted to get into a good college, I'd need grades as well as my football skills. She went on to explain that the pressure of being a freshman playing varsity ball might be overwhelming.

I had study hall as the last class of the day. Instead of going there, I was told to go to one of the tutoring rooms. They were soundproofed because they were also used as music practice rooms. These were small rooms with a desk, two chairs and a computer. I showed up a few minutes late because I wasn't sure where it was. When I walked in, I was blasted.

"You're late!"

I stepped back and saw my tutor was Suzanne Ball, a.k.a. the Ice Princess. I smiled. I guess she really was going to teach me things. She looked pissed, which confused me. Then I remembered she was a cheerleader and word was out Tracy was interested in me.

Cindy warned me off by telling me something was up with Suzanne. If it weren't for that, I'd make a serious play for her. Of course, we had the usual issues of her being in the social elite and a senior. Both seemed like insurmountable obstacles in creating a relationship. The final hurdle was the Ice Princess had been asked out by the best looking, most confident guys around, and she had turned them all down. I didn't stack up to that kind of competition.

"What are you mad about?"

"You're late."

Every guy knows the first thing a girl throws at you when they're pissed is usually not the real issue.

"Okay, I call bullshit."

Now that was probably not my wisest move.

"What do you mean, bullshit? I take being a tutor seriously. If you're not going to respect my time, I'll find someone else to tutor you."

"Whoa, I was late because I didn't know where the room was. I called bullshit because that isn't the real reason you're mad."

"All right, wise guy, why am I mad?"

I try never to ever fall for that one. I've had my mom pull it on me way too many times. She was the champion at this. I wouldn't confess to stuff she hadn't thought of. Suzanne was a lightweight compared to my mom. I gave her a small smile.

"Suzanne, I would never presume to tell you what you are or aren't mad about. I just know you aren't mad about me being late. Irritated, yes, but you're mad about something else."

"So you don't think I could be mad about you being late?"

"Of course you could. But let's be honest, is that really why you're mad?"

"No."

Now we're starting to get somewhere with this.

"Care to share, so we can work this out?"

"I'm not sure I want to work this out."

"Fair enough, would you prefer to yell at me and get it out of your system?"

This one took her back. Mom has used this technique on me, so I knew its effect. It made me take a step back and decide what I really wanted to do. Sometimes I *did* just want to yell, so I waited patiently while Suzanne figured it out. I wasn't expecting her to giggle, but that's what she did.

"You dork. I have no idea why I can't stay mad at you. I'd gotten myself all worked up so I could blast you."

"Tracy?" I guessed.

"Yeah, I figured if I came on tough I could smack you around and help you see she's not the right girl for you."

"I agree. Tracy isn't the best match. She's way out of my league, but I need to start with you. Are you comfortable being my tutor? If not, that won't affect our friendship, but I know we have a little more between us than a normal tutor and student would have."

"No, I really am fine with teaching you. Like I said before, what we did was a one-time thing."

"Well good; well, not really good. I'm glad you want to be my tutor. I have to say, you're one sexy lady and I'm a teenage boy. I get what we did was a one-time thing. But I can fantasize, can't I?"

I finally got a big smile out of her.

"Only if I can fantasize too," Suzanne stated.

"Who am I to stop you? So, here's the deal: you smacked me around and got me to see the light. I'll get my head out of my backside and at least talk to Tracy about whatever it is she has planned. I'll fantasize about the sexiest woman I know. You get to fantasize about the cutest freshman you know. Do we have a deal?"

"Well, I don't know about the sexiest woman part, but deal. Now get your books out and let's see what we need to work on."

Yeah, she thinks I'm the cutest freshman. Hey, you have to take your victories where you find them.

I found that Suzanne was a big help. My biggest problem had always been organization. I always waited until the last minute to write a paper or to study. She sat me down and taught me how to use my tablet calendar app to plan my days.

✧✧✧

My first day of varsity football was, let's say, interesting. I got my head handed to me. I was no longer the strongest or fastest, but I held my own. Word had gotten out about what I'd done in my first game, so the defense decided they needed to prove a point and put me in my place. Towards the end of practice, Coach Lambert called the offense and defense together to scrimmage goal-line plays. This drill could be brutal. Both sides wanted to prove who the best was.

"Y'all gather around here. Today we're going to make this interesting. We're going to put the ball on the 3 yard line, and if the offense scores then the defense will have to sprint to the 50 yard line and back. If the defense holds the offense, they have to run the same. If the offense fumbles and the defense recovers, it's one lap around the field."

Kevin Goode was our All-State middle linebacker and defensive captain. He was six-four and weighed 210 pounds. He was particularly well suited for the position. He was fast, strong and had a nose for the ball.

"You wimps are running laps today!" Kevin yelled.

The whole defense was whooping it up. Our quarterback was 'Magic' Mike Wade. He got his nickname for being a wizard at running the option.

"Okay, guys, huddle up. The last time we ran this drill, we ran six laps. I don't care what happens today, but *we are not fumbling*. Is that clear?"

We all nodded in agreement.

"Okay, Dawson, they're going to try to kill you. I'm not going to sugarcoat it. Kevin loves to crush the new guy, and you're it. Either we can keep the ball out of your hands, or we can see if you're man enough for varsity. What's it going to be?"

I didn't hesitate; challenge my manhood and I would respond.

"Give me the ball!"

"All right, you heard him. Veer right on two."

When we got to the line of scrimmage, I could see Kevin was prepared to blitz. Oh My God, he was huge. My adrenaline began to pump and I prepared to be creamed.

"Down. Set. Hut HUT!"

I exploded off the ball and hit the line of scrimmage and no Kevin. He had guessed wrong and blitzed to the left side. I walked into the end zone. Kevin went ballistic.

"God damn freshman just scored on us! Ladies, I am *not* happy. This isn't happening again!"

Magic got in Kevin's face.

"Shut your mouth and start running."

When they got back, we huddled up again.

"We got lucky on that one. Are you ready to run it again?" he asked me.

"Yeah, I think he's starting to piss me off."

The whole huddle cracked up.

"You think? Veer right on two," Magic chuckled.

Kevin wouldn't take any chances this time. He had the strong safety prepared to blitz the left side and him on the right. We would meet in the hole this time.

"Down. Set. Hut HUT!"

I exploded into the line and tried to keep as low as possible. Kevin did his best imitation of a freight train and did the same. We hit head to head; I felt every vertebra in my neck and back slam together; and white-hot pain exploded through me. The impact caused my helmet to come flying out of the pile. The only thing that kept me from fumbling was that I landed on the ball.

Kevin staggered back and fell on his butt.

"Son of a Bitch, Dawson! You smacked the crap out of me! I'm glad you're on our team. Boys, help him up."

I was surprised when the defense fought over who would help me stand up. I thought it would be best if I just laid there for a while. I felt guys pull me up and I staggered to my feet. To my surprise, the defense had me surrounded and they were all slapping me on my back. I got my balance back and Kevin was in my face.

"Kevin, man, I never want to play against you again," I said with as much sincerity as I could muster.

"I hear you, brother! You hit harder than anyone I've ever come up against."

Coach Lambert decided that was as good as it would get today and sent us to the locker room. Magic and Luke waited for me. I was still a little worried I might be hurt. I was unsteady, so they each took a side and guided me to the locker room.

"I've never seen Kevin even talk to an offensive player before. He considers them his enemy," Magic said with a big grin.

"My brother said you were tough. I would have fumbled like a little girl if I'd been hit that hard." Luke said, and Magic nodded in agreement.

"Can I tell you guys a secret? I would have fumbled if I hadn't fallen on the ball."

They cracked up. They got me to the trainer who checked me out and pronounced that I would live. He suggested I go sit in the hydrotherapy whirlpool tub to soak. I decided I'd had enough of school for one day and sent a text to Beth to see if I could use their hot tub, and she agreed. I then sent a text to Tracy to see if she wanted to join me. She had just finished practice and met me out in front of the school where Beth was waiting.

I felt like an old man as I walked up to them.

"Rough day?" Beth asked.

"I think they tried to kill me. Kevin Goode actually tried to take my head off. I'm not sure they found my helmet, it flew so far."

Both their eyes got big. They'd seen Kevin hit a running back.

I heard the squeal of tires as a classic Corvette came to a stop, and out jumped Bill Rogers. Tracy stiffened.

"Take Tracy inside and then go get help," I told Beth.

Beth didn't hesitate as she grabbed Tracy's hand and dragged her inside the school. Bill went to follow, but I stepped in front of him. I tried to be casual.

"Hey, Bill, long time no see."

"David, get the hell out of my way."

"Sorry man, but she's my girlfriend."

Okay, we had never really put a label on it, and we hadn't even gone on a date yet, but it felt right.

"What did you say?" Bill asked as he got a nasty look on his face. This was going south fast.

"I said Tracy Dole is my girlfriend."

I was amazed that my voice didn't squeak. The look he gave me left no doubt he didn't agree with that statement. He started to get the crazy look in his eye that scared everyone. I suddenly realized Bill was no longer bigger than I was. He was probably five-nine and weighed about 150 pounds. If my neck and back weren't messed up, I would've had a chance.

"The hell she is. I'm not done with that bitch. No one walks out on Bill Rogers."

My dad had always told me that if you ever got into a fight, throw the first punch and don't worry about fighting fair. I knew if this lasted more than a couple of punches, I was done. I could barely move. I could feel my neck and back stiffening as we stood there.

I'm not a fighter. The last fight I was in was in Little League when some jerk had tried to run Tami over when she covered second base. Bill was a completely different animal. His stock-in-trade was intimidation built upon a reputation for being a nasty fighter. Labor Day was still fresh in my mind. I needed to do something dramatic.

Bill squared himself and pulled his arm back to punch my lights out. I wouldn't beat him to the punch and I wasn't sure if it would have enough power to do any good, so I kicked him in the balls. I actually lifted him off the ground about four inches. I heard a girl scream, and in a flash, Tracy was there and looked as if she was going to kick his head off. As she pulled her foot back to punt his skull into next week, I grabbed her around the waist. Her momentum swung us around in a circle as she screamed profanities at Bill. Fortunately, or unfortunately, depending on how you look at it, Bill had passed out, so he never got Tracy's full message.

About that time, Kevin and three of his defensive players pulled up and jumped out of his car. He took one look at Tracy and smiled.

"Honey, David put him down, and we'll take it from here."

Beth pulled up in her car and I guided Tracy to the back seat. She was crying now and relieved. I looked back at Kevin and nodded.

"Thanks, man. I appreciate this."

"No worries, Dawson. We have your back anytime."

By the time we got to Beth's, Tracy was doing much better. She looked at me funny, but I was focused on getting into the hot tub because my back had really started to tighten up. I didn't have my suit so I just threw on a pair of shorts. Mrs. A offered to make us dinner, so I sent a text to Dad to let him know where I was and that I'd be home later.

I crawled into the hot tub and let the warm water relax every tense muscle. It was heaven. I felt my neck and back loosen. I did a few twists and my back popped back into place about six times. The headache that had been building started to go away. I leaned my head back and I must have dozed off.

Mrs. A and Beth came out with a plate of sandwich makings, a bowl of potato salad, and iced tea. I jerked awake when I felt cold water drip on my forehead. Beth held an ice cube over my face.

"Young Lady! If I weren't hurting right now, I would be tickling you. So be advised, when I get better I owe you one," I mock-warned her.

Beth stuck her tongue out at me and sashayed her cute little butt over to the table. I was starved, so I crawled out of the hot tub and headed for the food. Beth gasped and stared at me. Mrs. A chuckled.

"David, grab a towel."

I couldn't figure out what they were talking about until I saw where Beth was staring. My wet shorts had left nothing to the imagination. Thanks to Beth's little show, Mr. Happy had come out to play. My heart skipped a beat and I quickly grabbed a towel. I just smirked at Beth.

"Well, I guess I don't have any secrets from you anymore."

"David!" Beth screeched and turned beet red.

"Beth, you shouldn't tease the poor boy, he's injured," Mrs. A tormented her embarrassed daughter.

Beth turned on her Mom, not believing she had blamed her for my arousal. I snuck up behind Beth, circled her waist, and pulled her into my arms. She could feel my arousal on her butt, and I whispered loud enough for Mrs. A to hear.

"Baby, don't start something you're not willing to finish."

She spun around in my embrace. Her eyes were huge and I planted a kiss on her. About that time, Tracy came out and froze when she saw Beth in my arms and the lip-lock I had on her. I winked at her to let her know we're just having some fun. I broke the kiss and gave Beth an evil grin.

"You're bad. We are so not even now," Beth warned me.

Mrs. A gave us an amused look and I could see the wheels turning. I appreciated I had ratcheted up the sexy meter higher than I ever had before with Beth. We had flirted and badgered each other before, but I had never kissed her like that.

I walked up to Tracy, put my arm around her waist, and gave her a kiss on the cheek.

"You look nice."

Beth had loaned her a swimsuit and t-shirt. We grabbed plates and made sandwiches.

"Mrs. A, this looks great. Thanks for doing this, and thanks for letting me use the hot tub. I feel like a new man."

"How are you doing today, David? You were a little out of sorts yesterday."

The 'no secrets' thing really did apply to all the Andersons and me, so I wasn't surprised she would ask me directly about Tami leaving. Tracy gave me a strange look.

"Sorry I didn't tell you. Tami made me promise. She wanted to be the one to tell you," Beth said.

"No, you were in a bad spot. I know you'd have told me if she stopped keeping it a secret," I told her to take her off the hook.

Tracy looked even more confused. She didn't know Tami was going to Wesleyan in a few weeks.

"Tami Glade told me yesterday she's been given a scholarship to attend Wesleyan Academy. She wants to be a doctor someday, and this is a fantastic opportunity for her," I explained.

"You have to understand Tami and David have been best friends since I've known them. Heck, they're both so stupid I don't think they realize they love each other. For her to not tell him was kind of a big deal," Beth said.

I just waved it off.

"Water under the bridge."

I'm sure no one believed that, but they were polite enough not to call me a liar. I really needed to change the conversation. If I had to pretend this wasn't bothering me for another second I think I'd start crying. I finished my sandwich and decided to change the locale.

"Let's hit the hot tub again. My neck and back are still killing me."

Mrs. Anderson, Beth and Tracy all decided to join me in the hot tub. Mr. Anderson was traveling this week. He worked for UPS doing on-site quality assurance reviews. When I got in, Tracy and Beth were seated on either side and Mrs. A was seated across from me. I have to say, Mrs. A still had a killer body. She had Beth when she was nineteen and she was now only thirty-seven. She was in her prime as a woman. Her looks gave me a glimpse into how nice Beth would look at that age.

However, I have to say the body I was interested in was Tracy's. Beth had given her a white string bikini. I would have to thank Beth later. I started to become aroused when she lost the t-shirt. Tracy was five-nine with long dancer's legs and athletic. Tracy was one of those rare girls who had both a great bottom and large breasts. Normally girls seem to have either one or the other.

Mrs. A turned on the tub jets and I just moaned in pleasure. After several minutes of total bliss, I felt the water shift as Mrs. A and Beth crawled out of the tub. Beth smiled and winked at me as she and her mom headed into the house. After a few more minutes, the tub jets stopped via the timer. I started to get hot, so I crawled out of the tub. Tracy checked me out. I knew my shorts were putting me on display. For some reason I wasn't nervous that Tracy was getting an eyeful. I knew from the locker room I had nothing to be ashamed of. I guess I passed the test because her eyes finally met mine and she smiled.

"I need to cool off. I'm going to take a dip in the pool," she said.

She got out, slid her hand into mine, and led me to the pool. The Anderson's pool was nice. It had an area to swim laps. It also had an area that sloped down like at a beach. You walked into a few inches of water and then it gradually went to five feet deep. When we first got in the water felt like it was freezing, but after a minute, it started to feel good.

I leaned against the wall when I felt Tracy invade my personal space. Her large breasts brushed my chest before the rest of her slid up against me. I wrapped her in my arms and just moaned. She had a very intense look in her eyes.

"I want to thank you for what you did today. Bill scares me. I also want to thank you for stopping me. I'm afraid I would have done something I would've regretted."

"It was all I could do to hold you back. I'm just glad you and Beth listened to me and got out of harm's way. I don't know what I'd have done if either of you had gotten hurt."

"David, I know we've known each other since kindergarten," Tracy said, as she got serious. "However, I didn't really notice you until Saturday when you showed up with the Ice Princess. I've been asking around about you."

"Oh really, heard anything good?"

"You'd be surprised. I actually talked to Tami Glade about you for nearly two hours."

I wasn't surprised Tami would put in a good word for me. I'd do the same for her if the roles were reversed.

"She's one of your biggest cheerleaders. What has surprised me is everyone comments on what a good guy you are. I know you went through a rough patch last spring, but by all accounts, you've come out of that just fine. I guess the point I'm trying to make is you've shocked me."

"Is that good?" I asked.

"Absolutely. I have a habit of going out with bad boys. Bill was the most recent and probably the worst one. I think I'm ready for a nice guy, but I need to take things slow."

Mr. Happy would not be pleased with that. I think I'll wait to tell him; he doesn't listen to me anyways. I could think of three things I'd like to be doing with Tracy right now that didn't involve talking. Emotionally, though, I wasn't ready for a full-blown relationship either. I could see falling hard for her. She was a stone-cold fox with a wicked sense of humor.

Every guy has his ideal girl. Mine was Peggy Pratt. The only thing Tracy lacked was red hair, green eyes and alabaster skin with freckles, but Tracy surpassed Peggy by having a curvier body. The other thing that pushed Tracy past Peggy was we're only a year apart in age. The last thing I ever wanted to do was to hurt Tracy. I had seen time and again how expectations, when set too high, ended up killing a relationship. Eventually someone couldn't meet the expectations and the other person was hurt.

"Aren't we getting a little ahead of ourselves here? I mean, we've spent less than three or four hours actually talking to each other. I'd bet you've talked more to Tami than you have me."

She seemed relieved.

"I agree 100%. I want to spend time with you and get to know you. I want to take things slowly. I've been way too wild, and I'm afraid I'm starting to get the wrong kind of reputation. But I have to say, David Dawson, I'm falling for you. I know it's fast, and that scares me. I've never had anyone affect me like you do.

"I think the main thing is your quiet confidence. I see you talking to beautiful women and you just take it in stride. A perfect example was you flirting with Beth. She's one of the prettiest girls at Lincoln High. I don't know a single underclassman who could flirt with her and hold their own. If we do end up going out, you'll have to deal with what comes with me. I'm hit on a lot, but I think it'll be alright because you'll also be hit on. As long as we understand that at the end of the day we come back to each other, I'll be okay."

Did she just give me the green light to date other people? Had she put a subtle claim on me? I think the answer to the first question was, let's see where things go. The answer to the second was 'yes.'

"Trace, I like you. I like you for reasons that matter to me. You have a great sense of humor, you're smart, you keep me on my toes, and you're cute. You check every box I have and then some, but I don't want to mislead you. I'm not in love with you. I am in lust, yes, but not in love, yet," I said.

"If you were in love with me I'd be running for the hills. Look, I don't want to put a label on us yet, but I want you to be aware that everyone one at school will be looking at us as a couple. Will that be a problem?" she asked.

"What do you mean?"

"Well, I'm aware you're involved with some other people."

Now we would address the elephant in the room. I had to give her credit for not being afraid to talk about what concerned her.

"Okay, I'm going to tell you everything and let you decide if you want to jump aboard this crazy train. I think this'll either scare you off or not, we'll see," I said as I tried to gauge her reaction. "Yes, I've been involved with other people recently. This is all new to me. I know you think I come across as confident, but honestly, I'm trying to find my way. The other girls have been just fun, no strings attached, me trying to find what works for me," I explained.

"At the start of school, I recruited the help of my big brother and his girlfriend to help transform me from nerd into something more. Sometimes I don't even realize what a transformation it's been. When you showed interest in me, it scared the heck out of me. You're so far out of my league I have to get down on my knees and thank God that you even talk to me," I finished in a hurry.

"I don't know where you get that. You're a good-looking guy. Thank you for being honest with me. I see now that if I'm going to go out with you, I'm going to have to get my own act together. It's obvious I've come off as someone you think is above you. That is so wrong. I have the same insecurities and flaws everyone else has; I just have more practice at covering them up. If we're being honest, you're out of my league. I was a little surprised you gave me the time of day after the way I used to treat you," Tracy said.

This conversation was too intense. I needed to lighten thing up.

"Nope, all you have to do is wiggle your butt and smile at me and I'm yours. I'm a guy, after all," I said as I winked at her.

"I think I can do that," and she rubbed herself against my chest to prove the point.

What were we talking about? Oh, yeah!

"Look, let's not build up a lot of expectations. I'm sure I would disappoint you. Can we keep it casual and see where it goes?" I asked.

"Deal. Now let's go thank our hostesses and see if one of them will give us a ride home."

✧✧✧

When I got back to my new bachelor pad over the garage, I noticed Dad had installed an intercom. I should let everyone know I was home, so I pushed the button.

"Just wanted to let you know I'm home and going to bed."

I was ready for bed when I heard the door downstairs open and someone come up the stairs. It could only be my mom, because everyone else would knock. I sleep naked, so I pulled the covers up to hide my lower half. Mom looked at me with concern. Oh boy, I could do without this.

"What's going on with you and Tami?"

That was the question, wasn't it? I was tired and afraid I would lose my temper. Mom has a way of pushing my buttons, so I decided to delay this conversation.

"Tami is leaving to go to school at Wesleyan Academy. She'll be leaving the first of October."

"Are you guys talking again?"

"I think so. We had a long talk yesterday, but I'm afraid it'll never be the same. Mom, I think I really messed up and I don't know how to fix it."

"Don't worry, that girl loves you. There's no way you can mess up. She just needs to have a little space to get used to the idea of you not being around. I'm sure she's hurting as much as you are, and the change will be hard on both of you."

"I know, Mom. Not everything can be about me. I need to think about what's best for her. I just don't want to lose my best friend."

Mom gave a tight smile.

"When did you grow up?"

"I haven't. I'm just a fifteen-year-old kid trying to get through each day as it's thrown at me."

"I sometimes forget that."

"Mom, before you leave, could you put muscle cream on my back and neck? I took a pretty good hit today in football, and it's killing me."

She agreed, and we chatted about other things as she helped me. I thanked her, and she left shortly thereafter. I was sound asleep before she made it back to the house.

✧✧✧

Chapter 10 – You Take My Breath Away

Tuesday September 10

The next morning I knew I had a problem. The muscles up and down my spine seized up and I couldn't move. I broke out in a cold sweat and moaned when I heard Mom on the intercom.

"Breakfast is ready."

I prayed it would only take a little time before someone came to find me. I'd had a cramp before, but this was worse. I'd never felt so helpless in all my life. I heard someone knock on the door downstairs.

"Come in," I cried.

Thank God, someone came to check on me. It was Greg. At this point, I didn't care who it was. The pain was so intense I didn't know if I would pass out or throw up. Greg slowly came up the stairs.

"Mom's worried you're going to be late for school."

"I need help," I whimpered.

I could feel myself going into shock. Greg rushed to my side.

"What's wrong?"

"Can't move, football, please help," I begged.

Greg took charge. He recognized I was in real trouble. He yelled down the stairs.

"Tami, dial 911 and get an ambulance."

"What?! Is David all right?"

What a dumb question. No, I was not all right!

"No, he's not. Now call 911 and go tell Mom."

I saw the edges of my vision go dark and bright flashes. I lost my battle to stay conscious. The next thing I knew I was lying in a hospital bed in traction, pumped full of muscle relaxants. Wow, I felt good. I needed to get a supply of these meds. I looked around the room to get my bearings, and I saw Tami was the lone person in the room with me. She was reading her math book, studying.

My eyes narrowed and I got a scowl on my face.

"I'm mad at you."

I shocked her. She looked around for reinforcements, but no one was around.

"Yes, I know you are."

The side effect of the drugs was I had no inhibitions. This must be how my mom felt all the time.

"Why are you leaving me?"

Oops, didn't mean to put it that way.

"I'm not leaving you. I'm just going off to school. We're always going to be friends."

I felt my chest tighten up. It made me sick to think of Tami not being here. If it hadn't been for the drugs, I would have curled up into a ball and died. I needed to lance this boil or I was headed for a nervous breakdown.

"Look, just tell me we're going to be all right. I don't really care where you go. But you're not acting like my friend."

That did it. She was in tears. I just lay on the bed, and it felt like I was a bystander to a terrible car wreck. In my drug-hazed mind, I knew I'd messed up even more. Mom and Dad heard the commotion in my room and came in. Greg wasn't too far behind. They saw me fuming, Tami crying, and Mom was true to form.

"David, what did you say to her? You will ask for forgiveness this instant!"

I felt like a caged animal. I was trapped in the bed with no way to get out of there, so I lashed out.

"All of you *get out of this room!*" They looked at me as if I had two heads. "I said... *get out!*"

Mom was not to be deterred.

"You little shit. You'll apologize to everyone. I've had enough of your attitude."

Luckily, a nurse came bustling in.

"All out! You, out! We cannot have you agitating the patients. Until further notice this room is off-limits to all guests," my nurse ordered.

"What do you mean? I am his mother! He's a minor under my care!"

The nurse got into Mom's face.

"I said *out!*"

To Dad's credit, he pulled Mom to the door. Tami and Greg had already beaten a hasty retreat. Once everyone was out, the nurse came over, looked at the monitors, and after a quick check looked me in the eyes.

"Okay, I need you to take deep breaths and try to calm down. I'll make sure they stay out," the nurse promised.

I slowly started to relax. I gave the nurse a weak smile.

"Thanks, I was feeling a little trapped."

She just nodded. I wanted to know about my condition.

"So, how bad am I?" I asked.

"You're okay. You just had severe muscle spasms. Your x-rays don't show any real damage. It looks like you were in a car wreck."

"Football," I supplied.

"That makes sense. The doctor wanted to see you once you woke up. I'll page him."

She made some notes on my chart and left. A few minutes later, a young man, who must be my doctor, showed up with my mom and dad in tow. As soon as Mom came in, she glared at me.

"I won't cause any trouble. I'm just worried about you," she said, sounding reasonable, so I knew I was either dying or the pod people had taken my mom.

The doctor looked at her, then at me and just shrugged.

"David, it looks like you took a direct hit to the head that compressed your spinal cord. There doesn't seem to be any damage. What you experienced was severe muscle spasms. I'm going to release you in a few hours and give you a supply of muscle relaxants. I want you to talk to your team trainers, work on stretching, and get massage therapy for the next few days. Then on Friday, I want to see you again. If everything looks good, I'll clear you to play football again."

Mom couldn't keep quiet.

"No, you will not be playing football!"

Dad caught my look of defiance and grabbed my mom's arm to stop further outbursts. The doctor took in the standoff and snorted. I think he'd heard the same thing before. I was trusting Dad would fix this for me, so I didn't express my opinion of Mom's plan. The doctor continued and helped tilt the balance in my favor.

"Like I was saying, using the football team's resources will help you get well *free of charge*. If you need to use the hospital facilities for rehab, I can get the nurses to put together a fee schedule."

There was one thing Mom was, and that was tight when it came to money. I just kept quiet; I was sure it would blow over by tomorrow.

Two hours later, I was unstrapped, put into a wheelchair and given a supply of meds. Did I mention I really liked these meds? They put me in a great mood and I felt very mellow. The only bad side effect was I had a motormouth with absolutely no filter. My poor dad tried to keep a straight face as Mom got some of her own medicine on the trip home. About halfway home I was told I was to be sent to my bachelor pad and I was never going to get out. It was a good thing my dad had a calming effect on my mom or I think she might have kicked my butt.

✧✧✧

Wednesday September 11

The next morning I let Greg and Tami drive me to school. I really had no choice: Mom wouldn't allow me to ride my bike.

Before school started, I went to see the training staff. There were three of them. Mr. Hasting was the head trainer and I gave him the doctor's recommendations. He called in our newly minted trainer, Ms. Grimes who looked like a volleyball player. She was five-eleven and had short brown hair. She took me into the training room.

"Give me your meds."

I didn't expect that. I reached into my duffle bag and gave them to her. I gave her a questioning look as she took them and locked them in a cabinet.

"These are the type of pills people like to steal. We're required to lock them up when they're on school grounds. If you need any, let me know and I'll get them out for you."

"Can I have some to take home?"

"I'll give you some at the end of the day. Now we're going to get you ready to play Saturday. Let me call the office and let them know where you are."

She went over and used the phone to check me out of my classes. While she did that, she had me go change into my shorts and t-shirt. When I came back, she handed me a pill and had me take it.

"You're going to need this."

That didn't sound good.

"Ms. Grimes, these pills have a side effect," I warned her.

She smirked. I think she knew what it was.

"Let's just say I get a little chatty and say things I would never normally say. So please don't be offended if I say something inappropriate," I said.

We started out on stretching exercises. After about forty minutes I was glad I'd taken my pill. My back and neck started to feel better. Ms. Grimes told me to take my shirt off and get on the training table. I grinned at her.

"You're such a dirty girl. You just want to get your hands on me."

"I see someone's medication is kicking in. Get your butt up on the table so I can make you pay for your smart-ass comments."

I crawled up and she was putting some kind of smelly oil on her hands. I wrinkled my nose.

"You're not planning on using that on me?"

She just grinned and started rubbing my neck. The oil started to generate heat. It felt soooo good.

"I take it back. You can rub that all over me."

Ms. Grimes was very good at giving a massage. She would find all the tight places that hurt and work them until it felt like a twisted rubber band suddenly released and straightened out. Once she was done with my back, she started to work on my feet. By the time she was done, I was sound asleep. I woke up in time for lunch, and as I staggered into the training office, I went up to Ms. Grimes and gave her a big hug of thanks. I'm not sure she expected that, but I played it off as if I was still feeling the effects of the pills.

✧✧✧

Friday September 13

The rest of the week was uneventful. I stretched and rehabbed through Thursday. On Friday, the doctor cleared me to play. We had a rare Saturday afternoon game, so on Friday we did a quick walk-through, and then were told to keep out of trouble.

I intended to do just that, but tonight I was to escort Tracy to her birthday party. Tracy met me at the door of her house, and I stood open-mouthed. She had on a sundress and it was obvious she didn't have a bra on. Dear lord, her breasts should not be allowed anywhere near a 15-year-old boy. They were spectacular, and when she moved they would give a slight jiggle that had Mr. Happy suggesting all kinds of naughty things. I started to think he had some good ideas. No wonder he did my thinking every now and then.

She looked at my reaction and gave me a tight smile. I figured I'd better recover before I became the lecherous walking hormone I was acting like.

"Tracy, you take my breath away."

I gave her a peck on the cheek and walked in the house, leaving her at the door to wonder what had just happened. Her dad had seen the whole thing and tried not to laugh at his daughter's shocked reaction.

I stepped forward and introduced myself.

"Evening, I'm David Dawson."

Now it was his turn to be shocked. I doubt any of Tracy's friends had ever walked up to her dad and introduced themselves. He took my hand.

"Tom Dole. Are you the Bemoc my daughter's been talking about?"

I gave him a mock look of surprise.

"Sir, I'm surprised your daughter would tell you her pet name for me."

"Touché, I really don't want to think about that." I hoped that the Big Man on Campus thing was laid to rest. "I hear you got promoted to varsity after you set the freshman rushing record last week."

"Yeah, it's pretty cool, but I got my head handed to me in the first practice."

"Really? I saw the hits you were putting on Washington last week. I wouldn't think the step up would be a problem for you."

"Have you ever met Kevin Goode? We met head-to-head in a goal-line drill. I think he outweighs me by a ton," I explained.

Mr. Dole got a pinched look on his face as he remembered high school football.

"I remember those drills. Did you fumble?"

“No, I fell on the ball.” I said, which made Mr. Dole crack up.

I heard Tracy behind me.

“Oh, David! Come here!”

It sounded like I wasn’t supposed to spend all my time talking to her dad. Someone needed a little attention. Her dad recognized the same thing.

“Sounds like you’ve been summoned. I’m in charge of the grill; how do you like your steak?”

“Medium rare,” I answered.

“Okay, I’ll pick out a nice one and save it for you. Now go make my daughter happy.”

“That is my sole goal tonight,” I said with a grin.

For my first talk with a parent of a girl I was interested in, that went well. I walked up to Tracy.

“What’s up?” I asked.

Tracy stood by a good-looking guy I didn’t recognize. He was a little taller than I was and had on preppy clothes. His sweater said Doers Academy. It was an exclusive boarding school in the next town over. Before Tracy could introduce us, I heard a familiar female voice.

“You never called me.”

She walked up to me and gave me a steamy kiss. I went bright red and I heard both Tracy and the boy next to her gasp. It was Robbie King from the sandwich shop. Once the kiss ended, I just stood there with a dumb expression on my face. Robbie decided to have a little fun with me.

“I mean seriously, you leave a girl all hot and bothered and then don’t call. What kind of guy does that?”

I shook my head, gathering my thoughts.

“I guess I deserved that, but I just figured you were too old for me.”

I was slugged by both Robbie and Tracy who said, ‘David!’ in unison.

"Hey, I can't help it that she's old," I stage-whispered to Tracy.

Preppy-boy was cracking up.

"Yeah, my sister's old."

"Darryl!"

He got the same treatment from the girls.

"Hey, Darryl, I'm David. I hope you're not offended I hit on your sister?"

That got me a look from him as he tried to put two and two together and hoped it wasn't four. No brother really wants to think about his sister in a sexual way, but this was too good of an opportunity to pass up.

"Actually, you'd be doing the family a favor. We can't seem to marry her off."

"So you hit on Robbie? When did this happen?" Tracy asked, obviously wanting some dirt.

"I went into the sandwich shop she works at. I asked for her phone number and she gave me a bogus number."

"The VD clinic?" Darryl asked with a twinkle in his eye.

"Yep, she felt I needed it."

"Well, after seeing the girl you were with I figured you might want it," Robbie said, to get a little revenge.

"You hit on my sister while you were with another girl?" Darryl asked, as he gave me a look of awe.

I'd get Robbie back. It might not be right now, but I could be very patient. I decided to own it.

"Yeah, the girl I was with wanted a threesome, so we asked Robbie," I said. Robbie's eyes got big, so I finished, "... and that was when she gave me her real number."

"You slut," Tracy said. "I guess things *are* different in college."

"Big boy, anytime you need a third for a threesome, you give me a call," Robbie said as an evil glint came to her eyes.

The look on Darryl's face got everyone to laugh. I knew when I was beat.

"You win, you win," I said as I waved my hands in surrender.

I was surprised to find that Tracy's birthday party wasn't a full-blown bash. She told me later the confrontation with Bill Rogers made her decide to invite just a few friends. It turned out the only other guy was Darryl. Besides Tracy, there was Robbie and three of Tracy's cheerleader friends: Mona Wingman, Sammie Goudy and Kim Sun. I was at least acquainted with everyone but Darryl, but I was starting to warm up to him.

After everyone got there, Tracy moved the party out to the pool. She had teased me about wearing my X-rated shorts at Beth's, but I decided I'd wear my board trunks. Darryl surprised me when he came out in a speedo with the Doer Academy crest emblazoned across his butt; not a good look. It wasn't that he was fat, but he was a solid guy. In my opinion, if you plan to wear a speedo, you need the body for it. You didn't want a muffin top for that look.

Tracy put on a nice one-piece that highlighted her best assets. Robbie wore a bikini. She had an athletic body, but her thighs were a little heavy. It looked like the college-freshman spread had visited her. Mona had the best bottom in school—well, after Cindy Lewis. Mona was only five feet tall, but dang, she had on a little bikini that left half her bottom exposed. Sammie wore a very cute one-piece. She was an attractive girl, but she had no curves. Kim had picked a very sheer bikini. She was a sexy Asian. When we got into the water, I could have sworn she was nude, because the suit matched her skin tones.

We all jumped in the pool, and Darryl and I found ourselves in the deep end while the girls looked our way and giggled. I really didn't want to know what they were talking about, so I decided I'd take the opportunity to see how Darryl knew Tracy. I guess the big question I had was did they have anything going on? I observed him check her out in a way that told me they were very familiar with each other.

"Are you going to have a problem if I hit on your sister?"

I think I surprised him, but I wanted to see if he took the bait. He didn't seem comfortable, but guys learn early not to cross the women in their lives when it came to their relationships. I knew his answer before he even said it. My goal was to make him think we weren't interested in the same girl.

"I guess that would be okay."

"Hey man, if you would rather I didn't, just let me know," I offered.

He thought about it for a while.

"Honestly, I would rather you didn't. She's in a new relationship with a guy I like. They're good together."

"Fair enough. Which girl are you interested in?"

He didn't hesitate.

"Tracy."

"Are you guys are going out?"

"No, but our families have been close for years, and this is the first time we've both been free. It's time we got together. Plus it's her birthday, and I plan on giving her some Darryl loving."

Well, so much for liking the guy. Seriously, 'Darryl loving'? I really did like Tracy, but we had no claim on each other. I didn't think she'd asked Darryl to come in order to hook up with him, but she had to know he had a crush on her. Girls were much better at noticing those things than guys are.

Before I got a chance to watch Darryl put the moves on in the pool, Mrs. Dole called us to dinner. They had a large outdoor table set up. Tracy sat down next to her dad and I think she expected me to sit on her other side, but Darryl slid into that seat. She had a funny look on her face, glanced at me and I just shrugged. I wasn't suffering because Mona and Robbie grabbed me and put me between them.

Mr. Dole looked at me and gave me a wink.

"Hey, David, help me get the steaks."

I got up to help him.

"So, Darryl is cockblocking you?" Mr. Dole asked when we got to the grill.

I burst out laughing and everyone turned to see Tom and me cracking up.

"Daddy, you be nice to David," Tracy said.

"We're fine, honey." He then lowered his voice so only I could hear. "You want to trade seats?"

"Thanks, Tom, but I think I have a great seat to watch this show. Darryl has a serious crush, and only Tracy can decide what to do about it."

He looked surprised.

"You're not worried?"

"Not really. I don't think he's as smooth as he thinks he is. Tracy's been hit on by the best of them. She'll eat him up."

"You know, I think you're right. Okay, you're going to play waiter."

He started loading up plates of fish, chicken or steak with him telling me who got what. Tom was great, for a parental unit. Over dinner, I decided I liked Mrs. Dole even better. Man, could she cook. Mrs. Dole had a garden and most everything came from that. We had corn on the cob, green beans with new potatoes, sliced tomatoes with fresh mozzarella, and a zucchini casserole. For dessert, we had layered butter pecan cake with fresh sliced strawberries between the layers and a buttercream frosting. Everyone sang happy 16th birthday to Tracy.

I will give Darryl credit for trying. All during dinner, he worked to get Tracy to talk to him. At one point it looked like he tried to touch her knee, but she snatched his wrist and put his hand back on the table. To her credit, she didn't embarrass him. He gave it one more shot after we sang 'Happy Birthday' when he leaned in to give her a kiss. She deftly turned and all he got was her cheek.

After dinner, I helped Mr. and Mrs. Dole clear all the plates. We then brought out her presents. While gathering them up, Mrs. Dole took me aside.

"Thanks for allowing Tracy to handle Darryl's advances. Tom and I talked about what you told him. Darryl and Robbie's parents are dear friends of ours. It has always been a pipe dream that Darryl and Tracy eventually would get together to join our families closer. But it's obvious Tracy doesn't have the same feelings for Darryl."

"I had an idea there was more to their relationship, so I wanted to give Tracy a chance to figure out what she wants. I'll have a quiet word with him and see if it's okay if Tracy and I show each other some affection. If he's not comfortable, can I give you a wink and you let Tracy know so she doesn't think I'm acting weird?"

"You're a very considerate young man. You have no idea how happy Tom and I are. Just knowing you two are getting to know each other is a relief. Some of her recent boyfriends had us worried."

"I know what you mean."

There was an outdoor fireplace by the pool. Tracy had started a fire and gathered everyone around so she could open her presents. Everyone seemed to have a good time except for Darryl. He drifted to the back of the crowd. I saw Robbie look over at him with concern, and she started to get up. I caught her eye and indicated I would take care of it. I edged up to Darryl.

"Is everything okay?"

"Everything's fine," he said, as he gave me a dirty look.

"Yeah, right. You don't look like everything's fine."

He shook his head and looked down.

"Tracy and I aren't going to get together."

"Sorry to hear that. Are you mad at her?"

That surprised him. I think he was just thinking about himself.

"No, I think I'm feeling more like a fool."

"Did she give you any indication before today that she might be interested in being more than good friends?"

He took a while to answer.

"You know, no, not really. Sure, when we were much younger we played some of the games like you-show-me-yours-and-I'll-show-you-mine, but that was just curiosity between friends. Over the summer, she was going out with some real jerk and both our families were concerned. I think it was just assumed I'd step in at some point."

"Sounds like a lot of pressure."

"It is. Now that we're talking about it, I think I'm somewhat relieved, but I'm disappointed. Every girl I date I compare to her, and frankly they come up short."

"Yes, she is lovely, and fun to be around."

He gave me a funny look.

"Can I ask you something?" he asked.

"Sure."

"Are you and she…?"

I thought for a minute and smiled.

"Yes. Are you okay with that?"

"Actually, I am."

I looked over at Mrs. Dole and smiled. Robbie had been watching and I could see her relax. Tracy caught my eye and I winked at her. She mouthed, 'Thank you.'

Darryl caught it all and he smiled at me.

"I want to thank you also. I see you were concerned about not only Tracy but also everyone else."

"I learned a valuable lesson the hard way recently. When you have people that care about you, if something happens to you it affects them also. You have people here who care about you."

"Things turned out bad?"

"Yeah, my best friend didn't speak to me for months. All our friends have had to choose sides like in a bad divorce. I found out they liked her better."

"Do you think you'll get it worked out?"

"Yes. We've made a good start."

"Well, give it time. I'm sure you'll figure it out."

"Darryl, seriously, will it be okay if you see me with Tracy later tonight?"

"I'm never comfortable thinking about Tracy with another guy, but with you I'm fine. To be honest, all I ever wanted is for her to be happy. David, be it today or two years from now, I'll have to see it and work through it. I would just as soon get it over with."

"Okay, but promise me you'll have some fun tonight. Did you see Mona in that swimsuit?"

Darryl's eyes lit up.

"Unbelievable!"

Mona turned around and gave Darryl an appraising look.

"Shit! I think she heard us," he said.

Everyone broke up. I think they all heard the whole conversation. I just threw my hands up in surrender when Mona gave me a dirty look. Then she broke into a big smile, so I figured I was safe. Girls really do like hearing they have a nice body. They just don't want to admit it to the jerk brave enough to state it publicly.

Tracy made quite a haul on presents. Her dad was tackled when he gave her a set of Mustang keys and told her they'd go down on Saturday to either pick it out or order what she wanted. Shortly thereafter, the party broke up. Tracy and I didn't rub our relationship in Darryl's face. I think he appreciated it. Tracy told me not to leave.

We went out by the fire and found Tom and Mary lounging in a large recliner made for two. Tracy and I claimed a love seat. I put my arm around her, and she pulled her legs up and folded her body into my embrace as she put her head on my shoulder. It was so natural and comfortable; it felt like we'd been doing this for years. She smiled at her parents.

"Thank you, this was the best birthday ever."

Mary was still concerned about how Darryl felt.

"Was he okay when he left? I saw you talking to him as he and Robbie were leaving."

"He is, actually. I guess David had a positive impact on him." She giggled and looked at me. "He said if you didn't treat me right he'd kick your butt. Robbie said if I dump you to have you give her a call."

I perked up.

"I'll keep her number on speed dial, just in case."

"Tracy tells me you offered yourself up as her birthday present," Tom said, and smirked when he saw my look of panic.

Poor Tracy, it was obvious that she was Daddy's little girl and that she told him everything.

"Daddy!"

I tickled her and she squealed.

"I think someone's sharing too much information with the parental units. I heard you told your dad your pet name for me!"

She got big eyes and stuck out her tongue. She was embarrassed for being caught, but she wasn't sorry for it.

"If the name fits..."

"What nickname?" Mary asked Tom.

"Bemoc." She looked confused, so he explained. "Big Man on Campus."

"It could be worse," Mary decided.

"Don't give her any ideas," I begged.

I continued the attack as she giggled and made a half-hearted effort to fight me off. She changed tactics and pulled me into a sizzling kiss. That distracted me and I heard her dad snort. I have to say Mr. Happy was very close to taking over my body after that kiss. It was a good thing her parents were there.

I broke the kiss and looked into her eyes.

"Girl, you're going to get me into so much trouble. You keep that up and your dad'll be chasing me out of here with a shotgun."

Her dad played along.

"Mary, where are the keys to the gun safe?"

"In the jewelry box on my dresser," Mary deadpanned.

Tracy eyes got big and then she realized they were kidding. Her parents and I had a good laugh and she eventually joined in. I don't think she was used to her guy friends joking with her parents. We spent another forty-five minutes getting to know each other and then I yawned. I needed to leave because I had a game the next day. I had to admit, I had a good time with both Tracy and her parents, Tom and Mary.

Tracy walked me to the door.

"Do you want me to give you a ride home?"

That's right. She had a legal driver's license now. I would have to make some plans that took advantage of this new freedom.

"No, I feel like walking. I need to stretch my back out before I go to bed."

She stepped out onto the front porch and closed the door behind her. She gave me a lusty look, wrapped her arms around my neck, and pulled me in for kiss. Everything about Tracy was comfortable. I wasn't nervous, or out of sorts, and I enjoyed being with her. We pulled our lips from each other. Soon our innocent little kisses picked up in temperature and intensity. If I hadn't promised to protect her virtue tonight, God only knows what I would have done.

"Wow. That was a great kiss. I wish I didn't have to leave."

"Don't. Spend the night with me."

I was a little confused now, but I had made a promise.

"I thought you wanted to get to know each other and take it slow."

That was the exact right thing to say.

"I said that because I figured you'd be like all the other guys I've been out with. They would've been all over me. But you, I don't know, it's as if we're doing a slow dance, and the lust is building. I don't know what to do with you. All my friends love you. If I wasn't interested in you, they all would be dumping their boyfriends and begging you to go out with them. And my parents! What did you do to them? They're so excited you're seeing me they *would* probably allow you to spend the night! I don't know if I want you to throw me down on the stoop and make love to me, or if I should run from you. I'm scared I'm going to mess this up."

Before she could have a complete meltdown, I kissed her again. Greg had told me once that a great kiss would short-circuit a girl's brain. I know it did mine. I wrapped my hands around her until I found her hips and pulled her tightly into me. I wanted her to know I wasn't a total wimp. If she was worried she didn't turn me on, I was sure she could feel the evidence that was pressing into her.

The next thing I knew she had pushed me up against the door as she groped and kissed me heatedly. The teasing had gotten us both worked up, and suddenly the dam broke. Tracy climbed up me and wrapped her legs around my hips, moaned softly and tried to put her tongue down my throat.

I decided to enjoy the pleasure and worry about everything else later.

She pulled at my shirt up in the front, so she could have access to bare skin. Tracy rubbed her hands over my chest before returning to kiss me. I recognized we might actually have sex on her front porch. I think if my back hadn't started to hurt, we would have.

"Oh, ouch! Baby, you have to get down."

She got a look of concern.

"Did I hurt you?"

"No. I'm okay. My back is still a little tender. Tracy, if we don't stop I'm going to ravish you right here—parental units be damned! I promised I wouldn't let this get too far. But if you continue, you have to understand I'm a teenage boy who wants nothing more than to be with you in every way I can."

She seemed to realize what a near thing it had been.

"Look, it's getting late and I have a big game tomorrow. Are you free tomorrow after I get back from the game?" I asked.

She gave me a one of her best smoking-hot looks.

"Yes, I'd love to go out with you."

"You just made my whole week."

I gave her a quick kiss and left before she lured me to her bed. When I hit the end of the driveway, I almost turned around and went back. It took every ounce of my willpower to leave.

When I got home, I took a long, hot shower. The water beating on my neck and back felt wonderful. When I jumped out, I took one of my muscle relaxants. I didn't want to take too many of them, because I was afraid I liked them too much, but I wanted to be ready for the game tomorrow.

✧✧✧

Chapter 11 – Tug on Superman's Cape

Saturday September 14

The pills gave me vivid dreams. I watched Tracy and Darryl by the pool, in the love seat by the fireplace. I could see her head in his lap. It was obvious she wasn't taking a nap.

Tami sat by me and tried to reassure me as I watched my girl have sex in front of me. Cindy and Suzanne laughed at my discomfort. Tom and Mary were cheering them on as Darryl started to moan.

How could everyone just watch this happen? Somehow, I was in that ambiguous state where I knew I was in a dream, but I couldn't wake up. Why would I dream this? Was it because I wasn't sure about Tracy and my relationship?

When I looked back at Tracy and Darryl, they were gone. Tami crawled off the love seat and knelt before me. Somehow, I was suddenly naked. She grasped my member and stroked it. She looked into my eyes, and watched to see what I would do. She gave me a mysterious smile and then took me into her mouth. It felt unbelievably real.

I could feel the dream start to fade. I fought to keep it going, because I was almost there. I looked down again. For some reason Tami was gone and Tina was in her place. Why had Tina not told me we couldn't go out? I was confused, but my dream lover was doing wonderful things to Mr. Happy. Even in my dreams he seemed to be in control. Cindy and Suzanne were now sitting right behind Tina. Every few moments they'd look up and smile at me as if I'd missed something.

The dream started to leave me. I could see the morning light through my closed eyelids as I woke up to, of all people, my dream girl, Peggy. Then all the girls left my dream-addled mind.

The lips on Mr. Happy did not!

Peggy?

"Oh God!" I yelled.

My eyes snapped open as my arousal overtook me. I jerked fully awake and looked down into Tracy's sparkling eyes.

"Did you like that?"

Was she kidding? Did I like that? Dear lord, this had to be the best way to wake up ever invented. Did I like that? "Yeah, it was okay."

I had to remember that if a girl cupped my balls after she gave me the best blowjob of my life, I shouldn't joke with her. I felt her slowly tighten her grip. *Oh, crap!*

"Tracy baby, that was incredible. You're the light of my life, uhmfff, pleeeease!"

Thank God, she felt merciful.

"I think I like you begging me," she said as she smacked my thigh. "The bus leaves in twenty minutes. Get your cute butt out of bed and get moving."

I just grabbed my shorts and t-shirt. I had already packed my duffle bag at school, so I was ready to go in under five minutes. Tracy had borrowed her mom's car. It turned out this was her first trip driving unsupervised. She made me nervous because she drove like a little old lady, but I didn't want to put any pressure on her and get us killed. We got to the parking lot with ten minutes to spare.

"Are you coming to the game?"

"No, we have a JV game here today and then I'm going car shopping with Dad."

I gave her a kiss.

"Thank you for this morning. That was the best way to wake up. I wouldn't go to this game if my dad were buying me a car. Are you going to pick me up?"

"Not sure. Text me when you head back. I want to hear how many records you break today."

"For you baby, I'll try to break them all."

✧✧✧

Well, it turns out, Coach had a rule of no practice, no play. I found out right before kickoff. We were playing a new school that had been put into our division. They moved down from 6A to 5A over the summer. Which might not have been so bad, but they had made it to the semifinals of state last year.

It was one of those perfect fall afternoons to play football. It wasn't too hot, and we had a huge crowd. Everyone had marked this game on their calendar as the game of the year. The only bad thing was it was so early in the season. You wanted to play a game like this towards the end of the year when both teams had had a chance to work out any issues they might have early. We were a decided underdog, being the away team and with all the injuries we had. They'd tuned up on one of the better teams in our division and beat them handily. All the papers predicted a rout, but you still had to play the game.

It was apparent they had a great defense. They read our veer as if they played against it all the time. The poor guy that had taken my spot had ten carries for two yards and three fumbles, two of which were deep in our territory. They took advantage of those turnovers and scored twice. We were down 14–0 at the end of the first quarter.

The good news was our defense played lights-out. If we hadn't given them the ball in the red zone, this game would have been tied. I saw Kevin and Magic both in a heated discussion with Coach Lambert. He seemed to relent.

"Dawson, get in there."

The refs got the ball set to start the quarter. We were third down and eight on our own 22 yard line. When I trotted out to the huddle, Luke smacked me on the helmet.

"Are you ready to kick some butt?" he asked me.

Before I could answer, Magic settled us down.

"Okay, veer left on two. And David, the ball's coming to you."

I felt my adrenalin start to pump.

"Down. Set. Hut HUT!"

You could hear the linemen grunt and the crack of pads as they dug in to influence their blocks. Magic slapped the ball into my gut and read the linebacker who had scraped off the nose tackle to fill the hole. I jerked the ball out of Magic's hands. The linebacker went low. In football, the man that could get lower and bring some power had a huge leverage advantage. I didn't hesitate. I went over him, stepped right in the middle of his back and broke out of the hole untouched. At first, I thought I had broken free, but they were well schooled and their pursuit caught me. As I went down, I saw the down marker. I felt I would be short, so I stretched to reach it. It would be close.

The crowd cheered, because you could feel this was a big play for both teams. The refs brought the chains out and the stick kissed the football, first down for the good guys! The next play called was veer left. This time Magic pulled the ball out of my stomach. The linebacker was pissed and intended to lay me out. Little did he know what was coming for him on the other side of the line of scrimmage. He should have talked to Kevin before he tried to bury me.

Have you ever heard the term *heavy hands* in boxing? It was where a certain boxer's punches had much more impact than others' do. This was especially true with body blows. George Foreman was a classic heavy-handed boxer. His body punches would devastate his opponents. It was the same way in football. Being hit by certain players just felt like every bone in your body was rattled. I did that. When I hit you, you knew it.

I think most of it was attitude. I just got into a zone and knew I would drive right through a player. I didn't just hit them; I would explode through them. So when the linebacker went to crush me, I coiled up like a taut metal spring and exploded through him. You could tell when one of these hits happened. There was a distinctive crack of the pads that could be heard above the crowd's roar all the way up to the press box.

Unfortunately for the opposing linebacker, I had gotten lower than he had. He also came at me at an angle. When I exploded through him, I took him off his feet and launched him five yards. He made one and a half rotations as he helicoptered to an awkward landing. You could hear an audible gasp as everyone in the stadium held his or her breath.

Magic had cut upfield inside the defensive end. The free safety had to step around his flying linebacker, so I didn't see there was any chance he could make the play. I did see the cornerback get on his horse, and it looked like he had the speed to catch Magic. I let Magic cut up the middle and I tracked down the corner. He never saw me. His whole focus was to prevent the touchdown. It was like those great punt returns where you see a guy fly down the field and he gets clotheslined. It was one of the most exciting plays in football.

I hit him with my head in his chest and my pads came up under his. I took him off the ground, and I heard him grunt as his feet went towards his head. He just went stiff and I saw him shudder as he hit the ground. I looked up, and seventy yards later Magic danced in the end zone. The funny thing was that when we headed to the bench, the defensive team swarmed me. I thought Kevin would pee his pants, he was so excited.

Luckily, neither player was seriously hurt. They both were ready to go for their next defensive series. It was never my intention to injure another player. Both plays were clean, so I wasn't worried about retaliation.

Those two plays turned the game around. In the first quarter, we had managed 34 yards of offense. From that point on, we gained 536 yards. I rushed ten times for 152 yards and scored one touchdown. Luke Herndon put up All-State numbers, 263 yards on 22 carries and 5 touchdowns. After I crushed two of their players, their whole defense had their heads on a swivel as they had to account for me on every play. Instead of trying to tackle me with proper technique, they started to dive and arm-tackle me.

We went home 63–14 winners over our biggest competition for our conference. Now we were one and one with the season looking up. If this were any indication, we could be playing in the playoffs for the first time in 13 years.

Someone caught the two plays on a cell phone and posted it to YouTube. The title was *What if Superman Played Football?* So guess what my new nickname was. The popularity of the video turned out to be good for Magic, Kevin and Luke as well. College scouts started to show up for our games.

✧✧✧

On the ride home, I sent a text to Tracy, but didn't get a reply, so I asked Luke if he'd give me a ride home. When we got back to the high school, there was a huge crowd waiting for us. Coach Lambert stood up as we pulled in.

"Boys, as you can see, success has its benefits."

We looked out at all the pretty girls who waited for us to get off the bus. From the look of most of the guys, having a crowd was something new.

"I'm sure there'll be some kind of party planned for y'all. I want you to remember you're all in training. That means no drinking."

That got some moans, but overall it went over well.

"I also expect you to look after each other. If you see someone doing something stupid, then man up and stop them. You hear me?"

"Yes, sir," we all responded.

"Okay, go meet your fans and have some fun. Just make sure it's the right kind of fun," coach said, and let us off the bus.

We found a party had been planned at one of the alumni's home. He had a farm at the edge of town. Luke wanted to go, so I told him I'd get a ride with someone else. As I started to walk home, I saw Greg and Tami. I instantly felt my gut tighten up. I stopped and tried to see if there was some way of avoiding them. Of course, Tami read me, walked over, and took my hand in hers. Every fiber of my being told me I didn't want to go with them.

"David, I love you, and I can't go on with the way things are. Please come with us so we can work this out."

I noticed we'd started to draw a crowd of onlookers. I looked back at Tami and saw my pain mirrored in her eyes. Enough! I had avoided this too long. I just nodded to Tami and allowed her to guide me to Greg's car. She pulled me into the back seat with her. Greg didn't say a word. He just got in the car and looked straight ahead. Before we left the parking lot, I'd broken down and clutched Tami to me.

I have no idea how long the car ride was. I just remember we stopped and Greg got out of the car. I didn't know I hurt this much. I'd worked myself out of depression over the summer to come home to find my main support system missing. Tami hadn't talked to me, and something was off about Greg. I suspected he was cheating on Cindy, and from the way Tami acted, I thought I knew who with. I took in a couple of deep ragged breaths to clear my head. Tami reached up and wiped a tear off my cheeks. I looked at her and asked her one question.

"Why?"

"You left."

I hadn't expected that.

I found we were wrapped in an embrace and I slowly disengaged from Tami. What about my exile to my uncle's farm had anything to do with this, I wondered. It was time to face this. I'd run from hearing why my best friend was with my brother.

"Okay, I'm listening. Tell me."

"Last spring, I was really mad at you. You were such a jerk I convinced myself I never wanted to see you again."

Okay, what she'd said so far was true.

"I agree. I wasn't pleasant company. You had every right to be mad."

"Then you had the trouble with Lily. It seemed like just a few days later you were gone. After hearing how you'd saved her, I wanted to see if things were better with you. Even though I was mad at you, I still cared."

It felt good to know. I think deep down I knew she cared, but the confirmation was nice.

"I know; this last week I've realized the same thing," I said. "We just aren't us anymore. We used to be close, but now you're more of an acquaintance. It hurts too much for you to hang around the fringe of my life. Either you're in it, or we need to part ways. But it'll kill me if we do that."

"David, that's sweet. Do you know if you'd said that to me last spring, I would've stood by you?"

That took me aback. I thought she hated me back then. The sad fact was I was so wrapped up in my own angst, I didn't have room for anyone else when all that was going on. I didn't know what to say to that, so I just dropped my head and tried not to cry. Lord, I was a wuss.

"Do you realize we've said we love each other more in the last few days than we did the previous nine years?" Tami said.

"Tami, can I say something before you tell me what's going on?"

She stiffened and nodded for me to go on. I think she was prepared for me to say I really didn't give a flying leap, that I was done.

"I was in a bad place when I went away this summer. I figured out I didn't like myself very much. I know it was stupid, because what 15-year-old has a good self-image? We're full of insecurities and self-loathing. My uncle worked hard to help me realize I'm okay."

"You look more than okay."

I gave her a genuine smile.

"You have to understand most of this is due to Greg and Cindy. This exterior is for show. Yes, I grew up over the summer, and hard farm work did my body good, but what's important is the inside. I was mad at the world and depressed beyond belief. Uncle John made me see that I needed to become okay with who I am. I'm still not there yet, but he helped me see that if I didn't forgive myself, I would never be able to forgive others. I came to terms with being responsible for what happened. My actions got me sent to that farm, and thank God my dad had the foresight to send me there. I think it saved my life. What I also learned there was that I love you."

I could tell this shocked her. I could see tears start to form, so I hurried on before I lost my nerve.

"I'm sorry I didn't talk to you. Uncle John took my cell phone and didn't give it back until I left. When I came back, I intended to tell you everything, but every time I tried to talk to you, you wouldn't give me the time of day. I know you needed to have time to see if I was for real or not. I'm the one who broke our trust. I'm the one who hurt you. I'm the one who caused all this pain. If it weren't for my actions, you'd have been comfortable in telling me about you and Greg.

"That's the part that hurts the most. I made you not trust me enough to tell me what was going on in your life; and to be honest, if he makes you happy, I'm your biggest cheerleader. I love Greg and you both very much and only want what's best for the both of you," I said.

She tried to interrupt me, but I needed to finish.

"Please, let me get this out before I can't. What really hurts is I missed my chance and I have no one to blame but myself. I thought you were the only one who could make me happy. You've always been the only one for me. I've always loved you, but we were just kids. I never wanted to ruin our friendship by making it more. A little piece of me just died when I figured out you and my brother are together.

"In the past few weeks I've met women who make me realize the love I have for you is unrealistic. I need to grow up before I fall as hard as I have for you. We'd be a red-hot nova that would burn out too soon. I need to take things slow and find something that'll last, so I want you to know I love you and wish you the best. I hope someday we can be good friends again. I'll keep working to make you proud of me and prove through my actions that I'm not a lost cause. I also realize I must move on. I can't be mooning over my loss. I'm a big boy, and I'll get over it," I choked out the last part.

I ran out of steam and the car was quiet. I started to get out of car.

"Come on, and let's go tell Greg I'm sorry. I want you both to hear it."

She grabbed my arm.

"David, wait. Greg and I are *not* together."

What was going on, then? Yes, I'd heard the words before, but I had no idea why they hadn't sunk in.

"Okay, I'm listening."

"Yes, we've comforted each other, because we missed you so much. Greg confided in me. He asked me to tell you today. David, you're going to be an uncle."

Were they messing with me? Tami was pregnant? Then it dawned on her.

"Wait! I'm not pregnant and Greg and I have not had sex!" she clarified.

"Oh thank God. Who then, Cindy?"

"No, Angie Connor."

"You mean the girl he was dating last spring? I thought she moved away."

"Yes, he loves her. She's going to have his baby."

"So Cindy's just a cover for him?"

"Yes and no. Cindy went through a bad breakup last year. She's convinced that she's done dating high school boys. She wants to wait until she goes to college. She's not completely dead, so she likes to have a little fun on the side. Greg does that for her. In return she's his cover for Angie."

I was stunned. I didn't know what to think. I think I surprised Tami when I stepped out of the car and went straight for Greg. For once, she had no idea what I was thinking. She jumped out the other door.

"Greg!" she yelled to warn him.

He spun around.

"I'm so sorry," he said before I reached him.

I put him in a bear hug. It took him a moment, but I felt him give a big sigh of relief and he hugged me back.

"I can't wait to be an uncle," I whispered in his ear.

He burst out laughing.

"When Cindy finds out I told you, she'll be all over you. She thinks you're hot and wants to hook up with you. I think Suzanne has been talking to her."

I looked at Tami.

"Okay, no more of this bullshit. I thought we had this worked out last Sunday. We're friends, and we're going to start acting like it. We have to make up for lost time and you're leaving me in a few weeks."

My phone dinged. I had a text message from Tracy.

'*Got car–where r u?*'

I sent her a text back.

'*My house in 20*'

I spent the next fifteen minutes listening to them tell me about their summer.

"Guys, I'm glad we cleared the air. But I need to get home so my girlfriend can take me for a ride in her new car."

Greg's eyebrows went up.

"Who's your girlfriend?"

"Tracy Dole."

I saw Tami give me a look. I wasn't sure what it meant, but I was sure I would find out later. I thought I'd better clarify Tracy's status.

"To be honest, we're not officially going out. We're just getting to know each other. Hey, Greg, can you give me a ride home? Tracy will be there in about five minutes."

"Yeah, no problem," Greg said.

When we got into the car, I turned to Tami.

"I hear you've been talking to Tracy about me."

"She just wanted to make sure you were for real."

"Thanks for putting in a good word for me. I know you, though. Give me your take on her."

If I ever needed the scoop on something, Tami always filled me in, so I knew she had the lowdown on Tracy. I wanted to see her perspective. She always had insights I would never even think of.

"She really is a sweet girl. She's the perfect one for you right now, because she's in no hurry to jump into a serious relationship. You dating her takes a lot of pressure off her also. You're the right guy for her in a lot of ways. She needs someone high enough on the social ladder to make a good match. I know that sounds shallow, but she is the head JV cheerleader, and everyone has expectations of who she can and cannot date.

"She needs someone who's confident and isn't going to be a jealous idiot. If you haven't noticed, she's drop-dead gorgeous, and you're the best-looking guy in the freshman class," Tami said.

"Hang on. I am *not* the best-looking guy in the freshman class."

Tami looked to the front seat.

"Greg, back me up on this one."

"David, I hate to tell you this, but you are."

"Great, my brother thinks I'm hot. Okay, let's agree to disagree on that one. Tell me more about Tracy."

"I'm sure she told you we talked for several hours. I like her. I was expecting her to be stuck-up. She's surprisingly grounded, and she'll be very good for you. There was one thing that shocked me, though."

"Do tell," I said, but wasn't sure if she was nervous about telling me in front of Greg or not.

"She thinks you're out of her league. She's afraid you're not the kind of guy to have a fling with; she thinks you might be *the one*, and she knows it's too soon to meet that guy. Tracy's right. You're that rare hot guy who doesn't even know it and who's caring. You're not motivated by just what's good for you, if that makes sense?"

"Yeah, you're the one everyone's talking about," Greg added. "If they didn't think you and Tracy were going out, they'd be lining up. Cindy has a huge crush on you. She wants to take you for a spin after what she saw you do with Suzanne."

Tami's head snapped to look at me. I was a little pissed.

"Greg, you dumbass."

"Sorry man, I just broke the Dawson Code. Unfortunately, this genie's out of the bottle. David had a threesome with Cindy and Suzanne."

"Greg, you are so going to hell for that."

We pulled up to our house and everyone piled out. I pulled Tami into a hug and kissed her cheek.

"Are you okay with me going out with Tracy?"

She gave me one of her heart-stopping smiles.

"To be honest, now I'm the one that feels like I missed out, but you were right earlier. Now is not our time. When we do it, it will be forever. I want you to go out and experience everything. When you come back to me, I don't want you to have any regrets."

✦✦✦

Tracy pulled up in her new Mustang GT Premium Coupe, black with a white racing stripe running down the center of the hood, roof and trunk. It had black leather interior with white trim. It was such a cool car, and Tracy rocked the look driving it. She jumped out of the car with a huge smile on her face. Tracy ignored me and went straight to Tami.

If she was going to ignore me, that was fine, we guys wanted to look at the car. I popped the hood and we were looking at the engine when I felt arms come around me, and I got a kiss on the back of my neck.

"To be honest, I didn't even look under the hood when we bought it."

Greg gave her a look of surprise. I just laughed at him.

"Dude, she's 100% girl."

"She is that. Tracy, can I have a ride?" Greg begged.

"Are you horning in on my girlfriend?" I asked, and gave him a mock glare.

Tracy tightened her hug on me. She felt wonderful pressed into my back.

"Who said I was your girlfriend? Come to think of it, you've made that claim twice now. Is there something I need to know?"

I quickly scanned my memory and realized that I'd said it during the fight with Bill Rogers.

"Well I, uhmmm, I guess."

"Give the 'stupid boy' a break. He doesn't know what he's saying half the time," Tami said.

I turned in Tracy's embrace so that she faced me and I could tell she was giving me a hard time. I gave her a quick kiss.

"Give my brother a ride, or I'll never hear the end of it."

Tracy smiled while Greg raced around to the passenger seat. Tracy must have gotten over her fear of driving because she zipped down our street. I grabbed Tami's hand and led her to what I now called 'my bachelor pad.'

"Come on. I want to take a shower and change before they get back."

She followed me up the stairs and crawled up on my bed just like she'd been doing all her life. I took my shirt off and threw it at her. She caught it in one hand and whizzed it by my ear. The girl still had an arm. I stuck my tongue out at her and I ducked into the bathroom before she could find anything else to throw at me.

"Could you pick out something for me to wear?" I asked.

I knew she secretly wanted me to be her Ken doll. I wanted her to see the clothes Cindy had bought me. I stepped into the shower and turned the water all the way to hot. It stung at first, but I needed it to relax my back and neck. I switched the showerhead to massage and let it beat on my stiff muscles. Once I was relaxed, I turned the heat down and lathered up. I reflected on what a great day I'd had. I loved to play football and felt like I contributed to the team. I also started to make some new friends.

I figured Tami and I would fall back into our friendship easily. It just wouldn't be the same. We were different people now, and there was an undercurrent of sexual tension. That tends to happen, though, when a guy's hormones kicked in and the girl started to show signs of becoming a woman. What was a guy to do?

I brushed my teeth and combed my hair. I wrapped my towel around my waist and headed back into my bedroom. Tracy and Tami were on my bed, seated Indian style. Half my closet was spread out on the bed. It seems someone's best friend was getting help. They were doing what girls do, talking. I've learned you don't even want to know what it was about. When they finally noticed I was in the room, Tracy gave Tami a big smile.

"Oh goody, the show's about to start," Tracy stage-whispered to Tami.

I felt two sets of eyes burning into me as I grabbed my boxers and socks out of the dresser. I didn't turn around.

"You know I can hear you."

"Come on baby, give us a show like you gave me on the web cam," Tracy said, being a bad girl.

I figured I could tease her a little.

"Girls, don't start something you can't finish."

Tami was no help.

"I think he's scared. And I know he couldn't handle both of us."

I turned around.

"Oh look, I think we got a rise out of him," Tracy said.

I glanced down. They sure had.

"David, honey, I haven't seen little David since I was ten. Give us a little peek," Tami cooed.

I grabbed the clothes they had picked out and I started back towards the bathroom. I dropped the towel in the middle of the bedroom so they could get a good view. Both girls squealed in delight. I just got dressed in front of them. I didn't try to make it sexual.

"What's the plan? I'm starved," I announced.

"Mom and Dad want us to come over for supper. I invited Tami so that they could meet your best friend."

This was a great plan because I loved Mrs. Dole's cooking, but I had hoped for some alone time with Tracy. What guy in his right mind brings a girl he loves on a date with another girl? I suddenly realized I didn't have any condoms.

"Hey guys, I have to run in and talk to Greg for a minute. I'll meet you at the car."

I bounded down the stairs two at a time, ran in the back door and found Greg in the kitchen eating cookies.

"Hey big brother, can I talk to you for a minute?"

"Sure what's up?"

"I need some condoms."

"How many do you need?"

"I'm hoping I need thirty, but I think that might kill me. How about six? I'll get you a new supply on Sunday."

Greg shot milk out of his nose.

"Are you serious, you can go six times?"

"Hell, no, but a guy can dream."

When he got back gave me a handful of condoms.

"I only have five. You'll have to do something else for the sixth time."

I grabbed them and hurried out the door. When I got to the car, Tami and Tracy were ready. Tracy looked confused. Tami used her Jedi mind trick on me.

"He's being a good Boy Scout."

"What does that mean?" Tracy asked.

"Always be prepared," Tami said.

It took Tracy a moment to puzzle it out and then she went scarlet. We loaded up and went to Tracy's house. When we got there, Tracy's mom was at the front door.

"I was just about to call you. Dinner's ready," she said, and then saw Tami. "Hi, I'm Mary, you must be Tami."

"Yes, nice to finally meet you."

I gave up, my best friend talks to everyone. The evening went much the same as Tracy's birthday party. Tom and I spent half the night talking about everything from football to my summer on the farm. I was surprised at how much I enjoyed spending time with Tracy and her parents. The three ladies really seemed to hit it off.

Dinner was fantastic. Mary made pizza and a fresh garden salad. Tom offered me a low-alcohol beer, but I turned it down. I didn't want to get back into old habits.

Tami wasn't shy about it and had a couple at dinner. She covered for me by saying I was in training.

The only interesting thing that happened was towards the end of the evening. We were sitting out by the fireplace. I sat down in the love seat. Tracy crawled up onto my lap, turned to Tami and patted the seat next to me. Tami joined us and they both leaned in and gave me a kiss on the cheek.

I heard Mary giggle and whisper something to Tom. I looked at both the girls and smiled.

"What was that for?"

Tracy kissed my nose.

"That was for being such a sweet guy. Do you know how many boys would agree to going on his first two dates with the girl's parents?"

I really hadn't thought about it, but even though it was weird, it felt good. I looked in Tracy's eyes when I felt Tami take her finger and turn my chin to her. She gave me a peck on the nose also.

"And how many boys would let their best friend come on their second date?"

True, even weirder.

"How about tomorrow we take you all waterskiing? We have a cabin about thirty minutes from here, and we could make a day of it," Tom offered.

Tami looked at me excited, but Sunday was church and I'd made a commitment to Mom and myself that I'd go with her. I turned to Tom and Mary.

"Thank you for the invitation, but I have a prior commitment. I must go to church tomorrow. I'm sure Tami would love to go."

Tracy looked at me with concern.

"You'd be okay with that?"

"Of course I would. Tami's a tremendous athlete and loves all kinds of outdoor activities. She'll have a blast. In addition, if I'm going to be spending time with Tracy I want you all to get to know my best friend. She's very important to me."

Mary got a little misty-eyed.

"That's very considerate of you. Are you sure you can't get out of church?"

"Before this summer I would've jumped at the chance to go skiing over church. I'm working hard to become a man whose word means something. If I say I'll do something, I plan to do it, even if a better opportunity comes up. I made a promise to my mom that I'd go with her to church each Sunday, and just for full disclosure, going to church isn't a burden for me. I need it in my life, and I wouldn't want to disappoint my mom."

Tracy had a serious look on her face and surprised me.

"You're such a dick!"

What the heck was that about? I furrowed my eyebrows, trying to figure out what I'd done wrong.

"We're supposed to be taking it slow. Then you say things like that and all I want to do is fall in love with you," Tracy explained.

"I think I'm falling in love with him too," Mary said.

"Hey!" Tom and Tracy said at the same time.

I knew this was serious for Tracy.

"Tracy, I'm not trying to make you fall in love with me. I respect that you want to take it slow and see where this goes. To be honest, that's the best thing for me too. Please don't feel pressured in any way."

That only seemed to make it worse. I looked at Tami for help and she just smirked.

"Hey, 'stupid boy'! Just shut up and kiss her."

So I did. It took a few moments until Tracy relaxed, but she really started to enjoy it. It's not the best move when you hear the parental units chuckle while you have their daughter in a full-blown make-out session. I broke our kiss.

"Am I forgiven?"

“Yeah, you’re forgiven,” Tracy said.

It was almost midnight, so Tracy took us home. After we dropped Tami off, we made out for a while in Tracy’s new car. I found the Mustang wasn’t designed for any serious action. I looked at the clock and it was 1:30. Tracy quickly took me home and I promised to spend time with her on Monday.

✧✧✧

Chapter 12 – Holy Shit Batman!

Sunday September 15

I woke to a girl screaming.

"David, you're naked!"

I sat straight up to find Peggy Pratt in my bedroom. I looked at the clock and it read six a.m. Only a couple of hours sleep! What? Wait! What was Peggy doing in my bedroom?

"Get out of bed," she said. "I'm your running partner!"

I threw my pillow at her.

"Get out and let me get dressed, you pervert."

I'd forgotten that I was assigned a running partner and they would start today. The training staff hadn't told me who it was going to be. I quickly went to the bathroom and threw some water on my face. I got dressed and met her in my little living room. Without saying a word, she bounded down the stairs. When we got to the driveway, she broke her silence.

"Okay, let's stretch first."

Peggy ran me through some basic stretching exercises to get us loosened up. Then she just took off. I had to scramble to catch up. I set my position just behind her so I could watch her butt as we ran. She saw what I was up to and gave me a dirty look. We got to the park and she took off towards the playground. We played follow-the-leader. She ran up the teeter-totter and then down the other side. I had to pull it down, so I could run up. She then had us swing on monkey bars and bounce over benches. It was a lot of fun.

We came to an obstacle course. She stopped and looked at her watch. She then looked at me.

"Go!"

It started with the staggered tires that you had to high-knee your way through. Next, I found telephone poles that were cut at different lengths you ran over. Then there was a rope bridge followed by a rope swing. There were several other obstacles, and the final one was a twelve-foot wall. When I was done, I collapsed at her feet.

"Four minutes thirty-eight seconds. Not bad for a rookie."

I gave her the finger.

"Let's see you do better."

She took off like a shot. After I saw her speed through the first couple of obstacles, I just fell back and tried to catch my breath. In an incredibly short amount of time she was back, smiling at me.

"One minute fifty-nine seconds."

She pulled my sorry butt to my feet. We jogged back to my place.

"Thanks for running with me. I'm sorry I forgot we were starting today."

"Here's the deal: I expect you up and waiting for me out front at six, Sunday through Thursday. If you aren't there, I'll wake you up, and you won't like it."

From her evil grin, I knew I would be ready tomorrow.

✧✧✧

After I showered, I headed down to the kitchen and found my mom in her bathrobe. She looked bleary-eyed and nursed a cup of coffee. I looked at the clock.

"We need to get going if we're going to make it to church."

"Do you mind if we skip it?" she asked.

I suddenly felt myself get pissed. I made a conscious effort not to show it.

"Yes, I mind; go get ready."

She went upstairs and was down shortly. We barely made it and had to sit in the back. Every six weeks the youth pastor did the sermon. I really enjoyed Pastor Dan's services. They always seemed to relate to me. I think it was because Pastor Dan was only twenty-two.

Today's sermon involved some of the kids from Sunday school. Mrs. Kelly was in her early twenties and taught the eight-and-under group. They were cute as they fidgeted in their Sunday clothes. They sang a couple of songs, danced around, and got everyone to clap for them.

"Mrs. Kelly, what have you been teaching this fine group of boys and girls?" Pastor Dan asked.

"We're learning about the resurrection."

This seemed to please Pastor Dan.

"That's great. Today's sermon is on the resurrection." He turned to the kids and asked, "Who can tell me more about the resurrection?"

A cute blond-headed boy raised his hand. Pastor Dan pointed to him.

"Before you answer, please introduce yourself," Pastor Dan said.

"I'm Wayne Hole."

"How old are you, Wayne?"

"Eight."

"Are your parents here, Wayne?"

"Yes, my mom and dad are right there."

They stood so everyone could see them. This kid handled the audience like a pro.

"Can you tell everyone what the resurrection is?" Pastor Dan asked.

"Sure, if you have one for more than four hours you need to go see the doctor."

Pastor Dan dropped the microphone with a loud thud and bent over to laugh. I laughed so hard I had tears running down my face. Wayne looked a little concerned, and Pastor Dan could see his distress. He picked him up and gave him a big hug. They were talking and the little boy smiled from ear to ear. Dan then let him down and he ran over to his parents.

It took several minutes to get the crowd back under control.

"Well, folks, someone famous once said never work with children or animals. But I have to say if I didn't work with kids, I wouldn't get near the joy I feel right now."

✧✧✧

On the way home, I wanted to stop at the pharmacy to buy condoms. I was always a little nervous about what Mom would say on any given subject. So I was rightfully nervous with my intended detour.

"Hey, Mom, we need to make a stop on the way home."

She was in a good mood from the sermon.

"Sure, where to?"

Here goes nothing!

"The pharmacy."

"Okay."

What, no third degree? We pulled up to Glasson Pharmacy and I went to run in.

"Hang on. I need to get some things too."

Okay, don't panic. Maybe she would go one way and I could go the other. When we got to the front of the store, all hope was lost.

"Do you need help picking them out?" Mom asked.

My mother does not suffer fools well. So the question was, did I play dumb? Or tell her what's up? She gave me the 'stupid boy' look.

"Who does your laundry?"

What did that have to do with anything?

"You do."

"Where does Greg keep his condoms?"

Heck if I know? Okay, yes, I am a 'stupid boy.' She knew he was out of condoms.

"Okay, but I'm not sure I need help with this."

Please don't go with me to do this.

"Come on. This'll be fun."

She headed to the back of the store by the pharmacy counter. After she got about three steps ahead of me, I gave up and followed. Who knew there were so many choices? Mom and I started to look at the different boxes.

"May I help you?" a female voice said from behind me.

I turn around to see Kim Sun standing there with a smirk on her face. She had on a smock and a name badge. Oh, could this get any worse? Yep, count on my mom.

"Hey, Kim, David's buying condoms and we need help figuring out what he needs."

"No problem, let's start with size. David, do you know what size you need?"

Both of them turned to me with straight faces. What was she talking about? These things came in different sizes? I could feel my face going crimson.

"I, eh, sorry, what do you mean by size?"

Kim looked at my mom and shook her head. My mom seemed to agree.

"A condom is meant to fit snugly on the erect penis, and should cover it completely. I need some idea of length and girth so we can get you fitted correctly."

They both look at me expectantly.

"Well, I, uhmmm, not really sure."

Kim looked at me then at my mom.

"Okay, no problem."

Thank God! She pulled out a cloth tape measure from her pocket.

"Mrs. Dawson, do you want me to measure him, or would you like to use the restroom to measure David?"

I must have gone pale because both Kim and Mom broke out laughing.

"You should see your face," Mom said.

I think the only thing that kept me from running out of the store was shock. Kim pulled out a twenty-four pack and handed it to me. I grabbed another one.

"Sorry, David, looks like you don't plan on coming back anytime soon."

"You got that right!"

When we got home, I pulled out a twenty-four pack and turned to Mom.

"Here, this is Greg's box."

Mom got a big grin.

"I think you just made my day." As she walked in the back door, I heard her yell, "Greg, I have something for you!"

✧✧✧

When I got home, I helped Dad build some shelves. He then put both Greg and me on yard duty. Greg got the riding mower and I ran the weed eater. We were done in about thirty minutes. Dad had a small list of repair projects that needed to be done. Greg and I split the list. As we worked, we talked about insignificant things. We just got into the business of being brothers.

After we were done, we went in and watched pro football. The early game was the Bears vs. the Lions. It was a surprisingly good game. The Lions were a better football team than in the past. They'd also cut down on the cheap shots they had to rely on last year.

I didn't realize Greg had gone to my game. He was still fired up about my play.

"Have you seen the YouTube video?"

I'd chatted with Tracy and Tami on my tablet while we watched the game. They seemed to be having a lot of fun waterskiing. I handed it to Greg. He pulled up the video and we both watched it. The title rolled across: *What if Superman Played Football?*

Then the music started to build and a voice-over came on.

'Kal-El was born on the planet Krypton.'

There was a scene from DC Comics that showed the baby superman.

'*Jor-El sent his only son to Earth before the destruction of Krypton.*'

There was now a shot of the planet as it exploded, and then a shot of the baby as it was found in a field.

'*Now he has grown into a teen named David Dawson.*'

It showed me standing by the sidelines.

'*Let us see what happens when mere mortals play football against Superman.*'

I hadn't seen the two plays. Greg bounced in his seat when I stepped over the linebacker and got the first down. Then I flinched when I hit the same linebacker on the next play, and then again when I crushed the corner. It then showed the plays in slow motion three times. As soon as the video ended, I sent a text to both Tracy and Tami with the link.

By dinnertime, I was already getting #Superman messages. My phone had chirped so much, I sent Tami and Tracy a message and told them I had to turn off my phone.

✧✧✧

I was sound asleep when I felt someone get into bed with me. We had a security light on the garage, so I could make out that it was Tracy. I didn't say a word. I just pulled her to me. She knew from the day before that I slept naked. She pulled the covers down, and took me into her mouth. She was very talented and kept me on edge for fifteen minutes. I started to moan and whine my frustration. I ran my fingers through her blond locks, and relished the sensation her hot wet mouth had on my erection. I was in heaven. I don't think anything could top yesterday, but Tracy had a few more tricks up her sleeve.

She could sense when I got close. I moaned a warning.

"Ugghhh, look out!" I warned.

She did a trick that had me thinking, 'Oh my!' I tried to hold off and my muscles started to get sore from the effort. She knew what I was doing.

"David, my jaw's getting sore," she complained.

I nodded down to her and she went back to work. I just let go. I remembered the first rule Cindy had taught me: you couldn't have yours until you made sure the girl was satisfied. I pulled Tracy up to me and gave her a passionate kiss.

I went to work on Tracy. I used everything Cindy and Suzanne had taught me. Once I had her playbook down, I quickly returned the favor.

"Oh David! Oh, Oh, Oh, David! David! I'm there! Oh David!"

I wiggled down her body. Her eyes got big.

"Are you planning, you know?"

"Hell, yes, I am."

She shrieked as I dove between her legs and started to pleasure her. I adored the taste of her arousal, but it wasn't the taste or her exquisite beauty that aroused me. It was her reaction as she whimpered and moaned my name while she writhed on the bed. She was having the time of her life. Giving her this much pleasure was the biggest turn-on I had ever experienced. There was nothing more arousing than when I watched as Tracy had her release. She begged me to do more.

"Ohmygod, ohmygod, ohmygod," she started babbling, while she breathed rapidly.

This was going to be a big one. I found her G-spot. I think she tried to tear my ears off. Then she got vocal.

"David! Oh, David!" Tracy begged.

She made a strangled sound and then collapsed. As she started to calm down, I got up, went to the bathroom and washed my face. I came back in and grabbed two bottles of water out of my dorm-style fridge. She grabbed the bottle and greedily sucked down half of it before she said anything.

"Holy shit, Batman, where did you learn that?"

I just smiled at her.

"You know I'm not going to talk about other people like that."

"No honestly, tell me, I want to thank them personally. Was it Suzanne?"

I just shook my head.

"Are you ready for round three?" I asked.

Her eyebrows went up.

"I'm in so much trouble, aren't I?"

"Yes, you are."

I had a condom pack out and I opened it. She stopped me.

"Let me."

She rolled it on then lay back as she spread her legs wide, a clear invitation. Her pubic hair was neatly trimmed and she was obviously aroused. I crawled between her legs, and she reached for me and grabbed me at the base. When she had me where she wanted me, she pulled me into her. I got the head in.

"Yes! Do me, David!" Tracy begged.

I pushed steadily until I hit bottom. Dang, she was tight. I used the technique Suzanne had taught me: I ground into her as I did little circles with my pelvis. Once I felt she was ready, I slowly pulled out and then several shallow strokes and then a couple of long deep strokes. On the second deep stroke, she lost it. She wrapped her legs around my waist and dug her heels into my backside. Her hands formed claws and she raked my back. I lost all reason and just acted on instinct.

Her grip released and I grasped the back of her thighs and bent her in two. Her knees touched her gorgeous breasts. I concentrated on getting her off. I began to take long strokes. Tracy reached up, grabbed my head and locked her eyes on mine. She started to moan.

Oh dear God, I moaned with her. I then made some kind of sound like a bull elephant in full charge. I lost my cadence, and, I don't really know. I hadn't expected it, but she had put me over the edge. My joy sent Tracy over the edge as well. Her muscles clamped down on my shaft like a vise. She threw her head back and screamed. I was sure people dialed 911 at that very moment. I collapsed and rolled off her body.

Tracy recovered before I did, and snuggled up to me and kissed my ear.

"Thank you."

It took me a moment to be able to respond.

"What for?" I asked.

"That was by far the best sex I've ever had. If I'd known you were this good, I never would have suggested we wait. Good God, where did you learn to do all that?"

I just chuckled.

"Don't laugh, you're awesome."

"Oh, it was all you."

"What do you mean?"

"Have you looked at yourself in the mirror lately? You're a stone-cold fox. Your hot little body inspired me to want to please you. I could never be this good without you, and it's not only your looks. I feel your desire for me in your soul. Knowing you want me makes me work that much harder to please you. And you want to know the best part?"

She was out of her funk now.

"What?"

"Next time will be even better."

"Oh God, I am so screwed!"

"That's the idea."

✧✧✧

Monday September 16

We cuddled and talked for hours. Finally, we dozed off at about two. She woke me up at three and we went at it again. This time was gentle and slow. We both had a nice orgasm and fell back to sleep. At five I woke her up and we went two more times. When I looked at the clock, it was almost six. We got up and jumped in the shower together. I ran down to meet Peggy to run, and Tracy gave her a sly smile as she jumped into her new car and went home before her parents woke up.

Peggy gave me a look.

"Should I even ask?"

"No, but let's see if I can catch you."

I lunged for her and she squeaked and took off. She teased me all the way. Peggy got her revenge because I was dry-heaving when we got home. She just chuckled as I collapsed in my driveway, and her cute butt went down the street to get ready for school.

Five minutes after I got back to my room, my mom was in my bedroom. Oh Crud!

She went over to my trashcan and counted condom packets. She gave me a smirk.

"I don't think your dad would survive if he tried to do it that many times."

Okay, not what I expected.

"I have just one favor to ask of you. See this window?"

Oh shit! It was open.

"Next time, please make sure it's closed. I think the whole neighborhood is horny after your little show last night."

She was up and out of my bedroom before I could even respond. I stripped out of my running clothes and relaxed for just a moment and fell back to sleep.

✧✧✧

I woke as Tami shook my shoulder.

"Get up. You're going to be late for school."

I looked at the clock and jumped out of bed. I suddenly realized I was naked. I hesitated for a split second.

"Oh, hell, screw it!"

I just ran into the shower. A minute later, I got dressed. Tami, nosy bitch that she was, did the same thing my mom did and counted condom wrappers. I gave her an evil look and she just smiled. I grabbed my books, grabbed Tami's hand and dragged her down the stairs.

Greg was waiting for us.

"Who was with you last night?"

I looked confused and then said with a straight face, "Tami, of course."

They looked at each other in shock as I claimed shotgun. She climbed into the back seat and smacked me in the back of the head. I deserved it, but I was in such a good mood it didn't matter. They both knew the truth. Apparently, Mom didn't know the Dawson Code. She had spied a new Mustang in the driveway and figured it out. I would neither confirm nor deny their suspicions. I was confident Tami would have Tracy cornered before lunch to get the full story.

When we got to school, I hurried to my locker because we were running late. I got halfway down the hall when I heard a sexy voice.

"Oh, David."

I was hip-bumped by Mona, and on the other side of me was Sammie. They each grabbed an arm and escorted me to my locker. When we got there, we found Kim waiting. To say the two of them walking me to my locker caught everyone's attention was an understatement. I followed my brother's advice: "If in doubt, shut up and wait." They had me cornered at my locker.

"Okay, spill it: what did you do to Tracy?" Mona asked.

What were they talking about?

"I have no idea what you're talking about."

"Her mom is taking her to the doctor this morning because of something you did."

I sprinted out of the pack and headed to the exit. I looked back and all three girls glared at me. When I hit the exit, I pulled out my cell phone and called Tracy's number. On the second ring, her mom answered.

"Hello, David."

At least she didn't sound pissed.

"Mary, is Tracy okay?"

I think I aged about ten years as I waited for her response.

"Yes, David, she's fine. When she got home this morning she told us what you did last night."

"Okay?"

Yes, okay. Shoot me now.

"She made me take her to get on the pill this morning."

OHHHH! I knew three little bitches who were going to get some payback.

"Let me guess: Tracy put her three friends up to scaring the crap out of me?"

I heard Mary chuckle.

"No, it was actually Tom's idea."

"I think I wet myself. Let him know he got me good."

✧✧✧

Our lunch crew had expanded. We now took up a couple of tables, with both Tracy's friends and mine. Right before lunch I got a text from Tracy that said her mom let her stay home all day. She planned to catch up on her sleep. It was all I could do to keep my eyes open, and she got to take a nap. I was just a little jealous. When I arrived at the lunchroom, I saw Tami had our two crews organized and meeting each other. The three dead-to-me cheerleaders gave me a knowing looks and I just flipped them off. They all busted out laughing.

I noticed Cindy decided to eat by herself at the other end of the dining hall. I walked up behind her.

"Hey, kitten, anyone sitting here?" I asked in my best sexy voice.

"Get lost, dirtbag," she said without looking up.

I slid into the seat. She looked up, and when she saw it was me, she smiled.

"I'm a dirtbag, am I?" I asked.

"No, I just get hit on, and it's easier to be a bitch than to deal with it." It then dawned on her. "You're actually talking to me?"

"Yeah, I figured, when Greg told me you wanted to take me for a spin, I should come over and we could check our schedules to see what works." I pulled out my tablet and pulled up the calendar app. "How does Wednesday work for you?"

"Dork!"

"What, did Greg misinform me?" I asked as I tried to keep a straight face.

"No, but he's starting to share too much information."

I wiggled my eyebrows.

"No, I think he's sharing just the right information. You want me to describe everything I did to our Princess after you left the room? She taught me some things I think you'd like, and then later she held an advanced class."

She was getting turned on. She did the girl thing where they asked you twenty questions. This was usually a mood-killer, and I think that was why they did it.

"Don't you have a girlfriend?"

"Nope."

That one surprised her.

"Really? I thought you and Tracy Dole were boyfriend and girlfriend."

"Nope."

"If I asked Tracy Dole if you were boyfriend and girlfriend, what would she say?"

"Good question. I think you've done this before. She's made it clear we are quote, unquote, 'just getting to know one another.'"

I had to hand it to her; she was a little bulldog.

"Have you two talked about this since last night?"

Shit, I think she had me there.

"Hmmm, no, we've not talked about anything like that since then, but I have received a text message."

"What did the text say?"

"That she was staying home the rest of the day to sleep."

"Were you the cause of her not having enough sleep?"

"Maybe."

Now she had me. It was decision time. I had to say it didn't look good for the home team.

"David, I have to admit I'd gladly take you on as a casual romp. Suzanne went into great detail about how much she enjoyed it. But what I won't do is be the cause of breaking up any relationship, no matter how uncertain it is. So you have two choices: either you make it clear what you have with Tracy is just sex, or you get her permission."

I knew I was playing with fire here, but this was one of the four girls I would make a firm commitment to, and to find out she was interested was such a huge turn-on. I had gotten to know Cindy and understood what she had with Greg was just casual. She never looked at Greg like she looked at me right now, so I went for broke.

"Cindy, you're right. Tracy and I are on the verge of moving to the next level. Hell, she went this morning to be put on birth control, because of last night. Is there a chance she and I would be great together? Yes, I have a special place for her in my heart, but to be totally honest, we don't know each other all that well. We come from two different worlds.

"Are there other girls who interest me? Yes: you, Peggy, Suzanne and Tami. I've talked to Tami and she says she's not interested in going beyond friends. Peggy's more of a fantasy than a reality. I haven't talked to Suzanne. So, I'm putting it to you: I have strong feelings for you. I've told the same thing to Tracy. I want to make something clear: if I decide I'm with someone, then I'm with them, no questions asked. You're a very special girl. I realize we have an age difference, but I don't mind going out with an older woman. I also realize you're going away to school next year. I honestly don't expect we'd survive a long-distance relationship. But if you're looking for something right here, right now, for the next eight months, then I'm your guy. I'm giving you the chance to say 'yes' and not look back and say 'what if?'" I asked.

"Wow. You little shit. You're not giving me an easy out here, are you?"

I just stayed silent. I didn't know what I was more scared of, a 'yes' or a 'no.' I know beyond a shadow of a doubt that eight months with Cindy was worth everything. Nevertheless, when she left in eight months, would I survive without her? I also knew she didn't care about our age difference. She'd grown up enough that the whole age-difference thing didn't bother her. Then she gave me a look and I knew it wasn't going to be.

I smiled at her, got up, and left. I didn't need her to say the words. It would be too hard on both of us. The last thing I wanted to do was hurt her. I headed to a quiet place on the quad where I could be alone for a few minutes before I put my happy face on and faced the world. I also knew I wouldn't talk to Suzanne. I couldn't go through two of these in one day. I'd be thrilled if Tracy wanted to go to the next level in our relationship, but with Cindy, I didn't want to be the one to ask, 'what if?' At least now, I had my answer.

I got to my hidden spot and found Tami waiting on me. How did she do that? Hell, even *I* didn't know I would bare my soul to Cindy until I saw her. Tami pulled me into her arms and just held me. I'd become such a frickin' wuss. I finally broke away from Tami and took a deep breath.

"Tell me about your day with Tracy," I asked.

She knew what I needed and rambled on about how much fun they had. Tracy's parents have a great cabin right on the lake. They'd spent the day teaching Tami to ski. She went on until the lunch bell rang.

✧✧✧

After dinner, Tracy came by. She took a chance and found me in the bachelor pad. We made love. Neither one of us mentioned our status.

✧✧✧

The rest of the week was routine. Everyone just assumed that Tracy and I were a couple. The first time I saw Cindy, she looked a little down, but she put on a smile for me. Before football each day, I would spend an hour with Suzanne, being tutored. The funny part was we spent the majority of the time talking to get to know each other. After football practice I would head to Beth's for a soak in the hot tub. About half of the time, either Tracy or Tami would join me. It was nice to get reacquainted with the Andersons.

On Friday night, we played a weak team and cruised to victory. All the starters only played one half. The only bad thing was the backup quarterback tore ligaments in his thumb. It looked like his season was done. Coach Lambert told me I would try out as the backup quarterback. The JV team was doing well, and he didn't want to bring up their quarterback just to ride the pine.

The fun thing about being the backup quarterback was you got to be the scout-team quarterback and play against the first-team defense. It was sort of like sandlot football, because you played with a new offense each week.

The other thing of interest was the Marching Band's annual fundraiser would be a bachelor auction. Beth was on the fundraising committee, so she roped most of the cheerleaders, including Tracy, into finding guys. They ganged up on me and I talked several of the football players into helping.

✧✧✧

Chapter 13 – The Bet

Saturday September 21

I finally made my first Pilates class at the park's fitness center. A very fit twenty-something brunette taught the class. She was charming and happy to see me there. She and Ms. Kim were good friends. I looked around and there were some smoking-hot older women in the class. When things started, it looked like a calm and peaceful activity. Soft music played as the instructor walked me through all the machines that helped you move your body correctly. There was even a huge ball I would lie on and do movements.

It was a piece of cake. There were no heavy weights or long runs. It was just peaceful music and focused core strength and flexibility exercises. I had no idea the little brunette was Satan's spawn. After an hour and half with her, I felt like I'd completed an Iron Man. The sad part was I paid for the privilege to attend the class. After I sat in the sauna, I paid more money to get a massage. Ms. Kim was a dead woman on Monday.

✧✧✧

Saturday night I finally got to go out with Tracy without her parents. Well, let me clarify, for half of the date. Mary had planned dinner. Tracy said it was the price of her going on birth control. I was a little confused because if I were her parents, as soon as I saw the losers she used to go out with I would have wrapped her in Saran Wrap and locked her in her room.

Tracy came by and picked me up. My mom and dad wanted to meet her, so I had her pick me up at the house. When the doorbell rang, Greg sprinted to the door and greeted her. He was his usual suave self and he made her giggle before she reached the kitchen. I was *shocked!*

shocked, I tell you! when my mom acted like a normal human being.

Please note this was the same mother who loved to make me uncomfortable. She knew Tracy and I were doing the deed. Poor Greg and his first girlfriend still brought back memories that made me shudder. Mom made him bring her to dinner. During dinner, there were comments like, 'Greg doesn't like girls who wear too much makeup' and, 'Do your parents know you wear skirts that short?'

It was the most entertaining dinner I've ever been to, because I was out of the line of fire. If you're not the target, some of Mom's zingers are funny. The one we still talk about occurred when Greg thought he finally was going to escape with his date and they were headed for the door. Mom intercepted the poor girl and said, "If I never see you again, it was nice meeting you." Mom got her wish.

When Tracy saw me, she came up and did a very girl thing: she straightened my new hairstyle. Apparently one of my curls wasn't right.

"Thank you, that was driving me nuts," Mom said.

"I really like his new haircut, but he has no idea how to style it right. You'd think they would take the time to show him when they did it," Tracy complained.

"I know, and his new clothes. I'm thinking of putting tags in them that tell him what goes with what. I swear I have to send Tami up to make sure he's dressed right."

"Thank goodness she's helping. Did you see him on Thursday?" Tracy asked.

"Was that plaid with stripes day?"

Okay, so Mom didn't make my girlfriend cry. I was used to her abuse. I think Greg was disappointed. I wiggled my eyebrows at him and mouthed, 'Angie's next.' He went a little pale. After the girls had agreed my makeover had been a success, we were safely out the door and on to face her parents. They now knew I had slept with their little girl. This should be fun.

"Mary, I can't find the key to the gun case!" Tom called out when we walked in.

"That's okay honey, I moved it."

Mary came up and gave me a hug. It was obvious that Tom and Mary were pulling my chain. Tom came down the stairs and before I could shake his hand, he had me in a bear hug. I guess we'd be okay.

Tracy took my hand and we walked into the house. We went to the back patio and I found it was burger night. I understood we were in fact holding hands. The touch of her small hand in mine just felt right. I got a goofy grin when I looked down where we were joined together and she smiled. It was one of those special smiles couples have for each other. I wondered if this was what falling in love felt like.

I mentally had to put the brakes on. We'd agreed to keep it casual, and I was thinking love. I knew if we didn't take it a step at a time and work to both be on the same page, we were going to fail. I didn't want her to feel trapped or forced to have feelings before she was ready. I think at this point I loved Tracy, but I wasn't sure I was *in love* with Tracy. While I was musing about our relationship, Tom asked me to help with the grill.

I steeled myself and Tracy gave my hand a squeeze to wish me well. Tom must have gotten the short end of the stick because he got to give me the sex talk. I looked back and both Tracy and her mom were missing in action.

"I just want to come right to the point. Tracy has shared some intimate details about your relationship with each other. If it's okay, I have a couple of questions?"

"Yes, sir."

"David, when did we get to 'sir'?"

"When you asked me about my sex life."

"Okay, fair enough. Did you use a condom each time you had sex with my daughter?"

"Yes, sir."

"Good. I don't know how to say this, but I have to. It appears one of her past partners has given her an STD."

How do you respond to that? Greg had done me a solid with insisting on the use of condoms, and I knew this was extremely difficult for her father to share with me.

"Thank you for telling me. My concern is I've had both my mouth and fingers in contact with your daughter's vagina."

He flushed. I knew this wasn't easy for him, but he continued in kind of a stilted manner. I think he was just trying to get through this.

"Thank you for being honest with me," he said. "Let me give you some facts before you get too worried. Tracy has chlamydia. It's the most common STD in women under the age of twenty-five. It's a bacterial infection. It can cause many different complications for a woman, including causing them to become sterile. Chlamydia is known as a 'silent' infection because most infected people show no signs of having it. It's estimated 1 in 15 sexually active women in this age group has it."

"Odds are you don't have it. In men, the most common location of this STD is in the urethra. We can have you tested quickly. All we need is a urine sample," he said, as he pulled out a container and directed me to the bathroom.

When I got back, he shared some more information with me.

"The treatment for chlamydia is a seven-day course of antibiotics. During that time, you do not have sex with anyone. That's why from Tuesday on, Tracy hasn't had any sexual contact with you. I have a friend who's willing to test your sample tonight. By the time you get back from your date, you'll have your results. If we find you have this infection, we'll arrange for your treatments to start on Sunday."

"Tom, thank you for explaining everything," I said.

Honestly, I don't know whom I would rather have heard this from. I was glad he had all the facts, or I think I would have been going nuts right now.

"One more thing I have to ask you, and I know this is very personal." I just nodded. "In the past week have you had sexual contact with anyone other than Tracy?"

"No, sir."

"I didn't think so, but I had to ask. Let's find the girls and have some burgers."

I went into the kitchen, took Tracy into my arms and whispered into her ear.

"Thank you for having your dad tell me. I just did the test and he's going to get our results back by the time we get back tonight."

I gave her a kiss on the forehead and we went together to the patio. I could feel the relief come off Tracy in a wave. I later found out she assumed I'd dump her when I found out. She was also scared I would be sharing this information with other people. She needn't have worried on either count.

Okay, I must change the subject back to the burgers. I had decided if Tom ever dumped his wife, I'd marry her. She had stuffed the burgers with blue cheese. Now I wasn't a huge fan of blue cheese, but when put into the center of a burger and then done on the grill… Oh, my, you have to try it!

Tracy had originally suggested that we go see a movie, but I couldn't sit still while we waited on the results, so we went and played Putt-Putt Golf. I know, it was a stupid game, but I needed something that kept my mind busy and was fun. We had a blast. The sad part was she kicked my butt. I was stuck on the windmill. I kept hitting the stupid blades.

We then hit the local Dairy Queen. She had a banana split and I had the Peanut Buster Parfait. We were lounging at one of the picnic tables when Mona showed up with her date. It turned out to be Kevin. Kevin is a big boy, and to see him with little Mona was amusing. She saw us first and came bounding up. I gave her a dirty look because I was still pissed about the trick they'd played on me.

"That wasn't very nice Monday."

Kevin showed up about that time.

"Dawson, how's it hanging, man?"

"Hey, Kevin, are you with this evil little girl?"

"Yeah, she put me under her spell and talked me into buying her ice cream."

"Hello, Gorgeous," Kevin said to Tracy.

"Hey, Kevin, how's it hanging?"

Kevin snorted when he realized how crude that sounded. He looked at Tracy and me.

"Sorry guys, I need to work on my manners. I've been hanging out with too many jocks," he explained, and then he turned to me. "Dawson, I'm so going to kick your butt on Monday."

"Did you see who we're playing this week?" I asked.

"Eastside."

"And what offense do they run?"

"West Coast. Oh shit, you're going to be passing the ball all over the field."

"Yeah, I bet you I throw four touchdowns before you even touch me."

Kevin was fired up.

"No way, Dawson, you are so going down!"

"So, is it a bet?"

"Yeah, loser has to carry the winner's bags to the Eastside game."

"Deal."

Tracy and Mona were confused. Kevin helped enlighten them.

"Dawson is now our backup quarterback and, as such, he runs the scout team against the number one defense.

Ever since he almost killed me, coach hasn't let the number one offense scrimmage against the number one defense."

"What do you mean he almost killed you?" Mona asked.

"Didn't you tell them?" Kevin asked with a glint in his eyes.

I just shook my head. He was on a roll.

"Dawson, on his first day of practice, comes strutting in, so it's my job to take him down a notch. Coach set up a goal-line-stand scenario guaranteed to keep the little shit from running away, so on the first play I get the signal from Magic that the play's going left. I forgot his left was different from mine, so this little cocky freshman just walks into the end zone.

"It's a good thing he didn't disrespect his elders and do a little dance. He just took the ball and handed it to the center. I have to respect that; he has some class. The next play Magic gives me the same signal and I know where he's going. I give him the Kevin special 'welcome to the team' hit. Every back that has gotten that has fumbled the ball. What does this piece of work do? He hits me so hard he puts me on my ass. The defense *loves* him for it. He's the toughest dude I've ever played against, and he's only a freshman."

I smirked at Kevin.

"You want to know a secret?"

"What?"

"If I hadn't fallen on the ball, I would've fumbled."

"I knew it! That's okay, we still love you."

"See if you're saying that come the end of practice on Monday."

Kevin and Mona went to get their ice cream.

"Was that story true? Did you really put Kevin on his butt?" Tracy asked.

"Yeah, but the way I remember it, he hit me so hard my helmet flew off."

She looked at me with a new respect.

"I had no idea you were so tough."

"Have you seen my Superman video?"

"Yeah, but that wasn't real, was it?"

"I'm afraid so."

She gave me a big kiss. I noticed that after Kevin and I'd talked, most of my ice cream was gone. I looked at her and she smiled.

"I let Mona eat it while you two were yapping."

Oh well, at least she left me some of it. We went back to Tracy's to get my results. Thank God, they were negative. I was now a firm believer in wearing a condom.

✧✧✧

Sunday September 22

After my Sunday run, I went to church, and Pastor Dan met Mom and me in the lobby after the service.

"David, do you have a minute?"

"Sure, Pastor Dan, what can I do for you?"

"Would you be willing to be a youth counselor for the Christmas vacation ski trip?"

My mom stepped in.

"When is it? How long? And how much will it cost?"

"The group will be gone from December twenty-ninth till January second. The counselor's trip is free. They only pay for the odd snack or drink they get on their own."

I had a question.

"What would I need to do?"

"You'd be responsible for a cabin. There should be four to six in each cabin. Your job is to be a good example and just make sure nothing terrible happens."

I looked a little skeptical, so Pastor Dan jumped back in.

"Look, the kids asked for you. They see you as a role model and I've watched you with them. You talk to them as equals, and you don't bully them around."

"He'll do it," Mom said.

I looked at her suspiciously and thought about rejecting the offer out of hand, but I didn't have the funds to go skiing on my own. I looked at Pastor Dan and nodded my agreement. I smiled, because I was going skiing!

✧✧✧

Sunday afternoon Coach Lambert worked with the scout team to walk them through Eastside's offense. It was normally just seven or eight players, the skill positions and the center. I was instructed to get there early. I was surprised to see Magic there with Bill Callaway.

"Hey, guys, where's Coach?"

Magic took charge.

"Coach wanted you to work on your passing and, since Bill's our top receiving backup, I wanted him to get a little work too. Let's hit the field and just throw the ball around and see what kind of arm you have."

I stopped on the sideline and put on my cleats. I noticed Bill had top-end cleats. They weren't what we were issued by the school. I knew Bill was a junior. Unfortunately, he wasn't all that big for a receiver. He was five-eleven and 160 pounds. Coach Lambert liked his receivers bigger because he used them to block. The two guys who started were both over six feet and 200 pounds. The one thing Bill had over them was speed. He was the fastest guy we had on the offensive side of the ball.

Magic had us spend ten minutes just tossing the ball back and forth as he coached me on my technique. Once he felt my arm was loose, he got us started.

"Bill, I want you to go down ten yards and do a buttonhook."

Bill flew down the field, I let the ball fly, and he made a hard cutback to find the ball right in his chest. The ball bounced off him and Bill dropped it.

"Hey man, you're making me look bad," I teased him.

Bill grinned at me.

"Dang, you ripped that one. I wasn't ready for it. Let's do it again."

Bill lined up and took off. When he hit ten yards, he cut, and the ball was there. This time, though, he had his hands up, caught it away from his chest, and then tucked it. He tossed it back.

"Okay, I think you have some skills," I said, which got a big grin on Bill's face.

Magic turned out to be a good coach. Bill and I worked on a variety of pass routes and I started to be confident in my ability to make the throws. Bill made me look good, because he had tremendous hands. All I had to do was get it close. After about forty-five minutes, the rest of the players showed up. When everyone was there, Magic pulled us all together.

"Okay, Coach can't make it today. However, we have a personal stake in this game. The opposing linebacker is my cousin. He's been talking smack since they beat us last year. I will not lose this game."

We all nodded our agreement.

"They run a West Coast-style offense and they lost their first game. Then they changed quarterbacks. Some California kid took over and they're a different team with him at quarterback. They need to knock us off to tie us in the conference standings. If both of us win out, they'll get the automatic berth in the state playoffs due to head-to-head play. I need you guys to push our defense. This is the only game they'll play against this style of offense, so your job is to kick ass in practice. And I hear one of you has upped the ante."

He looked at me and I fessed up.

"I bet Kevin we would score four times before the defense even touched me."

Bill offered his lofty opinion.

"Dude, you're a dumbass."

Magic looked at me.

"Okay, big shot, how are we going to score four times before Kevin gets his hands on you?"

I grinned and gave them my plan. After I laid it all out, they all just shook their heads. Tomorrow's practice would be interesting.

✧✧✧

When I got home from practice, I sent a text to Tami to jump onto video chat. I turned on my tablet and she was waiting for me.

"Hey, I need your help."

She looked bored.

"Okay, go to your closet and I'll help you pick out your clothes for tomorrow."

I scowled at her.

"That's not what I need help with. Well, yes it is, but I need your help with something else."

I quickly told her my plan for tomorrow's practice. She got an evil grin. This was right up her alley.

"Okay, David. I have to get busy. I'll see you tomorrow."

"Hang on."

I got up and went to my closet. She just laughed and selected my clothes for the next day.

✧✧✧

Monday September 23

On Monday when I got to school, there was a buzz. Word had gotten out about my bet with Kevin. I made it until lunch before Kevin tracked me down.

"What the hell are you doing to me?"

I played dumb.

"What are you talking about?"

He seemed agitated.

"You've been telling everyone about our bet!"

"Oh, that. I wanted to make sure everyone got to see you go down today," I said, and gave him my best cocky look.

Our friends at the lunch table couldn't hold it in anymore and broke out laughing. Kevin got red and stormed out of the lunchroom.

"Dawson, you're a dead man walking!" Kevin yelled back when he reached the door.

"Do you think we went too far?" Magic asked.

"Nah, he'll get over it. I just need to get him out of his comfort zone for four scores. If he's on his game, I'm dead."

✧✧✧

When we got to practice, Coach Lambert talked to us before we hit the field.

"This week's game is a big one. We're facing the best team we'll see before the playoffs. What makes these guys dangerous is their speed. They're fast on both sides of the ball. That's normally our strength, but I have to say I think they may be faster than we are, so we're going to have to be disciplined in our roles. You all know your assignments. If you do them, we'll be fine."

Coach looked at his clipboard.

"Now the scout team has been offered the challenge of running Eastside's offense, and apparently there's been a little bet made. The offense must score four times before the defense touches the quarterback. I have to hand it to you, Dawson, you got a set on you. Best of luck today."

We jogged out to practice and I made a point of being right next to Kevin. When we hit the field, he came to a stop. I stopped with him as players ran around us. There were actual fans waiting to see our practice. Tami had come through.

Kevin looked at me and grinned from ear to ear. We both loved game day. I was a much better game player than practice player. I wanted to make this feel as real as possible. Coach wouldn't make it easy on me. He set it up so we would start on our own 20 yard line and had to drive the length of the field. He had the assistant coaches be our referees for the game.

One of the coaches placed the ball in the center of the field and blew his whistle. I had everyone huddle up.

"Okay guys, this is the big time. We're going to use their aggression against them. They're going to be coming for me full-out. I'm going to need some time for this to work. Draw right on three. Pay attention, 'cause I want to get them to jump offsides. Ready, BREAK!"

We ran everything on the two count so there was never a problem with anyone knowing the count. Kevin knew it; heck, the whole defense knew it. We lined up in a four-receiver set with me in the shotgun. I saw that the defense prepared for full-out blitz. We needed to slow that down or I would never have time to throw the ball.

"DOWN. SET. Hut, HUT, HUT!"

The defense jumped the gun as we had planned. The refs threw their flags and we gained five yards. Kevin screamed at the three guys who'd moved before the snap.

We huddled up.

"Okay, good job, they'll quit trying to jump the count now. Bill, did you see them cheat the safety up?"

"Yeah, let's hit them with a slant where he's supposed to be."

"Good. Now pay attention. We're running this one on first sound. It'll catch them flat-footed. Ready, BREAK!"

We lined up in the same formation. The safety on Bill's side started to creep up. I knew Kevin planned to have him blitz.

"DOWN."

The center snapped me the ball and I saw the safety break through the line clean. I zipped the ball to Bill and he caught it in stride. No one would catch him. The crowd erupted as Bill walked into the end zone on a 75-yard score. Bill did a little touchdown dance and Kevin went ballistic. I knew that was Kevin's pet peeve, so I'd instructed anyone who scored to do a little dance. My goal was to goad him into mistakes.

The safety slammed me to the ground, so I never got to see the results. I grinned when I saw the yellow flag lying by me. Coach Lambert slammed his clipboard on the ground and chewed out the defense.

The next series started on our 35 yard line because coach had carried over the roughing-the-passer penalty. We knew the defense didn't want to be embarrassed again. Kevin was too smart for that. Therefore, I ran three straight buttonhooks to Bill. We were now on the 50 yard line. Kevin yelled at his defense that if we walked down the field with the same play and scored, he would kick all their asses.

The next play was a thing of beauty. Bill ran the same buttonhook. I pumped the ball and Bill juked the defender and sprinted by him. I felt the defensive end closing on me, so I let loose. The ball traveled forty yards in the air and Bill pulled it in for our second score. Bill did a better dance this time and got a ten-yard unsportsmanlike-conduct penalty. I didn't care, because I saw Kevin go beet red.

It was like putting a red cape in front of a bull. He was fuming. This time he changed to a dime package to prevent the long score. They placed the ball on our 10 yard line. I changed our formation to pull both running backs into the backfield, flanking me on either side.

We planned to show the defense our running game. Eastside ran a zone-read option. It was very similar to the veer in that you made reads on how the defensive players reacted, which in turn determined where the ball goes. In theory, both offenses should gain nice yardage. I hadn't wanted to pull out the running game out so soon, because the odds of the defense touching me went up astronomically with me running the option.

The first play was a simple dive up the center. The key to this offense was to establish a steady diet of inside plays. Our scout team was seriously outmanned, so I couldn't expect this to work for any period of time. The run surprised the defense and we picked up eight yards.

On second and two, I saw Kevin grin. He knew he had this bet won. All he had to do was make me keep the ball. We ran the same play and gained the two yards we needed for the first down. The crowd started really to get into it. I heard chants of "Dawson, Dawson, Dawson!" Kevin didn't like that, but I had a big grin.

The next play we ran to the left. I had the right-side back go in motion to the left to lead the toss. We had them outnumbered and the back almost broke it. He picked up nineteen yards. We were now within striking distance. The scout team was fired up. They had never had any success against the first-team defense before. The next three plays I just dinked and dunked short passes and forced the defense to make plays. We picked up another eleven yards.

We then ran the zone read again. This time I pulled the ball from the dive in the center, and I saw the defense shift to intercept me as I moved down the line. Kevin had fire in his eyes and I thought 'Oh Shit.' I cut back and followed the fullback into the hole. The defense parted like the Red Sea. I was ten yards past the line of scrimmage before anyone even came close. The fullback blocked a corner just before he got to me. I only had one corner left who had me dead-to-rights. I put a move on the poor kid that had his feet crossed and he tripped himself. I found myself standing in the end zone. I think I did a better dance than Bill.

I handed the ball to the ref and went up to Kevin.

"Dude, get back into your defense and play us straight-up. You have size, talent and experience all on your side."

Coach Lambert called time and pulled the defense around him. I have never seen him more passionate than he was at that moment. When the defense came back out, we looked over from the huddle.

"Oh crud, I think the jig is up," Bill said.

Yep, Kevin was focused, and being the heart and soul of the defense, so were they. It happened on our second play. I dropped back and didn't see the defensive end break free, and he hit me from the blind side. Kevin and the defense had won their bet. From that point on, the defense played much better. Coaches let us play another series and then switched to first team offense against the defensive scout team. Our offense had no trouble scoring at will.

At the end of practice, Coach had us gather around.

"Dawson, get up here."

I came up front and the defense all jeered me.

"I want to thank this young man for making us better today. We needed a wake-up call and he gave it to us." The team gave me a good ribbing. "Kevin, get up here."

Kevin came up with a big smile on his face.

"Son, well done on getting the boys focused. If we had this happen Friday, we would've lost."

Kevin looked at the team.

"Actually, I have to give credit to Dawson. He talked to me after the third score and got me to realize he was using smoke and mirrors to beat us. I have to say, though, if he ever pulls this kind of crap again I'm going to kick his butt!"

I just put my hands up in mock surrender. Coach let us go and we all hit the showers. When I came out the locker room, Tracy and Tami were waiting for me. I had to appreciate Tracy. She wore, what looked like, sprayed-on jeans and a top that was too tight. She bounced into my arms and gave me a sizzling kiss. I guess half the team must have seen, because they all made rude comments for the next several weeks.

✧✧✧

After practice, the three of us went to Beth's so I could soak in the hot tub. All three of us had gotten smart and left swimsuits at the Anderson's house. Mrs. A just threw the suits in the wash with the rest of their stuff. I soon found myself relaxing with three gorgeous women.

I looked up and Beth gave me a strange look, which clued me in that something was up. She looked at the other two girls and I knew she didn't want to talk in front of them. Our habit was to spend thirty to forty-five minutes alternating between soaking and jumping in the pool to cool off. Then we would head home for dinner.

After we had all gotten dressed, I pulled Tami and Tracy aside.

"Hey guys, something's up with Beth. She needs to talk to someone, so I'm going to eat dinner here at the Andersons.'"

I gave Tami a kiss on the forehead and Tracy a real kiss. I found Beth a few minutes later sitting in the den. Beth jumped when she saw me.

"I thought you'd left."

"No, I invited myself to dinner."

I waited her out to see what was wrong. We'd played this game a few times and she knew what I was doing, so she told me.

"I've been feeling lonely. Seeing you with Tracy has made me realize what I'm missing."

Beth was a mystery. She was the head cheerleader, and every guy at school would jump at the chance to go out with her. The stereotypes didn't fit Beth. You'd think the head cheerleader should date the star quarterback. I had never known her to date a jock. She seemed more attracted to the artistic types.

"When was the last time you went out on a date?"

"I went to Prom, but that was just a setup. He was the cousin of one of my girlfriends. The last real date was New Year's Eve when I met that guy skiing."

That was over nine months ago. I remembered the guy, because he was on Christmas break. I think he was a music major from Dartmouth. What I needed to do was find her a cute band geek.

"Can I ask you something?" She nodded. "Do you have anyone in mind?"

She blushed, so I knew there was someone. This was good news. Of course, the guy in me wanted to just solve the problem and call him, but I knew from experience that wasn't how girls worked. I'd have to figure a way to get the guy to notice her.

"Okay, tell me who."

"Gary Baxter."

I gave her a look that said I didn't know who that was.

"He's a senior, cute and kind of quiet. He's also in the band."

"Does he know you're interested?"

"No, I've given him some hints, but I'm not sure he realizes I want him to ask me out."

"Want me to talk to him?"

You'd think I had shot someone.

"No!"

Then it hit me: the band fundraiser.

"How about this: you're recruiting bachelors for the band fundraiser. Why don't you get him to volunteer?"

She jumped right in with the plan.

"Then I could bid and win a date!"

She squealed, launched herself from her chair to mine and wrapped me up in her arms. It was amazing to see her smile all through dinner.

✧✧✧

Chapter 14 – The Comeback Kid

Tuesday September 24

I woke with my usual morning wood. My eyes were still closed, but I felt the presence of a warm female body in my bed. I felt a wave of pure bliss. In my sleep, my right hand found a handful of breast. This was almost better than waking up to a blowjob. Sleep started to leave my brain when I became aware I had no idea who was in my bed.

To my surprise, it was Tami. She had apparently borrowed one of my t-shirts. I was a little embarrassed to find myself pressed against my best friend's butt. I could tell by her breathing she was awake. I made no move to let her go, but I did let my hand slide onto her belly and I kissed her neck.

"Good morning."

She turned her head and we kissed. I could see she was emotional. She would leave me on Sunday. This wasn't a teenage hormone-induced hookup. This was the intimacy of two people in love, who were familiar with each other as only best friends could be. We had never had any sexual contact beyond a kiss, but this held the promise of what someday might be like.

I heard the downstairs door open and someone walked up the stairs. My bedroom door opened and Peggy walked in. It was time for my run. When she saw me naked with Tami, she blushed.

"Oh, sorry."

"Peggy, it's okay," Tami said, to ease her embarrassment. "We're just friends. I'm leaving Sunday and I needed to be close to him." She swatted my bottom. "Now, ready to run and let me talk to Peggy."

I jumped out of bed, covered the important stuff and hurried into the bathroom. Somehow, girls could make me feel helpless. I wasn't sure why I was so embarrassed. I sleep in the nude. If someone walked into my bedroom unannounced, they would figure that out. Peggy saw how I slept the first day we ran, so the little minx was trying to get a peek.

I came out of the bathroom, dressed, to find the two of them talking. Of course; Tami knew everyone.

"Peggy, you're terrible."

"Shhh, he's back."

They both looked at me like they were little angels. Peggy had warned me if I wasn't ready to run, she'd do evil things to me. I think I might want to sleep in just to find out what those things might be. Then again, maybe not.

"Okay, I don't think I really want to know what that was all about."

Tami shook her head.

"No, probably not. Come on, we need to stretch and then run. Today's a distance day," Peggy said.

I just groaned and followed her to go run.

✧✧✧

When I got to school, Tracy had waited for me. She had Luke backed up to a wall and was flirting with him. He looked a little uneasy. When he saw me, I put my finger to my lips to indicate that he shouldn't let her know I was there.

"How come you don't have a girlfriend?" she asked.

I wrapped my arms around her and kissed her ear.

"So, I don't see you for a few hours and you're looking for an upgrade?"

She twisted in my arms and gave me one of her patented mind-erasing kisses. I swear when she did that I forgot everything.

"No, silly, I'm trying to set him up!"

Luke caught on, and arched his eyebrows. I think he thought Tracy had come on to him.

"Anyone we know?" I asked.

"Of course, Kim," Tracy answered.

I smiled at Luke and I could see there was interest there.

"Good girl, I think he likes the idea."

"Yes, I do like that idea," he said, and then looked at Tracy. "Has she expressed an interest, or are you just testing the waters?"

"Oh, there's interest. She's waiting by your locker. Go ask her out."

Luke gave us a sheepish grin and went inside.

"So you're working as a matchmaker now. I think I like this."

I wanted to go watch the show, but Tracy steered me to her locker. I slipped my hand into the back pocket of her jeans. She looked back and smiled. I felt her slide her hand into the back pocket. I kissed her nose and we worked our way to her locker. Several people had noticed us walking in like that. When we got to her locker, she gave me a hip bump and I let her go.

"Hey, I almost forgot. Dad has tickets to the Florida/Kentucky game this weekend. He wants to know if you want to go."

"Wow! That sounds great!"

"Dad's boss is a Florida booster and has tickets to all the games. He's not able to go this weekend, so he's sending his top people as a kind of thank you for job well done."

"How come I get to go? Shouldn't your dad take you or your mom?"

She snorted at the ridiculous idea.

"If you haven't noticed, my dad likes you. Plus, he's been bragging you up to the point his boss has set up an appointment with Florida to look at possibly recruiting you."

"What?"

She had to be pulling my leg. She seemed perplexed by my confusion.

"David, I don't want to sound harsh, but at some point you're going to have to come to terms with you being a star. Everyone agrees you have the size and speed to make it at the next level. You're the most punishing runner my dad's seen at this level. If you continue to develop, there's no ceiling for your talent. The main thing I see you lacking is belief in yourself."

When did Tracy get this knowledgeable about football? Then I grasped what a stupid question that was. Tracy was motivated and smart. She'd watched a lot of football when cheerleading. She was also a Daddy's girl. She would spend time with him watching football.

"But…" I stammered.

"No buts. You already are showing leadership abilities. Luke is amazed at how you've brought the team together just by your example. The next step is to accept the mantle of a leader. You took a big step towards that on Monday by almost running the defense off the field with the scout team."

"Okay. You've obviously figured this out. Will you help me?"

Her whole face lit up. I instinctively knew Tracy wanted to find the right guy to get her out of this one-horse town. It wasn't that she couldn't do it herself. She was looking for a partnership where her talents would help them both become more successful. Tracy wanted to be part of the *it* couple.

"You were born for this, weren't you?" I asked.

"You know what, I think I was. We, you and I, working together can make a formidable team."

"Do you have any thoughts on where to start?"

"Yes, actually, you need to shine on scout team. Why don't you see if you can't get some upgrades at a few of the key positions? From watching yesterday's practice, if you had a decent center and another receiver, they'd never have touched you."

Okay, I didn't know any other girl who would have been able to figure that out. I was quickly realizing there was more to Tracy than I knew.

"I'll talk to Coach before practice. Maybe I can use a couple of the backup cornerbacks."

"Now you're thinking."

The bell rang for first period. I walked Tracy to her class and then hurried to math. I had some things to think about. The biggest issue I had with this was it seemed too self-serving. I understood that mindset was more Tracy's. I needed to figure a way for this to work for me. I had to convince myself that excelling on the scout team was going to benefit the team as a whole. If I could see this helping everyone get better, I think I'd be fine with it, but if it was just about me I knew it wasn't going to work.

✧✧✧

Before lunch, I sent a text to Tracy and Tami inviting them to spend some time with just the three of us. We only had a few days left before Tami left, and I wanted to spend as much of it together as we could. Both girls thought it was a great idea, and we ended up doing that for the rest of the week.

For the majority of it we tried to keep it light and happy. We scheduled out when visits and video chats would work. Then there were times when the realization of what was happening hit us, and there were some tears. Tracy helped us keep it from getting too gloomy, and we appreciated her help.

✧✧✧

Tutoring took an unexpected turn. Suzanne was helping me with World History when I noticed she was acting funny. She was distracted and squirmed in her seat. Then it hit me: she was horny.

"Emperor... What are you looking at?" she asked suddenly.

"Okay, enough studying. You need my help more than I need yours today."

"What are talking about?"

I picked her up and sat her on the edge of the desk. I dropped to my knees before her, and with one swift motion, I reached under her skirt, hooked my thumbs over the top of her panties and yanked them to the floor. She gasped as her v-shaped patch of trimmed white pubic hair was exposed. The sight brought memories of our first session flooding back. I lifted her thighs and rested her calves on my shoulders.

"Scoot forward," I ordered.

I looked up and she panted in anticipation. In a flash, it came to me: she wasn't trying to stop me.

Suzanne moaned as I got to work. She reached down and ran her fingers through my hair. She was so responsive to everything I did.

It was a magnificent thing to see. She'd thrown her head back and her hands fluttered, not knowing what to do. I wanted to just rip my pants down and have my way with her. I knew I couldn't do that to Tracy. Somehow that would be crossing a line I wasn't ready to go past. This was about helping a friend in need.

We started to come back to our senses when I realized I smelled as if I just came from a whorehouse. She looked down at the mess and laughed at me.

"It's your own fault."

"Laugh it up, Chuckles. You wouldn't be happy if the tables were turned."

I sat down on my chair in a huff. She slid off the edge of the desk and straddled my lap. She took both her palms, put them on my cheeks, pulled my face to hers, and kissed me.

"Thank you. I needed that."

She crawled off my lap and gave me another kiss.

"See you tomorrow."

✧✧✧

I ran into the outer locker room and Ms. Kim stopped me. Oh, crud!

"Hey, slow down. How was your Pilates class?" she asked, and then she smelled me. "David! You nasty boy. What have you been doing?"

I just snorted at her.

"Give me a minute. I'll be right back."

I washed my face and changed into my shorts and a t-shirt. I came back out with an awkward grin. I owed her for sending me to Pilates. I was still sore from Saturday.

"I can't believe you made me pay for that torture. And where did you find that sadistic instructor, anyways?"

"You are such a wuss. Linda said she took it easy on you."

"The hell she did. By the end I was hoping she'd just shoot me and put me out of my misery."

"Give it time. The results are worth it."

"I know, but the soft tranquil music and the slow stretching and controlled breathing kicked my butt. I should trick some of the other guys into going. There're a lot of hot chicks there."

"I see your plan. After Linda's done with them they won't even be able to look at all the women."

"You think *I'm* a wuss. Just imagine Magic. He'll be crying like a little girl."

"Better yet, Kevin. You have to let me know when you're doing this. I want to be there to watch the aftermath."

She was as evil as that instructor was.

"Okay, deal."

She smirked at me.

"Nice deflection. Who were you banging before you got here?"

I raised my eyebrows. I liked her. She talked like a guy.

"Let's just say a friend needed a little help."

"You're a little man-skank!"

I just grinned as she retreated to her office.

✧✧✧

Before practice, I shared Tracy's ideas of how to improve the scout team with Coach Lambert. He agreed this was a critical week and he would get us some players to help test the defense. I was a little surprised he took our ideas seriously. Most teachers don't seem to take a student's suggestions well.

"Y'all think you can push the defense?"

"Give me two or three more guys with speed that can catch the ball, and I can give the first team defense a serious challenge. Coach, Eastside is dangerous because we're not used to someone putting the ball up 40 times a game. If they get our defense on their heels, we could be playing catch-up all game long."

"David, I like you. Now don't go repeating that."

"Yes, sir."

"I also like what I saw yesterday. At our coaches meeting, we watched the film, and we're going to be making some changes where you get to throw the ball a couple of times a game. Bill shined also. Now I don't see him as an every-down receiver in our offense, but on pass plays he makes a hell of a deep threat."

"Coach, to be honest, Bill makes me look good. He catches everything thrown to him. In addition, if you'd change the blocking assignments and not make him pick up a linebacker, he can more than hold his own on the defensive backs. He just needs to learn how to screen them. He doesn't have to muscle people to be effective."

"Boy, you sound like my damned assistants. If I wanted this kind of advice, I'd go ask them."

"Sorry, Coach."

"Don't be sorry. If enough people are telling me something, it might be time I listened. Now get out of here before you start to irritate me."

"Yes, Coach.

✧✧✧

At practice, Coach gave us our starting center and two small cornerbacks who were almost as fast as Bill. They didn't have great hands, but they could make you look bad if you didn't play with discipline. Coach Engels finished with the freshmen and came to help the scout team practice.

"The West Coast offense is supposed to test the defense. It uses short downfield passes that are designed to turn into big gains after the catch. What we're going to help the defense learn is to keep everything in front of them and then close quickly. Bump and jam the receivers to disrupt their patterns. The more physical you are with their receivers, the less effective they are," Coach Engels explained.

"Normally, we use the running game to open up the passing game. We wait until they start cheating up and then we do a play-action pass and catch them for a big gain. With the West Coast, it's just the opposite. They try to get you cheating back to play the pass, and then run on you," he continued.

"The biggest mistake teams make is thinking they should blitz the quarterback. The offense is designed to have quick, accurate throws, not giving the defense time for an effective rush. What you end up doing is giving them an advantage in numbers and you get burned. How we can make a blitz work is to run a fake blitz. The quarterback is trained to dump the ball into the vacated area. Coming up to blitz and then stepping in front of the receiver can help turn a game around," Coach Engels said to wrap up our learning session.

We only had twenty minutes to practice Eastside's plays before we faced the first-team defense. The scout team gave the defense fits. They could no longer just key on Bill. Coach Engels helped them a lot, and by the end of our session, we were struggling. When practice was over, we all had big smiles on our faces. We had a blast running the wide-open Eastside offense.

✦✦✦

I didn't get a chance to go to Beth's and use the hot tub, so I set up a group video chat with Tracy and Tami. We chatted about our days until it was time to go to bed. Tracy dropped off first.

"Are you going to come over again tonight?"

"Do you mind? I just want to be with you as much as I can over the next few days. Even if it's only while we sleep," Tami answered.

"Not at all, I'll just put on some shorts before you come."

"'Stupid boy,' you better not. Half the fun is feeling you naked, spooned against my back. Plus, Tracy knows and is fine with it."

Yes, Tracy would be okay with it. Since we weren't in a relationship, I guess we could do whatever we wanted. It felt like I was waiting for the other shoe to drop and she'd be off with the next bad boy that crossed her path. I knew if I ever found out she'd been with another guy, I would be done. I hated she was giving me the freedom to be with other women. The Mr. Happy did too much thinking for me as it was.

However, it wasn't as if I was going out to find new partners. The only person I could see anything happening with outside of Tracy was Suzanne, and that would only be something like today. She seemed to need some relief. We both knew it was just sex, and neither of us was pushing for the 'just friends' label to change.

Any guy at my school would be thrilled to be in my position. Two of the hottest girls were spending quality time with me on what I hoped would be a regular basis, but neither relationship seemed to be going anywhere deeper than friendship and sex. I'd never been in love, but I would like there to be at least a hope that it would happen. The best I could expect was for Tracy to get over her demons so we could have a real relationship.

"You win. Buck-naked it is. Why don't you come over now, so we can fall asleep with you in my arms?"

I was almost asleep when Tami showed up. Without a word, she stripped down to just her panties and skipped the t-shirt. She crawled into bed; with me on my back, she put her head on my shoulder. She ran her hand up and down my chest. I was on the edge of sleep when I felt her grasp my member. I just moaned my approval. Tami just held me, and once I got used to it I went to sleep.

✦✦✦

Wednesday September 25

I woke to find I'd had a wet dream. There was cold spend all over my stomach. Tami was awake; she saw the horror on my face, and she gave me a wink.

"Sorry, I think I played with it a little too much. You really seemed to enjoy it."

I shook my head.

"I wish I was awake to enjoy it."

"We can't right now. Peggy's in the living room waiting for you."

"Crap, did she see me like this?"

"Yes. You need to start setting your alarm, so you don't keep showing her your wiener."

I looked at the clock. It showed 5:45.

"Hey, she isn't supposed to be here until six."

She just laughed at me as I went and took a quick shower to clean myself up. I was ready by six, and Peggy and I did freestyle running.

✧✧✧

When I got to school, the rumor mill was in full swing concerning Luke and Kim. They were 'the new couple' and everyone wanted the latest gossip. I was afraid Luke and Kim might kill Alan when he started asking them questions nonstop. I hoped Jeff would give him a few whacks to slow him down. I was glad Tracy and Tami skipped the normal lunch routine with me so we could say goodbye to Tami.

Football practice was fun, and we had a few more recruits on the scout team. Everyone was having a good time with me throwing the ball all over the field.

✧✧✧

Thursday September 26

Come Thursday, it was pretty much the first-string offense playing on the scout team. Coach let us play almost all practice because we kept pushing the defense. I finally threw back-to-back interceptions on fake blitz plays and Coach decided to end things on a high note for the defense.

I caught Coach Engels after practice.

"Hey, Coach. I just wanted to thank you for helping us with the West Coast stuff."

"It was a lot of fun. I was surprised all the first-stringers wanted to play scout team. What did you offer them?"

"Nothing, they just saw us having good time and wanted in. I was glad to see that Coach Lambert let them. If we get into a two-minute drill situation they all got some experience. Hopefully we're never down where we need it."

Coach Engels got serious.

"You should really think about switching to quarterback next year. In the spring, you might enter some seven-on-seven tournaments and go to some quarterback camps. If you continue to grow and learn the position, you'll be able to play at the next level."

"You really think so?"

"Well, nothing is ever 100%, but if you work hard, I do. You've had a lot of success early. My biggest fear is that you'll become complacent. You have to be careful of everyone telling you how good you are and believing it. There's always going to be someone bigger, faster and more skilled. But I know you can outwork anyone."

"I'll keep that in mind."

✧✧✧

I came home at ten to find Tracy in her cheerleading uniform doing her homework in my living room. I think it was every boy's fantasy to sleep with a cheerleader. The ultimate fantasy was to do one in their uniform. Tracy always seemed to take my breath away. I sometimes found it hard to believe she was only sixteen.

It still was hard to accept that she'd go out with me. Well, there was the problem: she really wasn't going out with me. In my head, I knew we'd agreed to take it slow, and it was for the best. Neither of us was ready for a committed relationship. It would be easy to fall deeply madly for her. If she asked me anything, I'd probably do it for her.

Her ex, Bill Rogers, had done something to her that had caused her to change. Whatever it was, it was holding her back from giving me her heart. I knew she cared for me and she hadn't dated anyone else, but there was always doubts that lurked in the back of my mind, that little voice that told me she wasn't really mine; that Tracy only used me to heal herself. I was afraid I was her rebound.

I wanted to talk to Tami about this. The rebound would explain so much. The thing that sucked was the rebound guy never got a real chance. I was probably stupid for seeing her now. I should have waited and let some other poor sap go through this phase of her healing. Tracy saw me; her smile momentarily lifted my sadness. I dropped my book bag. She was seated on the sofa and patted the seat next to her. I sat down and she gave me peck on the cheek.

"David, we need to talk."

Those four words are every man's nightmare. All my insecurities about our budding relationship came flooding back in that instant. This was it, she was going to dump me. She saw the pain in my face, closed the distance between us and gave me a hug.

"I'm sorry, it's nothing bad. God, the look on your face, you'd think I was leaving you."

She could see from my expression she got it right.

"I just wanted to talk to you about this weekend," she explained.

"Oh, sorry. I'm just feeling a little fragile today. Can you make me a promise? Can you never use the 'we need to talk' line on me? Every time I hear it, I cringe."

"I promise. Are you okay?"

"Now that I know you aren't dumping me, yes. What do we need to talk about concerning this weekend?"

"I want you to be clear we're not officially boyfriend and girlfriend. And before you say anything …" she said as she put her finger over my mouth to keep me from talking, "this weekend you may have the opportunity to hook up with someone. If that happens, I want you to have a good time."

I think she expected me to fight her on this. But that simple declaration crystalized in my mind that we weren't going to make it. Whenever a girl tries to pawn you off on another girl, it means that your relationship is over. She was trying to make herself feel better by finding her replacement. The sad part was most of us don't even realize it until it was too late. The funny thing was now that I knew we weren't going to last, I relaxed. I had two choices. End it now, or enjoy what was left. I picked option two. I felt my spirits lift.

"Okay, if you want me to bag some college chick, I will. Do you want me to give you details?"

I saw the smile leave her face and her eyes cloud over as she realized what she'd just done.

"I hadn't really thought about it."

"That's okay. Let me know if you do. Was there anything else you wanted to talk about?"

She bit her bottom lip and no longer would meet my eyes.

"No."

I got up and headed for my bedroom.

"Okay, I'm tired. Tomorrow's a big day, so I need to get to bed. You're welcome to join me."

I didn't wait to find out what her answer was. I undressed and crawled into bed. I'd given up and almost drifted off to sleep when I felt my bed move. I was surprised when she didn't touch me. I lay there for a while, and I heard her softly crying. I rolled over and looked at her.

"What's wrong?" I asked.

"I'm losing you, aren't I?"

Why lie?

"Yes."

"I've been such a bitch. You're the nicest, most loving, thoughtful guy I've ever met, and I'm messing this up. When you asked if I wanted details, I understood what I did to you. I came in to say I'm sorry."

"Look, tomorrow's a big day. I'm going with your dad to Kentucky. Sunday, Tami leaves. Let's get together on Monday and work this out."

"David, when you step onto that plane and until you come back, let's consider ourselves on a break. I'm serious. If you bang fifty hot college babes while you're away, I'm fine with that."

I felt better. Maybe we *could* make it.

"Your poor dad isn't going to know what to do when they start lining up. Do you think your mom will give him a get-out-of-jail-free card for the weekend?"

"David!"

I closed the gap between us and kissed her. She could kiss. She arched her neck, so I could give her little butterfly kisses from her neck to between her breasts. I felt a warmth and pleasure that this beautiful creature was in my arms and needed me. She pulled my head back up and we kissed for what seemed like days. I kissed her lips, her jaw, and her neck. I rubbed her arms, caressed her cheek.

I reached between us to see if she was ready and found she was. I quickly put on a condom and slid home as she wrapped her legs around my waist. I gripped her hips and I ground her body against me. Her moans got louder. I looked up to see my window was open. Oh well, showtime. Moonlight filtered through the curtains as it kissed Tracy's skin. I could never walk away from this. We were perfect together.

I would like to say we went several rounds, but all the pent-up emotions drained us both when we finally came. The last thing I remembered, before falling asleep, was Tracy had wrapped her arms around me with her head on my shoulder.

✧✧✧

Chapter 15 - Can We Do That Again?

Friday September 27

I woke up to find two girls in my bed. Tami had joined us sometime last night. She slowly stroked my morning wood. I arched my eyebrows and she winked at me. I let her have her fun. She quickly had me on the edge. Tracy woke up and gave Tami a dirty look.

"What are you doing to my man?"

I chose that moment to climax. Both girls shrieked at the first jet and then broke into giggles. Tracy gave her a mock scowl.

"Give me that, Rookie."

She grabbed a condom and gave me a few strokes to make sure it wasn't going down. She put on the condom and she straddled me. She gave a satisfied grunt as she bottomed out. I leaned over and gave Tami a quick kiss. I grinned when I saw that Tami was embarrassed.

"I think I like the new you. Naked sleepovers, playing with me, a little threesome. You're the best friend ever."

"Whoa there, 'stupid boy,' nobody said anything about threesomes."

Tracy scoffed.

"Hate to break it to you, but giving a guy a hand job and then watching another girl take him is a threesome. I bet if you ask real nice he'll pop that cherry of yours."

Tami's eyes got big.

"Don't even think about it, David. It's not happening today."

"I'll wait. I need to get you something for Christmas anyways."

Tami grabbed my pillow and tried to smother me. I had no idea the lack of oxygen could cause such an intense orgasm. It felt like I had a seizure, the way my whole body quaked. Luckily, Tami got concerned and pulled the pillow off my face or I might have blacked out. They both looked at me as I shuddered from the aftereffects. I finally was able to put a coherent sentence together.

"Oh my God! Can we do that again?"

✧✧✧

Our small town was a bedroom community for the city that housed the State University. A majority of the professors and their families lived here. The surrounding area was dotted with farms. I liked that everybody was friendly. There was a mix of intellectuals, who worked at the university and area tech firms, and blue-collar people. You never had to worry about locking your doors. The only bad thing was if you did anything wrong, it beat you home.

A small town like this loved high school football. Being a football player meant everyone knew you. If you don't believe me, try to walk all six blocks of our downtown with a player. It would take you over an hour to get from one end to the other. With all the idol worship, it was surprising how down-to-earth most of the players were. Were there some that thought they're God's gift? Surprisingly, very few, because the rest of the team would take care to knock those players off their pedestals.

The worst thing our teammates might do was drink some beer or get a girl pregnant. You never heard of them breaking into cars or doing drugs because most were good boys and the town loved them. Tonight the town showed them their support. By 6:30, the stands were packed for our 7:15 kickoff. The vaunted offense of Eastside had everyone worried. The weather predictions said it was supposed to drop to the mid-40s with the possibility of heavy rain. The townsfolk knew that as long as there wasn't any lightning, the game would be played.

Kevin and Mike ran us out for warm-ups. We then broke apart and ran some drills. This gave me a chance to check out Eastside. It didn't take long to figure out who their new star quarterback was. He was a blond kid who was almost six-six. He looked comfortable dinking short passes to his ultra-quick receivers. Our defense would have to have a heck of a game to keep up with this bunch.

I looked up into the stands and noticed several recruiters. They were easy to spot with their jackets blazing their school's logos. I'd bet they were here to see the California kid play. I hoped our guys could get some good exposure. Before I could spot my friends, we were herded back into the locker room.

I found Kevin in a deep discussion with several of his defensive players.

"Hey, guys, sorry to interrupt, but can I make one suggestion?"

They just looked at Kevin, and he gave me a nod.

"I was watching the game films, and that big quarterback was never touched. On the first play call a safety blitz to his blind side and put him on his butt, even if it means a penalty."

"What happened to playing disciplined?" asked Kevin.

"He just looks so cocky and smooth in warm-ups. We need to shake him up and have him wondering when's the next time he's going to get hit."

Kevin just nodded his thanks and I went over to where the offense was having their pregame meeting. Magic was getting the team fired up.

"Remember what got us here. We're going to need to score tonight to stay in this game." He focused on me. "Double D, I want you to run and hit like a man possessed. Luke, I expect you to have a huge game. You big guys hold your blocks. They're quick and pursue like crazy. If you lose your block, look for someone else to hit."

Coach Lambert and the rest of the staff came in.

"Okay, y'all gather around. I just want to say I'm honored to be part of this team. You boys have worked your butts off. I've never had a team that I'm prouder of, so win or lose, you're all winners in my book. Okay, so let's cut the crap. I want to win this game. We win this one and we control our destiny in getting a playoff spot at the end of the year. If Eastside wins, they'll have the tiebreaker of head-to-head. We'll have to run the table and hope that they lose.

"I know y'all know this. I remind you of this so you know what's on the line. This community loves you. For some of you this could be the highlight of your high school football career. We all know how everyone likes to brag about how they did," Coach said.

This got a laugh because we'd all heard people talk at family gatherings.

"This is your moment to shine. Go out there and win this game. On three, team. ONE, TWO THREE, TEAM!"

Luke and Kevin led us out. The cheerleaders had made a big paper banner, and the marching band was lined up to feed us to our side of the field. When the bandleader saw us come out of the locker room, the school song started and the fans were on their feet. Kevin and Magic ripped through the banner and you could feel the excitement in the air. I don't think my feet touched the ground as I floated to our sideline.

Our captains went out to the center of the field and met their Eastside counterparts. Everyone shook hands and the referee did the coin toss. Eastside won the toss and deferred the choice to the second half. We elected to start on offense.

While our kick-return team was getting ready to receive, Magic and Luke found me. We made a point to talk before the first offensive series of each game. Magic took the lead.

"Normally we'd run veer right and give the ball to David to start the game. His big hits set the tempo. Today I want to run the same play, but I'm going to pitch to Luke and catch them cheating."

"Are you sure? David's had a lot of success knocking heads," Luke suggested.

"I think it's a brilliant idea. Magic can sell it and I'll try to cause some havoc. You need to show them they aren't the only ones with speed," I said.

It was time to join the offense on the field. The kickoff had gone through the end zone, so we would start on our 20 yard line. When we lined up, I saw that Eastside was in their three-four defense. That meant they had three down linemen and four linebackers. It would allow their speedier linebackers to chase down our veer offense. The nose tackle was huge. He must've been six-four and weigh close to 250 pounds. In high school, that was a big kid. He was lined up in the center-guard gap on the right side. He cheated over, because they'd done their homework. They expected me to carry the ball on first down.

"Down. Set. Hut, HUT!"

My adrenaline pumped through my blood stream as I saw their plan was to make a huge pile in the center of the line so I had no room to run. The nose tackle tried to tie up both the center and the guard so the two inside linebackers could meet me in the hole. Their defensive tackle on our right side pinched down to try to cause more disruption in the middle. This was a huge gamble on the first play for the defense. If we ran the option to the outside, they were vulnerable.

Two things went right at the same time. Magic made one of his Houdini moves that hid the ball from the defense. The second was our right tackle let their tackle loose and picked up the outside linebacker. This left Magic and Luke two-on-one with their cornerback. The receiver on that side slid over to cut off the pursuit from Eastside's safety.

I met all three of their defensive players in the hole at the same time. You could hear the crack of pads over the moan of the crowd as they thought I'd been stopped. I found myself under a pile of bodies, and I could hear the Eastside players congratulate each other over a well-executed play. Then the crowd noise told me Magic and Luke were doing their thing. The crowd suddenly erupted and I knew one of them was running free. When I finally got out from under the pile, Luke was handing the ball to the official and we were now up 6–0. The extra point made it 7–0 in favor of the good guys.

On the ensuing kickoff, Eastside was able to get the ball out to their 32 yard line. They lined up in their four-wide-receiver set, and their big quarterback was in the shotgun as he looked over the field. On the snap of the ball, we jammed their receivers on their right side. You could see their quarterback wait for them to work themselves free. When he saw that wouldn't happen, he did his checkdown and shifted to the left side of the field. He noticed right away that the slot receiver had come free and was open on a crossing pattern. The quarterback just released the ball when our safety took him off his feet. The safety's pads came up under the quarterbacks off arm and buried in his ribs as he was slammed to the ground. The pass went off target and was incomplete.

At first, I thought their quarterback was done, because he just lay on the ground. The crowd went from being ecstatic to being quiet for fear he was hurt. Before the training staff could come out, he waved them off and one of the linemen helped him up.

You could see he wasn't happy. He screamed at his linemen. I think Kevin saw the same thing, and I knew if there was blood in the water, Kevin would blitz to take advantage. On the next play, Eastside lined up in another four-wideout formation. This time at the snap of the ball, our defensive tackles ran a game where they crossed, which caused confusion with the offensive line's blocking assignments. Their quarterback floated to the right to buy himself some time if we ran the same safety blitz. The cross allowed the tackle on the right side to break free, and Eastside's quarterback suddenly had him in his face.

Kevin did a delayed blitz, and when their quarterback spun back to the middle neatly to avoid the tackle, he was met head-on with Kevin. Our All-State linebacker showed why he would receive that honor. Kevin put his helmet on the ball and made a perfect tackle that crushed their quarterback. I knew how hard Kevin could hit, and the California kid was not getting up from that.

They got lucky when one of their linemen landed on the fumbled ball. After a delay, they were able to get their star off the field. The next play they ran a dive up the middle and then punted the ball. They had a great kicker. He booted the ball over our kick returner and it rolled out of bounds inside our 15 yard line.

We came out and Magic called veer right again. It worked pretty well the first time, so why not. This time the nose tackle played it straight up, and it looked like they were in their base defense.

"Down. Set. Hut, HUT!"

I powered into the hole and Magic gave me the ball. The nose tackle slapped my thigh as he tried to bring me down. I ran through his arm tackle and met one of the inside linebackers head on. He was too high, so I lowered my shoulder and ran him over. He slowed my momentum enough so that the other inside linebacker and the outside linebacker both hit me to bring me down. After everyone got off me, the linebacker under me hopped up and gave me a playful smack on my helmet. We grinned at each other when the umpire ran up and slid in between us.

"Okay, okay, okay, we're going to have a clean game tonight."

We both were having great time. We were two gladiators who'd be clashing all night, and we just gave each other respect. I never felt more alive than when bodies slammed into each other. I could tell my opponent was a kindred spirit. We'd have fun as we found out who was the best.

"Any problems?" Magic asked as we huddled up.

"No, we're just having fun."

He just called the play.

"Student body left, on two."

Student body left was a sweep. It was made famous by John McKay at USC in the mid '60s. It was named 'student body' because of where the students were seated in the stadium. The play looked like they were running into the student section.

"Down. Set. Hut, HUT!"

Magic pitched the ball to Luke and I led the sweep along with a tackle. The sweep play wasn't a great call against a fast team, and this was no exception. Their corner made a great play and dropped Luke three yards behind the line of scrimmage. We were now in a third and long. This was an obvious passing down and something we weren't very good at doing. I wasn't surprised when Coach sent in Bill at one of the receiver slots.

Magic got the play from the sidelines and when he came into the huddle, he was grinning.

"Okay Double D, let's show them your arm. Student body left special on two."

This was the same play, but I would get the ball and pass it. It was one of the new plays Coach Lambert had put into our playbook this week.

"Down. Set. Hut, HUT!"

I caught the pitch and everyone acted like it was a run. This caught Eastside off guard, because they'd dropped back into their zones. When they recognized it was a run, I heard their linebacker screaming.

"RUN, RUN, RUN!"

As a group, they hesitated and turned to pursue. Bill had disguised his speed and acted as if he was supposed to block the safety that now covered him. The safety pushed past him to support the run. We'd waited for this opening. He took off, now wide open. I stopped and planted my feet and threw as far as I could. Bill hadn't slowed down. He was confident I could get him the ball. Our fans had never seen us attempt such a long pass. There was an audible gasp as they saw the high arcing spiral fly to Bill. I had overthrown him and I could see him put on an extra burst of speed. He dove to try to make the catch, and he once again made me look good. He came down with the ball and the back judge signaled a catch on their 30 yard line. The ball had traveled 50 yards through the air. The crowd was on their feet, and I think they were the loudest I've ever heard them. As I trotted up field, my new buddy ran with me.

"What the hell, man, that wasn't on any of our scouting reports."

"I thought you guys knew how to cover the pass," I teased their linebacker.

"Keep it up, Chuckles, and I'll have to put you down."

I gave him a shove and we both laughed. By then I found Bill, ran over, and gave him a high five.

"Sorry man, I guess I got a little excited."

"No worries. Next time I'll run faster," Bill assured me.

Magic called for the huddle. Over the next three plays, we were only able to gain 8 yards. Our kicker came in and nailed the field goal. We were now up 10–0. From there the unexpected happened. The game turned into a defensive struggle. We were able to move the ball up and down the field. When we got close to scoring, their defense would stiffen and stop us. We were able to get one more field goal. They got lucky right before halftime and on one of their little dink-pass plays our defender fell and it was off to the races. We went in at halftime with a 13–7 lead.

At halftime, we made some adjustments and came out ready to win this game. Eastside received the kickoff and made it out to the 20 yard line. Their star quarterback was back in the game. He made a tremendous difference. They marched right down the field and scored to take a 14–13 lead.

We needed an answer, and Magic got us all together on the sideline before we went out.

"Guys, this is a crucial series. Let's focus and run our brand of football. Okay, no huddle, veer right on two."

We waited for the head linesman to set the ball and we sprinted out. Eastside didn't pay attention.

"Down. Set. Hut, HUT!"

Eastside sprinted to their positions when the ball was snapped. Magic slapped the ball into my midsection and I found their nose tackle standing in the hole. He was trying to figure out what to do when I hit him square in the gut and lifted him six inches off the ground. The hit made a tremendous clack as my pads delivered the impact. The crowd groaned as they saw the huge guy go flying. I stepped through the hole to see my new buddy running full tilt. I gathered myself and turned into his hit and there was another crash of pads. Eastside's linebacker caught the brunt of the hit on his shoulder and he no longer had the grip to bring me down. I powered past him into the open. One of their speedy corners caught me around the waist and I dragged him along when two more defensive backs caught us and brought me down after a 32 yard gain.

I handed the ball to the back judge and looked back to see Eastside's training staff rush out to take care of both players. I jogged up to their linebacker.

"You okay, man?"

"Yeah, it's just a stinger. When I get some feeling back into my arm, I'll be back to repay you for that one," he promised. He looked over at their nose tackle. "I think you might have killed Glen, though."

I was sure I had just knocked the air out him. Their staff didn't look too concerned, and after a minute they helped him up. Our crowd gave each player a respectful applause as they made it to the sideline. We were able to get within field goal range, but our kicker missed the kick wide right.

Right before the end of the third quarter things got ugly. Their big quarterback proved he could throw more than just short passes. They ran a pretty hitch-and-go that our corner bit on and suddenly the score was 21–13.

The kickoff was short, so we were able to return it. Our returner made a nifty move to avoid a tackle but let the ball separate from his body. An opportunistic defender punched the ball loose and we turned the ball over on our 18 yard line. Two plays later it was 28–13 as the third quarter ended.

The next kickoff went through the end zone, so we got the ball on the 20 yard line. It was as if the football gods had conspired against us. As we took the field, it started to rain. Magic came out and showed all the confidence that none of us had at that moment. I recognized a true leader and prayed that one day I would have the strength to show his resolve.

"Okay, settle down. I know we've only been down this much once this year, and we lost. That is not going to happen today." He looked each one of in the eye until he was confident that we agreed. You could feel the whole huddle relax. "Veer left on two."

"Down. Set. Hut, HUT!"

Eastside overplayed the dive, so Magic pulled the ball out of my gut and continued down the line. I saw a flash as a linebacker slipped through our line and crushed Magic. The ball came loose and the same linebacker was on the ball. They had recovered on our 15 yard line.

The crowd was in shock when after four plays we were down 35–13 with a little over 13 minutes to play in the fourth quarter.

Coach Engels grabbed Bill and me and had us warm up. The training staff was all around Magic, and it looked like he had a concussion. Kevin, Luke and the other assistant coaches had a heated discussion with Coach Lambert. I could tell he was pissed when he threw his clipboard on the ground and his headset went flying. A decision was made and Coach Lambert yelled.

"Offense, gather around! We're down three touchdowns. I have been convinced to run the scout-team offense for the rest of the game. Coach Engels is most familiar with this offense, so he'll be calling the plays. I am proud of you boys for working so hard this week. Now let's go out there and get back into this game."

The kick-return team had done a good job and gotten the ball to the 31 yard line. We huddled up and I called the play.

"Base four cross right long on two."

We lined up with four wideouts and I dropped back into the shotgun. The Eastside defense went wild trying to figure out what we were doing so they could get in the proper defense. Our crowd who was wet and cold at this point and had been headed to the exits stopped and turned to watch something they'd never seen before.

"Down. Set. Hut, HUT!"

"PASS, PASS, PASS!"

As I set up to throw, Bill was in the slot and one of the defensive backs who'd practiced with the offense was on the outside. On the snap of the ball, they both sprinted 10 yards straight down the field and then crossed. The outside linebacker that tried to cover Bill ran over their cornerback when we executed the cross. Luckily, we didn't touch either player, or it would have been an illegal pick play. Bill ran up the sidelines and I hit him in stride. Their safety had a chance, but our wide receiver gave him a brush block and Bill walked into the end zone. After the extra point we were down 35–20.

We rushed off the field to get with Coach Engels. I was happy to see Magic was waiting on us with his helmet in hand. The training staff would steal your helmet if you weren't cleared to play. Coach got all of us in front of a marker board.

"Good job. Now what they'll do is go into their dime package. This'll pull their outside linebackers and replace them with defensive backs. This is where Luke will shine. We're going to run their version of the option until they pull at least one of the defensive backs and respect our ability to run the ball," Coach Engels said, explaining his strategy.

"From now on treat this like a two-minute drill. We need every second on the clock to win this thing. If you hear 'Blue' instead of 'Down' we'll run the pass version of the play. If you hear 'Green' it'll be one of our special plays."

Coach Engels diagramed the two plays. It wouldn't be easy to have only three offensive plays, but they were set up to be free-flowing, and it was up to me to make the right reads. I had no idea what happened on the field until Coach Lambert called, 'Offense!'

We found ourselves pinned back at our 8 yard line. We lined up in Eastside's base four-wideout offense. Magic came in as the slot on my left with Bill in the slot to my right. The ball was snapped back to me, and Luke and I moved as one to the left. One of their defensive backs slashed into the backfield and tried to tackle me high. I hit him with a straight-arm that knocked him off his feet. Luke and I turned up the field. Three of their players had me in their sights, and just before I was hit I pitched the ball to Luke.

Luke almost broke it. He was pushed out of bounds just short of the 50 yard line. This gave us a chance to huddle up. The entire crowd, which had been heading for the exits, was back in their seats and cheering.

We got into the huddle.

"Okay Luke, it's time you learn what I do. We're going to run the option to the right. Luke, you find a gap between the tackles. If it isn't there, I'll step outside. Magic, you trail the play, and if I need to pitch, you're the man. On two!"

"Down. Set. Hut, HUT!"

I rode Luke into the hole and saw both linebackers zeroed in on him, so I pulled the ball and turned up the line. Their defensive tackle shed his block. I went to step inside of him when a cornerback hit me, taking me down for a one-yard loss.

I jumped up and tossed the ball to the head linesman.

"Line Up, Line Up!"

"Down. Set. Hut, HUT!"

We ran the same play but this time when I pulled the ball from Luke I followed him and used him as a lead blocker. I picked up 16 yards and we were now on their 35 yard line.

"Down. Set. Hut, HUT!"

They were ready for the inside play. I pulled the ball out of Luke's stomach and ran down the line. Two players converged on me and I turned and tossed the ball to a streaking Magic. He turned the corner to find one man to beat. I swear the poor kid lost his jock when Magic put his move on him. Magic scored and the extra point made it 35–27.

I started to get tired. I went over to grab a drink and looked at the clock: six minutes to go. We had a chance at this. On the kickoff, disaster struck. One of their speedy backs ran it all the way back and we soon found ourselves down 42–27 with just under six minutes to go.

We got the ball on the 20 yard line to start the next series. We came out and lined up. They had changed from their nickel to their base package. Back to the passing game.

"Blue. Set. Hut, HUT!"

I set my feet and one of their defensive backs had played back, so I threw the ball on a rope to the outside. I hit our wide receiver in stride right in the hands. He dropped it. I noticed Eastside's coaching staff pull that cornerback. I moved Magic over to the outside on the right along with Bill.

"Blue. Set. Hut, HUT!"

This time Bill went down ten yards and did a buttonhook; I hit him just as he turned. Bill was ready and caught the ball. We hurried to the line of scrimmage. The head linesman held up the clock until the yard markers could be reset.

"Blue. Set. Hut, HUT!"

I watched as Magic's defender went to jam him. Magic was strong enough to fend him off and break into the open. I hit him in stride and Magic was in the end zone. I looked over and saw the flag.

"LINE UP! LINE UP!" I yelled.

I looked at the clock and we had just over four minutes to play. The call was offensive pass interference. Everyone was in position when we were given the 'start clock' signal by the referee.

"Green. Set. Hut, HUT!"

It was time for our special play. We needed to score soon. I dropped back and Bill ran the buttonhook to perfection. Luke had snuck out of the backfield, and as soon as Bill was tackled he pitched the ball to Luke who went untouched for the score. After the extra point, we were now within striking distance at 42–34 with three minutes and 40 seconds left in the game. The crowd went wild and I could see the Eastside players get nervous.

The rain was starting to be a problem. The field had gotten soft, and the cold temperature caused me to have problems gripping the ball. When we came off the field, the training staff went to work putting longer cleats on the skill player's shoes. I was given a fanny pack with a warmer in it to help with my hands. The backs and receivers were given gloves.

We watched as Eastside's quarterback proved his worth. He methodically moved the ball down the field, eating up the clock. I saw Kevin line up to blitz. The Eastside quarterback called an audible. On the snap of the ball, Kevin dropped back and stepped in front of their intended receiver and intercepted the ball. He had learned his lesson in practice. We had first and ten at our 36 yard line with a minute ten seconds left in the game.

As we lined up, I saw they had their dime package in. I turned to Luke.

"Outside left."

"Down. Set. Hut, HUT!"

I don't think anyone thought we would run the ball. We were 10 yards down the field before we met any resistance. I saw their defensive back play the pitch, so I stepped inside of him. I was hit hard from the side by my buddy. I guess this was his payback.

We quickly lined up. The referee had stopped the clock so that the yard marker could be set. I looked at the clock: we had 48 seconds left, and we were 54 yards from scoring. I looked at Bill and nodded.

"Blue. Set. Hut, HUT!"

He ran a 15-yard down-and-out. I hit him just before he stepped out of bounds. We now had 40 seconds and 39 yards to go. The clock had stopped, so we huddled up.

"If we get caught in bounds we'll call time. Let's catch them by surprise. I'm going to call Blue, but we're running the inside option. We still have three time-outs, so be ready to call it."

"Blue. Set. Hut, HUT!"

I handed the ball off to Luke. He found a hole and broke free for a seven yard gain.

"TIME! TIME! TIME!"

The umpire stopped the clock. We were now at the 32 yard line with thirty-four seconds left. The offense jogged over to talk to the coaching staff.

Coach Lambert was as excited as we were.

"Gol Dern It, y'all are going to win this thing. We have two time-outs. USE THEM! I want you to run the outside option and get a first down. We then have four shots at the end zone. I want all four receivers to go long and Luke to sneak out about 7 or 8 yards and be the last option.

"Blue. Set. Hut, HUT!"

Luke and I sprinted down the line. I saw they were stringing us out to eat up clock. I cut up and took on two of them. There was a resounding crack of pads. I stumbled forward and picked up the first down. The referee blew his whistle to stop the clock. One of the Eastside players was slow to get up, so play was stopped to help him off the field.

We were lined up on the 29 yard line with thirty seconds to go. I jammed my hands into the fanny pack so I could get them warm. I had a huge grin on my face.

"IT'S SHOWTIME!" I shouted.

My counterpart from Eastside pointed at me.

"Dawson, you're dangerous."

"You have no idea. Blue. Set. Hut, HUT!"

Bill and Magic went straight up field and at the 5 yard line they cut to opposite corners of the end zone. I lofted the ball so Magic could run under it. He pulled it down and the crowd went wild until the back judge indicated that he'd caught it out of bounds. I couldn't see where his feet were. It didn't matter because we didn't have instant replay in high school.

"Shake it off. HUDDLE UP!" I called.

I smacked Magic's pads.

"Good catch. We have twenty-three seconds. We can get three plays in if we need to. I want Magic to move to the right outside position. I want you and Bill to run a crossing pattern and I'll either be throwing to the goal post or the corner," I said, and then we lined up.

"Blue. Set. Hut, HUT!"

I looked up to see my buddy had decided to blitz. I smiled as I released the ball for the corner. I was sitting on my butt when I saw Bill go up for the ball and start to bring it in for the score when one of Eastside defenders made a spectacular play and punched the ball out. My hands went to my head.

"FRICK!" I shouted

The crowd moaned when the saw the incomplete pass sign. My buddy helped me up and shook his head.

"That's two you should have had."

We had twelve seconds left. I called time out to get my head back into the game. We trotted over to the bench. Coach Lambert was talking to Coach Engels, and they agreed on a course of action.

"Boys, they're going to pack the end zone. I want you to run the same play, but this time I want you to dump it to Luke in the flat. Luke, punch it in. If he's stopped, we have one last time-out. Twelve seconds is plenty of time."

We trotted out on the field. My buddy nodded to me and I did the same to him. Twelve seconds and this thing would be over. The crowd stood and gave both teams a standing ovation. They'd gotten their money's worth tonight. Win or lose, this one would be barbershop talk for years to come.

"Blue. Set. Hut, HUT!"

I dropped back and looked at the clock as it ticked down. I pumped to the end zone and then turned to find Luke 9 yards down the field. He was met at the five yard line.

"TIME! TIME! TIME!" I yelled to get the clock stopped.

The ref blew the clock dead with three seconds left. We were five yards from scoring. We found chaos on the sideline. Half the coaches wanted to run the ball and the other half wanted to pass.

I stepped into the middle.

"Stop! Roll me out and give me the option to run or pass," I said.

Coach Lambert looked at me as if he was seeing me for the first time.

"At least someone around here is keeping their head on them. Coach Engels, you have a play like that?"

"Yes, sir."

He pulled out a marker board and drew out a play. The ref came over.

"Coach Lambert, it's time."

We came out and Kevin reported in as a running back. There was no way we could keep him off the field for this play. His job was to give me time to throw the ball. There wasn't anyone I would rather have my back. Luke was moved to a slot receiver. All four receivers were on the wide side of the field. Bill was the closest to the ball, then Luke, then Magic, and then on the far outside was the tallest wide receiver we had.

"Blue. Set. Hut, HUT!"

Luke went straight to the back of the end zone and then started to work his way to the left. Magic made an aggressive move straight at one of their backs and then did a quick turn just across the goal line. Right before Magic's move, I had drifted to the right when I heard a tremendous clash of pads behind me. I ignored them, knowing that Kevin would protect me. I ripped the ball to Magic and it was there when he turned. The ball hit him square in the chest and bounced out of the end zone. Bill was doing a slow drag in front of me as my outlet. The ball bounced up and he snagged it out of the air. I heard the gun go off to indicate the end of the game. Bill planted his outside foot. He was going to score. His footing gave way and he went down on the one yard line.

Final score was 42–34. I was exhausted after the game, and I helped Bill up. He had tears running down his face. I gave him a hug.

"Buddy, we weren't even supposed to be in this game. We play them again and we win."

"But I lost the game."

"Bullshit. I threw the pass too hard for Magic. I threw the ball out of bounds. I could go on all day about what-ifs. You made a hell of a play just to make it possible for us to have a chance. So quit hanging your head and go have fun tonight. Tonight you're a football god, and some pretty girl is going to show her appreciation."

"You think so?"

"Hell, yes. Now let's hold our heads up high and go show some sportsmanship and congratulate Eastside on giving us a game to remember."

✦✦✦

Chapter 16 – Kentucky

Friday September 27

When I exited the locker room, I saw Tom standing back behind a crowd of parents and well-wishers. I was shocked when they all stopped talking and clapped. We'd come very close to winning the game, but time ran out. I was still flying high after the thrill of scoring three touchdowns in ten minutes of play. I would replay the last play in my head for a very long time. I knew Bill was crushed he hadn't made it into the end zone, but we were lucky to even be in the game, let alone have a chance to win it.

I worked my way through the crowd and found Tracy standing by her dad. I broke into a big smile as I took in her sexy cheerleading outfit. The JV cheer squad had been part of a special halftime routine. I dropped my duffle bag, and she rushed into my arms and gave me one of her patented mind-erasing kisses. I heard some girls giggling, and then Luke Herndon must have come out of the locker room.

"Dawson, get a room!"

The crowd laughed and I felt my cheeks start to glow. I grabbed my duffle and Tracy and I went hand-in-hand to meet her Dad.

"You guys ready?"

"Yes, Daddy, let's go."

As we worked our way to the parking lot, I was surprised to see so many fans had still hung around. They didn't seem to want to leave. I was a little nervous about all the attention I'd gotten until I looked over and saw Tracy just beaming. This was what she lived for. She had the star football player on her arm as we walked out of the game, and all the fans had taken notice. When I saw her reaction, I relaxed and made it a point to introduce her to everyone that greeted me. If I hadn't been going with her dad tonight, I would have been a very lucky boy. She quivered with excitement when we got to the car. Tom popped the trunk and I dumped in my bag.

Mary was in the front seat when Tracy and I slid into the back.

"Hey, David, you played a great game tonight. I had no idea you could play quarterback. How's Mike?"

On the last play, one of his fingers on his throwing hand had been injured.

"I'm not sure how bad Magic's injury is. From the looks of the training staff, it's not good. I really hope he gets back soon. It's a lot of pressure running the offense. I'd rather just run over a few people and contribute that way."

Tracy smacked my arm. I think being the freshman starting at quarterback on the varsity fit her plans better.

"Don't sell yourself short. You played great tonight."

I gave her a kiss as a reward. We all chatted about the game on the way to the airport. There was a separate terminal for small and corporate aircraft. I'd never flown before, so I started to get excited about my first flight. The owner of the firm where Tom worked was a University of Florida alumnus. He had a block of eight tickets for every home and away game. He'd given Tom two tickets for tomorrow's game at Kentucky.

Florida had a good team this year and I looked forward to seeing them play. This was also the first college game I'd ever been to. Tom said we might be able to meet some of the players before the game. His boss sometimes got field passes because of his booster level.

The only thing that put a damper on this weekend was that Tami was leaving on Sunday and I wouldn't be getting back until late afternoon. There was a chance I might not see her until she came home for Thanksgiving. I didn't even need to ask Tami if I should go on this trip. She would have just called me a 'stupid boy' and made me go anyways. I would call her tonight when we got settled into the hotel.

When we got to the airport, Tom pulled around the little terminal and drove onto the tarmac. There were three other cars there. It looked like we were the last to arrive. The trunk popped open and I went back and pulled out our bags. Tom's bag was one with a telescoping handle and wheels. Tracy grabbed it and we followed to where Tom and Mary talked to the group making the trip. I was introduced to six other men who all worked with Tom at Rigby, Thompson and Associates. Their boss, Mr. Rigby, wasn't able to make this trip. As they all talked, Tracy and I went to where the ground staff was loading the bags.

"I wish you were going with us," I said.

She looked sexy as hell in her cheerleading outfit. That seemed to be the right thing to say, because she gave me a kiss that curled my toes.

"I wish I was too. If I was you would get so lucky tonight you don't even know."

We looked into each other's eyes and my hands were on her hips. I pulled her closer so she could feel what I thought about getting lucky. I then let my hands slide around and I cupped her perfect ass. Her eyes got very big.

"You're such a naughty boy. You realize my mom and dad are only ten feet away."

I kneaded her bottom and grinned at her. I jumped when I heard someone clear their throat. When I turned around, I found her mom and dad with big smirks on their faces.

"Time to go, Romeo. Give my daughter a kiss and get your butt on the plane," Tom said.

As I was frozen in stunned silence, I felt Tracy grab my butt, which made me jump.

"Paybacks are hell," she said.

I gave her a menacing look, then broke into a smile, and gave her a kiss.

"Are you picking me up when I get back?"

"You bet. Now go have fun with my dad."

We all got on the plane to leave.

✧✧✧

The airplane seated twelve, and all of Tom's work-mates headed to the front. Tom indicated two seats towards the back where we would have privacy. The seats reminded me of home theater chairs. They were covered in nice leather with large armrests with cup holders. Once we were seated, the pilot came onto the intercom and told us the flight to Lexington would take an hour and a half. Tom and I settled in, and shortly we were airborne.

Tom seemed excited about something.

"I've been talking to Joe Phips about your running game. He's the recruiting coordinator for Florida. When you threw your third touchdown tonight, I called him again. He's setting up a workout for you tomorrow morning. If you're everything I think you are, they'll start recruiting you."

I was in shock. I thought this weekend was just to get to know Tom better and see a football game. It now had a lot more meaning. To be honest, I really hadn't thought a lot about college other than for an education. I figured I'd worry about it my junior year. When we got to the hotel in Lexington, I needed to call Tami and get her advice.

"Dang it, Tom, do you think there's a little pressure on me now? Florida's one of those dream destinations for football. I'd hate to mess this up after only playing less than a quarter of high school ball at quarterback."

"Don't worry about it. Joe's job is to identify talent early. They're not asking you to come in and play next week. They'll want to see you develop over the next three-and-a-half years. At this point you're just a prospect."

"I'm a prospect who's done nothing to this point."

He gave me an appraising look.

"David, you're going to have to grow a pair. You're a damn good player and your confidence is going to have to grow if you ever plan on leading your team to the playoffs. Magic isn't coming back in time to salvage the season. You're it.

"Have you noticed all the recruiters who've been showing up to your games?" Tom asked.

"Aren't they there to see Luke, Mike and Kevin?" I asked.

"In part. Even though they're making offers to those three, they weren't coming until you had your superhero game. Those three owe you big time. Tonight I saw you throw, off your front foot, a fifty-yard pass that hit Bill in stride. Your throwing mechanics suck. You're doing everything just off your arm strength alone. If you ever get your technique down, you'll be a high major prospect.

"Combine your potential at quarterback and your toughness running the ball and you're the perfect college quarterback. Currently your only obvious problem is your height. Most major programs are looking for someone at least six-two," Tom said.

"It just seems like this is too soon," I complained.

"Like I said, you need to man-up. Tell me, how many freshmen are starting on a team with this level of talent?"

I thought for a moment. Luke had pulled it off three years ago. Mike and Kevin hadn't started to play varsity ball until their junior year.

"I'd guess not many."

"You'd be correct. The only other one I can think of is the freshman back over at Washington. He's starting, but not putting up near the numbers you are. By the time he's a senior, he'll be a beast. The problem with him right now is he doesn't make everyone around him better. You do. Luke's numbers have almost doubled since you started. The whole offense is better. Hell, since you went all superhero in your first game, the whole team is better. You have the potential to be special. I wish you could see what I see. You know I love Tracy. For her to be going out with a good guy, he has to be good looking. You have the looks to be the poster boy for a program, and if you don't think that plays into it, you're nuts. Big-time football is all about marketing and selling tickets," Tom told me.

"Okay, I'm not sure how to take that last part."

"Look, tomorrow is just a look. Nothing is written in stone. Hell, by the time you graduate, Florida will probably have a new coaching staff. So get your head out of your ass and have some fun with it. If you have to, just play the role of a big-time recruit; then own it. You have nothing to worry about."

I felt myself relaxing. Tom was right. I needed to look at this as an opportunity and just get over my fears of inadequacy. It was time to either put up or shut up. If I failed, I would just dust myself off and move on, one day at a time, right?

✧✧✧

When I was settled in at the hotel, I pulled my tablet out and sent a text to Tami to jump on the video-chat. I could see she was in her living room as she kicked back and watched a movie with her mom.

"Hey, Gorgeous, you all packed for Wesleyan?"

"Almost. I was stressing about getting everything perfect, but Mom reminded me that all I need to do is call you and you can just run it over."

"Really? And how long a drive is it?"

"Just a couple of hours, it's no big deal for my *best* friend to drive over to come see me."

"If you need me to come see you, all you have to do is ask. I'll drop everything. You just say the word. Only problem is I don't have a driver's license."

"There is that. The move is so much easier knowing you're in my corner."

“I have some news,” I offered.

“Spill it.”

“I’m working out for the University of Florida tomorrow. If the workout goes well, they’ll start recruiting me.”

“Bullshit.”

She could read me, so she could tell that I told her the truth.

“I swear, David, you just fall into it, don’t you?” she asked.

“Yeah, I was thinking I should go play the lotto. I need some cash.”

“So tell me, how did all this happen?”

“Actually, it’s all through Tom Dole. His boss is a booster. He called their recruiting coordinator and arranged an informal tryout. I about had a cow when he told me on the flight here, but he calmed me down. I just figure I’ll go with it and have some fun. He told me to pretend I was some big-time recruit and to own the place. It actually sounds like fun.”

“That’s great advice. I know you. You worry about stuff like this and overanalyze it to death. When it comes time, you’re a different person. You just exude confidence. Do me a favor: don’t get caught up in the surroundings. I want you to focus on the task at hand and do your absolute best.”

“I hear you. I do tend to get distracted. I’ll treat it like a game and just get into the zone.”

“What time are you getting back Sunday?”

“Probably late afternoon. What time are you going off to school?”

“Mom’s going to take me and spend the night. I can’t move into the dorm until Monday. She wants to leave around five at the latest, but I can get her to wait. I really want to see you before I leave.”

"I'm hoping we'll be back before three. Tracy's picking me up. Is it okay if she comes along?"

"Of course, 'stupid boy,'" Tami answered.

"You had to get one last 'stupid boy' in. I'm going to get even when I see you."

She stuck her tongue out at me. We chatted about a few other things and then decided we better log off. I was keeping Tom up.

✧✧✧

Saturday September 28

I was up at six so I could go run. The hotel was on the edge of campus. I talked to the desk clerk to get an idea of the layout so I could plan my route. It was going to be a beautiful Indian-summer day. The Kentucky campus was impressive. I really enjoyed my three-mile run. After I got back and stretched, it was almost seven. I decided against swimming today and headed up to the room. Tom was just getting out of the shower when I came in.

"Did you go run?"

"Yeah, I kept it light and ran three this morning."

He just looked at me as if I had two heads. I jumped into the shower and was ready to leave before Tom got dressed. He didn't seem like a morning person.

There was a restaurant attached to the hotel. When we were seated, Tom filled me in on the details for the day.

"Joe has made arrangements with the Kentucky staff to provide you with some gear for today. Kentucky has a couple of quarterback prospects coming in for their campus visit today. They're letting you do some drills with them. It'll give Joe a chance to do a quick evaluation. Then the rest of the day is ours to enjoy."

Our server interrupted our conversation. She was obviously a coed who'd had a little too much to drink the night before. She was cute, so I naturally went into flirt mode.

"What can I get you boys to drink?" She was focused on Tom.

"Coffee."

She turned to me and did a double take. She actually smiled.

"You have too much to drink last night?" I asked.

"Sugar, you have no idea. Are you in town for the game?"

"Yes, and I'm doing a private workout. They're trying to decide if they want to recruit me or not."

"Let me guess—you're a quarterback," she said as she rolled her eyes, since she obviously had heard that line before.

"You must get hit on a lot to be so jaded."

"You wouldn't believe me if I told you. Stand up," she ordered.

I arched my eyebrows and smiled as I slid out of our booth. When I got up, I pulled my shirt up so she could see my six-pack. I sat back down and she seemed a whole lot more interested.

"Oh, my, you're a sexy one, aren't you? My only concern is you might be too young, and I'd go to jail for what I'd like to do to you."

Tom cleared his throat to slow us down.

"I think your dad wants to eat breakfast."

"Not my dad, but he's right. I need to eat something before I go work out."

"Oh, I think I like you. What are you having?"

"I want two large milks; an orange juice; two sausage, egg and cheese omelets with wheat toast and home fries," I ordered.

Tom looked shocked. I just shrugged.

"They're trying to bulk me up."

Tom ordered and we settled in for breakfast. As we were leaving, she gave me her phone number and told me she was off at one. Tom just shook his head as we headed over to the athletic center. The Kentucky staff was very gracious. They set me up with everything I needed for the workout. They pointed me to one of their practice fields, and Tom and I got there early. I was glad because it gave me time to stretch out and run to get warmed up.

Tom and I were goofing off when I saw a blur run past me.

"Hit me long."

Without thinking, I dropped back and threw a forty-yard bomb that hit the receiver in stride.

"Man, you're fast! I wish I had someone like you to throw to," I said as he came up and I shook his hand. "David Dawson."

"Mike Ware. Kid, you have a cannon for an arm. I don't recognize the name. Are you a late addition to the workout?"

"They added me last night."

"Let me go get someone you can throw to. I think they only have me and Tim scheduled." He jogged off, and five minutes later Mike was back with Tim and Jack.

While we waited for everyone to get there, the three of us goofed off with them running routes. The three guys were shocked when a group of Florida coaches showed up. Tom took me over to introduce me to them. Joe Phips was the former coach at Kentucky before he joined the Florida staff. He recognized the three guys I was throwing to. He went over to talk to them as Tom introduced me to Brad Peace. He was the offensive coordinator and quarterback coach.

Joe jogged back and he went up to Coach Peace.

"Hey, we need to move this workout to a more private setting. David's for real and we don't need the Kentucky staff watching this."

"Seriously?" Coach Peace asked.

What was that supposed to mean?

"Yep. Mike tells me David has a strong arm and is accurate with it. He has terrible footwork, but for a freshman has a good upside. He also had him throw all the other key passes and he made them without any effort. I want to get our own receivers and video team."

Kentucky's coaches and recruits showed up. Joe saw Mike hurry over and talk to one of the coaches. Joe and Coach Peace looked at each other.

"Shit," Joe said.

I was easy to pick out, because I had on Kentucky gear. Two of the Kentucky coaches came over. They turned out to be Don Berta and Ned Braun. Don was Kentucky's recruiting coordinator and Ned was their offensive coordinator and quarterback coach.

Don and Joe stepped away to discuss the situation. Mike had clued the Kentucky staff in on what was going on. Joe and Don came back laughing. They came up to me and Joe led the discussion.

"David, Coach Berta and I have agreed to go ahead with the workout as planned. We really never hold workouts on other campuses. They were just doing it as a favor because I was the coach here in 2012. Are you okay with that?"

"I don't see why not. I might look silly throwing with seniors, but I told Tom I'd just do it for the fun of it."

Don looked at me funny.

"What grade are you in?"

"I'm a freshman."

Don got a worried look on his face. Joe broke into a big grin and clued me in.

"He's worried you're going to make his recruits look bad, and they're going to be pissed when they find out you're a freshman."

"Don, I won't tell them if you don't."

Don looked a little better. Shortly all three of us prospects were running drills. I did as Tami said and just focused on what I was doing. I didn't pay attention to how well the other two were doing. They had paired me up with Mike. We were running a drill where Mike would go downfield ten yards and then do a buttonhook. He'd dropped the ball three straight times. I noticed Mike had dropped a lot of balls, and I'd finally had enough of it.

"God dammit, Mike! Catch the ball with your hands, not your body."

Mike got in my face.

"Listen, Sport. Learn to take a little off the ball. You don't have to rip it in practice."

"Bullshit, Mike. I haven't even ripped one yet. Hell, my high school receivers catch better than you do."

His face went beet red.

"Okay, Wuss. Let's see what you can do."

"You better get your hands up or this is going to hurt."

"Whatever. Do your worst."

What I didn't realize was that everyone had stopped to listen to our exchange. Mike did his route and on the break, I let loose. It sounded like a fastball. To his credit, Mike caught the ball. He was grinning from ear to ear.

"Dawson, you're a freak."

I then heard the Superman music start. Oh hell, no. Tom had the other two recruits and the coaches all watching my YouTube video on his cell phone. Everyone's head snapped up and Joe started to chuckle. I just turned around and Mike and I continued the drills. After we were done, Mike took me aside.

"Look, sorry about earlier. They have us deliberately drop passes to see how you'll react. You're the first recruit ever to dress me down. You handled it just right. You called me on it and coached me up to help me do better. You caught me off guard because I'm not used to being told I don't catch as well as a high school kid, but it got me motivated. What they're looking for is leadership."

"I was just trying to get you focused. This is a big deal for me, and I wanted to do my best."

"Look, you're young. If you work hard, you're going to be scary-good. Arm strength can't be taught. Let me give you a tip for the rest of the day: get the recruits to like you and show leadership. If you do that, they'll make you an offer just on that alone. Your development will take care of itself."

"So how do I get them to like me?"

"Get them laughing. Tease them some, but don't be mean. Get them to laugh at themselves. If you want them to follow you, let them know you care about them." He smirked. "Heck, the same thing works with girls."

Mike took me back to the training facility, and I took a shower and changed. When I came out, Tom had waited for me.

"Okay, that went pretty well. Both coaching staffs agree you're nowhere near ready. They said you telegraph your throws, your footwork is terrible and you have to shorten your release. The good news is they both are going to start watching you. I thought Joe was going to cry when I told him you play on a team that runs the veer option."

"Well, I guess that means mission accomplished. I want to thank you and your boss for setting this whole thing up. Even if this trip never turns into anything, that's fine with me. I'll always remember that you did this for me. Now feed me! Growing boy here," I said with a big grin.

✧✧✧

The one thing I'll give the University of Kentucky was the hot chick ratio; it was phenomenal. Every time I turned around there was one better-looking than the one before. I found I liked Kentucky more and more. We picked up our tickets at the will-call window and were informed that the Kentucky staff had left me a field pass. I went up to where

Tom was sitting so I knew where to find him, then headed to the gate to let me on the field.

Waiting at the gate was a very pretty coed named Marcy. She was assigned to be my chaperone. She explained that recruits were assigned someone to show them around. Normally it was someone on the team, but I was a last-minute addition. Marcy played volleyball. To be honest, I thought it was just fine that I had gotten Marcy.

"What are we supposed to do before the game starts?"

She gave me an irritated look.

"I guess I could show you around."

"What's wrong?"

"I need to run. Sorry, I'm being a bitch. I don't know why I agreed to come in."

I thought about it for a minute. Kentucky had lost something like twenty-six straight to Florida. I could really care less about the actual game.

"Do you need to run sprints or distance?" I asked.

"Distance."

"What's your pace?"

"I do six-minute miles."

I hate to run with someone that runs at a different pace than I do. Her pace was a little slower than mine was, so I could relax.

"How far?"

"I need to run three today," she said.

"Okay, get me some gear and I'll run with you."

She looked surprised.

"I sleep in a pair of my brother's shorts and t-shirt. That should work."

We walked to her dorm room and she gave me the clothes. I changed in the restroom. The shorts were fine, but the t-shirt was tight. When I got back to her room there were two other girls ready to run. They all giggled when they saw the t-shirt. Someone made a rude comment about me looking like a gay porn star. I just shrugged and told them to get moving.

Turns out all three girls were freshmen on the volleyball team. Sue and Janet were twins. I honestly couldn't tell them apart. They were strikers and nearly as tall as I was, and they were cute. Marcy was a setter. She was defiantly doable. I would rate her a solid seven. All three girls were very athletic-looking and I enjoyed their company. When we got about a mile and half into our run, the t-shirt got to be too much. It had started to restrict my breathing, so I just pulled it off.

I had been running behind the girls so I could check out their butts. Marcy turned back to make some comment when she saw my change of attire. She tripped and started to go down. I grabbed her waist and picked her up before she hit the pavement.

"Whoa! You okay?" I asked.

"Dang, David! Catch me, I think I'm falling!" one of the twins said.

I set Marcy down. She was a little shaken up. She nearly had done a face-plant on the sidewalk.

"Thank you. That could have really hurt."

She seemed to be okay. I smiled at them.

"Okay, I've looked at your cute butts long enough. If you can catch me you can have mine."

The three girls squealed and the race was on. I made a point of staying just out of reach. Marcy almost caught me when she cheated and took a shortcut through a parking lot. I finally led them back to their dorm and we all collapsed on the lawn. When we caught our breath, we helped each other stretch. I think the girls were being a little free with their hands. We went in and all took showers. Then Marcy and I headed back to the game.

When we got back, it was halftime and the band was playing. Florida had the game well in hand and the crowd was thinning out. I took Marcy into the stands and found

Tom. He gave me a funny look when he saw me with Marcy.

"Look, Tom, see what Kentucky gave me for my recruiting visit? What do you think Florida'll give me when I visit them? I bet it's some crummy baseball cap."

Tom didn't miss a beat.

"I'm not sure that's going to fit in your suitcase."

"I hadn't thought of that."

Marcy smacked my arm.

"Tom, I'm Marcy. I'm David's guide for the day. We're supposed to make sure our guests stay out of trouble, but this one has been more trouble than he's worth. He made me chase him all over campus."

"Yeah, she got two of her friends and they tried to grab my butt, but I was too fast for them."

Tom was chuckling.

"David, you're not very smart, are you?" Tom asked.

"What do you mean?"

"I think the whole object is to *let* them catch you."

"No way! They dressed me up like a gay porn star, and then chased me all over the campus. I'm not sure I would have been safe with any of them if they'd caught me. I had to wear them out first."

Now the whole section cracked up as Marcy just shook her head. Tom wasn't sure what to do with me. Our row had thinned out so everyone scooted down to allow Marcy to join us. I put her next to Tom so she could explain what really happened. Towards the end of the game, Tom asked Marcy what her plans were for me for the rest of the day.

"We normally take the recruits to the athletic dorm and feed them. Then we have a social gathering that lasts till about midnight."

Tom looked at me.

"That's plan A. Plan B is going with me and the guys I work with to dinner, and then we head to the hotel. Which do you want to do?"

"Hmmm, spend the evening with my hot chaperone and go to a party, or spend the evening with you and six other old guys and listen to you talk about work. I think I'll go with the hot girl."

"Thank God. I was afraid I was going to have to feed you again. Marcy, I hope you have plenty of food, because this one's a pig."

"Love you too, Tom."

✧✧✧

Marcy and I went to the football dorm after the game. Marcy was something of a social butterfly and seemed to know everyone. She introduced me to so many people I stopped trying to learn their names. We finally found the rest of the recruits. The two quarterbacks started to give me shit about having a girl chaperone. There were ten recruits visiting this weekend. The chaperones left to talk to the recruiting staff to update them on how things had gone. Once we were alone, the ribbing began in earnest.

"Dude, how do you rate? We all got guys who play for the team."

"When you filled out your weekend form you were supposed to check the box whether you were gay or not. I checked 'not,'" I said.

"You're so full of shit. They told us there's supposed to be a party with plenty of cooter for all of us."

"Did you all bring condoms?" I asked the other recruits.

They looked confused.

"Guys, think about it. If these girls'll do all of us, what do you think they do every week when a new batch of recruits come in?" I asked them.

"Dammit, Dawson, now you've ruined that for me. I hadn't thought of that."

"I'm just saying I'd double-wrap it if I was going to take one of them on," I sagely offered.

"Don't listen to him. These are supposed to be some hot chicks."

I looked at them seriously.

"Guys, all kidding aside, but do you seriously want to risk going home and giving your sister a venereal disease?" I asked with a straight face.

It took a while, but finally one of them got it.

"I'm not banging my sister!"

"Hmm. Looks like you're the only one," I said, as I tried hard to keep from laughing.

The chaperones came back to find me at the bottom of a dogpile. Marcy helped me get up after the others had gotten off me.

"Why am I not surprised to find you at the bottom of this?" she asked.

"I don't know. I guess they don't have a sense of humor."

She could see them all smirking at me, so she knew we were just having fun.

We went on a tour of the facilities before dinner. During the tour, every one of the recruits managed to get their chaperone aside to ask for condoms. Then we all ate dinner in a private room. During that time, Don Berta stuck his head in the door and indicated that Marcy should join him. A minute later, she came back in, grabbed me by the scruff of the neck and pulled me out of the room. For some odd reason, everyone else found that highly amusing. We found Don in the hall.

"I hate to ask this, but why do all of these guys want condoms?" he asked me.

"They all want to have sex, of course."

He looked at Marcy. She just shrugged. He looked at me again.

"Are you saying that you don't want to have sex?"

"Of course I do. I just planned ahead."

He still looked confused.

"Coach, what would happen if one of your recruits got a nasty STD and took it home with him?" I asked.

That got his attention.

"Look at it as a marketing tool," I continued. "If each recruit was given a six-pack of condoms in his welcome bag, how cool do you think they would think Kentucky is?"

"Okay. Come with me!" he ordered.

"Shit, what did I do wrong?" I asked, and immediately regretted the language.

"Nothing. I'm taking you up to my office, so I can give you an offer letter. We can't give you an official letter of intent yet. However, I want you to know we're serious about you coming to Kentucky. Plus, I can't have you working with Joe to out-recruit me for the next three-and-a-half years."

Marcy suddenly realized that I was a freshman in high school. Crud!

"Marcy, run over to Health Services and bring back sixty condoms," he said to her, and waved his hand to shoo her out the door.

Her eyes got wide as saucers, and her mouth was moving, but nothing came out.

"Just go! Tell them I sent you. Have them call over here if they have questions."

He dismissed her with another wave. She shook her head, and left without a word.

"I'd like to be a fly on the wall when Marcy asks for sixty condoms," I said as I followed him up to his office.

"Yep, I probably should have sent one of my staff." He chuckled to himself momentarily, and then turned serious again. "Okay, I want you to know that we don't normally make offers to freshmen. I talked to Coach Lambert, and he sent over some game film. You show a lot of potential. We'll be recruiting you as a quarterback. We also talked at length about your leadership skills. I have to ask; did you really tell the whole coaching staff to shut up before the last play of last night's game?"

"At the time it seemed like what needed to be done. Someone needed to make a decision and we didn't have time for everyone to be fighting."

"Well, from what Coach Lambert told me, you did the right thing. All the recruits like you. A couple have asked where you plan to go to school. We would love that to be Kentucky."

"Coach, let's be honest. Is this just something to one-up Joe, or are you serious about me coming here?"

"Smart boy. I'd be lying if I said Joe doesn't play a part in this. Kentucky is an up-and-coming program. We need to get in early with players we feel have potential to be great. We may not win all the battles, but we think if we can get to know you over the next few years, you'll come to find that the University of Kentucky would be a great destination."

"Okay, if you're serious about offering me a scholarship, I'm not going to turn you down. So far, you're the only one who's asked me to the dance. I would be happy to consider Kentucky."

I came back into the dining room and showed everyone my offer letter. One of the quarterbacks who was seated next to me was John Phillips.

"David, I'm so mad at you. You walk in and do a workout for Florida. Now I see you here with an offer. Kentucky's my dream school. Look, I'm a damn good quarterback. But the buzz is if you come here, I'll be riding the bench."

"John, I'm a freshman. At the most you'll ride the pine just one, maybe two years if you redshirt."

"You cocky little twit, thanks for telling me. At best you'd be backing me up since I'll have that job well in hand by the time you hit campus," John bragged.

"Yeah, right, I hit campus and you're done. Seriously though, John, if this is your dream school, then go talk to your chaperone and let him know."

John nodded and I saw him take his chaperone into the hall. The guy on my other side asked what was going on. When I told him, he shared with the next guy, and so on. Pretty soon I was the only one in the room eating my dinner. When Marcy came back, she looked around the empty room and gave me a look. I just shrugged. She did a quick one-eighty and left to find out what was going on. After a few minutes, she came back in with a huge smile on her face.

"You are so going to get lucky tonight. I'll help you find the pick of the litter and make sure you're walking funny come sunup," Marcy offered.

"I've been learning to 'dine at the Y.' Do you think you can find one who'd be willing to give me some pointers?"

"Oh, dear, I'm going to end up taking you home tonight, aren't I?"

I just smiled at her.

Over the course of the next twenty minutes, recruits came back one at a time, each with a big smile on their face. Each time one came in, I got up and congratulated him. I talked Marcy into getting me another steak, because I was still hungry. They were all amused at how much I ate. The last guy to come in was John. He had tears in his eyes and I got up and gave him a hug. Coach Berta followed John in.

"I want to be the first to welcome you all to the Kentucky family. In a few minutes, you'll be joining your families and going over to the booster reception. We'll spend some time there and then go to something a little more laid back. Don't worry, your families will stay with the boosters. We all owe David here special thanks. He's gotten you all a gift. Marcy, will you hand them out? Please don't open your bag until everyone has theirs."

They all waited until everyone had a bag and then they turned to me.

"Okay, guys, open them," I told them.

They all got big stupid grins on their faces when they saw what was inside. I opened mine and counted. I looked up in dismay.

"Only six?"

John cuffed me on the back of the head.

"You oversexed dork. If you need more than six, come see me and I'll give you some of mine."

We all followed Coach Berta to the main lounge. All the guys rushed to show off their letters. John and his dad had tears of joy. I think his dad was more excited than he was. It didn't take long for them to pull me in and start to introduce me to their parents and brothers and sisters.

John had a hot sister who was my age or a little older. When he saw me smile at her, he physically got between us.

"No way, Dawson, my sister wouldn't survive you. I am *not* explaining that to my parents."

I got a big grin on my face when I saw the sudden interest his sister showed me. John turned around and saw the look in her face.

"OH, FRICK. I just did that to myself, didn't I?"

I reached out my hand to introduce myself.

"Hi, I'm David... eeeek..."

John had picked me up, thrown me over his shoulder, and was physically hauling me to the other side of the room as he said, "NO, NO, NO, NO," over and over again. What he didn't realize was that his sister had followed him. When he put me down, she stepped around him.

"Hi, I'm Alice. Ignore the big jerk behind me."

"Nice to meet you, Alice," I said as I pulled out my bag of condoms. "They gave me six condoms. Do you want to go see if we can use them all? John said if I run out, he'll give me some of his."

"OH DEAR LORD, PLEASE SHOOT ME NOW!"

John knew when he'd lost, and went over to talk to everyone else. Alice was bent over laughing.

"I've never seen him so frustrated." She calmed down and took a deep breath. "You've been all he can talk about since this morning. You must have put on some show. He and dad have wanted him to come here since he was born. Now he's worried he'll be riding the pine."

"I know. He seemed relieved when I told him I was only a freshman. I want to tell you I'm sorry about the rubber remarks. I was only saying that to pull his chain."

She winked at me and then looked pissed.

"JOHN, COME HERE!" she yelled across the room.

He came running over to see what I'd done to piss off his sister.

"David won't use his rubbers on me now. What did you say to him?"

"Nope, I'm not getting involved. Alice, you're on your own with this one. Don't say I didn't warn you," John said as he stormed off.

After talking for a few minutes, Alice and I made a point to hold hands. It was a good thing her parents were cool and saw we were just tormenting John. Marcy showed up and told us the bus was ready to take us to the booster party.

✧✧✧

Chapter 17 – We Need to Get a Move On

Saturday September 28

We worked our way to the back of the bus. Marcy sat across the aisle from Alice and me.

"So, David, it didn't take you long to replace me."

I winked at Marcy.

"You never told me if you're in or not."

Alice gave me a confused look.

"Earlier I told Marcy I've been learning to go down on a woman, and I was looking for someone to give me pointers," I enlightened her.

Alice nodded and then leaned over to talk to Marcy.

"Would it be okay if I came over to watch?" Alice asked.

I jumped right in before Marcy could go into shock.

"That's a great idea. After I make Marcy climax so much she's just a puddle of exhaustion and no longer any fun, I could practice on you."

We both turned to stare at Marcy. I saw her eyes go big and she took a moment to gather herself. I could see she was looking flushed. She suddenly came to a decision.

"Okay, I'm in, if you're both serious."

I looked at Marcy.

"Give us a minute."

She got up and moved up a couple of seats. I liked Alice and didn't want to toy with her feelings. It was one thing to tease and joke around, but something told me she might be a real friend. Maybe more than that someday; who knew? The other thing I needed to consider was John. I could tell he really loved his sister. I liked John, too, and wanted to become friends with him. If I messed things up with her, I was sure it would hurt our friendship.

"Alice, we've been playing some games up to this point. I like you and John. I don't want to do anything to jeopardize our friendship."

She looked deep into my eyes and then shocked me.

"Kiss me."

I didn't hesitate. I brushed her lips with mine and then eased into a slow, sensual kiss. She ran her hand up and brushed my jaw. It felt like an electrical shock. I parted my lips and found her tongue caressing my lips. We soon chased each other's tongue in a game of tag. We didn't have a lot of time, so I broke the kiss and looked her in the eye.

"Wow, thank you. That was special," I said.

"I like your confidence. There's something about you. Hell, less than two minutes after meeting you I was chasing you across a room."

"I think we both owe John. If he hadn't tried to stop me from meeting you, we would never have been curious."

"It's the whole forbidden-fruit thing. It did pique my interest."

"What's it going to be?" I asked.

She grinned.

"I'm in." She raised her voice so Marcy could hear her. "Marcy, we're in."

Alice and I went back to kissing. It remained pretty PG-13 until Alice grabbed my package. After that, it was game on. Somehow, Alice lost her panties before we got off the bus. I stuffed them in my back pocket. Luckily, Marcy let us get off first, and noticed the lacy garment peeking out of my pocket and stuffed it in so it didn't become a problem.

✧✧✧

The bus pulled up in front of a large two-story brick home that looked like it was built in the late '20s or early '30s in a Colonial Georgian style. It was the President's home. The place was full of people who just reeked of money. This was the core group that kept the athletic department afloat with cash.

I pulled Alice into the mixer and scanned the room. I was surprised to see one of my favorite actors, Lori Winnick. She was a gorgeous woman for being in her mid-40s. A man about her age had her cornered. I heard Alice and Marcy gasp as I made beeline to Lori. Alice had no choice but to follow me because I had a firm grip on her hand. I glanced back to see Marcy rooted in her spot, not sure what to do.

"Excuse me, Miss Winnick, I wanted to come over and introduce myself and my date for the evening. This is Alice Phillips, and I'm David Dawson."

The man talking to her looked irritated, but I didn't detect any irritation in Miss Winnick. She shook both our hands and then looked at Alice.

"I follow recruiting pretty heavily. Are you related to John Phillips, the All State quarterback who's visiting this weekend?" Lori asked.

Alice's smile was infectious. It was obvious she was very proud of her brother.

"Yes. John received an offer today, and he accepted. Kentucky has always been where he wanted to go to school. He and my dad are over the moon that he's coming here. He would love to meet you."

Lori suddenly realized she hadn't introduced the man standing next to her.

"I'm sorry, this is Teddy Wesleyan. He's a major donor, and I'm trying to talk him into helping me with a project."

"Sir, are you the same Wesleyan as in Wesleyan Academy?" I asked.

He finally seemed to warm to our interruption.

"Yes, my great grandfather started the Academy in 1941."

"My best friend, Tami Glade, just received your first scholarship. Sir, you've no idea what a difference this is going to make in her life. You won't be disappointed you picked her to be first. She'll make you proud. Would it be okay if I shook your hand?"

"Yes, I met Tami at the banquet when it was announced. We have high hopes for her."

He shook my hand and was happy to see his money was going to good use. Miss Winnick smiled at him.

"Teddy, it looks like you're in a giving mood," she prodded.

"Okay, Lori, I'll fund it."

She grinned and gave him a big kiss, lucky bastard. She turned to Alice.

"Come on, I want to meet your brother."

She grabbed Alice's hand and they worked their way through the crowd. I said my goodbyes to Teddy and found Marcy where I'd left her.

"What the hell, you're here ten minutes and you're talking to Lori Winnick as if she's your best friend?" Marcy asked.

"I know. That was a big mistake. The bitch stole my date."

"I see that. Let's go see if we can get her back."

"Nah, leave her alone. I think she's having the time of her life."

I grabbed Marcy and made her go with me as I made the rounds of the room to meet the donors. My dad had always made Greg and me do this type of thing. He said you never knew when something like this would pay off. We eventually made it to a library where we found Miss Winnick in the middle of all the recruits and their families. Alice was right beside her, and they were having a great time. When I walked up, Alice gave me a wink.

Lori was laughing at something one of the recruits said.

"Okay. Where is this mystery David guy? I have to meet him."

Alice smiled and pointed at me. Lori gave a look of mock horror.

"You, you are so bad. You got them condoms as a gift?"

"Hey, we're talking about teenage boys full of hormones away for a weekend where there are hot college girls running around. If something were to happen, better safe than sorry."

"I hear you have your own YouTube channel. I want to see it. Something about you being Superman," Lori said.

"You guys are so going to die," I said as I gave them all a dirty look. "Okay, I have it in my favorites in my browser."

I hit play on the video and handed to Miss Winnick. It was fun to watch her reaction as the video played. She looked at me with concern.

"Were those boys okay?"

"Yes, both of them were uninjured, just a little shook-up," I assured her.

Marcy made an announcement.

"Okay, the bus has been pulled around to take the guys to their social gathering. As soon as it drops them off it'll come back and take everyone else to the hotel."

As Marcy got the recruits headed to the bus, I went with Alice to talk to her parents.

"I'm too young to drink or go to a party like the rest are. Marcy's going to take Alice and me to get something to eat, and we're just going to hang out for a while. I just want to make sure it's okay if Alice comes with us."

Mrs. Phillips seemed to be the decision-maker. I was glad it wasn't her dad. Dads never wanted to see their daughter in any potential situation where a guy like me might violate them.

"Do you want to go with David?"

"Oh, yes. I like him, Mom. I want to get to know him better before he has to leave."

"Aren't you worried about the long-distance thing?" her mom asked.

"Sure I am, but right now we're just seeing if we can be friends. I want to spend the time to find out," Alice responded.

"Okay, Sweetie." She gave me an evil look. "Do you have enough condoms?"

"I hope so. If I need more than six, call the paramedics." Whack. "Ow!"

"DADDY!"

"No, I deserved that one. Sorry, Mr. Phillips," I said.

"You kids better get running before my husband decides to overrule me. Have fun."

✧✧✧

We came out as the bus pulled away. To my horror, John wasn't on the bus. He was talking to Marcy. My perfect evening for my first official threesome was going up in smoke. I was almost 100% sure Alice wasn't going to do anything in front of her brother. John saw the look on my face as we got near and started laughing.

"Don't worry, Dawson. I'm not here to mess up your plans. Alice would cut my nuts off with a rusty spoon if I did that. I'm just not the partying type. I'm going to head back to the hotel with Mom and Dad."

I thought about making another condom joke, but the last one got me smacked. I think the shtick had played itself out.

"I don't blame you. I really can't afford to mess around with drugs or alcohol during the season. My team has too much at stake for me to be doing something stupid."

He walked up to Alice and kissed her forehead. It was nice to see two siblings who really loved each other.

"Alice, you have a good time tonight. I'm not going to worry about you because you're with David. I know he'll treat you right."

"Thanks, John. I'm glad you introduced us. He really is trouble, isn't he?" she asked.

"Yes, he really is, but I know you can handle him. You've been handling me for the last sixteen years. Are you coming to the hotel tonight?"

She smiled.

"We'll see. Love you, big brother."

"Love you too."

We walked to Marcy's dorm. I swear she was skipping. When we got there, we had to sign in. We took the elevator to Marcy's floor, and when we got off there were fifty or so people milling around. Three of the dorm rooms had been turned into bars. The good news was the girl-to-guy ratio was fifty to one. The bad news was I was getting a lesbian vibe from about half of the girls. I found it funny when Alice plastered herself to my side. I think she didn't like the appreciative looks some of the girls were giving her.

We worked our way to Marcy's room. When we got there, she threw a red scarf over the lamp to give us some mood lighting. The roommates had worked out a way of using bungee cords to make their two beds into one large one. I could see Marcy was starting to hesitate. It was one thing to think about a guy going down on you. It was another to go through with it. I let go of Alice's hand, closed in on Marcy and pulled her into my arms.

I whispered in her ear.

"Don't worry, Baby. This isn't going to be weird or uncomfortable. You're a sexy girl, and I'm going to give you one climax after another until you tell me to stop. I promise you'll have fun. Now take your clothes off so I can give you what you need."

Where that came from, I'll never know. I felt her shiver in my arms and then she pulled away and stripped. Nothing sexy, she just took off her clothes. While she did that, I took off everything but my boxers. I pulled out the bag of condoms and put them on the bedside cabinet. If they were needed, I wanted them handy. She crawled onto the bed and settled in. I followed and crawled on top of her and let my weight settle. I wanted her to feel all of me as I kissed her.

We just kissed gently for the next few minutes. Nothing was rushed or frantic. I think she expected me to mount her as soon as we entered the room, but I really did want to practice pleasing a woman. Tonight was all about their pleasure. I could tell when Marcy started to become aroused when she moaned into my kiss and allowed her legs to open so my hips could settle between her legs. I rolled off to the side so I'd have access to her body. I allowed my hands to explore as I found all her little trigger points.

I broke our kiss so my lips and tongue could help my hands heighten her arousal. I felt the bed shift as Alice crawled on. I was disappointed to see she'd found her panties and put them back on, but that was all she had on. Her body was every teen boy's wet dream. Her long firm legs came together to form God's gift to butt-lovers. If I hadn't promised Marcy she was first, I would have tackled Alice. I smiled at Alice.

"Are you ready to see her pleasured again and again?"

Alice's eyes got big and she nodded yes.

"Marcy, you ready to go to heaven?" I asked.

"I'm so close right now. Please make me happy, you've been teasing me forever."

I moved down so my head was between her legs. I allowed my hot breath to bathe the inside of her legs. I lifted her thighs so her womanhood opened for me and her knees were around her shoulders. I didn't do anything until I felt her relax. Once she did, I trailed my hand down her jaw and she moaned.

"Humphhh."

I went to work on what I'd been taught. It was almost too easy. Three, two, one, SCORE!

"AAAACK! GAAWD! OOOOOOHHHH CRAAAAP! Huuumpphhhh."

Alice was looking at me as if I were evil incarnate. Marcy twitched at odd intervals as she recovered. I smiled at Alice.

"Round 2," I said.

I went back to work, nibbling and licking all around her sex. When she started to get close, I attacked her bud. I let my tongue strum her in a rapid one, two, three, four rhythm. She found her own rhythm.

"Oh Gawd Damn, OH GAWD DAMN, OHGAWDDAMN, AAAAAAAHHHHHH!"

I stopped when she began to breathe as if she were an old-style freight engine as it struggled up the side of a too-steep mountain. I started to worry she'd pass out on me. She was covered in a light sheen of sweat that made her body glisten erotically in the low light. Her hair was a tangled mess from her throwing her head from side to side. When her breathing finally slowed down, I crawled up by her ear so I could whisper.

"Are you ready for Round 3?"

She took her hand and slapped the mattress twice.

"Marcy, are you tapping out? Are you done?" I asked.

She nodded and curled up into a ball. I picked her up and moved her to the side of the bed. She was sound asleep when I laid her down.

Alice smiled at me.

"Dammit, David, no guy who looks as good as you do should eat the peach like that."

I reached down, grabbed Marcy's panties, and wiped my face off. I lay down so I faced Alice.

"Did that scare you a little bit?"

She bit her lower lip.

"Would you rather we made love?" I asked.

"Is that okay, David? I'm not sure I'm ready for what you did to Marcy. I've never had anyone do that to me before."

"But you have made love?"

She was acting all shy, like a little girl. It started to be sexy as hell. She nodded.

"I'm really horny right now. Are you ready for me?" I asked.

In answer, she peeled down her panties. I pulled my boxers down, letting my member slap against my stomach. I pulled Alice into an embrace, and my manhood pressed between our bellies. I felt the heat from her tight little body everywhere we touched. It felt intimate. We were almost there. I reached to grab a condom but she stopped me.

"Baby, are you sure? Are you protected?"

"Yes, I just want to feel you."

I *really* wanted to make this right. I seemed to fall for girls very fast, and Alice was catching me off guard. When I first met her, I figured we would goof off and tease John. The most I'd been hoped for was to make a new friend, but every time she looked at me and we touched, I felt us get closer. With her willing body under me, I felt myself opening up to her so I could give her my all.

I suddenly thought of Tracy. I think I loved her, but she kept pushing us just outside the relationship zone. We were in the 'everything but' zone. We had sex that was unfrickinbelievable. Tracy's body was a solid ten. I loved her parents and we are all good friends. Hell, Tami even liked her. If she would let me, I would commit to her in heartbeat.

I then remember that Tracy and I were on a break, and why. Right then I knew Tracy and I weren't going to make it in the short run. Down the road, maybe, but as rebound guy there was no way. I got the vibe she was scared of a relationship right now, and the closer I got, the more she'd push me away. I was sure we'd be friends. Maybe even friends with benefits; but we wouldn't be lovers for quite a while.

Alice had come out of left field and knocked me off-kilter.

"Look, a condom isn't just to protect you from getting pregnant. Let me do right thing here," I urged.

She nodded and I put one on. I kissed her with all the passion I felt; her hips lifted up, and her legs spread. I slid back until my member was free and the tip settled into the folds of her sex. The head began to stretch her entrance. In one smooth motion, I eased half my length into her hot little oven. When I stopped, she exhaled loudly as I moaned in pleasure.

"Oh, David," she moaned in my ear, and I felt I was close.

I heard myself moaning.

"You're perfect."

"So good."

I could see the signs of arousal. I slowly started to move. She responded by wrapping her legs and arms around me so that she could get maximum contact with my body. Alice started to chant in my ear.

"Oh, David, I love this. Oh, David, I love this."

We had sex two more times over a two-hour period. The last one was just wild monkey sex. Sometime during the second one, Marcy got up and left the room to give us our privacy. When we finally collapsed, we cuddled and didn't say anything. We just enjoyed the afterglow of good sex.

Alice started to tremble. I wrapped my arms around her, suddenly concerned that something was terribly wrong.

"This shouldn't have happened. You weren't supposed to make me feel like this. It was just supposed to be friends having a good time. I want you so bad my chest hurts. I had one orgasm after another. You've ruined me. You're leaving in less than twelve hours. What am I supposed to do? At first, I thought it was just the sex talking, but I know it's more than that. Why did you make me feel so much? Why do I know I can't live without you?" she asked as her lips quivered.

I pulled her tight against my chest and just rocked her while she cried. She finally fell asleep in my arms. A little after midnight Marcy came in and crawled into bed with us. She snuggled up to my other side and fell asleep on my shoulder.

✧✧✧

Sunday September 29

I woke up and looked at the clock. Shit! It was 7:30 and we were supposed to meet everyone at eight.

"Wake up, girls, we need to get a move on."

I grabbed a towel and shampoo and sprinted to the showers. Both girls came into my shower and giggled as we hurried to wash each other. I'd had fantasies about two girls in a shower. This wasn't the time for it, though.

At least we weren't the last ones to show up. John gave us some funny looks. I would let him take it up with his sister. Alice was in a much better mood this morning. We just enjoyed the time we had. I'm not really sure about all that went on, because Alice and I were so focused on each other. When I had to leave, I walked her over to her mom and let her comfort her. I felt like hell having to leave her. I know I left a little piece of my heart behind.

✧✧✧

I met Tom at the hotel at ten and we checked out. We were airborne by eleven. Tom wanted to talk.

"So, how did you like Kentucky?"

"Don't get me wrong, I love the college and the people, but if I become good I want a shot at a national title. If Kentucky's even close, I would go there."

"Do you want to go to Florida sometime this fall?"

"I can't, it would jeopardize my standing with the NCAA. I can't have a booster fly me on their private jet. Especially since Kentucky has already made me an offer."

"What? They seriously made you an offer?"

"I know. I think they're crazy too. They told me my intangibles were off the charts. They loved my competitiveness, my focus and my leadership abilities. They told me to find a real quarterback coach, like yesterday. They were almost as happy as Joe was when they found out we run the veer option. They said in a worst-case scenario they would play me at fullback or switch me to defense. But the offer is solid as long as the coaching staff is there."

"What type of offense do they think you need to run?"

"They're suggesting a pro-style offense. They had Coach Lambert send them video. The staff watched me almost pull a rabbit out of a hat on Friday. We were trying to run the West Coast offense. They said it didn't fit my style. It needs a super-accurate short-range dink-and-dunk kind of guy. They liked it much better when I was throwing downfield. My mid to long throws are my strengths. I guess Coach Lambert is looking to find someone who can retool our offense without making us crash and burn. Kentucky has come up with no one. Maybe you can talk to your Florida contacts and see if they know of anyone."

"I'll call my boss and see if he can help. How did the thing with Marcy work out?"

"We had a good time. I actually met Lori Winnick. She's great. I also met Teddy Wesleyan. He owns the academy that Tami's going to attend. He helped get her the scholarship. I decided not to go to the party. I figured there'd be too much temptation to drink or do other things. I ended up going to Marcy's and spending the night, and before you ask, we didn't go all the way. Sorry, that may be more detail than you want."

"I'm sure Tracy will appreciate that." He saw my look and understood. "Just give her time. She loves you to death. She just needs to get her head on straight and let it happen."

"I know, Tom. I'll wait on her. She's worth it." I hope.

✧✧✧

Chapter 18 – There it is

Sunday September 29

I didn't call or text Tracy when I got back. I think Tom knew there was trouble in paradise, so he got one of the partners to drive us home. I stopped in, talked to my folks for a couple of minutes, and then told them I was going to go say goodbye to Tami. They told me that Uncle Jim was going to be arriving on Monday. I went up to my apartment, took a quick shower, and changed my clothes.

I sent Tami a text, grabbed my bike, and rode over. Today was truly a day to celebrate. One of our own was escaping our small town. Most of us fled once we graduated high school. I think the biggest fear was you would become a lifer. My goal had always been to escape with Tami. She was just getting to do it sooner.

I stopped at Jerry's Ice Cream and got a quart of vanilla and a container of hot fudge. I knew Tami and her mom loved Jerry's soft serve. As I paid, I got a text that let me know Tracy was at Tami's house. I suddenly didn't want to go. This afternoon was for talking things out with Tami. A big part was what I should do about Tracy. It wouldn't be possible to be open if she was there. I suddenly felt cheated. I guess it was my own fault for not getting a ride from Tracy when I got home.

I wouldn't let our issues get in the way of my saying goodbye. The emotions of the day finally caught up with me and I felt sad. My best friend would be moving an hour and a half away. I know we joked about me coming to see her, but we both knew I didn't have a car. The only way I could do it was by either train or bus.

Tracy's Mustang was parked at the curb. I pulled my bike into Tami's garage and walked in the back door. A long time ago, we started to treat each other's homes as if they were our own. Neither one of us even thought about knocking. I went to the cabinet that held the bowls and got out four. I made ice cream with fudge for all of us. I found Mrs. Glade watching TV in the living room. I handed her a bowl and a spoon and leaned down to let her kiss my cheek. It was our little ritual.

There was no Mr. Glade. She had found herself pregnant as a senior in college and had broken up with Tami's father a few weeks before she found out. Their breakup had been bad, so she never told him about Tami. When Tami was 12, she decided she wanted to meet her father, but he wouldn't see her. I remember finding her crying at odd times for a while after that. I'd just hold her, not knowing what else to do. We never talked about that now.

I went back to the kitchen and got the other three bowls. I didn't even ask. I just knew Tami was in her room. I was about to nudge the door open when I heard Tracy.

"I think I'm losing him. He's going places, and I'm afraid I'm going to hold him back," Tracy whined.

"Tracy, get your head out of the sand, David adores you. He already knows more than you give him credit for. He knows you're not perfect and that you have stuff you need to work through. Don't you realize his demons are just as big, if not bigger, than yours are? If you'd trust him, he could help you more than you know, and in turn, you can help him."

Tami had gotten herself worked up.

"It makes me sick when I see you pushing him away. Don't you know he's the greatest guy you'll ever meet? You two together could seriously have something. You're the perfect couple. But you're acting like a spoiled bitch, and you're going to mess this thing up."

Wow, I hadn't heard Tami this pissed since seventh grade when Jimmy Ellison tried to bean her in Little League. I had to pull her off him when she charged the mound. She was mad for weeks that I stopped her from kicking his butt. I still smiled when I thought about this little girl as she beat the heck out of the big stud athlete. I made a point not to mess with her after that.

"Look, Tracy, he and I need to talk when he gets here. I'll talk him into giving you another chance. If I know him, he'll bring us ice cream. When we're done I need you to leave."

"Okay. I know you need to say goodbye. My mom keeps telling me I'm getting in the way of our relationship. I think my mom and dad would like to date him. I'm just feeling a lot of pressure. Is it okay if I call you about David? I know he's your friend first and foremost, but I need advice," Tracy said.

"Call me anytime. If I feel uncomfortable I'll tell you, and we can figure it out from there," Tami said, then paused. "David's a smart boy. Don't tell him I said that." They both laughed. "He knows I talk to you. He also knows I only want what's best for him. He trusts me. I take that trust very seriously because he gives it to me unconditionally; so you're right, I will probably always side with him, and I think you know that. But that doesn't mean I can't be your friend as well."

I went back down the hall and made some noise. Tami opened the door and let me in. She looked at the ice cream and realized it was a little melted. She smirked at me because she knew I'd eavesdropped. I made a point to go up to Tracy and give her a hug and a kiss.

We settled in and ate our ice cream. It was a little quiet, so I figured I needed to get the conversation started.

"I met Lori Winnick last night."

Both of them looked at me to see if I was lying. Tracy looked at Tami.

"I call bullshit," Tracy said.

Tami looked at me and nodded.

"Nope, he's telling the truth. I think we want a little more detail than that."

"She was at the University of Kentucky's President's home for an alumni fundraiser. I talked to Teddy Wesleyan about you getting a scholarship to his school."

Tracy was about to call bullshit on that one. Tami stopped her.

"Nope, he's still telling the truth."

Tracy shook her head.

"How do you know that? Next he'll tell us that he found a couple of chicks and had a hot threesome."

Tami looked at me and snorted. She'd better not confirm that one. Tami was my human lie detector. She'd been able to look at me and tell if I told her the truth since I was eleven. I'd had to stop playing cards with her because she could read me so well. Thank God, she covered for me about the threesome.

"I'm not sure about that one, but he has even bigger news, don't you, David."

It wasn't a question, but a statement.

"I had a tryout with both Kentucky and Florida for football. Florida has agreed to start recruiting me."

Tracy screamed, jumped into my lap and gave me one of her mind-erasing kisses. I smiled at Tracy when her kiss finally stopped. We looked into each other's eyes with our foreheads touching.

"Come on, David. Give her the really big news," Tami said.

"The University of Kentucky offered me a football scholarship to play quarterback."

"There it is."

"How did you know there was more?" Tracy asked as she turned to Tami.

"Simple: up to the Kentucky offer, David meeting Lori Winnick didn't tie the story together."

We finished our ice cream, and I promised Tracy I'd call her when I left Tami's house. I could tell Tracy didn't want to leave, but she knew she couldn't get between us saying our last goodbye. We walked her to her car, and I again promised to call her. I guess we're having our talk tonight.

✧✧✧

When we came back to Tami's room, she pulled me into her arms and just held me. I picked her up, lay her on her bed, kicked my shoes off and got in bed with her. As soon as I was on my back, she crawled on top of me and wrapped me in a bear hug. Her head came to rest on my chest. I heard her chuckle.

"I thought you were going to crap when she guessed about the girls. Do you have pictures?"

"You're awful. You know me too well."

I handed her my phone. She could get to the pictures faster than I could.

"How many girls were chasing you? Are those twins?"

I told her about our run. Then she found a picture of John Phillips.

"Who's the hunk?"

"That's John Phillips, All State quarterback and all-around nice guy. You'll like him. I think he and I are going to be good friends."

"I'll say I like him, he's really cute. Good lord, you did his sister, didn't you? Don't even answer that."

How she figures things out was a mystery to me. She flipped through and found one of Marcy in a ball.

"What the heck did you do to this one?"

"I pleasured her until she begged me to stop."

Then her eyes got big.

"What's John's sister's name?"

"Alice."

"You're screwed. That girl loves you. What're you going to do about it?"

"Same thing I'm going to do with you?"

"What, sleep with me and then leave me?" Tami asked.

"If that's what you want."

She got very quiet. This had been building for the past week. Tami had gotten bolder and bolder with her sexual advances. I knew she would do the right thing for both of us, so I hadn't worried about it, but I knew that she was working herself up to something. We had never crossed a certain line because of our friendship.

Tami wasn't afraid to experience anything. I loved her adventurous side. I'd have missed out on so much if she hadn't dragged me along. Sex was the first thing that I had done first. I regretted not being here this summer, because I was sure she would have taken my cherry if I had been.

I know when we did make love it would mean the world to both of us. There'd never been any doubt in either of our minds that someday it would happen. Tami told me once we would someday not just be together, but she would marry me and we would have three kids. I was sure she knew if they were boys or girls and the names of our future children. She thought I was too much of a 'stupid boy' for us to be together now. She was in this for the long haul and planned to be the last girl I was ever with.

Our feelings for each other went far beyond just friends. They had grown since we declared our love for each other at Beth's. If I thought that for a moment we could have our relationship now, I'd drop all other girls in a heartbeat. My attraction to her was beyond the normal boyfriend-girlfriend thing. This was born from an almost lifelong conversation. Being this close and knowing what might happen had caused my chest to tighten. I could feel the raw emotions just below the surface.

I think this last week had been about Tami exploring her sexual side. She was about to leave and wanted me to be her first. She knew I would treat her right. My own sexual awakening had been the catalyst. She'd made a point to talk to every one of my partners. Anyone else doing that would have pissed me off. If I knew her, she'd talked to them in great detail.

Tami got out of bed and started to get undressed. I followed suit. As soon as she was naked, she pulled my head down and kissed me. I got out a condom and put it on. She laid back on the bed and spread her legs as an invitation. We didn't say anything. We no longer needed words. I started kissing her all over. She stopped me.

"David, I want you in me now."

I smiled at her.

"Tami, for once, shut up. This is something I'm good at; let me make it special for you."

She moaned deep in her throat as my hand slid slowly up the inside of her thigh in an electrifying caress that culminated with my long, lean fingers stroking her. I felt her sex part and she was wet and hot, waiting for me. She had craved me for the past week. I could tell my lips made her squirm. Tami was almost as responsive to my touches, licks, and sucks as my Princess. My touches set her on fire. I decided not to tease her and pushed her through her first orgasm. I could tell she was close, so I let my tongue caress her sex to help her through her first release.

I wasn't counting on Tami being a screamer.

"David! What are you doing to me?"

I didn't realize I was holding my breath. I let it out in one long, slow breath. I was sure Tami was in for a talking-to later since her mom couldn't have missed hearing her moan, but now was about us saying goodbye.

Tami started to come back to me when I attacked her with everything I'd learned. My Princess had been a very good tutor. Tami soon had several small releases, and I could tell she was building to a big one. When she was just on the edge, I stopped.

"That's it," I said in my best Barry White voice. "Show me how much you want me."

She was right on the edge. Tami was very athletic, so when she grabbed me by the ears and pulled me up to kiss her, I was in position to enter her as the tip found her slot. I wasn't concerned about any problems with our first time. I was there when she fell on my bike and that issue went away. I also knew that she wasn't the type to do slow and easy. I slid up and slowly entered her.

"Yes! We are really doing this," Tami cried.

I looked at her as if she were possessed. I waited for her head to spin around and her to levitate off the bed. I started to move, which caused her to have an orgasm. I watched in amazement as she began to have more. She started to roll through another and another and another. I'd never seen someone have multiple orgasms so close together. The whole time her headboard slammed against the wall, and she wailed as if I were killing her. Crap, her mom had to hear that. If I hadn't been so involved now, I would've died of embarrassment.

Tami grabbed my face and forced me to look her in the eyes. She had an expression on her face I'd never seen before: raw lust. I drowned in the pools of her brown eyes. I felt our connection deepen in ways I'd previously only hoped for; I was deeply, madly in love with Tami Glade, and she was in love with me. Her legs started to curl back until her knees almost touched her shoulders.

She got a fierce look on her face.

"Yes … faster… Yes … Yes … harder …" Tami chanted over and over again.

I couldn't last much longer as I felt myself build to a tremendous release. My abdomen screamed as I followed her commands. Sweat dripped off my nose as my hips continued to swing. I had no idea that sex could be so physical. Suddenly Tami closed her eyes, her whole body went rigid, and her legs shot straight out. She then started to shake as I pumped a couple more times to bring myself over the edge. She made a strangled sound as we both shuddered in our sweet release. When we were done, we were both rag dolls as we collapsed into each other's embrace.

"Jesus, that was intense. And you waited to do this until right before you leave," I scolded her.

I had always known this would be magical. Tami and I had a connection that was going to make sex addictive. I rolled off her so I didn't crush her. I grabbed my boxers and headed to the bathroom to dispose of the condom and to grab a warm washcloth. Thankfully, Mrs. Glade had made herself scarce. I came back and gave Tami the washcloth.

She gave me a sheepish smile.

"You were right. You're better at that than I am."

"What? We need to mark our calendars. Did Tami Glade just admit that David Dawson was better at something than she was?"

She held up her hands in defeat.

"I'll admit that you're the master—for now."

"I can't wait until you're better at this than I am. I think we'll end up killing each other when that happens," I said as I gave her a wink, and headed back to the bathroom.

I got in the shower and cleaned up. By the time I got back, Tami was in shorts and t-shirt. She and her mom were laughing. It was almost five, so I went downstairs and made tomato soup and grilled cheese sandwiches, two of our favorites. I took everything upstairs.

"Then he tells me to shut up, he's better at this than I am, and let him make it special for me. I'm glad I let him take charge," Tami shared.

I gave up. I would never understand women. Both laughed, so I figured I would survive.

"Look, he made us dinner," Tami said.

There were rules about grilled cheese sandwiches and tomato soup. The soup must be served in a coffee mug and you dunked your sandwich. Once the grilled cheese sandwich was gone, you then drank the soup. No spoons needed. During dinner, they didn't talk about what had just happened and I didn't talk about my issues with Tracy. Tami knew I'd overheard their conversation and trusted me to take it from there. I also didn't want to bring up someone else right after we just possibly had the best sex of my life.

After dinner, I took the cups downstairs to wash. I was cleaning up the kitchen when Mrs. Glade came up behind me and wrapped me in a bear hug, similar to what Tami did. I just stood there and let her bury her face into my back. I then felt her shaking and I knew she was crying. I twisted in her embrace, pulled her into my arms, and kissed her cheek.

"You know I love her. If she'd have me, I'd marry her tomorrow, but we both know that we need to grow up. Actually, I need to grow up. When that happens, we'll be together for the rest of our lives. Mrs. Glade, I want you to know I think of you as my family. If there is ever anything you need, please let me know. Even if it's just to talk about missing our girl."

Tami had heard the whole thing and rushed in, and we sandwiched her mom in between us.

"I love you, Tami Glade."

"I love you, David Dawson. Hurry up and grow up so I can marry you."

"When you think I'm ready, you let me know and I'll make it happen."

"Okay, deal."

Her mom looked at the clock. It was time for them to go. I hauled out the last bags and we had a long, tearful kiss. Tami got in the car and I watched as she disappeared down the street. It felt like a piece of my heart had left me, but I knew that at some point it would come back.

✧✧✧

I got home to find my mom and dad in my apartment, drinking a glass of wine. I smiled when I saw them. Only one thing would make them flee the house.

"Let me guess: Uncle Jim came early."

My mom smirked.

"He got it in one. Greg's already threatening to move in with you. We told him we have first dibs. Your dad plans to replace this couch with a futon or hide-a-bed."

I decided to change the subject because I knew my mom was serious. If I weren't careful, they *would* move in, so I told them about my weekend. I don't think Mom and Dad realized I actually might be good at football. Neither of them was really into sports other than my dad watching it on TV. I would need to invite them to a game so they could see me play.

My phone rang, and it was Tami.

"Hey, Coward, call Tracy."

"Okay."

I hung up and dialed Tracy.

"Hey, Gorgeous. How was your weekend?"

She was not in the mood to chat.

"Can I come over?"

"Sure. Mom and Dad are hanging out in my apartment, having some wine. We'd love to have you."

"Okay, see you in ten."

Well, shit. The parental units didn't even slow her down. I guess we would have this conversation tonight. I quickly gave my parents the Reader's Digest version of what was going on with Tracy and me. I explained my rebound theory and how she gave me the green light for the weekend. I told them about Alice, and then that Tami and I had finally gotten together.

My mom poured herself another glass of wine.

"You're a bigger slut than your brother."

My dad just buried his head in his hands.

"She'll be here in about four minutes. Any advice?" I asked.

"Do you think that if this wasn't a rebound, you might get serious with her?" Mom asked.

"Yes, she's everything I'm looking for."

"Then break up with her."

"What?" Tracy and I said at the same time.

Tracy came in and she sat down next to me. My mom may not have the smoothest way of saying things, but she was usually right. We both looked at her and waited for her explanation.

"You're both great kids. I can see where you'd be crazy-attracted to each other, and if what I hear coming out of that window is any indication, your sexual chemistry is great. But you're both damaged goods. If you try to make a go of it, one of you is going to do something ridiculously stupid and possibly ruin your relationship from ever working in the long term. David says that you two could have something special. I tend to agree. But right now may not be the best time for either of you."

She turned to Tracy.

"You're going to keep playing this non-relationship card until you drive him away."

She turned on me.

"You aren't going to keep it in your pants."

I wouldn't touch that comment with a ten-foot pole. Tracy and I both blushed as we realized that the elephant in the room had been pointed out concerning both of us.

"You're 15 and 16 years old. Back off the relationship and let yourselves be friends for now. When you both have healed, then get back together." Mom said with a scowl. "But I know you, David. You aren't going to take my advice. I just hope you two don't mess up so bad that when you break up you can never come back together. You two have strengths in different areas. Together you'll make each other a better version of yourselves."

Mom grabbed my dad's hand.

"Come on, Daddy-O. I think I've had enough wine to handle my brother now. You and Greg may want to go grab an ice cream. I'm about to lay down the law and reclaim our house."

When my parents left, Tracy and I just held each other. I knew we weren't going to follow my mom's advice. Someday I may wish I had. I gave us until Thanksgiving. Until then I would enjoy every moment with Tracy I could get. I decided to stop asking for a relationship. I would focus on what we did well together, make myself the Big Man on Campus that she wanted, and have lots of sex. We could agree on those three things. If I had enough sex with her, the problem of my wandering would go away.

✧✧✧

Chapter 19 – I Can't Do This Alone

Monday September 30

I woke to find Tracy still in my arms. We didn't talk last night. We simply held each other until we started to make out. Our lovemaking the previous evening had been gentle. It had brought us closer together, but in the backs of our minds, I think we both knew that our relationship was running on borrowed time. The problem with knowing a relationship might be ending is it puts you on guard. No one wanted to get hurt. With that in mind, I kissed Tracy awake.

"Morning, Stud. I think I like waking up this way."

"I'd love to wake you every morning with a kiss. Of course, at some point your dad's going to have my balls when he figures out your sleepovers are with me."

"Tami's right; you are a 'stupid boy.' Dad knows exactly where I am."

I let that just roll over me.

"I need to tell you a few things about the weekend."

I saw her eyebrows inch together for a fraction of a second. She was good at hiding her emotions. If I hadn't looked for it, I would never have noticed her concern.

"I was with three girls this weekend, one of which you may not be happy about."

Now she wasn't hiding her concern. I could see her puzzling it out. Her eyes snapped up.

"Tami," she guessed.

"Yes."

"Do you love her?"

"Yes, I think I've always loved her. I'm not sure if it was a one-time thing, but we're not together. If we ever get together, it'll be way down the road. I want to be clear though, that if she should ever ask, I would sleep with her again."

I could see a kaleidoscope of emotions cross her face. It took her several minutes to work through her feelings on this. I think she realized that if Tami asked, I was hers. The question was, would Tami ever ask? I stayed quiet to allow her to work through what I had just told her.

"David, I need to think about you and Tami. I take it that the other two were when you were at Kentucky."

"Yes."

"Look, I can't complain about those. We were on a break. Hell, technically we were still on a break when you slept with Tami. But we both know Tami's not just any other girl."

"You're right, she's not. Can I suggest something?"

"If it'll help, I'm all ears."

"Call Tami. She'll be honest with you and let you know where things stand." I chuckled. "And when you find out, let me know."

That got a smile out of her. Then she got a concerned look on her face.

"How many girls have you slept with?"

I looked her right in the eye.

"I won't tell you who, but are you sure you want a count?"

She nodded. I went through the list in my head. Tina was my first, and then Suzanne. I wasn't sure if Cindy counted. I think I would just count actual orgasms. Either I gave them an orgasm or they gave me one, so that left Cindy off the list. There was Tracy, Tami, and the two girls at Kentucky.

"Six, counting you," I told her.

She was taking this in when it dawned on her that I might want to know her count; that caused her to blush.

"Do you want to know my count?"

"Actually, absolutely not," I told her.

I glanced at the clock and saw I needed to get downstairs for my run with Peggy.

"I want us to work out. I have serious feelings for you. Right now, I need to get downstairs, because Peggy will be here in a few minutes for our run. Can we get together after school and really figure this out?"

"Yes, let's do that."

✧✧✧

I took a quick shower. When I came back, Tracy was gone. I got dressed and found Peggy waiting. She decided today was a distance day. We were in a good rhythm and just ran. There was something about running where you could clear your mind. Normally Peggy was chatty, but I think she sensed my mood and left me to my own thoughts. I finally noticed that Peggy was starting to tire, and she was giving me a funny look.

"What?" I asked defensively.

"You do realize that we just passed the ten-mile mark?"

I was shocked because I didn't even feel winded. I'd just settled into an easy pace that seemed to eat up time and distance. I actually felt refreshed after I'd allowed my mind to relax and come to some decisions.

"Shit, you're kidding me."

The most we'd ever done was six miles for our morning run.

"Nope. You were in such a zone I just kept us going. We don't have a meet this week, so I was enjoying the run also." Peggy ran cross-country.

We jogged back to my house and stretched. She came up to my apartment and I got her a Gatorade. Peggy wasn't meeting my eyes.

"You need to find someone else to run with you."

"What, did I do something wrong?" I asked.

I loved to run with Peggy. In addition, I still had a huge crush on her.

"Settle down. I love running with you, but you need someone to push you. Your pace today was 15 seconds per mile faster than I normally run, and you were just gliding. You need someone who can push you closer to a five-minute mile pace. I still want to run with you on freestyle days, but I can't get you to where you need to be on distance days."

"Okay, I'll talk to my trainer and let her know. I'm going to go take a shower. Why don't you start bringing a bag and you can just shower here? Greg can take us to school. That'll save you a trip home."

"Won't Tracy mind?" she asked.

"I can't see why. It's not as if she doesn't already know you've seen me naked. If she had a problem, I'd have heard about it by now."

"Okay, I'll bring my bag tomorrow."

When I got out of the shower, Peggy was gone. I sent a text to Tami and wished her a good day. I sent another text to my Uncle John to let him know I was offered a scholarship to Kentucky. I sent one to Alan and Jeff to let them know I was going to be at lunch today. They'd felt a little uncomfortable without me there. They weren't yet used to my jock and cheerleader friends. I sent a final text to Lily to see if she'd help me set up a Facebook page for my recruiting.

✧✧✧

I was zoned out in second period World History when one of the office secretaries gave the teacher a note.

"Mr. Dawson, you're to report to Coach Lambert's office."

Everyone gave me looks as I packed up my things. I'd never been summoned to the Coach's office during school before. I ran through all the possible reasons I would be called to his office. I decided to go with the flow. I found

Coach Lambert's door closed. I was undecided as to what to do when the door suddenly opened.

"Come on in, Son."

Coach indicated a chair for me to sit in. He was quiet for several moments.

"Magic has broken his middle finger and won't be back for at least three games. The coaching staff has agreed that our best option is to have you play quarterback."

I figured they would bring the JV quarterback in to play varsity. He at least had a year under his belt, as he had played freshman ball. I was grateful for the opportunity.

"Coach, I'll do my best."

"I know you will. The problem is we've decided that if you're going to start, we'll need to change our style of play. If we do that, then Magic won't be coming back to play quarterback."

My heart sank. I didn't want to do anything to hurt my friend. He had a potential scholarship offer based on his football skills. Without the scholarship, he'd most likely go to the local junior college, because it was cheaper.

"Son, I know what it means to Magic and his family. To be honest, he was a long shot to get a scholarship. The recruiters aren't looking for a veer-option quarterback. I sat down with him and his family on Sunday to map out his options. He has a much better shot of getting a scholarship playing cornerback. If he switches now, he can play immediately."

"Is he okay with this?"

Coach smiled.

"Actually, he's fine with it. He just loves the game, and even Kevin is pleased to see an offensive player coming to defense. I never thought I would see that."

"What did you need me for?"

"Joe Phips found us a coach who might help us. He's asked to see you run some drills before he agrees. At first, I told Joe a thing or two. But he sent me this guy's résumé, and the list of quarterbacks he's coached reads like a 'who's who' list."

"Who is he?"

"Bo Harrington."

"When does he get here?"

"The tryout is scheduled for noon. He's flying in. If he likes you, he has plans of moving here temporarily. Coach Engels has agreed to put him up for the rest of the season."

"Is Bill free to help?"

Bill was the junior receiver that I'd been working with on the scout team.

"Yep, he's getting dressed as we speak. Why don't you get changed; we're going to do this in shorts and t-shirts. Don't forget your helmet."

I found Bill in the locker room. I remembered my promise to Alan and Jeff and sent a text to tell them what I was doing. Bill looked nervous.

"What the hell is your problem? You look like you've never done this before."

He gave me a sheepish grin.

"Up yours, Double D. This is my shot to play, and I don't want to mess it up."

I cuffed him on the back of the head.

"Come on. I'm going to throw some balls at you and see if you can still catch them, before it's showtime."

I took Bill out to the football field and we started to run some patterns. I had him run through the workout I did for the University of Kentucky. I heard the noon bell ring and still no Coach or Bo Harrington. Bill caught everything I threw at him.

"I'm going to put some heat on a few. Think you can catch 'em?"

"You bet."

Bill started with a basic buttonhook. As soon as he broke, the ball was in his chest and bounced three yards away.

I heard someone behind me.

"Shit, that's going to leave a mark."

Bill was rubbing his chest.

"I know, you warned me it was coming. It was my fault," Bill said.

I had expected someone who was retired or close to it. It turned out Bo Harrington was in his mid-thirties. He came up and shook my hand.

"You must be David."

"Coach Harrington?"

"Yes, sorry. Coach Lambert and I have been up in the press box watching you run your drills. What I haven't seen is something long. It's Bill, right?" Bill nodded. "Can you run a deep post, say 35 yards?"

"Yes, sir."

Bill ran down about 15 yards and broke for the post. He was at full speed, so I lofted a soft one that he could run under. He pulled it in stride and jogged back.

Bo looked at me.

"Okay, I want you to put a little something on it this time. A ball in the air that long is going to draw a crowd, and you're going to get Bill killed."

Bill ran the same play, but this time I fired the ball on a rope. Bill snatched the football out of the air and came back to line up again. Coach Harrington had him come over to us instead. He looked at Bill.

"I just have a couple of questions, and I want Bill to answer them if you don't mind." We both nodded in agreement. "His balls don't sail or fall short?"

"It usually isn't that he throws high or low, it's he'll throw a fastball and it'll bounce off your helmet or pads."

"How is he at leading you? Do you have to wait for throws?"

"No, if anything he makes me hustle to catch up to a ball. But that's more me being lazy than where he puts the ball."

"Okay, that confirms what I saw in the game film." Bo turned to me. "David, are you willing to work your butt off?"

"What are we talking about?"

"You know, you're the first one who's ever asked me that. Usually I get a snap answer of yes. Let me guess, you get good grades too?"

"I do okay, A's and B's."

"Coach, don't let him fool you, he's a nerd," Bill offered.

"We're talking extra sessions working on your footwork, throwing motion, reading defenses, learning to make all the passes. Outside of what you're already doing, you'll be working two to four hours a day, and six to eight hours on the weekends."

"Aren't there rules against being coached only a certain number of hours?"

"If I was going to be working for the high school, yes, there would be, but you're going to hire me. You can have all the personal training you want."

"Okay, I'm a fifteen-year-old high school kid. How am I going to afford you?"

He looked at Bill.

"Go hit the showers, David and I need to talk."

Bill looked concerned, but he did as he was told.

"Okay, David, this is where we find out how serious you are. If you go to state and win, that's nine more weeks of football. I'll be working with you in practice through Coach Engels. We'll be spending an average six hours per day, seven days a week. That comes to a little over 375 hours of work. This will take me away from my other work to devote to your career. My normal billing rate is $125 per hour. Let's ballpark this at $50,000."

Crap! That was a lot of money for anyone, not just me.

"What about subsequent training throughout high school and college?"

"We can either do this on an hourly basis, or we can negotiate a set rate that won't exceed a certain number of hours."

"Okay, I know you know how old I am, and that I can't sign a contract with you. I also know my parents won't commit to something like this. How're we going to make this work?"

"There are benefactors who are willing to pick up my fees for this year. After that you and I would need to work something out."

I was worried about some things. I didn't want to feel obligated to someone to the tune of $50,000.

"Can we meet after practice and talk about this?"

Bo shook my hand and we agreed to meet. We exchanged contact information, and he told me he was scheduled to be at practice tonight to get things started. I went into the locker room to get my cell phone. I called Tami. She'd know what to do or who to call.

"Hey, Tami, I need your help."

"I'm kind of busy, can it wait?"

"No, give me five minutes, and then tell me what to do and I'll be out of your hair."

"It sounds serious."

"It kind of is."

I spent the next 15 minutes explaining it to Tami. She took a lot of notes and told me to go to class and she'd call me back. I was told to keep my phone on in case I had to deal with something right away. Coach Lambert gave me a note to give to my teachers to allow me to have my phone on during class. I was in time for English when my phone rang and it was Tami. I waited to answer until I was in the hall.

"I talked to Tom Dole, Tracy's dad, and he's agreed to be your lawyer. He'll do this pro bono. I emailed him a copy of Coach Harrington's resume and references. Mary has agreed to call them. Tom says to set up a meeting for seven, and have Coach Harrington meet you at Tom and Mary's."

"Anything else?" I asked as I took notes.

"Are you sure you want to have this guy help you?"

"I don't know yet. He's going to be at practice today. I guess I'll know more after that. You read some of the testimonials. What do you think?"

"If he's for real, then I'd do it. Think of it as a scholarship. I'm able to pursue my dream because I'm getting financial aid. Let Tom help guide and keep you out of any eligibility problems."

I could hear someone calling her.

"Hey, David, I have to go. Call me after your meeting."

I went back to English and tried to focus on what was being taught, but I failed. The good news was I had forgotten about my problems with Tracy.

✧✧✧

Mondays are usually a light practice where we're introduced to the upcoming opponent. It was also a heavy conditioning day. I hated Mondays because I got bored. Today was the exception. Coach Lambert started practice by introducing Bo Harrington and the staff change of Coach Engels taking over the Offensive Coordinator position. Magic was moved to defense. He then split the offense and defense up and let the defense do their usual preparation.

Then the offense was told to put on gym shoes and meet on the basketball court in shorts and t-shirts. As we came into the gym, we were handed new playbooks. Coach Engels had us gather together to explain the offensive scheme change.

"We're changing our offense to be more pass-oriented. It was the coaches' decision that David wasn't ready to run the veer. Normally we wouldn't change a scheme just for one player. We looked at bringing up a quarterback from the JV or freshman teams, but it was decided that wouldn't work. Friday's game against Eastside convinced us our best chance of making the playoffs is to play David and to play to his strengths. We've brought in an expert to get us up to speed in Bo Harrington. Let me turn this over to Coach Harrington."

"Earlier today I worked with David to see if he has what it takes to run this offense. After watching him throw, and also watching the game film, I found he has the skills to run this offense well enough for you to win. I'm considered a 'fixer' in the business. I come in and solve problems, be it a quarterback having confidence issues, recovering from injuries, throwing motions, and so on."

"What I'm going to do is get you all up to speed on the new offense. Your homework assignment is to take this playbook home and learn the first ten plays. Today we're going to work on a basic play, the down-and-out. We'll spend all practice running through all the variations that can be run against the defense you'll be facing Friday. This may seem like overkill, but what you learn in the gym today will apply to all the other plays we will put in this week."

"Tomorrow we'll take it to the field. The first half of practice will be devoted to the same play. We'll run it until we're comfortable with it. If this is the only play we learn this week, I'm fine with that, because we can win with it. For those that don't believe me, we'll run this play against your number-one defense on Wednesday. We'll run the play until they can stop it. What you'll find is they won't be able to."

"Are there any questions before we get started?" Coach Engels asked.

One of the current starting ends, Jim Davis, raised his hand.

"Coach, is there room for ends like Doug and I? I know when we were running the West Coast scheme we were deemed too big and slow."

Coach Harrington stepped forward.

"Actually, there are several places for big guys like you. First, you'll cause mismatches with smaller defensive backs. We'll also be playing a tight end. Your size and blocking ability will be needed there. Finally, we need a new fullback. He needs to be able to block and catch the ball. So don't worry, we have plans for your unique skills."

Coach Engels then described the new offense. He had a large markerboard to show the play designs.

"We're going to keep this simple. Our basic formation will be run out of the shotgun and use the run option, similar to how Eastside ran theirs. Most of you have the basics of that down, and we're confident that Luke and David can run that on the fly. We aren't scrapping our whole offense. Don't be surprised when we switch to running the veer offense under certain circumstances."

We spent the remainder of practice running the down-and-out and the variations for that play. My head hurt when we finally were done. It was already 6:30, so Coach Harrington just gave me a ride to the Dole's home. On the way, we picked up some fast food.

✧✧✧

We arrived at Tom and Mary's right at seven. Tracy answered the door.

"Hello, Gorgeous."

She slid into my arms and proceeded to erase my mind. I guess she really did it this time, because I heard Tracy's dad clear his throat to bring me back to the present.

We went to the living room and I introduced Bo to Tom, Mary and Tracy. Tracy wasn't letting go of my hand, so we sat down on the couch with her mom. Tom and Bo sat in two leather side chairs.

Tom started the meeting.

"Bo, Mary checked your references and we're impressed with the results. I have a couple of questions. The first is concerning the benefactors that are paying your fee. Are they affiliated in any way with a college?"

"It's my understanding they are all local businessmen and women that are doing this to support the high school football team. My contract isn't specifically for David, even though I'll be spending the majority of my time working with him."

"Do you have a copy of the contract I can review?"

"I have one with me. The only stipulation is that you may not share who's providing the backing."

"Okay, let me get a nondisclosure document put together and you and I can review the terms of the agreement. Are you okay with that, David?"

"I'm okay if you are. My concern is eligibility in college. Secondary is high school eligibility."

With that said, Tom and Bo went to Tom's office.

"Mom, can David and I have a moment?" Tracy asked. "We need to talk about a few things."

Her mom just smiled and went to the kitchen. I turned to Tracy.

"I had some time to think this morning while running. Let me say a few things and get them out, and then you can let me know what you think."

"Okay, I was hoping you'd go first."

"I bet you were." I kissed her. "First off, this non-relationship status is causing me some problems. After thinking about them, they're my problems and I've come to grips with them. Relationships fail because of expectations. If my expectation is that we're boyfriend and girlfriend, and yours is that we're just friends with benefits, we won't make it."

Tracy nodded.

"Okay, so what should we do about that?" she asked.

"Simple, either I accept your expectations or we end the relationship."

Her eyes got big and I kissed her before she got upset.

"Tracy, I've decided to accept your definition of our relationship. I know that if I pressure you it'll not end well. You'll feel trapped and resent me. My mom is right, one of us would do something stupid."

"David, I'm so relieved!"

"Hang on, we still have one major issue to work through, and that's me and other women. Are you okay with me having other friends with benefits, specifically Tami, Suzanne and possibly Cindy?"

I was worried because I wasn't willing to give her the same freedoms about this one. I couldn't handle the thought of her with another guy. Call me a hypocrite, but I wasn't wired to be able to think of her with another guy.

"Before I say yes or no, tell me about Suzanne."

"Suzanne and I are friends. She doesn't want a relationship. She does become sexually frustrated at times, and I help her out."

"Okay," Tracy said. "What about Cindy?"

"There's nothing right now. But I don't think it would take much for something to happen."

"I'm fine with that. I am also fine with Tami, even though I'm scared that I'll lose you to her. But I want you to tell me beforehand if you find anyone else. What about me, are you willing to allow me the same freedoms?"

"Tell you what: if either of us decides to sleep with someone else, we talk beforehand. If we do sleep with someone else, we also agree to use a condom. If either of us slips, we agree to full disclosure. The only way this is going to work is if we communicate."

"I can live with that. Are you okay with the non-relationship status?"

"Actually, I'm getting there. I think what I figured out was the uncertainty of where our relationship was going was causing us both to pull away. Tracy, I care about you. You're worth waiting for, and I hope you feel the same way," I told her with utmost sincerity.

"Let's put it this way: if my mom wasn't in the other room listening to our conversation, I'd be ripping your clothes off and showing you how much I care about you."

Her mom looked around the corner with a sheepish grin.

"I know I'm a terrible person. I just care about you both, and I want you to be happy."

Tracy got up and gave her mom a hug.

"I want to thank you for calling Bo's references. I'm assuming they were good," I said.

"Every one of them praised him and felt he helped them become better players. The only negative I heard was that he expected your focus to be 100% on football. It sounds like you're going to have to set some boundaries so you get your schoolwork done and have time for a social life."

We heard Tom and Bo laughing as they came out of the office.

"I pulled up the High School Association rulebook on the Internet and there are no rules against a paid consultant. The way the contract reads it's for the team, and not you. That being the case, I don't see any eligibility issues," Tom said.

"Tom, are there *any* issues I should worry about?" I asked.

"I read the contract and it doesn't pertain to you, so I think you're covered."

"Coach, what's next?"

"What's your schedule?"

"Sunday through Thursday I get up and run at six. On Sunday, I go to church. I have Pilates on Saturday at eleven. PE is weight lifting and conditioning."

"Starting tomorrow I want you at the high school at six. We need to start working on making you a quarterback. I'll also pull you out of PE and we'll work after practice. On Saturdays, we'll work out before Pilates. You'll have Saturday afternoon off unless you want to work on something. Sunday afternoon is film day. We'll watch game film and then also watch portions of your practice sessions."

I looked at everyone. It was sinking in that I was going to be buried in football for the next several weeks. I turned to Tracy.

"Are you going to be okay with this?"

She looked shocked that I would ask her.

"David, this is for you and your future. I don't have any right to comment on this."

"That's where you're wrong, Tracy. You're important to me, and if I'm going to do this I need your support and for you to be a part of this. I can't do this alone."

Her smile was like the sun coming out after a thunderstorm.

"Of course I'll support you. We'll figure this out together."

"Sounds like we need to celebrate. I baked an apple pie," Mary said.

I looked at Bo.

"Mary's the best cook. It'd be a mistake not to try her pie."

We spent another hour at the Doles'. I wasn't a big coffee drinker, but with apple pie and a scoop of vanilla ice cream, I loved everything. I think by the end of our dessert Tom was worried I'd run off with Mary.

Tracy gave me a ride home and we talked for hours. I sent a text to Peggy to let her know that our running plans were on hold. Tami sent me a text, and Tracy and I jumped onto video chat and gave Tami an update. She let us know what her class schedule was and about her roommates. She loved the campus, and I could tell she was excited. Our lives had chosen to pull us apart for now, but good things were happening.

✦✦✦

Tuesday October 1

Tracy's period had started earlier today, so we just cuddled and fell asleep in each other's arms. At 5:30, we got up, and she dropped me off at the school before she went home. I was on the field by six.

I was met by Coach Harrington and a video crew. They had three cameras set up. One camera was on a ladder behind me, one at my side, and the last was pointed at my feet in front of me.

"We're going to have you drop back and pass the ball 20 times. I'm filming it so you can see what you're doing. We'll then start making some adjustments."

Bo pointed to garbage cans he'd put at different points on the field. They had numbers lying in front of them. They were placed in each spot the down-and-out play would have receivers.

"I'll toss you a ball as if it's snapped to you, and then you'll listen for the number I call out. Your job is to make the throw to the appropriate garbage can."

We quickly ran the drill. By the end, I was feeling good because I had hit the target on the last eight balls. It was harder than it looked to throw a football 25 yards and put it into a garbage can. Some of the cans were tilted up so you had to drop them gently or they bounced out. The video was downloaded to Bo's laptop and we went through it pass-by-pass. I have to say, the next hour and a half was very informative. To his credit, Coach Harrington didn't point out everything that was wrong. He just pointed out a couple of flaws that we could work on this week.

The good news was I was now very coachable. I think that was the point of this exercise. Too many people counted on me. Everyone from Coach Lambert to my teammates to the community somehow were invested in how well I'd play. Even Coach Harrington had something on the line that was directly related to how I played quarterback.

✧✧✧

I took a shower and went to Coach Lambert's office. He motioned me in and I sat down. He was finishing a call.

"Yes, he just came in. I'll see you in a minute," he said when he hung up. "Coach Harrington is joining us."

We only had to wait a short time and Coach Harrington came in and shut the door behind him.

"How was this morning's training?" Coach Lambert asked.

"After watching the film, I realized how far I have to go," I admitted.

"Good to hear. Is there anything I can do to help?" Coach Lambert asked.

"Actually, there is. Can you show me what we're working towards, so I can have something to compare my progress to? I'm not talking about comparing against what I can achieve in the next few weeks. I want to compare against the best."

Coach Harrington pulled out his laptop.

"You have PE right after lunch. Come back here for PE. I wanted to show Coach Lambert this morning's film. I'll also show you both what we're working towards. Now get out of here."

✧✧✧

I was the first one to our lunch table. Today was some kind of gray mystery meat in gravy over runny pseudo-mashed potatoes. I felt my stomach rumble, so I took the gamble. Greg was the first one to join me.

"Hey, Bro, long time no see. How's Uncle Jim?" I teased him.

I'd lucked out and hadn't seen Uncle Jim for more than five minutes. He was the baby of the family and acted as if everyone should take care of him. We all loved him, but he was the most self-centered person I knew. Greg gave me the finger.

"He's the biggest slob alive, and he snores. I swear Mom's going to kick his ass."

"I'd like to see that."

Alan and Jeff sat down.

"Hey, guys," I said.

"Nice of you to grace us with your presence," Jeff said, giving me a hard time.

"So how was Kentucky?" Alan asked, digging for dirt.

"Okay, one at a time. Jeff, it's good to see you. Alan, Kentucky was awesome. Every time I turned around there was a better-looking girl. The campus is crawling with babes. I also met Lori Winnick."

Everyone else started to join us.

"Tell us about the hot chicks," Tracy said as she sat down next to me.

I blushed.

"Busted," Alan said, as he cracked up.

"Yep, you guys suck. You're supposed to give me a heads-up."

Jeff gave me a superior look.

"The foundation of a good relationship is open communication."

Tracy gave him a look.

"You've been watching too much Dr. Phil."

Luke sat down.

"So, your boyfriend is keeping secrets."

Tracy turned to him.

"He's not my boyfriend. We're just close friends."

✧✧✧

After lunch, I went to Coach Lambert's office, only to be directed to a conference room. The coaching staff was all waiting for me. Bo Harrington was sitting next to a projector. There was an open seat between him and the screen and he indicated that I was supposed to sit in it. As soon as I sat down, they dimmed the lights and ran through the highlights of my morning session.

"David asked me to show him what we're working towards. I'm going to show you film of Jeff George. In high school, he was the first winner of the Dial Award as the best high school player in the nation in 1985. He's who we're going to use as a model for David's development."

The film started showing Jeff when he was at the University of Illinois. Coach Harrington let it run several plays before he stopped.

"Jeff George was the number-one draft choice in 1990. The reason he was drafted that high was because of his arm strength and quick release. The ball is out of his hand in one smooth motion."

I could see him glide back and stand tall in the pocket. He made playing quarterback look effortless. I now had something to model my play after.

✧✧✧

The rest of the week was much of the same. I would have been lost in my classes if it hadn't been for Suzanne and my tutoring sessions. She seemed to be able to keep me focused on what I needed to survive scholastically. The rest of my life was football. Even lunch hour was turned into seven-on-seven drills organized by Magic and Luke.

The one thing that stood out that week was my video chat with Alice and John Phillips. I'd gotten home from practice at a quarter till eight when I got a text from John. I sent him a message back telling him to jump onto video chat. I turned on my tablet and connected to find Alice and John seated at their kitchen table.

"Hey guys, good to see you."

They both had big smiles, and it was good to see them. Alice winked at me.

"Hey, David," Alice said in a sultry voice.

John wouldn't take the bait.

"Shut up, Alice, you can talk to him in a minute. I hear you got a coach."

"Wow, you're well-informed. I just started working with him today."

"Dad's thinking about hiring someone to help me. Do think your guy is helping?"

"Why don't we talk in a week or two and I can tell you more. So far, I know *everything* about what I'm doing wrong. Text me when you and your dad will be around and I'll fill you in."

"How much is it costing you?"

"He's here through the rest of the season and will stay if we make the playoffs. It isn't cheap. He's charging almost $50,000."

John whistled.

"Dad won't spend that much. Is this guy some kind of guru or something?"

"He's a 'fixer.' His list of clients is impressive. You saw how bad my technique is. Why don't you talk to the coaches at Kentucky and see what they recommend?"

"That's a good idea. I'm going to jump off so you can talk to Alice."

She gave me another wink, letting me know that we were going to play with him again.

"Hey, Stud, I've been a good girl."

"Oh, Baby, so did you get your mom to show you how to get *all* the Popsicle in your mouth?"

I saw a dishtowel fly into view and hit Alice in the head.

"Dawson, you suck! Quit trying to corrupt my little sister!"

"Love you, John!"

Alice cracked up.

"Okay, he just left. I miss you. We need to figure out how to see each other."

"I don't know. I can't even drive to come see you until this summer when I get my license. For now, we'll just have to chat like this."

"You look dog-tired. Get your rest and we'll talk this weekend."

"I look forward to it."

✧✧✧

Friday October 4

The game this week was away at Lakeview. They had a bad team this year and we expected to win. Our fans filled their stadium by driving the 20 miles in a huge caravan. It turned into essentially a home game.

I was nervous before the game, and what made it worse was everyone was leaving me alone. We won the toss and decided to receive. The kickoff team gave us the ball in a decent field position. We'd only been able to put in three pass plays so we didn't have a very deep playbook. My first pass sailed high and was intercepted.

When I got to the sideline, Coach Harrington found me.

"Good, we got that out of the way. You're going to have that happen. No big deal."

His relaxed attitude calmed me down. The rest of the game was the most fun I'd ever had playing football. We never punted and Coach Lambert didn't take us out in the second half. We played the full game to get experience. The final score was 70–6. I threw ten touchdown passes and completed 46 of 52 passes for 635 yards. The only running play we did was when I kneeled down to end the game.

✧✧✧

Chapter 20 – Bachelor Auction

Friday October 11

After the Lakeview game, I buckled down and did everything Bo Harrington wanted. If I wasn't in school or church, football consumed ninety percent of my day. If I was lucky, I found an hour a day right before bedtime for myself. I spent most of that time talking to my friends on video chat. Tracy snuck out a couple of nights and we spent the night together. I loved having my apartment over the garage.

Tracy and I were becoming a team. She understood the demands on my time and she did a lot of little things that were a big help. One example was her mom would make me an egg sandwich each morning that I would eat right before first bell. She was also the keeper of my schedule. Throughout the day, she would text me where and when I needed to do things.

I also put her in charge of my recruiting and social media requests. The Lakeview game had caused a media frenzy. Headlines across the country read '*David Dawson, freshman quarterback for Lincoln High, sets State single-game passing record.*' She was quoted in an AP article and even made the evening news. She was a dream as my press secretary and the media loved her. You could tell she had a real future in broadcasting. She soon had all the reporters eating out of her hand and kept them off my back as much as possible.

Recruiters started to make noise too. Joe, from the University of Florida, planned a trip to this week's game. State started to recruit Luke, Magic, Kevin and Bill. They wanted us as a package deal and pushed me to come see their campus with the other four. I talked to Tracy about it and we agreed that it wasn't in my best interest because State wasn't a winning program, but for the other four it was a perfect fit. We agreed we would play along to help them out. Tracy created talking points where she or I mentioned our excitement at the possibility of continuing to play with our friends in college.

Tracy worked with Lily to set up all my social media sites for my recruiting. They worked with the coaching staff to put together videos of the Lakeview game and highlights of some of my plays. My Superman video had nearly eighty thousand views. It was Lily's idea that made everything have a Superman theme. My tweets and postings on Facebook had a similar theme. Anything that needed my input on she sent to Tracy.

The thing that surprised me most was that girls started to become brazen in their approach to me. Saturday night I woke up to some random girl crawling into my bed. Luckily, she wasn't a serious stalker. She was in a sorority and one of their pledge tasks was to take a picture in bed with a football player. Even though it was somewhat funny, my parents agreed to put a lock on the apartment and floodlights with motion sensors. When I related the story to Bo, he was in shock that we didn't have a lock on the apartment. I explained to him that in our small town the only people that had locks on doors were the ones trying to hide something.

Even though Tracy and I had formed a team, there still was the issue of the non-relationship. Neither one of us mentioned our concerns, but they were still there. For the most part, things were good for us. I was ready to take on Mount Vernon in tonight's game.

✧✧✧

Mount Vernon rolled into town with a four-game win streak and featured one of the better defenses we would see all year. They were in the race for a playoff spot, and a win by either team would go a long way to locking up a place. Last week they played Eastside and won 14–10. That was the fewest points Eastside had scored since the California kid took over their offense. The media made a big deal out of our weak competition last week and that everyone would find out if I was for real this week.

All the hype had caused the school to bring in temporary bleachers for each end zone. Mount Vernon also planned to bring their marching band. The town had called the State Police to help with crowd control since our six deputies weren't going to be enough. After the game, it was estimated that nearly ten thousand people had attended.

In the locker room before the game, I put on headphones and listened to rock music. I do that before tests and games to pump me up. Coach Engels, in his role as the new offensive coordinator, called the starting offense together.

"Okay, is everyone here?" He looked at me and I counted ten other noses, so we were all there. I gave him a nod.

"I wanted to talk to everyone and give you the first play of the game. We're concerned that David's on edge early in games. Last week the only low point was the opening interception. I think we need to see the old David." I could see the guys starting to grin. "I think we need to run Student Body Right with David keeping the ball." There was a collective, "Yeah!"

Coach Engels smacked my shoulder pads.

"I want you to hit someone so hard that they can hear it up in the press box!"

Coach Lambert called everyone together and we could see the rest of the team wanted in on the secret. One of the local clergy led us in a team prayer, and then we were surprised when Coach Lambert didn't launch into his normal pregame speech. He just turned to Coach Engels and in his best soft southern drawl asked, "What's the first play of the game?"

"Quarterback keep, student body right!"

The whole locker room erupted and Coach Lambert led us out to the field. Coach Engels held me back as the rest of the team ran out and broke through a huge banner as the band played our school song. Mount Vernon was already on the field. As the crowd quieted down, Coach Engels told me to join the team. The announcer came on.

"Introducing the new state single-game passing record holder... DOUBLE D... DAVIIIIID DAAAAWSON!"

Talk about embarrassing. Football was a team sport, and if I'd known they were going to single me out I would never have let Coach hold me back. Of course, when I got to the sidelines I was met by Kevin, who hated all forms of hotdogging. He just grinned at me, and I nodded to let him know that we wouldn't be doing that again.

I peered across the field and saw the sun start to set with the distant clouds tinged in orange. The light breeze and the crisp autumn air made it a perfect night for football under the lights. We won the toss and elected to receive. The kickoff team muffed the return and we were on our own 3 yard line. The old USC play was not a good choice to run in a situation like this. It was slow to develop, and if a team blitzed, you could potentially be taken down behind the line of scrimmage.

We didn't bother to huddle up.

"Blue. Set. Hut, HUT!"

The center almost hiked the ball over my head. I had to leap to get the ball, and when I brought it in I was four yards deep in the end zone. Their defensive end had shed his block and bore down on me. I lowered my shoulder and exploded through him. The distinctive crack of pads had the crowd on its feet, because I should have been brought down for a safety. Fortunately, the impact was enough to bounce the big defensive end backwards. He went to wrap me up and missed. The video of the play was hilarious. It looked like the poor kid tried to hug himself as he fell on his butt.

Mount Vernon started the game with five defensive backs. When our linemen got into their secondary, it was over. They punched me a huge hole and I broke free. The place went nuts. I was suddenly in the zone. Hitting the defensive end and putting him on his backside was what I needed. I had only green grass in front of me when their safety made a great shoestring tackle at their 15 yard line. The next play I threw a quick screen to Luke, he found a seam, and we were up 7–0.

From that point on, the game was almost a repeat of last week. I settled in and we picked them apart. Working with Bo had improved my technique to go along with my arm strength. My throwing motion wasn't there yet, but I was getting rid of the ball much faster. I only had to scramble twice all night. They learned their lesson when I broke a twenty-yard run when they tried to blitz. We as a team had worked hard and added six more pass plays and three running plays. We racked up over 600 yards of offense with a little over 400 of it passing yards. Final score was 49–0.

That was my most satisfying win. We crushed a good team that we had to beat. Fox Sports highlighted the game, and when the Monday morning rankings came out we'd jumped from number ten to number three in Class 5A statewide.

✧✧✧

After the game, I went out with the team to Monical's Pizza. This was the first time I'd participated in an after-game get-together. Tracy's dad had reserved the restaurant's banquet room for the team.

When I came out of the locker room, Tracy had waited for me. When she saw me, she broke into a huge smile that made me glad she was smiling at me.

"Hey, what do you have me doing tonight?"

She wrapped me in her arms and gave me one of her patented mind-erasing kisses. This was the life. I was sore from playing a game and now in the arms of the most amazing girl. She had her Mustang parked right by the door, so we raced to get in.

"Here's the schedule for the next 24 hours. We're going to Monical's Pizza. I've arranged for a couple of the recruiters to 'bump' into you. In addition, that cute girl you like at Channel 15 is going to be there for a quick interview. Tomorrow you have seven-on-seven drills and then Pilates."

I moaned when I heard about Pilates. That sadist was going to try and kill me.

"In the afternoon you have the Band Fundraiser Bachelor Auction and then the party for the fundraiser Saturday night."

I gave her my best puppy-dog face.

"You are going to bid on me, right?"

I'd volunteered for this when Beth ambushed me earlier in the year. It was all part of her scheme to get Gary Baxter to ask her out. Tracy knew I wasn't looking forward to doing it, and I made her promise to bid on me. In years past, if the bachelor's girlfriend bid on him, the rest of the girls backed off. My worst nightmare was to be up on stage and no one bidding on me. Tracy was getting sick of me asking her about it. She just stuck her tongue out at me as we pulled into the parking lot.

"Wow, this place is packed. Why don't you park across the street at the bank so your car doesn't get dinged up?"

We were halfway through the parking lot when Tracy stiffened. I looked where she gazed and Bill Rogers glared at us. We didn't slow down and made it into the restaurant before he could do anything. I knew that at some point he and I would have to settle this. Tracy didn't need that creep harassing her. As we got inside, I turned to her and pulled her into my arms. I could feel her shaking. I stroked the back of her head and told her everything was okay and that I loved her. When I felt her relax, I let her go. She smiled at me, and the Tracy I loved was back.

We entered the main dining room and 'bumped' into Joe Phips, the University of Florida head recruiter. I smiled when I saw him.

"Joe, how're you doing?"

"Not bad. I was in the neighborhood and decided to take in a game. I see Bo Harrington has been a big help."

"Yes, he's worked hard with the team getting them ready. Hey, have you met my right-hand gal, Tracy Dole?"

"Hi, Tracy, we've spoken several times on the phone." He gave me a smirk. "Do you even have a cell phone?"

I blushed.

"I do, but Tracy won't let me give out its number, so you can stop trying to get her to give it to you."

He put his hands up in defeat. Tracy winked at me.

"I only give that number out to schools that have made offers."

Joe took it well.

"Touché. If we were to make an offer, how would we get it to David?"

Tracy slid her hand on Joe's arm and they went to have a private chat. Before I took a step, the cute Channel 15 Sports girl ambushed me. She was just out of college and covered the local sports scene. The station had launched the careers of many big-market broadcasters. She didn't introduce herself; she just had the cameraman hit me with the lights and shoved a mic in my face.

Tracy had briefed me on how to handle this tonight. Monical's had set up an area that showed the school colors and our logo. I also wanted to get Kevin, Magic, Luke and Bill together. I needed Tracy there so if the interview got out of hand, she could step in and stop me from saying something stupid.

I ignored the reporter's question and caught Tracy's eye. She broke away from Joe and gathered the guys. I turned back to the reporter.

"Sorry, let's get out of the way of people trying to get tables and move over there."

"David, we're on deadline. I don't have a lot of time."

I just smiled at her and started walking over to the stage. I could see she wasn't happy, but she had no choice but to follow me. I jumped on stage and the crowd quieted down so they could hear. The cameraman blinded us with his light again.

"David Dawson, freshman star for Lincoln High, had another stellar performance tonight. How do you feel tonight's game went?"

"It all started on the first play. Our coaching staff had a brilliant game plan and called a run. The offensive line played lights-out all night. I think they only touched me a couple of times. Then these two guys lit it up." I pulled Luke and Bill forward. "Luke Herndon had another All-State performance with over a hundred yards receiving and a hundred yards rushing. Bill Callaway caught everything I threw at him. He's by far our most improved offensive player."

"Some would say you're the most improved," she said to interrupt me.

"No, Bill's the man. Our defense held one of the best teams in the state to no score. 'Magic' Mike Wade held their leading receiver to one catch for five yards. Kevin Goode, our defensive captain, had 10 tackles, 3 behind the line of scrimmage."

"There's a rumor that you five are trying to package yourselves to attend the State University."

"I'll let Ms. Tracy Dole answer that."

Tracy came up and slid her arm around my waist.

"Tonight, State made scholarship offers to all five players you see up here. Coach Lambert and his staff have informed me that Mike Wade, Kevin Goode and Luke Herndon have all verbally accepted. Bill Callaway, being a junior, is waiting to make his decision, and freshman David Dawson is strongly leaning towards State."

"Is it true that Kentucky has made David an offer?" she asked.

"Yes they have, and David is very impressed with their program, along with several others. The State offers have made him take notice, though." Tracy said.

"I saw the University of Florida attended tonight's game. Have they offered?"

"The staff at the University of Florida got in early on David's recruitment and they're evaluating him, but as of now they're waiting."

The cameraman turned off the lights and the crowd clapped for the guys. I hugged Tracy and her big goofy smile and my mug made the front page of the Saturday paper. The headline read '*David Dawson and girlfriend Tracy Dole.*' The rest of the night was a blur. At one point, I actually got to eat some pizza. I organized several teammates to walk us out to Tracy's car and we saw Bill and his thugs back off. She took me home and we were done for the night.

✧✧✧

Saturday October 12

I still couldn't believe I'd been talked into the bachelor auction, but Beth was in charge, and when she asked, I couldn't say no. I found myself with nineteen other 'volunteers.' I was happy to see Gary Baxter was one of the guys. I had helped Beth create the plan to get Gary in the auction so she could win the date with him. The clueless doofus would then see she liked him. I wasn't sure what the attraction was, but he seemed like a nice guy, and if Beth wanted him, I hoped she'd get him.

The way the auction worked was the winning bidder would receive one date with the bachelor. The bidder planned and paid for the date. The bachelor was responsible for being a perfect gentleman and showing the bidder a good time. In years past, many new couples had been created this way. This gave the girls a chance to show their interest in the bachelors. Let's be honest, most of us were clueless. The girls also seemed to have an unwritten rule that if a bachelor were dating someone, then their girlfriend would bid twenty-five dollars and win the bachelor. Tracy and I had agreed that she would make the minimum bid so I would fulfill my obligation.

Beth had put me in charge of recruiting football players to help and I'd done pretty well. I talked Magic, Kevin, Bill and Luke from the varsity squad. From the JV Suzanne got her little brother Jim. I use the term 'little' loosely, because Jim was six-five and weighed nearly 250 pounds. If he could ever get coordinated and gain some foot speed, he'd make a heck of a lineman. From the freshman team Luke's little brother Mike had joined Bert and Tim. All told, if you counted me, I had gotten nine of the twenty bachelors. I'm sure these guys would have fun with this. They were all good guys and the band needed the funds, so it was a win-win.

This year's auction was at the school auditorium. Beth, being in charge, had volunteered to MC and one of the band members' dads was asked to be the auctioneer. Beth made us all show up two hours early, and she and the cheerleaders had us learn an opening routine complete with costumes. When I saw what the costumes were, I almost turned around and left. But Magic called me a wuss, so I sucked it up and stayed. The basketball team had loaned us warmups and the swim team had gotten us Speedos. In practice, it was apparent that not everyone should wear a Speedo.

Standing backstage, I started to get nervous. Luke could see me pacing and stepped in front of me to get me to stop.

"I can't believe you. You're mister cool and confident on the football field, but get you in room of girls and you fall apart. You do know that Tracy's going to bid on you and end this thing for you, right?"

"I do. Thanks for the pep talk," I said, but wasn't sure I believed him.

I sucked in a deep breath and then let it out very slowly, as I concentrated to calm down. Luke was right, Tracy would bid on me and all the other girls would step aside. It was some kind of girl code that I didn't understand, but everyone had told me that, so I had no idea why I was nervous. It might have had something to do with Tracy and me not actually going together. She kept saying we should go slowly. This was while we screwed our brains out every chance we got. By all appearances, everyone thought we were a couple.

Tracy had never given me a reason to doubt her feelings for me. She never even looked at other guys, but in the back of my mind, something just wasn't right. Every time I had brought the subject up, she had been consistent in her mission to go slowly and make this relationship work for the long haul. It had nothing to do with the sex; sex with Tracy was fantastic. I had nothing to complain about in that regard. Her friends all liked me. Her parents treated me as if I was part of the family. Since football blew up, we'd made a good team, but there was something that had held her back. I knew the issue was with me. I don't think I fully accepted the non-relationship status.

Part of me wanted to push ahead and force the whole boyfriend/girlfriend discussion. I was sure if I did, she'd bail on me. If I were wasting my time with Tracy, wouldn't it be better to find someone else? Hell, my mom even told us that we should break up and then get back together when we grew up. My mind had gone in circles with no apparent solution in sight. I took another deep breath and held it in. I then slowly released it. I needed to slow down and just take this one day at a time.

It was now getting close to showtime, and the music was pumping. Magic came bouncing back.

"There must be a couple hundred girls out there and they're ALL hot!"

One of the stagehands called out, "Line up, we're one minute away."

I saw Beth on the side of the stage as she got her microphone hooked up. She saw me and gave me a wink. Through the curtain, you could see the house lights dim and then go out. The girls started to clap rhythmically. Beth walked out on stage, and when she hit her mark, they lit her with a spotlight.

"Ladies, are you ready for this?"

The girls were treating this like a rock concert. I wasn't expecting the volume they could put out. When the crowd quieted down, Beth continued.

"I'm Beth Anderson and I'll be your Master of Ceremonies tonight." There was polite applause. "I want to welcome you to the fifth annual Bachelor Auction hosted by the Marching Band. This year's proceeds will be used to offset the cost of the band going to the Orange Bowl in Miami, Florida. They've been invited to the New Year's Day Parade. They'll also be attending the game on January third which is part of the BCS Bowl Championship Series. So ladies, dig deep tonight, and let's see how much money we can raise for this worthy cause."

The music started to play *You're Sexy and You Know It*.

"Now, let's meet your bachelors!"

The noise level went through the roof. The stagehands pulled back the curtain and Gary Baxter strutted out and hit his mark. "Gary Baxter!" He then headed to the right to give us room to come out. I was next. I did my best catwalk imitation. "David Dawson!" I headed to the left. Next was Magic. "'Magic' Mike Wade!" It didn't take long before we were all on stage. "Let's give a big hand to our bachelors. Without them volunteering, this event would not be possible."

Beth stepped to the side of the stage, burlesque music began, and we began our routine, acting like bad Vegas showgirls. It didn't matter, the girls loved it. Halfway through we all took our shirts off. This had started to become fun. I think what kept me from being nervous was that the spotlights in our faces made it so I couldn't see the crowd. If I'd been able to see my friends, I think I would have died of embarrassment.

Beth was on my side of the line and stood next to me.

"I don't know, girls, I'm not sure I want to spend good money on a bachelor if I haven't seen the complete package. What do you think? Should we see more?" she asked.

"Yeah!" the crowd screamed.

She looked at me.

"Are you ready to take it off?"

I shook my head no.

"Come on girls! Encourage them to TAKE IT OFF!"

"TAKE IT OFF! TAKE IT OFF! TAKE IT OFF!" the crowd chanted.

We started looking up and down the line, and then a stagehand cued up dance music and we all ripped the breakaway basketball warmups off. That left us all in our Speedos, and we began to dance. The girls went wild. Magic cracked me up because he kept shaking his booty at the crowd. When the song ended, we all ran off the stage. We hurried to get dressed for the auction. Gary had drawn the short straw and had to go first. They had us dress in suits and ties.

While we dressed, the auctioneer was introduced, and he went over the auction process. The house lights were brought up so the auction staff could see the crowd. Several of the band members were placed in the crowd to help the girls bid.

They had us all come out and sit in chairs on one side of the stage. Beth brought Gary up and the auction began. It quickly became apparent that the band girls all had a crush on Gary. I could see the shock on his face as the bidding hit $100. We all were shocked when it hit $300.

Suddenly Beth was next to me and panicked.

"David, how much money do you have in your checking account?"

"What!? Why are you asking me that?"

"I don't have enough money to bid any higher!"

I could see the pleading in her eyes. Our well-crafted plan was going to go up in smoke because of a lack of funds.

"$350 going once, $350 going twice," the auctioneer announced.

"I have $500 in the bank."

"$500!" Beth shouted.

Well, shit. She'd just spent all my savings. Everyone turned to her, and Gary got a big smile on his face. The doofus finally realized that Beth was into him. That killed the bidding and Beth had won her date. She turned and looked at me, and the joy on her face was worth every penny.

Towards the middle of the auction, things got interesting. Suzanne's brother was being auctioned off but there was no bidding. I started to feel bad for him when finally someone opened with twenty-five dollars. I suddenly realized it was Suzanne. That couldn't be good if she'd had to bid on her own brother. I could tell he knew who'd bid, too. He put on a brave front, but I could see this was killing him. Then I heard a bid of $250. Everyone gasped. After the opening bidding for Gary, only one other bachelor had reached the $250 mark. This was high school here. None of us had a ton of cash.

I then saw who had bid: it was Tracy. I think every person in the theater's head snapped to look at me to see how I'd react. I suddenly felt physically ill. I jumped up and ran off the stage, sure that I would vomit in front of the crowd. It took me a few minutes to calm down. I was supposed to be next, but they skipped over me. I was taking deep breaths when Beth came back to check on me.

"I'm okay. It just caught me off guard. I'm sure she did it so that Suzanne and Jim wouldn't be embarrassed. That was a good thing she did."

Beth looked at me and we both knew I was full of shit. I needed to get it together and put on a happy face for Beth and her charity. I allowed her to guide me back to my seat. I was glad they took pity on me and had me go next. I wanted this day to end.

I got up, found Tracy in the crowd, and smiled at her. She gave me a half smile and then the bidding began, or for me, didn't. I thought Jim had it bad. Everyone sat on their hands. I looked at Tracy and she gave me a little shake of her head to indicate that she wouldn't bid on me. The only thing I could think of that kept me from bursting into tears was she'd run out of money.

The crowd started to get restless. Beth walked out to Tracy and I could see them talking. I then heard Tracy.

"I am not bidding on him!"

Beth turned to me. I took another deep breath, this time I found my center, and I felt the weight of the world fall off my shoulders. I mentally said a little prayer: 'God grant me the serenity to accept the things I cannot change; courage to change the things I can; and wisdom to know the difference.' I pushed all my feelings into a little box and hid it deep inside of me. At least now, I knew. It was the doubt that had been eating me up. I surprised everyone when I smiled, and they could tell it wasn't a forced smile, but a genuine smile.

I walked up to the auctioneer and took his mic.

"You heard her, ladies. I just got dumped in the most public way possible. There's no doubt I'm a free man. Please don't be mad at Tracy. I'm not. I honestly hope she'll be my friend after this. I think she and I make better friends than we do a couple, anyways."

I could see her cover her mouth and start to cry. That, honestly, was not my plan.

"Tracy, please don't cry. I'm not trying to be a jerk. I really do care about you and only want what's best for you."

Well, that didn't seem to help, and now I had several girls crying. Then Luke saved me. He came up and grabbed the mic.

"All the guys pooled our money and we have $278 we would like to bid for a guys' night out with a great friend we all look up to."

Then from the middle of the crowd, I heard a bid.

"$300!"

Everyone turned to see Cindy Lewis grinning at me. She was going to get so lucky. I would be the biggest slut and be her boy-toy on our date. I surprised everyone when I jumped off stage. Cindy was about six rows back. I didn't want to wait to go around so I stepped up on the armrest of the first-row chair and then the back. I stepped on the back of the next-row chair, and so on, until I reached Cindy. I've no idea how I didn't kill myself as I balanced from row to row. Cindy had a happy smile and her eyes were moist with emotion.

"I think you're happy to see me," she said.

I didn't answer her. I pulled her into my arms and kissed her. I was so happy that Cindy had picked me. I knew this wasn't going to be a forever thing. Cindy would be off to college next fall, but this could be a for-right-now thing. With Cindy, I had no doubts. I'd wanted her from the first day of school. I knew she liked me and I liked her. With Cindy, I realized I didn't need any labels. The difference was that there was no doubt in my mind.

When our kiss broke, I realized the place was quiet. I opened my eyes and I saw a sea of happy girls watching us. They all seemed to want what we had. Then someone started clapping and soon everyone was joining in. We both blushed, she grabbed my hand, and we worked our way to the aisle.

I looked around and saw that Tracy had left. It made me sad she felt she had to end things this way. If she'd just spent the time to talk to me, things would have been much better. We could've set each other free. I wish I knew why she felt the need to hurt me. It wasn't as if we were actually dating. I had followed her lead and not asked for more than she was willing to give. My concern was that if she was doing something this extreme, there had to be something wrong. I thought I should call her mom and dad and talk to them. I didn't want to see her going off the deep end and end up hurting herself.

Cindy led me to the table where she needed to pay for the auction.

"Hey, I'm going to go and change and I'll meet you here," I told her.

"Okay, I'll wait for you. Hurry back."

By the time I got backstage, the auction was over, and Magic, Luke and Mike were waiting for me. Luke was in typical big-brother mode. At some point, he'd adopted me as his little brother.

"Are you okay? That was brutal."

"I'm a little concerned about her. Are you guys going to the party tonight?"

The band had organized a party for after the event. It wasn't the group my friends normally hung around with and I wasn't sure if they'd be going.

"We are. Tomika wants me to go with her as our date," Magic explained.

Tomika was the cute girl who'd won the bid to go out with Magic. I knew he'd wanted to ask her out, but he'd been afraid she wasn't interested. I was glad to see she was moving things forward.

"How bad can the party be? We all are taking the girls who won the auction to get to know them. Plus if Beth organized it, I'm sure it'll be fun," Magic said.

"If Tracy shows up, could you spread the word to the guys to look out for her?" I asked the guys.

"What're you worried about?" Luke asked.

"Two things: first, she has a tendency to go for the bad boys. Bill Rogers still thinks she's his property, and if she hooks up with him, it would be bad for her. It could be even worse for Jim. He may try to protect her, and Bill and his gang would kill him. Suzanne is our friend and I don't want her brother getting hurt.

"The second thing is she might go completely crazy-town. I fully expect she'll sleep with Jim. Tracy is a sexual person. I've actually been a little surprised she hasn't been hooking up with other guys already. My concern is she might go wild and pull a train or something. It would destroy her reputation. If she wants to get a little freaky and do that in a private setting, that's one thing, but doing it in public would be terrible for her and her family," I said.

All three of them looked at me and could see the genuine concern in my eyes. They all nodded their agreement to help. I then smiled as I remembered Cindy.

"Now I have to go home and tell my brother that I stole his girlfriend."

Mike barked out a laugh and Luke turned on him. Mike's eyes got big as Luke gave him a hard stare.

"You better not get any ideas about *my* girlfriend."

"You better keep an eye on her, big brother. She's hot," he said, and he giggled like a little schoolgirl as Luke took off after him.

Mike dodged out of the room, laughing. I could tell Luke hadn't really tried to catch him. Magic just shrugged.

"She *is* hot," he offered.

We both laughed at Luke when he gave us a scowl.

✧✧✧

Chapter 21 – I Think I'm Going to Like Being Selfish

Saturday October 12

I found a quiet spot and called the Dole household. Mary answered.

"Hello."

"Hey, Mary, it's David."

"David, what can I do for you? Tracy isn't here right now. Actually, I thought she was with you."

"I need to talk to you."

I took the better part of five minutes telling her what had happened. After she got the idea, she stopped me and had Tom pick up another phone. They listened to my full story before they asked any questions. The first one surprised me.

"Are you sure you're okay?" Tom asked. "That was probably the worst way I could imagine her delivering the news."

"I really don't know. There hasn't been time for it to sink in. I'm sure at some point I'll find a corner and curl up into a tight ball. Tracy could have been the one. She and I fit. I understand we're young and the odds are against us, but I was happy when I was spending time with her."

"You don't know how happy Tom and I were that the two of you were together. I'm not sure what happened, but that jerk Bill did something terrible to our little girl. She lost her innocence. That's a terrible thing for a parent to know," Mary said, sounding sad.

"I'm worried about her. I've known for a while something was wrong, but I didn't want to admit it. Have you thought of maybe having her talk to a professional?"

I heard Tom sigh.

"We've been dancing around this for too long. Mary and I will sit down with her and figure out what to do."

"Okay. Just let me know if there's anything you or Tracy need."

"We will."

"I have to go. I'll talk to you later in the week."

After I hung up, I felt better. At this point I'd done everything I could to help Tracy. Now I had to focus on the girl who actually wanted me in her life. I said my goodbyes to the guys and went to find Cindy.

She was surrounded by my friends: Lily, Beth, Peggy and Suzanne. I was surprised that Tracy's cheerleading friends, Mona, Sammie and Kim, were there also. I thought about it for a second. The JV cheerleaders obviously knew Beth and Suzanne. They also knew me and I considered them all friends. I would have thought they'd all be with Tracy, since she seemed to be the leader of their group. I'd have to ask Cindy about that later.

Cindy smiled at me.

"Hey, I called Greg. I didn't want him to hear about it from anyone else. I think he's happier than I am."

"Thanks, I was dreading that conversation."

Mona came up and gave me a hug.

"Are you okay, David?"

"Thanks, Mona. You're a good friend. With you all at my side, I'll be fine."

Kim shook her head and looked at her shoes.

"We had no idea she would do that. I can't believe she'd try to hurt you so bad. She really doesn't know how lucky she was to have you. We hope you don't think any of us would be a part of what happened."

I hugged both Kim and Sammie. I pulled the three JV cheerleaders into a tight huddle.

"Listen, I don't hold any of you responsible for today." I looked each of them in the eye and I could see them relax. Beth winked at me over Kim's shoulder. "I've gotten to know the three of you over the last few weeks and I like each one of you. You're all great girls. Tracy's lucky to have you as friends. Today wasn't the Tracy we all know. Either something's wrong, or she has a good reason for what she did. It's important that the three of you are there for her."

Sammie gave me a measured look. Of all the girls there, she was the one I knew the least well, so I was surprised when she took me to task.

"Look, we all know you're not okay. You have to stop thinking about everyone else all the time. This is typical David behavior. Your natural instinct is to bend over backwards and accommodate everyone else, even to your own detriment. It makes you the perfect boyfriend, but if you keep this up you'll never really be happy. You have to take control of your life and do what's best for you. We know you have it in you. You wouldn't be a very good leader on the football field if you weren't selfish," Sammie said, as I gave her a look.

"That sounded worse than it is. Everyone needs to be selfish at times. If all you did is do what's best for everyone else, you'll never be truly happy yourself. Let me put it this way. What would be best for Luke? Letting him run the ball a lot more?"

I nodded my agreement to her statement.

"So why do you pass the ball? Is it so Bill's a star?"

I shook my head no.

"Are you doing it because you think it's best for the team?" Sammie asked.

"I guess that's it," I answered thoughtfully.

"I disagree," Sammie stated, confusing the hell out of me.

"You're more competitive than anyone I know. I watch the games, and I see you go into some kind of trance. When we see it, we know you're taking over the game. We can see you're not thinking about anyone's feelings. You're focused on winning. That's all you care about, and that's a selfish emotion. You need to understand that selfish does not always equal bad. There are times when you need to be selfish in your personal life for you to be truly happy."

"But I want what's best for my friends. I want to see you become the best version of you that you can be. And if I can help in some way, I want to help you," I defended myself.

She waved her hand indicating all the girls.

"We all know that, and that's one of the reasons we all like you so much. But we'd all like you even more if you were selfish now and then," Sammie said.

I was still not following her, and she sighed. She could see I didn't understand.

"Okay, selfish may not be the right term. I think you're hung up on the implication that being selfish means to do something at the expense of another. That's not what I mean. I think it'd be better to say you need to look out for your own self-interest. David, let me give you an example you might understand: how do you feel when you're helping one of us?" Sammie asked.

"It makes me feel useful. I love seeing you all happy."

"Then why won't you let us do that for you? Don't you think I'd find enjoyment in helping you through the pain you must be feeling? It breaks my heart to know that you're torn apart inside, and you won't even allow me to comfort you. We all are so sad about what occurred, but we're trying to keep a happy face on because you're acting like nothing happened," she said, and let her emotion show.

That rocked me. I had pushed my feelings down so hard I was afraid to let them out, and I cracked. It was like a giant spring suddenly unwound and I nearly collapsed. Sammie steadied me and I started to shake a little. I found myself biting my lower lip as I tried not become overwhelmed. I found myself in the middle of a giant group hug. How could Tracy have done what she did? I could make all the excuses in the world about us not actually going together, but let's face it: in my mind, we were; and to be honest, she thought so too.

I could also make excuses that this wasn't in her nature, but it obviously was, or how else could she publicly disrespect me like this? Why did I feel the need to comfort and protect her? We had agreed beforehand how the auction would go. She set me up to crush me in public. I couldn't wrap my mind around anyone being that cold and calculating. How had I missed it? She had gotten into my heart. With that insight, I started to get mad.

How dare she. I'd only shown her love and compassion. Had I been with other girls? Yes, we'd talked about that up front. Even though we officially weren't committed, we had at the very least a deep friendship. We had started to move towards more. She'd never given me any indication we had any problems. To humiliate me in such a public manner was unforgivable. No one would put up with that. I was such a wuss. Not two minutes ago, I defended her.

"FUCK HER!"

That simple declaration was what saved me. Sammie was right. I needed to do what was best for me. I'd been led around by my nose for too long. It started with Tami for all those years. I loved Tami to death, but I have to grow up and start taking control of my life. My problem was I didn't know how to put my feelings before everyone else's. To be honest, I wasn't sure what my feelings were, I always tried to keep them in check. Why did I keep them in check? What did I have to be scared of here? I know this change wouldn't happen overnight, and I wasn't sure I would ever be 100% selfish, but I needed to start to look out for my own self-interest.

"Did I just say that out loud?" I asked as I looked up sheepishly.

Sammie pulled me into her arms and kissed me. It was the right thing to do. It stopped me from thinking completely. She had her own version of the mind-eraser kiss that was quite enjoyable. When our kiss ended, I looked around, and all the girls had tears in their eyes and big smiles. I felt love from all of them and I realized that she was right. Their smiles kept me from feeling embarrassed about losing it. Friends who cared for me surrounded me. It would be okay. I kissed her again.

"Thank you. I needed someone to kick me in the butt. You're a special friend. Feel free to kick my butt anytime you think I need it."

"Okay, now go spend some quality time with Cindy, and we'll all see you tonight," Sammie said.

"Why, what's going on tonight?" I asked.

"You'll be at Beth's party and you're going to dance with all of us," Sammie ordered me. "You will get every guy's wet dream and get to flirt with the hottest girls in school. And if you're a very good boy, we might all let you kiss us."

I grinned.

"I think I'm going to like being selfish."

Beth smacked me in the back of the head.

"Listen, 'stupid boy,' there's no need for you to become a jerk. Don't think any one of us isn't capable of taking you down."

That brought a smile to my face. Beth needed to stay away from Tami and the whole 'stupid boy' thing. Cindy grabbed my hand and led me out of the auditorium. Before I got to the door, Beth yelled after us.

"Hey wait, I forgot to tell you that you have two dates."

I looked at Cindy and she gave me a Mona Lisa smile that was of no help.

"The guys paid their money, so you have to go on a guys' night out with them. Talk to Gary, he's organizing it."

That sounded like fun. Maybe I could get my *girl* friends to go.

"Hey, would you guys like to go spend an evening with all my bachelor friends?" I asked.

Beth was jumping up and down. Of course she did.

"Okay, Beth's vote doesn't count because she has the hots for Gary."

"Hey, no fair!" Beth complained.

They all smiled and nodded. The good news was with Beth involved I was sure Gary wouldn't mess it up. She would help him. Okay, she would plan the whole thing.

"Great. Beth, tell Gary I added to the guest list. I'm sure the guys will be fine with who all I added. You are, after all, the cutest girls I know."

"Sure, you're just saying that so you'll get kisses at tonight's party," Mona said.

"Of course, but you're all still cute. See you guys tonight."

We got into Cindy's car and we were leaving the school grounds.

"So where are you taking me?"

"Do you mean right now, or for our date?"

"Tell me about the date first."

"You're taking me to Homecoming. Greg was starting to crack under his role as my bogus boyfriend. I'm pretty sure the shit has been cheating on me."

"What happened to your rule? The rule of only dating guys your own age or older?"

"You poor, naïve boy, you never ask a woman why she changed her mind about something like that. Just be thankful I did. In addition, you wore me down. Suzanne keeps telling me about your tutoring sessions and I decided I needed some of your special attention too. Well, our Princess is the one who wore me down. You'll have to be extra nice to her the next time you two get together."

"Good lord, I don't know how much nicer I can be to my special tutor. You may have to come along and give me some ideas."

"You shit. You're just trying to get another threesome for yourself."

"You heard Sammie: I need to be more selfish."

"Well, in this case it'll work out for you. But I'm warning you right now that you better drink plenty of fluids, because I think the two of us are probably too much for you."

"Oh goodie, a challenge! My guess is our little Princess will be in the middle to begin with, and after we tag-team her she'll be a quivering mess. By then I'll be so horny you don't stand a chance."

"I agree about the first part, but let's just say, 'challenge accepted.'"

I didn't have to ask where our intended destination was, because we pulled up to my place. We went to the kitchen to grab a snack and sodas before we'd go up to my apartment. Mom and Dad were at the kitchen table. I figured I'd better break the news about Tracy to them.

"Hey, Tracy and I are no longer going out, so I stole Cindy from Greg and she's taking me to Homecoming."

I think if my parent's heads hadn't been attached, they would have snapped off. Of course, my mom has a way with words.

"What the hell?"

"I guess it's a little more complicated than that. Tracy decided to humiliate me in public at the band auction. By her actions, I think everyone would be fair in assuming we're no longer an item. Miss Cindy here saved me from having a bunch of guys bid on me. Thank you, by the way." I gave her a kiss on the cheek. "Cindy bought me at the auction as her boy toy and decided I was going to Homecoming with her. She called Greg and dumped him. That about covers it, doesn't it?"

Cindy nodded.

"Just about."

Greg came into the kitchen.

"Hey, Dumbass, I thought there was some kind of Bro Code that said you weren't supposed to steal your big brother's girlfriend."

My dad just started laughing when he saw the look on my mom's face, and she gave him an evil glare. She saw that no one was going to talk, so she just threw her hands in the air and walked out. Dad was still chuckling.

"Oh, David, how she hasn't killed you yet is beyond me. She would have taken me out years ago if I tried that with her. I wouldn't poke the bear too much, but damn that was funny."

Greg went up to Cindy and gave her a kiss.

"Hey, I'm not a dumbass like you were. Hands off of the girlfriend," I complained.

Cindy gave me a curious look.

"I'm your girlfriend now?"

Oh crud. Not her, too. Then I saw her and Greg try not to laugh.

"I'm sorry, I should've asked before I made that declaration. Cindy Lewis, will you be my girlfriend?" I asked.

"Of course I will."

That made me very happy. How hard was that? I would never understand Tracy. Thank God, she was no longer my problem. I grabbed our snacks and drinks and dragged her out of the house. I could hear Dad and Greg chuckling as we left.

✧✧✧

I took Cindy out the back door.

"Where are we going?" she asked.

"To my apartment."

"How did you swing that?"

"I asked."

"What does your brother think of you having an apartment and him being stuck in the house?"

I opened the apartment door and we went upstairs. As we walked up, I explained.

"He's jealous that he didn't think to ask," I said as we went into the living area. "What do you think?"

She took it in.

"You suck. Every teenage boy should have his own little love shack. Word gets out and you'll have girls sneaking in."

"Not in my wildest dreams, unless you're planning on it," I said as I arched my eyebrows.

"I just might. What's behind door number one?"

I saw her look at the bedroom door.

"Why don't you open it and see?"

She walked over and took in my room.

"Do I need an invitation?" she asked.

I walked up to her and kissed her.

"You were incredible," Cindy enthused as she wrapped her arms round my neck.

"You're pretty incredible yourself," I whispered in her ear.

The husky tone of my voice brought her up short.

"David."

Okay, I have nothing on sexy. With that one word, I was aroused.

"You just look good enough to eat when you say my name like that."

I felt her shudder as I pulled her tighter. I don't think she expected me to talk like that. Always before, she was in control. My assertiveness was turning her on.

"I may have to take you up on that."

"Count on it," I promised. I took her hand and guided her next to the bed. There was no more guessing what my intensions were. She could see the desire smolder in my eyes. She bit her lower lip and I saw a moment's hesitation. Using my foot, I pushed the door closed.

"Oh, God, David."

I nudged her chin back and left a trail of little butterfly kisses along her jaw and down her neck. I laid her on the bed, gently. I used the back of my hand to caress her cheek. I then stepped back and began to untie her tennis shoes.

Her socks quickly followed. I joined Cindy on the bed and let my lips slowly caress their way down her neck. She started to squirm, and I took the opportunity to unbutton her blouse. As more skin became exposed, my lips and tongue pleasured her. I mapped all her erogenous zones as I'd been taught. I found Cindy was a very receptive lover. Soon her white lacy bra was exposed. I saw the clasp was in the front and I popped it open. Cindy gasped when I attacked her breasts.

"You're so hot. I've wanted you ever since I saw you making out with my brother on the first day of school. I'm the luckiest boy alive."

Her face lit up, and she sat up and took her shirt and bra off. Her firm body was magnificent. There was no sag at all in her ample breasts. When she settled back on the bed, she grasped the back of my head and pulled me in for one of the best kisses of my life. There's something to be said about dating an older woman. I thought our previous kisses had been hot. This one really did make me forget my name. I felt goose bumps all over my arms. She broke the kiss, and her smile lit up my life.

"Someone's been practicing. Which of your little girlfriends taught you to kiss like that?"

"That's pure inspiration from being with you."

She snorted.

"I think we've taught you too well. Nice save."

She gasped as I bent down and let my tongue trail down around her breast, noting what turned her on. She seemed to like a teasing, gentle approach with little nips.

She soon had her fingers stroking my head as she guided me to where she wanted my oral attention.

"Oh God, that's it," she gasped when I found a good spot.

I felt her hands leave my head and she started to work my t-shirt off. I sat back and let her pull it over my head. She tossed it somewhere near the foot of the bed. She was almost panting, and her face was a mask of lust. As I sat up, she ran her hands over my stomach and worked their way up my chest. Her caresses turned me on.

"You keep that up and I'm going to ravish you."

"If that's all it taaahhh..."

I pushed her back and went to work. While I did that, I softly caressed her and paid special attention to what turned her on.

"Uhhhmmmm, you little shit. This is what you did to my little Princess, isn't it?"

I just glanced up and grinned. She let her head fall back and enjoyed the experience. I switched breasts out of concern for fair play. She seemed to enjoy that. She suddenly grabbed my hair and pulled my head off her.

"David, you're going to make me climax before you even get my pants off. We don't have all day and I'm not leaving until we do it."

Okay, she made a good point.

"Only one thing stopping me."

"Do tell."

"I promised I was going to eat you."

"Oh good God, take me now."

She ripped her tight jeans and underwear off all in one motion. Ms. Cindy Lewis was no longer playing any games. As soon as she was stripped naked, I used my strong fingers and let them dance firmly across her lower lips. She whimpered as I used a tender, gentle touch and she became aroused. My light caresses had her trembling. Her head fell back and she moaned as I teased her. My lips closed on her breast again, my tongue teasing it gently. My other hand caressed her sensitive jaw and neck. I nipped her nipple and she shuddered through her first orgasm.

"Uuughhhh."

I was impressed with her extensive vocabulary. Someone must have failed their SATs. As her arousal continued to build, I became more aggressive. She began to shudder and her gasps became louder as she started to get close. Her hands clutched the sheets. She was close as I lowered my head to her sex.

When my tongue came into play, her hands flew to the back of my head and pulled me tightly to her crotch. I think I may have ended up with a couple of bald spots if I'd not been careful. Her cute little gasps went straight to full-on screams of ecstasy. Anyone near would know exactly what was going on.

"OHHHMYYYYGAAWDIIIILLLOVEEEYOU!"

Her orgasm was spectacular. It seemed to go on and on and I just kept working to pleasure her until she was finished. When she was done, it was as if a marionette had had its strings cut. She just collapsed in the middle of my bed. Her eyes were unfocused and she lay there panting. I waited until I saw her eyes begin to focus. I remembered how we had tormented Suzanne.

"Are you ready for round two?"

She chuckled.

"Bring it on. Get out of your clothes. I want to see what Suzanne's been mooning about."

I stripped down to my underwear and decided to play with her. I was going to leave the size of my manhood a surprise. I grabbed her, rolled her over, and pulled her hips to the edge of the bed. She got on her knees so I could take her from behind. She turned her head so she could see me and I swatted her butt.

"No peeking."

"What?!" she complained.

"You heard me, no peeking."

She stuck her tongue out at me and then ducked her head. I knew she was trying to cheat. I grabbed a condom and used my teeth to open the package. I knelt down so she couldn't see and dropped my shorts. I put the condom on and fisted the head of my shaft into her slot. The sexual animal in me was wide awake and ready to go. I pushed into her in one steady stroke until I hit bottom. She was soaking wet and I met no resistance as we joined.

"Damn girl," I groaned.

"Oh, God, did you just shove a baseball bat into me?"

Her body hugged every inch of me in her warm velvet vise. I started to pull out when she began to beg.

"Please stop. I need to get used to your size. Suzanne, the little skank, didn't warn me you were so big. I'll have to talk to her later."

I began to rotate my hips gently to help her muscles accept me. I wouldn't last long. She let out a long hiss.

"Okay, slowly."

I grasped her hips and began to rock in and out of her. I took it slow and did long, steady strokes to get her used to me. It was a great plan, but I could feel that all-too-familiar feeling. I jerked out of her and tried to think of anything that wouldn't turn me on. The only problem was that one of the hottest girls I had ever seen had her magnificent bottom pointed up at me.

"DON'T STOP!" she demanded.

"Hang on, or I'm not going to be any use to you."

She gave me a grin as she realized what I was saying. I gathered myself and was ready to go again. This time I was in control. I needed to bring her off fast, so my right hand circled around her pelvis so that I could touch her sex. She whimpered and cried as she got close. I leaned over her and nipped her ear.

"I love you too," I whispered.

As soon as I said it, her orgasm hit, and when she jerked her head back to scream I felt I was already there. I felt the release that overtook all my senses. I heard myself scream.

"GOOODDD!"

We collapsed with my body draped over hers. We then got the giggles. I slid off and she crawled onto my chest.

"I should've dumped your brother a long time ago."

I tried to lift my head.

"Are you telling me my brother isn't as good in the sack as I am?"

"Oh, my, someone's ego is about to be too big for his own good. I'm not sure I should answer that question."

"Tell you what: you take whichever of us is better in bed to the party tonight."

"Let's put it this way: your brother has more moves than you, but he doesn't have your equipment."

I grinned.

"I can live with that. With you teaching me, I'm sure I'll learn the moves."

She smacked my butt.

"Ouch!"

"Get your lazy butt out of bed and come take a shower with me," she ordered.

Smirking, I took a deep breath and nodded. Still, it took me another thirty seconds before I had enough energy to sit up, but once I did, Cindy led me by the hand out of my bedroom and into the bathroom. Cindy climbed in first and I followed behind her. I was already half-aroused again. Cindy turned around.

"Does that thing ever rest?"

"Not when your gorgeous bod is anywhere near it," I said as I gave her my best leer.

There's something indescribably sexy about the way a girl's hair gets swept back and plastered to her scalp when wet. I grabbed the shampoo and slowly worked it in. She moaned as I massaged her scalp. I rinsed the shampoo out and I found myself holding my breath while I just watched her soaping up her body. Once she was lathered up, she leaned back into me and I used my hands to clean every inch of her.

It was her turn to do me. We couldn't seem to stop giggling as we played grab-ass. We quickly dressed and got ready for the party.

While we were dressing, she got a little bashful.

"David?"

"Hmm?"

"Did you say you loved me?"

My head snapped around and I saw her smirk at me.

"Yes, I did, but I think someone else said it first."

"Will you say it again?"

I thought about it for a moment.

"I'm sure I will, but I don't want to scare you. I think we both were just reacting to the orgasms. There should probably be a 48-hour rule. 'I love you' doesn't count if it's said within 48 hours of an orgasm."

"Good rule. I love you."

My whole day got better.

"I love you too."

✧✧✧

Chapter 22 – Free Agent

Saturday October 12

We went to Cindy's house so that she could change. I was watching ESPN and catching up on college football games when she came down. She was wearing her version of the little black dress. I was glad she'd picked out my clothes or I would've looked totally underdressed. She had me wear a fitted oxford short-sleeve blue-and-white striped dress shirt with tan pleated slacks and boat shoes with no socks. Not my normal style, but like every other girl I've met, she enjoyed picking out my clothes. Who was I to argue? She bought them.

"Cindy, you look spectacular. Every guy there is going to be jealous when they see you with me at the party tonight."

"Why thank you, David. Are you ready to go?"

"Absolutely."

✧✧✧

We pulled into Tracy's neighborhood and found the party at a huge home at the end of a cul-de-sac. The street was blocked off and there was valet parking. Not what you're thinking: band guys were parking the cars, and they kept the keys in case anyone was too drunk to drive home. Cindy slipped onto my arm and we walked up the street to the front door. The music blared and you could feel the beat of the bass through the closed door.

We walked into a huge living room with twelve-foot ceilings and marble-tiled floors. All the furniture had been pushed back against the walls. In one corner there was an area set aside with a drum set and amps. It looked like the band would provide the entertainment later. For now, there were a couple of people working as DJs and they played electronic dance music.

The one thing I noticed was that everyone was dressed for the party. Cindy wasn't the only one rocking the little black dress. We walked through the party to see who was there and slowly worked our way to the back patio. On the way, we stopped and chatted briefly with several people we knew. When we reached the patio, there was a full bar setup, which had three taps with different beers. The marching band parents pitched in for the bar setup each year, and this was rumored to be one of the best parties of the year.

The bar worked on a donation system. They technically couldn't sell alcohol, but you could buy tickets for a raffle. You had the option of using your tickets to 'buy' drinks and bypass the raffle. I bought $40 worth of tickets; that netted me 10 tickets. While I did that, Cindy found Suzanne and Beth. I interrupted them for a second to take drink orders and become their waiter for the night. They all wanted lemon drop martinis. I ordered a tonic with lime. I had never seen a martini made and was surprised when it was all alcohol. A couple of those and the girls would feel no pain.

When I got back, Kevin and Luke were talking to the three girls with their dates Mona and Kim. I asked them what they wanted and came back with their drinks. All four of them picked beer. When I made it back, they had taken over the pool-area tables and pushed them together. I went over to the ticket booth and bought another batch of tickets. I gave everyone another ticket and officially was done being everyone's waiter.

Suzanne and Cindy saved me a seat between them. I sat down and they both kissed me on a cheek and grabbed a hand to hold. Kevin shook his head.

"Double D, you're the only guy I know that can get dumped in such a spectacular fashion in the afternoon and by that night have the two hottest girls at Lincoln High School hanging on your arms."

"You leave David alone. We've all been waiting for him to become a free agent," Beth scolded Kevin.

Luke went to his friend's rescue.

"Come on, Beth. You have to admit that these two are smoking hot. It's almost an embarrassment of riches. You know I love David like a brother, but he's a freshman."

Suzanne looked at both Kevin and Luke.

"You boys forgot one thing: he's Greg Dawson's brother, and Greg's been teaching him to be a Dawson."

Luke choked on his beer, and it took the rest of the table a moment to figure out what she meant. I saw Kim whisper to Luke and he had to explain it to her. She turned bright red. I winked at Kevin and he shook his head.

Then the moment I dreaded finally arrived: Tracy and Jim were at the bar. I hadn't noticed, but Cindy squeezed my hand and used her chin to point them out. I just shrugged and continued my conversation with Suzanne.

"Hey, just so you know, your brother's here."

She spotted them in line. I gave her two tickets.

"He didn't see that he needed to buy tickets. Why don't you slip these to him so he doesn't look silly on his big date?"

"Why would you do that?"

"Simple: he didn't ask to be in the middle of this, and he's your brother."

She surprised me and gave me a serious kiss that left me toe-curled.

"Thank you, David."

I turned back to Cindy and I saw the look she and Beth gave me. They'd both overheard what was said. Beth was about to say something when Gary turned up. He pulled up a chair and Beth gave him a peck on the cheek.

"Hey guys, thanks for keeping an eye on Beth for me. Our band is set up and we'll start playing in about twenty minutes."

I looked around and didn't see Sammie.

"Hey, where's Sammie?"

"She didn't have a date and was worried that she'd be a third wheel," Kim said.

"Jeez, give me her number." I said, and Kim rattled it off as I dialed. "Hey, Trouble, it's David."

"David, why are you calling? Aren't you at the party with Cindy?"

"Yeah, Cindy's here, along with every other cute girl in our school except one."

"Yeah, right."

"Seriously, Kevin, Luke and I were just saying we need a girl we can throw at all the band geeks and keep them away from our dates."

Cindy and Suzanne both smacked me in the back of the head. I gave them both a dirty look. The good news was that I could hear Sammie giggling.

"Look, we all would like you to come. It's not the same without you here, and I promise if you come your dance card will be full all night."

"I'll only go if you promise to save me a couple."

"Deal."

I could hear her laughing as she hung up on me.

"Bitch, she hung up on me," I announced.

I got up to get Cindy another martini. Mona followed me up to the bar and I smiled at her.

"You need a ticket?"

"No, I still have one. Kevin and Luke are going to buy the next round," she said, and then looked serious. "Thanks for calling Sammie. She's upset with what Tracy did. She didn't want to come tonight because she's afraid she might say the wrong thing to her."

I snorted.

"She's not the only one. I honestly don't know what I'll say when I see her. My guess is I'll totally wuss out and let her off the hook."

"God, I hope not. That was one of the coldest things I've ever seen her do."

"Well, I didn't come here tonight to talk about her."

"One thing I need to warn you about: Sammie has a huge crush on you. Actually, Mona and I both do too; we've seen you with Tracy, and how good you were with her. Plus she gives you very high marks in key categories."

"You flirt."

Her ears were so red that Kevin yelled over.

"Dawson, don't forget you have your own date!"

I just waved over at him to acknowledge that his date was safe with me. I got Cindy her drink and sat back down at the table. Gary had left to go play while I was gone. We were having a good time when we heard the band start. Everyone gravitated to the dance floor.

This was the first party I'd been at since my disastrous party last spring. What a difference: I was sober and having much more fun than when I did drugs and drank. Sammie showed up near the end of the first set, and she bounced out on the dance floor and gave me a big hug. Cindy had a good laugh and asked her if she was trying to steal her date. Sammie almost bolted until she saw everyone around us laughing. I was even okay when I saw Jim and Tracy dancing. They looked like Beauty and the Beast. He dwarfed her. They seemed to be having a good time, and he was in lust big-time. I couldn't blame him; I was still in lust with her.

Once the set ended, we went back out to the pool area. Beth left some of the band people to save our seats so we were able to grab our original tables. As I settled into my seat, Suzanne sat in my lap. She leaned in and gave me a nice kiss. She giggled when I pinched her butt. The rest of the table was doing their best to ignore us, but I did get some sly looks.

"What has you all frisky tonight?" I whispered into her ear.

She sucked my earlobe into her mouth; that sent shivers down my spine. I saw Luke turn to Magic and mouth, 'Damn that's hot.'

"I want you to take me to Homecoming."

"Princess, I would take you in a heartbeat, but Cindy and I are going."

"I talked to Cindy, and she said I can go too."

She licked my neck and purred. Now everyone was watched us with their mouths open. Cindy and Beth smirked at me like they knew something. I was ready to throw caution to the wind, throw Suzanne on the table, and have my way with her. The little minx was driving me insane with her hot little body. I looked at Cindy for help.

"Suzanne!"

They locked eyes for a moment and did that weird girl-communication thing that always baffled me. I swear that with one look they could communicate a complete conversation. Suzanne wiggled her butt to let me know she felt my desire, and then went over and hugged Cindy and everyone could hear her stage whisper.

"Thank you, he's taking us both to Homecoming."

Luke smacked the palm of his hand to his forehead.

"Dawson, I give up. You're a rock star."

Everyone laughed at Luke. We could hear the band start to play, so I grabbed my two girls and we hit the dance floor. I tried not to embarrass myself as these two put on a show. There was a reason they were on the cheerleading squad. They had everyone watching us. After the second dance, I had to pee, so I excused myself and they continued to dance together. I found the bathroom by the kitchen open, so I quickly took care of business.

When I came out, Beth had waited for me.

"Hey gorgeous, you look great tonight," I said.

"You don't look so bad yourself. I see you jumped into the deep end with those two."

"Yeah, they're a lot of fun."

She got a serious look on her face. I couldn't figure out what she was thinking. I looked deep into her eyes.

"Hey, what's wrong?" I asked.

"I'm regretting not following Tami's advice. She called me after she heard about the auction and told me to forget about Gary and ask you out."

I was in shock. Not by Tami knowing about the auction—her network of friends kept her up to date on everything that went on—but that she would tell Beth to go out with me. I never got more than a 'friends' vibe from her. I wasn't sure how to respond, so I pulled her into my arms. I'd been friends with Beth the longest, since I literally grew up with her. It would be a nice, comfortable relationship. With Cindy and Suzanne, there was more passion, but there wasn't the foundation for a long-term friendship. She laid her head on my shoulder and began to talk.

"David, I know the timing sucks. I really like Gary and I know you like Cindy and Suzanne, but I can't stop thinking about you. I know Cindy and Suzanne aren't looking for a relationship. They both have plans to go away for school and have both been hurt in the past."

"You're right. I'm looking at them as short-term. I like them both a lot, and knowing we aren't in a long-term relationship is kind of a relief. I'm not over Tracy yet. She got deeper into me than I even know. It'll take me a while to get over her. Like with Tami, if I started something with you it would be serious. We are too good of friends for it not to be that way. I honestly love you more than you know. All you have to do is ask and I'm yours. My heart is in your hands."

She had tears in her eyes. She turned her head and gently kissed me. I felt a spark like static electricity when our lips met. Kissing Beth was different from anyone I'd ever kissed before. I could feel her longing for me and I felt our desire ramp up. Suddenly she pulled away from me and the reality of where we were flooded my mind.

"You're right, we can't hurt them. I like Gary. Hell, I spent $500 of your money to go out with him. Can you forget I ever asked?"

I hugged her tighter to me.

"Beth, you know I love you. You're one of my dearest friends. If and when we're both free, I'm looking you up."

She gave me a funny look, then pushed me back into the bathroom and locked the door. Oh, shit! Beth walked towards me with a wicked gleam in her eyes. I slowly backed up until I felt the toilet hit the back of my legs. Now what? There was nowhere to go.

"Beth," I tried to warn her off.

She put her finger on my lips to shut me up. She looked me in the eye as she unfastened my pants. I was in shock and didn't try to stop her. When she had them undone, she pulled my pants and boxers down around my ankles, and then pushed me back so that I could sit on the toilet lid. She grabbed a bath towel, folded it, and set it down in front of me. She then kneeled down on the towel, and when she was comfortably situated, she gently stroked me to full arousal.

"Beth," I croaked out as a whisper.

Her mouth was warm and wet. I could've erupted then and there, but Beth was deliberate, and slowly she sucked. I watched the top of her head bob up and down. She took her time and brought me to the brink several times. Somehow, she knew how far she could go, and then eased off. I was ready to explode.

"Beth, please, let me..."

She grinned and quit teasing me. "Beth!" was all I got out when I finally climaxed. It felt like she had drained my entire body of all my fluids through my penis. My breath came in exhausted gasps. What was that? I started to regain my senses and I looked down to find a very contented Beth smiling up at me.

"I've wanted to do that ever since you teased me at my house. I remember your gym shorts as you came out of the hot tub leaving nothing to the imagination. If Mom hadn't been there, I would have had my way with you then. I agree, when we're both free, we'll talk. For now, thank you for letting me fulfill one of my fantasies."

I just nodded as she got up and left. All I could think was '*wow!'* Who knew that my friend had that in her?

I went back out to the dance floor and Sammie grabbed me for her dance. I'm not big on psychic things, but I suddenly felt the hair go up on the back of my neck go up. Only one thing does that to me: Bill Rogers. I spun around to see Bill and three of his goons all look nervous and almost run out the front door.

"Princess! Jim!" I yelled without even thinking.

I grabbed Suzanne's hand and the band stopped playing as the two of us ran out onto the patio. We found several people crowded by the side of the pool house. I plowed through as I dragged Suzanne with me. We found Tracy seated next to Jim who was in a fetal position. It seemed obvious that Bill and his crew had beaten Jim. Suzanne rushed in and bumped Tracy out of the way so that she could check on her brother.

"Beth! Call 911! We need an ambulance!" I yelled.

I noticed that Tracy had a dazed look and was bleeding from her lip and nose. Her blouse was ripped, exposing her left breast. I quickly took my shirt off and put it on her. It was like dressing a rag doll. She had a faraway glazed look and I could tell she was deeply shaken. I sat her down next to the wall so I could check Jim.

Jim was unconscious. His hands were a mess. He obviously put up a good fight trying to protect Tracy. I unbuttoned Jim's shirt and saw the red marks on his stomach, side and back. They had kicked him when he was down. I quickly checked to see if anything was life-threatening. Jim didn't seem to be in immediate danger, so I got some crowd control in place. Magic had arrived with Kevin and Luke.

"You guys get the crowd back. See if someone can get clean towels, a bowl of warm water and a wash cloth," I said.

Suzanne sobbed when she saw the condition her brother was in. She tried to comfort Jim, who was now moaning. I was encouraged by his moans, but concerned he wasn't responsive. She was in near-hysterics.

"Princess, look at me," I said to get her attention.

She looked up.

"He's going to be okay. Keep him calm and do not let him move until the paramedics get here. He might have back or neck injuries from where they kicked him."

I switched to Tracy. She had a nasty gash on the back of her head. Cindy showed up with the towels. I had her take one of the towels and apply pressure to the back of Tracy's head. Tracy also had a nasty welt under one eye and her nose and lip were bleeding.

"Tracy, can you tell me what happened?"

"Ghhhaa, my head hurts."

"Baby, look at me, what happened?"

"Goddam Bill."

She slurred her words and was either drunk, high, or had a head injury. She seemed to have a hard time focusing.

I grabbed my cell phone and called Tracy's parents, and Mary answered.

"Hey, Mary, is Tom there?"

"What's wrong?"

She must be hearing the strain in my voice.

"Please get Tom on the other line."

"Tom, pick up the phone, it's David," she called.

I heard Tom pick up. I started to talk before he could say anything.

"Tracy and her date were beaten by Bill Rogers and his goons. Tracy has a head laceration. Her date was beaten unconscious, and it looks like they kicked the shit out of him once he was down."

Tom was all business.

"Did you call the paramedics?"

"Yes. They should be here shortly."

"Is this at the house down the street?"

"Yes, the one at the end of that short cul-de-sac."

"Okay, I'll be there shortly."

I broke the connection. I turned to Cindy.

"Do you know Suzanne's home number?"

She gave it to me as I dialed.

"Mr. Ball, this is David Dawson."

He seemed happy to hear from me.

"David, I've watched you play. What can I do for you?"

"I'm at the band party and I'm with Jim and Suzanne. Jim and his date were beaten tonight and we've called an ambulance. It looks like he's going to be okay, but he was knocked unconscious. He should be at the emergency room in 10 to 15 minutes."

I got lucky and the second dad of the night was all business.

"Okay, can you see that Suzanne gets a ride?"

"I'll have Cindy take her and they'll meet you there and give you the details."

He hung up. The ambulances showed up and the paramedics took over. I took Cindy aside.

"Hey, I hate to dump this on you, but can you take Suzanne to the hospital?"

"Of course. Aren't you coming?"

"Of course I am."

She clutched me and started to cry. I let her cry for a moment and then pulled her away.

"You have to be strong for Suzanne. You're her rock, and she needs that right now."

The paramedics quickly loaded Tracy and Jim. Tom and Mary followed them to the hospital.

I walked over to Beth and Gary.

"The police will be here once the paramedics radio in what they found. We need to do some damage control quickly. We've been serving alcohol to underage drinkers," Beth told Gary.

Gary realized the problem.

"Shit," he said.

He gathered up the party crew and had them going around with garbage bags, cleaning up. He had another group breaking down the bar.

"David, go make sure that the valets aren't giving out any keys to anyone that's even close to being drunk," Beth directed me.

"I'm going with Cindy and Suzanne to the hospital. If you need me, call," I said.

Beth hugged me and I promised to call her once I got any news. On the way out one of the party crew gave me a t-shirt from the event to wear. I got the girls together and we left. Cindy was arguing with the valet. I had told them what Beth had said, and they were checking everyone before they gave them keys. I got Cindy's keys and promised I would drive. I drove half a block and then switched back with Cindy.

My record for parties was dismal. The last two had ended with someone being carted out by paramedics. I was sure I wouldn't be on anyone's guest list anytime soon.

✧✧✧

My grandma was born at Regional General Hospital. It looked like a gothic mansion with modern wings added on.

It had to be ugliest hospital in the state. We parked and entered the emergency room. It was straight from the 1930s, with subway tile lining the walls and old-style lighting. It felt like you were walking into a Steven King story. Even though the building was in poor shape, the quality of care was top-notch.

Suzanne went to the desk to find out where her brother was, and the receptionist directed her into the family-only waiting room. She grabbed Cindy and my hands and pulled us through. When the guard tried to stop us, she told him we were family. From the look on her face, the guard just let us through.

Suzanne went to her parents with Cindy in tow. Tom headed me off. He looked relieved.

"They're both going to be okay. Tracy is getting some stitches in her hairline and Jim is responsive. It looks like he has some broken ribs. They're going to keep him overnight for observation. Tracy should be out shortly."

"Tom, I'm sorry I wasn't there for her. If I'd known Bill was around, I would've tried to protect her."

I heard my name called and as I turned around Tracy wrapped me in a bear hug. She had her face buried in my chest and she was crying. She said something, but I couldn't understand her. I just wrapped her in my arms and hung on. I looked over and saw Cindy and Suzanne smile. I was so confused.

Tracy looked up at me.

"I, I, I messed everything up. Please forgive me."

I felt my heart go out to her. Less than 24 hours ago, I had been in love with this girl. I didn't think I could jump back into that Pandora's Box of a relationship that had us 'not together,' but our lives were so intertwined with her helping with my recruiting and media obligations. I needed to sort this relationship out, but it couldn't happen in a hospital emergency room.

I kissed her forehead.

"I love you. Go home with your Mom and Dad and get a good night's sleep. Tomorrow I'll come over and we can talk about things."

"David please, can you forgive me?"

"Tracy, you don't even have to ask. I forgive you."

Mary had to pry her off me. Tracy's parents guided her out of the emergency room with her looking back every few steps to make sure I wasn't mad at her. When they got through the door, I felt arms snake around my waist and someone kissed me on the back of the neck. I turn around and found Suzanne smiling at me. I shifted in her embrace so that I could face her, and give her a quick kiss.

"How's Jim?"

"He's going to be fine.

"David, how did you know? How did you know that Tracy and Jim were hurt?"

"I just had a feeling. And when I saw Bill and his goons leaving in a hurry, I knew there was trouble."

She looked me in the eyes as she tried to find something. Today had been one of the worst days of my life. Tracy dumped me and then she and her date had been beaten by one of the vilest guys I knew. If it wasn't for my friends, I don't know if I would've made it through the day.

My mind went in several different directions. Cindy and Suzanne were a lot of fun, but we were just friends and would never be anything more. We might become even closer friends, but we all knew that this would end when they went off to college.

Beth was a wild card. I wasn't sure what to make of what she did with me at the party. I knew she'd been drinking. Could it have been a momentary lapse? Or did she really have feelings for me that went beyond friendship? I prayed that this wouldn't mess up our friendship. I didn't have many close friends, and I would hate to lose one.

The big one was Tracy. Could I ever take her back after the way she publicly humiliated me? The short answer was no. The problem was I'd come to rely on her and her parents. I'd become friends with Tom and Mary and could talk to them about football. My family had never supported me in anything beyond academics, as far as school went. I think Greg had been to one game. I wasn't sure I could have Tracy help me with my recruiting. Maybe Tom would have some ideas when I got to their house tomorrow.

Suzanne kissed me under the chin to bring me back.

"David, what are you thinking that has you so serious?"

"Sorry, I'm tired. I should probably find a ride home."

"Actually, Cindy's ready to go. I came over to thank you for tonight. I was having a great time until Jim got hurt. Thank you."

"I'm glad he's okay."

"I know you are. Be nice to Tracy. She's a bitch, but you're not that guy."

"I will. She and I are done, but I think she needs me as a friend right now. I can do that."

She gave me look that I couldn't read.

"David, you're a better person than I am. I know you two have some history, but it's only really been a few months. Before that, she wouldn't give you the time of day. All your other friends at least liked you. When I dated Greg, I remember thinking that when you grew up you'd be something special. I knew that you'd grow out of your awkward stage, and the girls would be chasing you. What counts is that you're as gorgeous inside as you are outside."

She had no idea of how insecure I used to be. I'd gradually started to get used to the idea that girls found me attractive, but there were days I still felt like the pudgy little geek I used to be. I still wondered why beautiful girls like Beth, Cindy and Suzanne would even notice me.

"Honey, what you have with Cindy and I is not a long-term relationship. At the end of the year we'll be off to college. We've seen enough long-distance relationships to know that very few ever work, especially if one of them is still in high school. College is so much different," Suzanne said.

"Then why? I don't want to hurt either one of you, and I don't need to be hurt."

"Cindy and I talked about this. First, you don't need to be in a serious relationship right now. There're two reasons for that: you've just had your first breakup. Predictably, the relationship that follows the breakup turns into a rebound. You use this kind of a relationship to blunt the hurt you feel. We're willing to help you through this because we both have been hurt, and know what you'll be going through.

"The other reason you don't need to jump into a serious relationship right now is that you're fifteen. You need to live and allow yourself to grow up. No one ever seems to marry his or her first love anymore. You'll have many relationships with many different and wonderful women before you find 'the one.' You may not believe me right now, but no matter however perfect she is, you and Tracy were never going to live happily ever after," Suzanne told me.

"Second is that Cindy and I aren't looking for anything more than fun. You know that we could have our pick of boys. Older guys are going to want more." I smirked at her. "Okay, some just want to get into our panties."

"Hmm, I would never have thought of that."

"Why do you think junior and senior guys go out with freshman girls?"

"Because freshman girls are clueless?"

"That may be true, but the real reason is that they're just looking to have some fun and then go off to college. So why can't girls do the same? Cindy and I have picked the hottest freshman and decided to have fun with him until we leave. The problem we have is that we've been in intense relationships that didn't work out. Part of those relationships was sex. You'll find once you're used to getting regular sex, you never want to go without."

"You're telling me I just need to have fun right now and allow two hot seniors to have their way with me."

She smiled.

"You got it on the first try, but I want you to know what we're offering is not just fantastic sex—and it'll blow your mind—but we have some expectations. We expect you to treat us right. If you wander, we expect you to use a condom. If you find someone you're potentially serious with, you have to tell us. Just because we're all friends doesn't mean we'll not develop feelings for each other. To be honest, we both have feelings for you now."

I smiled in return.

"As do I. I love you both. I may not be *in love* with you, but I have feelings for you."

"We know. Another thing is we may not always do things together. There will be times when you'll be with just one of us. Cindy and I will work out most of that, but if you have a desire for just one or both of us, we'll work it out. The key is communication."

"Okay. It sounds like you and Cindy have this under control."

She snorted at my blind acceptance.

"Cindy and I have been friends too many years. We'll try and not gang up on you."

"I'm not worried about that. To be honest, considering how busy I am right now, it'll be a big help if you guys figure out my social calendar. I promise to tell you if I feel like you're pushing me around, but it's a relief not to have to plan everything, and to really be honest with you, I trust you both. For some reason I never trusted Tracy 100%. But you and Cindy have always looked out for my best interests."

Cindy came up.

"What're you guys talking about? You look so serious."

I turned to her and pulled her into a three-way hug.

"We were talking about how you and our Princess are going to run my life. She's just laying down the ground rules."

Her eyes got big and she looked at Suzanne.

"Spill it."

I jumped in.

"It's pretty simple. You two will tell me where and when to be somewhere, and then we have awesome sex."

Suzanne tried to keep a straight face.

"I think he has a grasp of the situation."

Cindy didn't look like she was buying it.

"I think our Princess and I will have to catch up on this talk some other time. Right now, I'm beat. Let's get everyone home and get a good night's sleep."

We made our way to the parking lot. I crawled into the back seat and let my two girls sit up front and talk. To be truthful, I wasn't really paying attention to what they said. They talked in hushed tones and dropped me off first. I leaned over the seat, kissed them both goodnight, and thanked Cindy for winning the auction for me. I went up to my apartment and found my mom had waited up for me.

"Hey, Mom, what's up?"

She closed the book she'd been reading.

"I just wanted to see if you were okay. I know we talked about Tracy before. I just didn't expect it to end this badly."

"Mom, I was listening to you, and I agreed with you for the most part. If I'd known it would end like this, I would have broken up with her that night, but I try to see the best in people. I made a mistake. I have no one to blame but myself. I knew things were bad; I just had no idea she would react the way she did."

"Do you even know what set her off?"

"That's what's bothering me: I have no idea. I don't know what caused such a reaction. I'm going to talk to her tomorrow to get some closure. Can we talk afterward?"

"Okay, but you do know you can come to me or your dad, right?"

"I will. Goodnight, Mom. I need to get to bed. I'll see you in the morning for church."

Mom kissed my cheek and left. It took me quite a while to get to sleep, because I was thinking things over. Mom might be a little rough around the edges sometimes, but she always has my best interest in mind. Not once did she say, "I told you so." I eventually fell asleep with no idea what to do about Tracy.

✧✧✧

Chapter 23 – Are You Off Your Rocker?

Sunday October 13

I woke Sunday morning to my stupid cell phone chirping at me. Tami had texted me to jump onto video chat. I was a little surprised it had taken her this long to figure out my life imploded yesterday. I guess her network of informants must not be working. I pulled out my tablet and logged in. Tami was waiting for me.

"David, you look like shit."

"What do you expect first thing in the morning? Why am I talking to you at this hour? What time is it anyways?"

"It's six-thirty. I wanted to talk to you before you went to church."

"It's a good thing I like you. Church doesn't start until nine," I reminded her.

"I know, tough guy. You had a busy day yesterday. You get spectacularly dumped in front of over a hundred people. Then you get Cindy to bail you out of that mess. I hear you were seen with both Cindy and Suzanne at the party. Rumor has it you're taking them both to the Homecoming dance. Then Tracy and her date get beat up. Does that about sum it up?"

"You're missing that Beth professed her love for me and gave me a blowjob at the party."

She laughed at me. I just shrugged my shoulders. I was too tired to get irritated. Her laughter was infectious. I soon started to chuckle at my own predicament as well.

"Oh, I forgot. Then I saw Tracy when she was leaving the emergency room and I forgave her. I'm meeting her later today to work things out."

Tami howled, which made me laugh hard. The sad part was it wasn't funny, but it was either laugh or cry.

Between gasps, Tami let me have it.

"'Stupid boy,' I leave you alone for a couple of weeks and you accomplish this? I may have to move back home just to watch you dance through life. I can't believe you might actually end up better off after all this. How did you get a blowjob from Beth and that not blow up in your face?"

"She swallowed," I said with a straight face.

Tami's eyes got big as she took a moment to figure out what I just said.

"You're such a pig."

It took us a little while to calm down enough to talk. I had to wipe tears from my eyes.

"Beth scared the shit out of me. She cornered me in the bathroom, professed her love, and then she showed me how much. She'd had a few drinks. Luckily I talked her into waiting until we're both free before we do anything else."

"I bet you had no idea she was into you, did you?"

"No. I was completely shocked." Tami had an evil grin. "Dang it, Tami, why didn't you warn me she had those feelings?"

"If I told you about every girl that was hot for you, your ego would be so big I couldn't stand to be around you. You're better off not knowing."

"Hmmm, do tell. What I really need right now is more women in my life."

"Yeah, that would solve your problems. I'm glad Beth's feelings weren't hurt. She's a good friend. What are you planning for Tracy?"

I suddenly got serious. That was the question. I knew I didn't want her back, not right now. My emotions were still too raw.

"Tami, I had a friend tell me I need to start looking out for my own self-interest. Someday Tracy and I may be more than just friends, but not anytime soon. My biggest concern is that if she got pissed at me, she could do some damage. I've had her handling all my recruiting and press stuff."

"You don't have time to do that mess. You need to find someone you trust to help you. What about your mom and dad?"

"You know them; they don't pay attention to sports. They haven't even been to see me play. They've no idea what a circus my life is right now."

"Greg?"

"No, he has his own problems."

"Who do you trust?"

I looked at her, and she shook her head no.

"David, talk to Tracy. She might have a solution."

I smiled. Wouldn't that be ironic if she could figure this out for me? She was one of the smartest girls I knew. It was dumb enough that it might work.

"I'll ask her this afternoon."

"Call me after."

"I will. Hey, thanks for getting me up this morning. I really needed to talk to you. I love you."

"I love you too."

✦✦✦

I had to drag Mom to church again. Uncle Jim had gone home on Saturday and she was still a little on edge from his visit. His consulting job was done and the whole family was relieved to see him go. I think she hoped to sleep in, but we'd made a commitment, so she agreed to go.

I almost wished we'd skipped going. It started in the parking lot when a group of teens swarmed me and wanted to talk about football. One thing that I liked about Mom was she doesn't put up with much, and everyone knows it. When she rounded on the growing horde and she saw the look of panic in my eyes, she quickly scattered my well-wishers. She put her hand on my arm and walked me into the church. I could tell that people wanted to talk about football, but one look from Mom and people allowed us to enter the church unmolested.

Then we had one of my least-favorite services. Every year we have people come in who want to raise funds for missionary work. They prayed with the meaningless platitude, 'God will provide.' I just want to smack people when they say that. God doesn't hand out blessings out of the sky for things like this. He works through people. Ever think that just maybe that's why he said he would help those that help themselves? How about just doing something like, geez, I don't know, maybe get a job! God is not all about handouts just because you say 'God will provide.'

✧✧✧

On the way home from church Mom, dropped me off at Tracy's house. This wasn't a conversation I looked forward to at all. Dad had always quoted Shakespeare to me when I had a hard decision to make: 'To thine own self be true.' He explained that Shakespeare tried to tell us that you have to look within when you made a decision. You had to live with those decisions. So basically, you had to do what was right in your heart. You didn't make decisions based on what other people thought.

My heart told me that I still loved Tracy, but for *now,* we couldn't be a couple. It had been all I could do not to make a huge scene at the auction. I still couldn't fathom how she could dump me in such a public way. If it hadn't been for my friends, I would've either done something stupid, or curled up into a ball. I gathered my thoughts, took a deep breath, and rang the doorbell.

Tracy opened the door and we both just stared at each other. The bruises on her face looked worse than they did last night. We just looked at each other and didn't say anything until Tracy's mom, Mary, came to the door.

"David, come on in. Lunch is almost ready."

Tracy stepped out of the way and I followed her mom to the eat-in kitchen area where lunch would be served.

Mary was an excellent cook and she had a spread that had my mouth watering. She'd made a platter of fried chicken that was enough to feed ten people; homemade biscuits; mashed potatoes and pepper gravy; and green beans. Tom came in and we all sat down to eat.

Tom and Mary carried the conversation through lunch. Tracy and I were quiet. I couldn't tell you what was talked about. We kept glancing at each other and we were both nervous. The sad part was I didn't get to enjoy Mary's cooking. I barely touched it, I was so wrapped up in what I would say to Tracy. On the ride over, I had a whole speech planned, but for the life of me, I couldn't remember a word of it. Thankfully, lunch ended and Tracy grabbed my hand and led me to her room.

She had me sit on the edge of her queen-size bed and she quietly shut the door. She seemed to gather herself and then she turned to face me. I could see she was fighting not to cry. Her lower lip quivered and I could see the tears start to well up. My heart broke to see her in pain. I opened my arms and the next thing I knew she was in my arms, seated on my lap, crying. I couldn't help myself and I joined her. The raw emotions seemed to pour out of each of us.

"We need to talk," I told her.

She took a deep breath and calmed herself.

"I don't know what to say."

"Why don't we start with *why*? We'd agreed you'd bid on me." I said, and I bit my tongue not to say more.

"No," she said through tears. She got up and went to her desk. She had a copy of the Saturday paper with our picture and she handed it to me. I looked at it and looked back at her in confusion. "We agreed that we were not together."

I looked at the picture again and read the headline '*David Dawson and girlfriend Tracy Dole.*' Then it dawned on me: they had called her my girlfriend. My first reaction wasn't good. How was I supposed to control what the press said?

"Seriously?" I barked.

I saw her nostrils flair. That was a sure sign she was angry.

"You don't get it, do you? I'm not your girlfriend," she said with some heat.

"Well, you made that clear at the auction. I can't believe you'd do something like that," I shot back.

I don't think she'd ever seen me mad. I could tell she was shocked.

"David, I couldn't bid on you. I didn't want people to get the wrong idea."

"Are you off your frickin' rocker?" I felt myself losing control. "Instead of talking to me, you humiliate me in front of hundreds of people. I thought we were a team. A team works together. They don't turn on each other. I trusted you."

Then it hit me. I didn't trust her. That was what had been eating at me for the last several weeks, *trust*. In a relationship, if you don't trust each other, then it's only a matter of time before the relationship falls apart. I knew in that moment of clarity that I couldn't have her involved in any important parts of my life. I felt the anger drain from me.

They say that the opposite of love is not hate, but indifference. You have to care about someone to get truly angry with them. I realized that without trust we were done. There was no need to be mad at her. She had dumped me over a stupid caption in a newspaper. I took a deep breath.

"Tracy, you're right, we're not together," I said in a quiet voice with no emotions.

I could see the relief and then the confusion on her face. She hadn't expected me to react that way.

"Oh, okay."

"I just have one question: how do I get the recruiting and press requests switched over to me?"

"Lily would need to change the website."

I moved her off my lap, got up, and started towards the door. It dawned on her what I had just asked.

"Wait, that's my job, I handle all that for you. We don't have to be together for me to take care of that for you."

I could see that panic in her eyes. This was a part of our relationship she loved, but I couldn't have her taking care of something so important if I didn't trust her. I just shook my head no. Tracy flopped back on her bed and started to sob. I walked out of her bedroom and closed the door behind me. Mary met me at the foot of the stairs.

"What happened?"

I didn't want to tell her I no longer trusted her daughter, so I told her another truth.

"Tracy and I are not together. She's pretty shook up."

She squeezed me shoulder.

"Tom and I were pretty sure that was going to happen. I hope you know Tom and I like you more than just as Tracy's boyfriend. We've become your friends. We know you've always had Tracy's best interest at heart. If there's ever anything we can do, please call us."

I smiled. I liked them both, and through their help, many good things had happened. As far as football stuff went, I looked for their help even before talking to my own parents. I didn't want to lose that.

"Mary, can I talk to you and Tom for a moment?"

"Sure, he's in his office. Let's go talk in there."

We went in and Tom was busy reading a report. When he saw us, he knew my talk with Tracy hadn't gone well, just from our body language.

"I was afraid your talk wasn't going to end well."

"You're right, it didn't." I took a moment to gather my thoughts. "I need your advice."

They both looked at me and Tom laughed.

"I wasn't expecting that."

"Mary reminded me of something: I've become friends with you guys. I rely on you to give me guidance. With my relationship with Tracy over, I'm hoping that we can still be friends."

Tom didn't hesitate.

"Tracy is very important to us, obviously, but you didn't hurt her, and it took real guts to come here today and talk to her. Mary and I do like you, David."

"Well, my dilemma is that I'm buried in football. Tracy was helping with keeping track of my schedule and taking care of my recruiting and media requests. Last week alone she took something like 35 calls that, frankly, I don't have the time to handle. Tracy said she'd continue to help, but I think we can agree that she needs to focus on herself for a while."

Tom smiled.

"I might have a solution for you. We have interns who've been working for me; that project is just finishing. I only have busywork for them now until the end of the semester. Let me see if we can have one of them help you out."

Mary gave Tom a look.

"Is the one you're thinking of the same intern I met?"

Tom gave her sheepish look.

"Yep."

She just shook her head. Something was up, but I was just happy they might have a solution for me.

"I hate to run, but I'm meeting some of the guys to practice some seven-on-seven drills."

✧✧✧

Monday October 14

When I got to school who would have believed it, *Hell had frozen over*. That's right, Hell froze over! How did I know? Jeff told me.

"David, I thought you should know, Hell froze over."

Jeff usually wasn't one to make such biblical proclamations, so I knew it had to be something huge.

"What is it?"

Jeff looked around to make sure no one was listening. He pulled me over towards the entrance and turned me towards the parking lot.

I gave him a quizzical look.

"What am I looking for?"

Jeff just had a stupid grin.

"Wait for it."

Now I was clueless. Jeff saw something.

"David, get your phone out. You're going to want to get a picture of this."

Then I saw Alan wave at us. I waved back. Something wasn't right. He held hands with a real-life girl, and not just a girl, a cute girl. I guess my mouth hung open because Jeff nudged me.

"Close your mouth and take a picture."

As they got closer, I could see she wasn't just cute, she was VERY cute. She had silky long black hair that set off her coffee-latte complexion and was just coming into her figure. I would rate her a solid 8. In a couple of years she could be a 10. Jeff nudged me again and when they got close, I snapped their picture.

Alan made the introductions.

"Gina, you remember my best friend Jeff."

She gave him a smile you could tell was genuine. Her eyes sparkled. Jeff blushed under her attention.

"This is my other best friend," Alan started to say, but she stepped forward and shook my hand.

"David Dawson. Alan, you didn't tell me you knew *the* David Dawson."

My breath caught as her dark brown eyes captured mine. I guess I was still holding her hand because Jeff nudged me again.

"Oh, sorry," I said as I somehow gave her hand back and turned on Alan. "Yes, Alan, how come you never told Gina about me?"

Alan had that 'Oh shit' look on his face. He could see the spark of desire between Gina and me. He relaxed when he figured out I would never steal a girl he was interested in. Gina saw him blush and laughed.

"You told me about all your friends, but you didn't tell me that your *best* friend was the cutest guy in school."

Jeff and I had stupid grins on our faces as we watched the most socially inept person we knew deal with a girlfriend who was teasing him. Tami would have kittens when she found out she'd missed this. Alan looked like a carp out of water. Gina finally felt sorry for him, leaned over, and gave him a kiss on the cheek. Of course, I snapped another picture. I bit my lower lip as I tried not to laugh.

"Gina, my best friend neglected to tell me about you also. Did he tell you I just got dumped? Maybe we could go to lunch and get to know each other."

She didn't fall for my line.

"Oh, you're bad. I heard it took you all of half a day to get two, not one, but two of the hottest seniors to be your Homecoming date."

I arched my eyebrows.

"Hey, hey, I just wanted some scoop. I wasn't hitting on you," I said, but under my breathe I added, 'much.'

"I hear you prefer older women," she said as she gave me a sly grin and pulled out her phone. "I should hook you up with my older sister, Kara."

She showed me a picture of an exotic beauty. She was an older version of Gina but had piercing blue-gray eyes. My eyes got big and I just stared at her picture. Now she was a solid nine, maybe nine and a half. If she were as fun as her sister was, then she'd be a 10. This girl was stacked, which caused Mr. Happy to stir with arousal.

"When?" was my one-word question.

Gina's laugh was music to my ears.

"She should be home at the end of the month." Gina said as she gave me an appraising look. "She's going to like you."

I hugged Alan.

"You have the best girlfriend ever!"

Jeff and I looked at each other. Yep, Hell had frozen over.

✧✧✧

Yesterday I had called Lily and had her direct all the calls from my website to my cell phone. What a mistake that was. My phone had blown up. I turned it off during class. On my way to lunch I turned it back on. The little icon showed I had 17 messages. I planned to just listen to my messages when my phone rang.

"David Dawson."

"David, Joe Phips. I was actually looking for Tracy."

Joe was the Recruiting Coordinator for the University of Florida.

"Why, what did you need?"

"I was hoping she could send me your official stats for last game."

"Lily is posting them on the website this afternoon along with video highlights. Sorry I didn't get more time to 'bump' into you Friday."

"Hey, congratulations, by the way, that was a nice thing you did for your teammates. I talked to my buddy over at State and they're excited to have your guys committing. You and Tracy did a great job putting that together. We were also impressed with how you two handled the press conference."

I started to feel bad for Tracy.

"Tracy and I broke up."

"Ah, David, I'm sorry. I really liked her."

"Me too. So, when's Florida going to make an offer for the best freshman quarterback in the Midwest?"

Joe must have thought I was pretty funny.

"David, Tracy has that all worked out."

"What are you talking about?"

"She had several schools hold off on coming to see you until the State offers were accepted by your teammates. We snuck in last week to watch you play. This week the big guns are rolling into town: Notre Dame, Ohio State, Michigan, Michigan State, Alabama and a few others are coming this week to watch."

"Damn, I have the worst timing. She handled all this. I'm trying to focus on playing football."

"Don't let it get you down. I won't be back during the season. I have to wrap up this year's class."

"Joe, thanks for coming last week, it meant a lot to see you at my game."

"It was my pleasure. I just wanted to say your game is coming along. I can see Bo is helping. If you need anything, call me."

As soon as I hung up, the phone rang again. I just hit *end* and then called Tom. His secretary put me through.

"David, I have good news."

"Am I getting a personal assistant?"

"You sure are. She's meeting with Tracy and Lily after school and she'll meet you after practice. Sounds like a big contingent of scouts are coming to the Homecoming Game."

"Who is she?"

"Oh, sorry. Kendal Miller. She's working on her Management and Law degrees at State. We're opening an Entertainment and Sports Management division. This will be great experience for her."

"She can't start soon enough. Tom, thanks for this."

"I just have one piece of advice for you: don't hit on her."

"So that's what Mary was talking about. Is she cute?"

"Yep. Just so you know, Tracy was none too happy when she found out who the intern was."

"Dang it, I don't want to hurt Tracy."

"No, Mary talked to her. She's okay with it."

As I said, Hell had frozen over today. All I needed was an angry ex-girlfriend.

✧✧✧

After practice, Coach Harrington had me work on my footwork.

"On your toes! On your toes! Slide, slide, throw! Better. Let's end on a good note."

"Thanks, Coach. See you in the morning."

I pulled off my helmet and turned to head to the locker room when I heard Tracy.

"David!"

I turned towards Tracy and I saw she was with Lily and Kendal. I closed my eyes for a moment to calm myself. Kendal was in my favorite fantasy outfit, the naughty Catholic schoolgirl: short plaid skirt with fitted white button-up blouse. Kendal had model-quality legs and curves in all the right places. She had long, blond, wavy hair. She had librarian glasses, which was another one of my favorite fantasies.

I fought getting aroused. Unfortunately, it was a losing battle. I heard Lily giggle when she realized what was happening. My face felt like it was on fire. I kept thinking 'look in her eyes.' I opened my eyes and I saw Tracy smirk at me as Kendal came up to me with her hand out.

"Hi, I'm Kendal Miller."

I shook her hand and felt an electric shock when our hands touched.

"David Dawson."

I suddenly noticed all the team managers were behind me to watch us. I turned on them and gave them a look that caused the group of gawkers to scatter.

"David, can I talk to you for a minute?" Tracy asked.

Oh, crud.

"Of course."

Tracy led me a few feet away so we could have some privacy.

"You don't need this bimbo. I can still handle everything. I know everything that's going on and this is a big weekend. Now is not the time to make a change. You need me."

I had never heard Tracy whine before; she was normally much more confident. I also had never heard her call another girl a bimbo. This could turn into a real problem.

"Tracy, I think you were there when you broke up with me. I seem to remember you doing it in front of a big crowd."

"David, that was because we aren't together. It didn't have anything to do with everything else."

"I kind of think it does."

She actually stomped her foot.

"Uh uhhh."

Was she ten years old? I didn't want to piss her off, but she was on my last nerve.

"Tracy, let me talk to Kendal and see where you can fit in."

"Are you sure? I don't think you need her. I know you know I'm doing a good job."

"Yes, you are. Your dad and I talked, and he's helping out by loaning me Kendal. Give me a minute."

We went back to Kendal and I could see Lily roll her eyes. Great, I needed to take control of this.

"Kendal, it's nice to meet you. I see you've met Lily and Tracy. I hope they've been helping you get up to speed."

I had to give it to Kendal. She acted extremely confident, but she showed her insecurities by trying to run the show.

"Yes, the girls have been very helpful."

Uh-oh, did she just call them 'girls'?

"I'm fully up to speed and ready to go," she continued. "I'll transfer the calls to my cell. I need you to forward any messages you received today so I can follow up. Then we need to schedule a press release letting everyone know that I'll be handling your management."

"Slow down. You do realize I can't have an agent?"

"Sorry, I just worded that wrong. I'll fix that."

Tracy touched my arm. She could tell by my body language that I was about to lose my cool. I looked at her and she gave me a drawn smile. I started to understand what Tracy had tried to tell me, and Lily's look. My dad always told me that you praise in public and you reprimand in private.

"Tracy, Lily, can you guys give us a moment?"

When they stepped away, I turned to Kendal. I could see her confidence was shaken. I didn't want her to fall apart on me.

"Kendal, first of all, thank you for taking this on. You've been put into a difficult situation. My needs have popped up overnight and we're trying to find our way. Lily and Tracy have been doing an outstanding job of keeping me organized.

"Tracy and I had a personal relationship up until the end of last week. I'm sure you're aware that Tom is her father. I need someone I can trust to oversee everything. Tom suggested you could do it. I understand that this real-world experience will help you down the road. I want you to succeed. But more importantly, I want me to succeed," I said, and saw I'd only confused her.

"I'm sorry. I just look at you guys and you look so young. I'm having a hard time understanding how you've been doing this," Kendal offered.

"We may be young, but we've been doing okay. Have you seen the social media and website Lily's running?"

"Yes, I'm impressed."

"Then why would you want to take that over? You have a volunteer who's putting in countless hours to help me be successful. Do you have a better plan?"

"No. I mean, I do have some ideas."

"Do you have the time this week to do that with all the scouts and media coming in?"

"No, I see your point. But what about Tracy?"

That was the big question. I still didn't trust her. My best bet was to level with Kendal.

"Okay, this is why you're getting paid the big bucks." She chuckled at that, because most interns worked for free. "Tracy can either be a huge asset to us or destroy us. Saturday she dumped me in front of several hundred people. I'm having some trust issues right now. That's why you're here," I said, and gathered myself to continue. "Let me ask you, have you ever done a press conference?"

"No. But I was hoping to do some to get experience."

"I hadn't either. Tracy taught me how. If you let her, she can teach you how also. She's a natural and I think she'll eventually be in broadcasting. Pull some of the tapes and see how much I improved and how good she is.

"I guess what I'm trying to say is that I have a pretty good team in place. Things are getting bigger and more hectic. We need a full-time person to keep us organized. I need you to pull this team together and get us through this week. I'm leaving you in charge so I can play football. Can I count on you?" I asked.

"Yeah, I like the girls."

"Slow down, you have to get over this age thing."

"I will, and I do like them. I'll work it out with them. Do you think we need more help this Friday?"

"Why don't you talk to your team and figure that out?"

"In other words, quit bothering you with the details?"

We both smiled.

"Kendal, you're going to do just fine."

I could tell Tracy and Lily had eased over and listened to our conversation. They both had smiles on their faces, and Tracy mouthed 'thank you,' so I knew we'd be okay. With that, I went home to finish my math homework and ice my knees.

✧✧✧

I had just finished icing my knees. They'd been swelling because of the constant pounding they took. I jumped in the shower and was headed to bed when I got a text from Tami. I powered up my tablet and jumped on video chat. She was giving me her mock-pissed face, so I 'accidently' tilted the tablet so that she could see my semi-hard manhood. I heard a shriek and laughter.

"David, my roommates can see you."

"Nice package," one of them shouted.

"I missed it," another complained, so I had another 'accident' and got another round of shrieks.

I saw four faces looking at Tami's monitor. She shook her head at me.

"Guys, this is my best friend David. David, these are my roommates."

"Hey, roommates, you guys want to have some fun?"

"David, you be good," Tami said as she did her best mom voice, but she knew I was in a goofy mood. If she didn't want me messing with her roommates, I would have known.

"You want to see some more?" I asked.

Tami threw her hands up and her roommates gathered around.

"What are you thinking, Tami's best friend?" the brunette asked.

"How about we play Naked Dance Party!"

The cute blond ran out of view.

"I have the perfect music."

"Oh, crap. You just met my roommates and you talk them into dancing naked with you?" Tami complained.

I could hear the blond yell down the hall.

"Hey, Naked Dance Party!"

Tami had her head in her hands and her roommates were down to their bras and panties. The music started and they started to dance around, so I stepped back and did the same.

"OH GOOD GOD HE IS HOT!" one of them yelled.

"Oh my, he's naked!"

"That's Tami's best friend David."

"When's he coming to visit?"

I could see at least ten girls packed into Tami's suite. A couple girls had taken their bras off so I at least had some fun. The song came to an end. I jumped back into my chair.

"I love you, Tami."

"I love you too, David. I currently don't like you, but I do love you."

We signed off. I was sure that I'd pay for that one. I could tell Tami appreciated me goofing off with her suite-mates. She was still trying to fit in, and this would help them bond. At the very least, they would be nice to her just to get a glimpse of her naked best friend. What are best friends for, after all?

✧✧✧

Thursday October 17

I just finished my morning practice and was on my way into the school when Tracy called my name. It had been a weird week. She acted as if nothing had happened on Saturday. The only reminder was she still had some bruises on her face; the swelling for her split lip had gone down.

Her date, Jim Ball, came to school on Wednesday. I felt sorry for him, because Tracy wouldn't give him the time of day. I made a point to talk to him in private to let him know how sorry I was. He was a little awkward talking to Tracy's ex. On top of that, I was seeing his sister. I couldn't say we would ever be friends, but we were cool.

Bill Rogers and his goon squad had been arrested. Bill was apparently on probation for a drug-related conviction. The arrest and charges sent him directly to jail. Word was we wouldn't see him until he turned 18 in about three years. I'd talked to Mary and she told me that the news of Bill's incarceration had lifted Tracy's spirits. Mary said they'd arranged for Tracy to see a therapist. We all hoped she would help.

I slowed down to let Tracy catch up. She did her patented hip bump that always made me smile. She handed me a breakfast sandwich her mom had made.

"Tell your mom thanks."

"She worries you're not eating right," she said, as she gave me a mysterious look. I could tell she was up to something. "Kendal has a budget."

"Does she? What's the budget for?"

"We're going to have a hospitality tent for before the game. It'll be open to the public and we'll grill hot dogs. There'll be a band. Kendal wanted to just have it invitation-only, but I told her you'd want it open to everyone."

I had already heard rumblings from the freshman class that I was a snob. The girls were pissed I was dating seniors, and the guys didn't understand how much time I spent practicing. I was never around to hang out. I didn't need the whole town alienated by not including them in the hospitality tent.

"Thanks, Tracy, that was a good call. Is Kendal getting you guys help to pull this off?"

"I told her to talk to Beth. She's organizing her volunteers and she got Gary's band to play for free. We're allowing the Marching Band to raise funds for their trip at the tent."

I could tell they were up to something more.

"Just tell me. I can see you're up to something."

"We have uniforms."

With that, she unzipped her coat and I could see she had a polo shirt on. Over her left breast was her name, and under that it said 'Double D's Girls.' I arched my eyebrows.

"You like what you see?" Tracy asked.

I nodded my approval.

"Tracy, you're going to be the death of me. Is everyone wearing these?"

"Yeah, all the volunteers are getting custom ones with their names on them. They'll be wearing them to school tomorrow, so be prepared to catch some shit. We're printing up 5,000 t-shirts that say *Fan of Double D* that we're going to give away at the hospitality tent."

"Well, I'm a fan of your double D's."

She blushed.

"Remember, we're not together."

She got serious and leaned close to me.

"David, I miss you. I messed up and I'm sorry. I never knew what I had until I lost you. You could have cut me out of your life and no one would've blamed you. Because you haven't acted pissed, my friends are starting to talk to me again. I don't know why I acted like such a bitch and hurt you. What I found out was you're a much better friend than I deserve.

"Someday I'm going to get my life together. I don't think it's going to be anytime soon. When I do, you'd better look out. Mom talked to me about how I'd broken the trust between us. I see that now. You may never trust me again, but I'm going to work to regain that trust. You're one of the few close friends I have. If you ever need anything, please let me know."

We hugged each other and we were both a little misty-eyed. I think we'll end up being better friends. I still have moments when I was in a funk. Keeping busy, and being around Tracy and not being uncomfortable would be a big help. I still waited for the other shoe to drop. Given time, I hoped that feeling would go away. We broke the embrace.

"David, I saw you eyeing Kendal. Do you think she's sexy?"

"What was up with that outfit?"

"I know. Lily and I were cracking up when you saw her. We think she has the hots for you."

"Don't tell me that, I'm having enough trouble with women since you dumped me. What is up with everyone thinking they can grab my butt?"

"You're such a slut, you love it."

We headed into school and I could see everyone gave us strange looks. I was sure they all wondered if we were back together. She saw me smirk. She gave me a hip bump and headed to her locker. I knew we were stirring up the rumor mill. Let 'em talk.

✧✧✧

Chapter 24 – Homecoming

Friday October 18

Homecoming was finally here. As I walked to school, I could see my breath in the crisp fall air. This was my favorite time of year. I loved the feel of cool air as I sucked it into my lungs. All the trees were in full fall color. I understood why so many paintings were done to depict the changing season. The riot of orange, yellow and reds made the whole neighborhood look nicer. There was the faint whiff of someone burning leaves as they raked and disposed of the fallen leaves in their yard.

I could feel my anticipation for today in the pit of my stomach. I could just tell it would be huge for my future. Kendal told me that over thirty colleges would have representatives at the game. The media wasn't far behind. Fox Sports Network had picked us up as the regional High School Game of the Week.

Tonight's game would be a real test. Our state had six classes in football, based on school size. We were in 5A and the team we were playing was 6A, or the largest possible class. I think our athletic director was crazy to schedule the game. We had a return date in their stadium next year.

Lurking later in the evening was my date with Cindy and Suzanne. They were both acting a little weird. My guess was that we were featuring three football teams from past years for Homecoming. One of them was last year's team. They both had ex-boyfriends coming to the game. Both had been hurt, no, *really* hurt, to the point they didn't even date now. I'd been in middle school at the time, so I wasn't aware of what had actually occurred. I just knew that my relationship with them was just a short-term thing because of what happened. There was no real commitment. I knew I cared for them both, but I wasn't in love with either of them. That kind of relationship wasn't something any of us was ready for. For me, Tracy was still painfully fresh in my mind.

The school day went by in a flash. Everyone was excited about the game and the teachers seemed to realize it. There wasn't much in the way of learning accomplished. In last period, I had my tutoring session with Suzanne. There was no point in our session, so she had a suggestion.

"Come with me. Beth wants you to come see what they're doing with the hospitality tent before you get busy."

When we came out of the back of the school where the football field was, I saw a huge tent behind the far end zone. A banner read 'The Double D Zone.' The Elks Club had loaned us three of their big grills to cook the hotdogs. When we got there, Beth was all smiles. All the volunteers were cute girls in polo shirts that said 'Double D's Girl.' Kendal and Beth met us as we came to the tent. Beth gave me a hug.

"Thanks for letting us raise funds for the band."

"Thank Kendal and her team. They put this together."

"Actually, it was Tracy who suggested it." Kendal was learning to praise her team. "And thanks to Beth, the hospitality tent is going to be a success. David, before this gets started we all want to take a picture with you."

Beth got everyone gathered around. One of the local paper's photographers was early. He offered to take our picture. I spent a half hour going around and thanking each volunteer for helping. I was surprised when they handed me a shirt that just said 'Double D.' Of course, I stripped off and changed. Beth rolled her eyes at me.

✧✧✧

I ran home to get my suit so I could change into to it after the game. Mom was home, so I went into the house to say 'hi.' When I saw her, she had a weird look.

"What's up, Mom?"

"I didn't know you were good at football and how important it was."

"What makes you say that?"

"I just met with a man from Notre Dame. Could you really get a scholarship to play football?"

I smiled. I knew my parents weren't big into sports. Dad did like to watch the Bears and Cubs, but that was about it.

"If I continue to improve, yes, I might get a football scholarship."

She had a pained look.

"I'm not sure I want you playing football in college. College is for learning, not playing games," she said and then she saw the look that came over my face. "David, is this important to you?"

"It kind of is, Mom."

She looked stricken.

"I'm sorry, I didn't know that. The guy from Notre Dame says tonight's a big game for your future. Is that true?"

"Yes. There're going to be thirty or more scouts at the game to see how I play. If I do well, I could have my pick of schools to go to."

She seemed to come to a decision.

"Okay, your dad and I will come to your game."

She was surprised when I scooped her out of her chair and swung her around. She was giggling like a schoolgirl.

"David! Put me down."

I gently set her down and I couldn't stop grinning. She shooed me out of the kitchen and I went back to the school without a care in the world. My parents were finally coming to see me play.

✧✧✧

As game time approached, I started my pregame ritual. I had my headphones on, listening to rock music to psych myself up for the game. I was listening to a classic AC/DC song, *T.N.T.,* when Luke came up and wanted one of my earbuds. We were both bopping our heads. When the song ended, Luke was as fired up as I was. We were going to have a great game.

The weather was almost perfect for football. The temperature was in the mid-50s with a slight breeze. The sun was just going down and the stands were packed. Coach led us out and the place erupted. I love high school football. There's nothing like seeing your friends and family scream for you. I spotted Mom and Dad. They had 'Double D's Fan' t-shirts on. It looked like most of our side was wearing them.

When our captains went out for the toss, it was obvious the other team was big. It reminded me of a recent college game between Army and Notre Dame. At every position, Notre Dame outweighed Army by 20 to 30 pounds. It looked like they were men playing boys. We were in for a long night if we tried to play them straight-up.

We won the toss and elected to receive. Our kickoff return unit had worked hard. It gave many of our second- and third-string players a chance to play in front of their parents and friends. We had bodies flying, put on some great hits for a nice return, and were starting on the 35 yard line. Coach wanted to establish the pass, so we called our basic down-and-out play.

As we lined up, I knew I was going to be running for my life tonight.

"Down. Set. Hut Hut!"

Out of the corner of my eye, I saw their defensive end on my blind side shed his block. Bill broke his route and I released the pass. The defensive end grabbed my facemask and ripped my helmet off as he tried to take my head with it. I felt a sharp pain in my neck as I lay on the ground. I could hear the crowd erupt. Bill had slipped his tackle and scored.

The cheers quickly died down as the training staff rushed onto the field. Jill Kim got there first and leaned over me.

"Don't move."

Shortly after that, the head trainer, Mr. Hasting, was there to check my neck. They wanted to immobilize my head and cart me off. Screw that. I had a game to win.

"Stop! Just give me a minute!"

I rotated my head and heard my neck pop back into place; maybe not the best idea if you had a spinal injury. When I didn't feel any real pain, I sat up. I got up and jogged off the field and the crowd roared. I waved to everyone and quickly went to the bench to collect myself.

There was a personal foul on the play, which was assessed on the kickoff. Coach Lambert must have felt it tonight, because he called an onside kick. We recovered and had the ball back. When I jogged back to the huddle, the crowd went nuts.

Coach Lambert called another pass play. I had other plans.

"Okay, guys. I'm taking that asshole out of the game. We're running option left and I want you to let him go."

Our center gave our poor tackle a look.

"How would that be any different than last play?"

I took charge.

"Hey, we're a team. We'll all make mistakes, so cut it out. Just brush-block him and then get downfield and block somebody. On two, break!"

"Down. Set. Hut Hut!"

The defensive end was shocked when he wasn't even touched. His eyes lit up when he saw me come to him. He had a moment of confusion when I lowered my shoulder and ran right at him. He met me a yard behind the line of scrimmage when I drove through him. I exploded into his chest and you could hear the crack of the pads in the press box over the moan from the crowd. Mister Cheap Shot crumpled to the ground as I stepped over him.

Our tackle picked up their outside linebacker and got enough of him so I was in the open. I cut up field and surveyed their defense. Luke was a step behind me and all I saw was in the open field. I flipped him the ball and watched him sprint to the end zone. When I got to the sideline, Coach Lambert wanted to be mad at me, but he broke into a big grin.

From that point on, I put on a passing clinic. I looked like Fran Tarkenton from the old Vikings. I ran for my life all night and was put on my butt twelve times. I threw 58 passes and completed 46 for 585 yards. Luke ran for another 200+ yards. We had over 800 yards of offense and beat them 72–14. I was a man possessed. In the third quarter, Coach tried to take me out but I refused. He gave up and let me play the entire game.

That game made me realize how competitive I was. If their defensive end hadn't tried to tear my head off, I think we may have lost the game. When the final gun sounded, I collapsed from exhaustion and the release of the adrenalin that had been coursing through my veins all game. My teammates helped me up and we lined up to shake hands with the other team. Mr. Asshole—I never learned his real name—tried to take a swing at me, and his coach grabbed him before he could start a fight.

The fans were still in the stands, so we all went to the bleachers to thank them. They started chanting "Double D, Double D." I had a grin on my face as I hugged my mom and dad. The coaches finally had to come get us and drag us back to the locker room.

✧✧✧

When I got into the locker room, Coach told me to hurry up and change: I was wanted in the postgame press conference. I put on my suit on for the dance, so I looked very dapper. I was surprised to see Tracy at the podium giving out the stats for the game. Kendal must have decided she didn't want the limelight yet.

"As you can see, David Dawson is now here," Tracy said. "Coach Lambert will be out in a few minutes to give a statement. David will answer a few questions and then he has a dance to attend. If you have additional questions please see myself or Kendal Miller, and we will have David available for a nine a.m. conference call."

"Thank you, Ms. Dole. I want to give a brief statement and then we'll open it up for questions. Tonight, we played a fine team. As you saw, they had me on the run for most of the night. We caught some breaks and the game turned in our favor. Our defense played a heck of a game. On offense, Luke Herndon looked like an All State running back tonight, mostly due to the fine blocking of our offensive line. State is getting a fine player in Luke."

"How are you feeling?" one of the local reporters asked. "You took some serious shots tonight, especially your first play."

"Yeah, I thought he'd taken my head off. Once they figured out I wasn't going to die, our trainers put some duct tape on it and sent me back out. I think they were trying to let me know they were the better team. All the rough stuff did was fire us up. We used that play as motivation."

There were a few chuckles. Fox Sports was next.

"Your performance tonight will possibly vault you into the top 10 nationally among freshman quarterbacks. I see there are several college recruiters here tonight to see you perform. Did that have any effect on how you played?"

"Football's a team sport, and I'm lucky to play on one of the best teams around. My team makes me look good, so if I'm ranked it's due to them. As far as the colleges that have come out to see my fellow teammates and me, it's testament to the fine program that Coach Lambert has put together. They wouldn't be here if there wasn't talent on the field."

"David, I have to disagree."

I hated this guy. Jeff Delahey was with our local paper and was usually a jerk.

"I've been critical of the decision to change the offense and entrust it to a freshman. I've even questioned the level of your competition. I have to tell you, I've been covering high school football for 23 years, and tonight's performance rates in the top five I've ever seen. Do you think you can get any better?"

I didn't know what to say.

"Jeff, I think if you talked to Coach Lambert he'd tell you that I have a lot of room for improvement." That got a laugh. "At least, that's what he tells me in practice."

Tracy stepped up.

"Okay, Coach Lambert will give a ..."

I slipped out while she introduced Coach.

✧✧✧

By the time I got to the gym, the dance had already started. This year's theme was *Starry Night,* and they had somehow gotten the ceiling to look like the night sky. Round tables that would seat eight were strategically placed. They surrounded the dance floor and all had silver tablecloths on them. I edged around the gym as I looked for Cindy and Suzanne.

I caught a glimpse of white hair that could only be Suzanne on the dance floor. As I went a little closer to the stage, where the band was playing, I saw both of them dancing. They were smiling and having a good time. My breath caught in my throat when I saw their matching black dresses. They clung to their bodies in all the right places. They both looked gorgeous. I felt someone get close to me.

"Hey, those are their exes," Beth said.

I felt my stomach turn as I finally saw they were dancing with two guys I didn't recognize. If they were interested in getting back together with them, there was nothing I could do about it. I liked both girls, but if they needed to spend some time for closure, I was fine with that. I turned to Beth and she slid under my arm as I kissed her temple.

"Thank you for everything you did today. Did everyone have a good time?"

She wrapped her arm around my waist.

"Yes, everyone had a good time. We met our fundraising goal."

"That's great news."

"I'm relieved. I was getting tired of working on that."

I looked around.

"Where's Gary?"

She stiffened and I kicked myself because I could tell something was wrong.

"I don't know. He and I didn't work out."

I turned and looked her in the eye and I could see the sadness.

"Beth, I'm so sorry. I know you had your hopes up." I pulled her out on the dance floor. "Come on. If my dates are busy, I have time to dance with you."

She grinned and we worked our way onto the floor and started dancing. It wasn't long until I felt a hand on each of my butt cheeks and I turned to see Cindy and Suzanne grinning at me. Apparently, they had ditched their exes and joined Beth and I dancing.

"Dawson, you suck!" Luke yelled.

I just waved at him and he and Kevin cracked up. I was having the time of my life, dancing with the three of them. It felt comfortable to be with people that you liked. There was no pressure or worry like when I was with Tracy. I missed Tracy—there was something special about her—but this had no expectations. Anything that happened was fine.

With how busy my life was right now, this was a relief. When the song ended, a slow song started. The three girls smiled at each other and somehow decided that Cindy would dance with me.

I figured it was best to let them decide things. She smelled of jasmine. I closed my eyes and felt her body mold into mine. We gently swayed to the music, enjoying the moment. I felt her head turn and she kissed my neck which caused my eyes to open and pull back a little so I could see her angelic face. There was a twinkle of mischief in her eyes, which caused a twitch in my groin. She could make my knees go weak with just a look. I leaned down and kissed her.

Suddenly we were in our own little world with our lips locked. That twitch turned into arousal, and when she felt it, she let me know by her body movement that she approved. Just as I thought the first day of school when she kissed my brother, she was a 10. I was suddenly brought back to the present when someone tapped me on the shoulder.

"Do you mind if I cut in?" a male voice asked.

Cindy seemed to snap out of it and I saw her face go from lust to anger. I looked to the side and saw her ex looking uncomfortable. She gave him a look that would cause me to go find a place to hide, and I could see it had the same effect on him.

"Bryan, I tried to be nice and dance with you. You see I'm with my boyfriend. Go back to college and leave me alone."

She grabbed my hand and led me off the dance floor and we left Bryan in our wake. When we got to the table, she twirled around and planted a huge kiss on me. I thought that would be enough to give Bryan the hint he needed, because I saw him storm out of the dance. When our kiss ended, I was grabbed and turned. I found Suzanne as she pulled me into an equally hot kiss. When she finally let me up for air, Cindy slid in and kissed Suzanne. I heard several guys groan. I wanted to leave right now, but we had to wait because they were both in the running for Homecoming Queen.

When the song finally ended, we came to our senses and several people around us started to clap. We all were suddenly embarrassed. The girls giggled and left me to go to the bathroom.

I saw Kendal come in. She saw me and came over.

"Hey, Boss-man."

"Hey Kendal, when was the last time you were at a high school dance?"

"I don't even know." She looked around lost in her thoughts of dances past and then she turned back to all business. "We don't have to do a conference call tomorrow. Coach Lambert wants you to come in at ten to let the trainers work on you. There's no practice with Bo, so once you get done with the trainers you're free for the day."

"How did it go with the recruiters?"

"Interest is through the roof. Hey, your dates are coming back." I could see them entering the gym. "Good game tonight. I talked to several of the scouts after the game. They opened my eyes as to how good you are. I mean, I could tell you were a man among boys today, but they're thinking you have the potential to be one of the best. That's why they want to get in early. They know that when you're a senior, it might be too late to build a relationship."

I didn't know what to say. I guess I never thought in those terms. My focus had been on getting better so I wouldn't let the team down. I had ignored all the praise because I felt it was a distraction, but the jerk reporter's comments, and now Kendal's, made me wonder how good I might become. I knew that was the wrong way to look at things. Pride was one of the seven deadly sins. That wasn't what I was working so hard for.

"Kendal, one of the things you need to know about me is that I'm very competitive, but I'm not doing all this just for me. Tracy and I have worked hard not only to get me a scholarship, but the other guys as well. Of course I want to be the best I can be. I work hard at that, but the reason I have that goal is for the betterment of the team. People lose focus that football's a team sport."

"The guy from Alabama was talking about you being too unselfish. They said you shouldn't have pitched the ball to Luke. They said it hurt your running stats."

I laughed.

"If they'd argued it was stupid because of ball security, I would understand. I mean, I might've blown the pitch and we could've turned the ball over. I should've pitched him the ball when the defensive end had me in his sights. It was selfish of me to want to put a hit on him. I'm not perfect. I really wanted to take him out of the game, because I was mad about the cheap shot he took. I think I knew that once we broke into the open, and that's why I pitched the ball."

Kendal shook her head.

"I forget you're only fifteen and have the weight of the world on your shoulders. When I was your age I was worried if Danny Ellis liked me or not. You have people pulling at you all the time."

"I can only do what I can do. That's why I've turned the circus aspect of this over to you. I go to school and play football. Every once in a while I try to be a kid and have fun. Speaking of which, I'm at my Homecoming Dance, talking to you."

"I hear you. Go have fun."

I got serious for a moment.

"Kendal, I'm scared to death. If it wasn't for people like you, I could never do this. I want you to know I appreciate everything. Please let everyone that helped know."

"You got it, Boss."

Cindy and Suzanne came up and gave me a kiss. We decided to mingle. We ran in different circles and we wanted to have time to see our friends. I went to find Jeff and Alan. I eventually found them at one of the back tables. I should have known that they would gravitate to the edge of the action. No freshman wanted to draw too much attention to themselves.

Alan was with Gina. They made such a strange pair, but they seemed happy. To my surprise, Jeff had a date that he was currently ignoring. She didn't look happy. I caught his eye and he got up so we could talk. I lit into him as soon as he got close.

"What do you think you're doing?"

He got defensive.

"What crawled up your ass? What are you talking about?"

He had a right to be pissed, but he was blowing it with his date.

"Why're you ignoring your date?

He threw his hands up.

"She's being a whiny baby."

I looked out of the corner of my eye and Gina and Alan were joining us. Alan couldn't help but put his two cents in.

"He's right, she is being whiny."

I could see Gina give him a skeptical look.

"Okay, I'm going to explain something to you two. This is something that Greg taught me." That got their attention. Something coming from me about girls and dating they would probably ignore. If it came from Greg, the legend in their minds, then I was sharing a treasured secret. "This date is not about how you feel about your date. What's her name, anyways?"

Jeff looked as confused as Alan did. I could see a twinkle in Gina's eye.

"Her name's Sally. Why don't my feelings matter?" Jeff asked.

"Let me ask you a simple question. Do you want your next date to be after you graduate from high school?"

Jeff blew up.

"What are you talking about?"

I allowed myself a little smile. I turned to Gina.

"Gina, I need a woman's viewpoint. Do freshman girls talk to each other about the guys they date?"

"Yes, they do."

"If one of your sisterhood has a terrible time on a date, are they likely to go out with the guy that showed that girl a bad time?"

"No, they won't."

"Even if the girl in question was... what did you call her? Oh, yeah... whiny... and that was the reason the guy treated her badly?"

"Wouldn't matter, the guy would look like a jerk."

I turned to a stunned Jeff.

"This date is not about you. This date is about how all the other girls are going to look at you. This is about you getting dates in the future." I could see I had his attention. "Greg told me that on my first date with Tina that even if I had a bad time I had to make sure that she had a good time, so you suck it up and go pay attention to your date. She came to a dance with you, she got dressed up, and her friends are all jealous, so get your butt out there and dance."

He just nodded at me. It took him a moment to gather himself and he went over to the table where Sally was. We could see that she hadn't bought what he told her. After several minutes, we could see them both smile and he led her out to the dance floor.

I turned to Alan, who looked at me weird, so I made a motion with my chin to the dance floor and his eyes got big. I knew that Alan was terrified of dancing. I also knew he was more scared of messing up the best thing that ever happened to him, i.e. Gina. He grabbed her hand and pulled her to the dance floor. She turned back to me and mouthed 'Thank you.'

I went in search of more of my friends. I found the freshman football players all at a couple of tables. Bert, Mike and Tim were with their dates at one of the tables. They had an empty seat, so I sat down and shot the shit with them. Mike gave me a hard time about slumming it by hanging out with them. Since they gave me a hard time, I started to ask their dates to dance. After the second one, Mike and Tim threatened to tackle me. We all had a good time.

The rest of the night I found myself on the dance floor with a string of girls, many of whom I barely knew, but I think the guys had orchestrated the string of dance partners to keep me away from their dates. To tell you the truth, I didn't care why they did it. Right before it was time to announce the Homecoming King and Queen, my dates found me and saved me. I could tell that Suzanne was upset, but Cindy gave me a look to let me know we'd talk about it later.

Last year's King and Queen were on hand to pass their crowns on. Of course, Bryan was the previous King. He kept glancing over at Cindy, I wrapped my arm around her waist, and she gave me a strained smile of thanks. I expected one of my dates would be the Queen, but I was pleasantly surprised when they announced Beth and Gary as this year's royalty. I felt bad for Beth, because when everyone voted they thought they were a couple.

They had the traditional dance for just the King and Queen. You could see it was strained and Gary said something that pissed Beth off. She started to storm off the dance floor when Cindy gave me a shove. I swept Beth into my arms and she tried to fight me, but I just pulled her tighter to me. She broke down and cried, but I kept her dancing and she soon looked at me and smiled. We finished the dance and she was laughing by the time it ended. I had no idea where Gary had gone, but I was just happy to see that my friend wasn't sad.

We were both laughing when I took Beth to where Cindy and Suzanne were. Beth hugged Cindy.

"You sent him out there, didn't you?"

"He would have figured it out, but I gave him a nudge."

"Thanks for turning what could have been a bad moment into one I'll always remember."

"That's what friends are for."

They all three were grinning at me as I slowly turned red. If Cindy hadn't pushed me, I would've stood by and watched my friend's misery. Cindy had a good heart.

"She's right, what are friends for? I can only say I'm glad you three are my friends. I'm a lucky guy."

I saw Suzanne force herself to smile. Our eyes locked and I stepped forward and hugged her. I could tell that was what she needed.

"What's wrong?" I whispered.

She pulled back and planted a kiss on me that I was sure violated the school's PDA (Public Display of Affection) rule. When our kiss finally ended, Cindy giggled.

"Let's get out of here."

We made a hasty exit after I gave Beth a kiss on the cheek. She looked sad, but gave me a warm smile as my dates dragged me away.

✦✦✦

On the ride, I noticed that both girls were unusually quiet. It seemed like seeing their exes had reminded them of the pain they had both gone through. I'd never asked them about it before. Now I wasn't sure we had a relationship where I had the right to know. To be honest, I didn't really want to know about their past relationships. I could only see trouble in heading down that particular rabbit hole. I never saw the point in talking about people you used to date, not that I had many to share.

Now it seemed I might have to talk to them about it. If they were hurting and needed to be comforted, then I could do that. But how did I want this to work with the three of us? Did I want friends with benefits, or did I need more?

Emotionally I'd not dealt with Tracy. I'd been buried in all things football. I know there was going to be a day of reckoning. In the game tonight, I felt myself get so angry I wanted to injure another player. After the game, I said a prayer and thanked God that I hadn't hurt the guy. That anger had come from somewhere, and it made me someone I didn't like.

What I did like was that the anger triggered a focus I didn't realize I had. I dropped into a zone similar to the one I got into while I ran. It was as if muscle memory took over. I knew how much zip and loft to put into each pass. I could see where a receiver would be. I didn't even flinch when I was hit. Several of the shots I took were brutal. When my fellow offensive players saw me just keep getting up and shaking it off, they had upped their games. Everything seemed to work. We dismantled a physically superior team. If we could bottle this performance the rest of the year, we would be State Champions.

I was brought back from my thoughts as we slowed down in front of my garage apartment. We went upstairs and I could tell that Suzanne was having trouble. When we got into the apartment, I went into my bedroom and took off my suit. I grabbed a t-shirt and just my boxers.

I came back into my living room to find both girls hugging each other and crying. I went back into my bedroom and got them t-shirts and sweats with drawstrings. They went into my bedroom, changed, and came back out.

They both hugged me. I think even Mr. Happy realized we wouldn't have sex tonight.

"Look, I love you both more than you know, but you're both hurting tonight and I'm not the solution. You guys take my bed and I'll take the couch. You're best friends and you need each other's support."

Cindy caressed my cheek.

"When did you become so smart? We love you too, and you're right. I didn't know how to ask, but we need some time alone. Thank you."

Cindy took Suzanne's hand and led her to my bed.

✧✧✧

I grabbed my tablet, pulled the door closed behind me and went back to the living room. I sent a text to Tami to see if she was around. She sent one back saying she and her roommates were at a party. I replied to have fun. I sent one to Alice Phillips. She was home so we jumped onto video chat.

She was in the kitchen and I could see her family had just gotten home from her brother's game.

"Hey Alice, how did that All State brother of yours do tonight? Did he throw more interceptions than completions again?"

Poor John had been sacked hard in the previous game and they took him out as a precaution. Unfortunately, when he was hit the ball had landed in the wrong hands. This was the first chance I had to give him a hard time about it. He took the bait.

"I will tell you I put up All State numbers tonight." I could see his dad puffing up, and I knew John had had a good night. "I threw for three touchdowns and 280 yards. We won 28 to 24 over our crosstown rival. That locks up a playoff spot."

"Great job, John. Kentucky's lucky to be getting a player of your caliber."

Everyone but Alice seemed to take my praise at face value. She knew I was playing with her brother, and she played along.

“David, you should have seen him. He played the best game I’ve ever seen him play. He completed 26 of 48 passes with no interceptions. We had recruiters from Indiana, Vanderbilt, Rutgers, and of course Kentucky,” Alice bragged on her brother.

“John, that’s great. You keep that up and you might start your freshman year. That way you’ll get an extra year of playing time before I get there.”

Alice broke out into a big grin as both her dad and John gave me a dirty look.

“David, tell my brother and dad what you’ve done the last couple of weeks. Better yet, tell them how many recruiters came to your game tonight.”

“Alice, you know that I’m not like that. I want John to have his moment.”

Alice and her mom started to laugh. John rolled his eyes.

“Put me out of my misery. What did you do tonight, and who came to see you play?”

“We played one of the better 6A teams tonight. We’re a 5A school on the low end of enrollment in that class. I think they outweighed us 30 pounds at each position. Luckily, it was a home game or it could have been worse. On the first play, their defensive end literally ripped my helmet off my head. The training staff wanted to cart me off the field.”

John looked concerned.

“Are you okay?”

“You should have seen it. I was sacked 12 times tonight.”

I pulled off my t-shirt and I heard them all gasp. I looked down to see how bad it was, and I was black and blue all over. Man, this would hurt in the morning.

"Dude, why did they leave you in? They should have called the game if you guys were getting the crap beat out of you."

"I know. It was the absolute worst game for this to happen, too. I had 30 colleges at the game to see me play."

John's dad jumped in.

"Seriously, who all was at the game?"

I could tell from Alice's eyes that she was trying not to laugh.

"I had some independents, a couple from the Big Ten, some from the ACC and a few from the SEC. I even had a couple from the Pac 12."

John shook his head.

"Okay, quit being smug and tell us the highlights of the list."

"We had Notre Dame, Ohio State, Michigan State, Wisconsin, Alabama, Auburn, LSU, USC, Oregon and Texas all send representatives," I said with a straight face.

I could see John and his dad look like they'd eaten something that didn't agree with them.

"David, how bad was it? Did you guys even score tonight? You must have been so embarrassed," Alice said, laying it on thick.

"I threw 58 passes and completed 46 for 585 yards. We had over 800 yards of offense and beat them 72 to 14. One of the long-time reporters said it was one of the best performances he's seen in his 23 years of covering high school football. He also said I was one of the top 10 quarterbacks in the freshman class."

"Shut up," John's dad said.

His wife smacked him in the back of the head.

"Oh, I almost forgot. Fox Sports has us on as the regional High School Game of the Week. I think they're replaying it right now."

Alice jumped up, ran to the TV, and turned it on. Sure enough, the game was being replayed. I saw the men run in and I heard John.

"Oh my god! That's Alabama's coach. Good God, did David just forearm-shiver a linebacker and put him down?"

Alice came back shook her head.

"You're going to give my brother a complex. After he sees this game he'll be going to Indiana."

"Not that. Tell your dad if he lets you come to one of my games and spend the weekend I promise not to go to Kentucky."

I heard her mom laugh and she came into view.

"You make that promise and John will drive her himself."

She had an evil sparkle in her eye. I now knew where Alice got her sense of humor.

"I heard a rumor that you had Homecoming tonight and two seniors as dates? Any truth to that little tidbit?" Mrs. Phillips asked.

Crud, I was busted, and by the parental unit no less.

"There might be some validity to that rumor."

"I thought so. David, how are you going to explain Alice when she shows up?"

"Easy, all they'll have to do is take one look at her and they'll understand."

Alice gave me a dirty look.

"Not so fast. I don't share very well."

"Are you sure you want to have this conversation right now?" I asked while I raised my eyebrows.

She looked back to see her mom smiling at her. She got a sheepish look.

"No, that would probably be a bad idea."

It must have been time for a commercial because the men came back in. John looked sick.

"Please tell me you're not going to Kentucky."

"Your sister and I were just in discussions to solve that problem for you. I'll let her work out the details, but I might be persuaded."

John got a hopeful look, but I heard his mom say somewhere in the background, "Over my dead body. Sorry, John, but David's going to Kentucky."

I always felt good after talking to the Phillips family. They were all good sports and gave as well as they took. Alice would tease John for weeks. Our last game of the year was an away game almost two hours away. We would spend the night and come back Saturday. John had a Wednesday-night game, so they would have almost a week and a half before their first playoff game. It was a long drive for the Phillipses, but Alice had convinced her mom and dad to come to our game. John was the only one who wasn't in the loop. I looked forward to seeing both John and Alice again. We all were becoming good friends.

✧✧✧

Chapter 25 – We're Dead

Saturday October 19

I woke at 9 a.m. to find that Cindy and Suzanne had left sometime during the night. I jumped into the shower and let the hot water loosen my sore muscles. When I got out of the shower, I checked myself in the mirror and didn't like the view. Being blindsided so many times made me look as if someone had taken a two-by-four and beaten me. I ached all over and was a little hesitant to see what the trainers had in store for me.

I slipped on a pair of shorts, a t-shirt, and then put on some sweats on because it was only supposed to get into the high 50s today. I needed to go for a run to get my blood flowing and work out some of the kinks. I fell into an easy pace and dropped into my thinking zone. I missed my runs with Peggy. After football season, I would somehow figure out how we could do that again. She had a cute butt, and it didn't hurt that I had a crush on her. I knew that she'd also make a great girlfriend. She was a junior, and we could at least have a year and a half to build a relationship. Teenage years were similar to dog years, so that was almost forever.

Cindy and Suzanne were something else that I needed to figure out. I was embarrassed that I'd expected a hot threesome last night. One of the things Greg drilled into me was that you should not expect sex. If it was offered, treat it like a gift. Sex was a two-way street, or three-way, in last night's case. Be prepared, but don't force the issue. There was a lesson in there, but that was too much for me to think about right now.

What I couldn't seem to figure out was why I wasn't disappointed to find them gone in the morning. I started to get a nagging feeling of doubt in the back of my mind, that little tickle you felt that told you that not everything was as it seemed. Cindy had to know that her ex would be there. He was Homecoming King last year. When I got to the dance, both Cindy and Suzanne were dancing with their exes. Then they played it off as if nothing had happened. If nothing was going on with their exes, why had they both shown such strong emotions?

But what did I know? How would I feel if Tracy had been gone for several months and then showed up for a dance? Could I say I wouldn't feel anything? It was hard for me to judge because my emotions were still so raw from being dumped so recently.

Cindy said she was my girlfriend, but I started to wonder. Was I just a friend with benefits? Whatever Cindy and I did have didn't feel like boyfriend/girlfriend. We really needed to sit down and talk about our expectations. I could see being friends with benefits could work out. However, I didn't think any of the three of us was interested in a full-blown relationship right now. With all of my football commitments, I just couldn't see anything more working out.

By the time I got to school, I hadn't solved all of the world's problems, but I felt better about myself. When I walked into the training room, Becky Grimes and Jill Kim, our two assistant trainers, were there waiting for me. Jill was the one who took care of my strength and conditioning and Becky took care of injuries. They both saw that I was sweating and had a slight limp.

Becky gave me a hard look.

"Shit, I knew we should have checked you out last night. How bad is it?"

I pulled my shirt up.

"We're dead," Jill said, as she looked at Becky.

I could tell that they were both nervous.

"David, you have to tell us when you're hurt."

They each grabbed an arm and dragged me to the training table. They stripped my sweats and shirt off.

"Do you need to see all the damage?" I asked.

"Yes, drop 'em," Becky said with no hesitation.

I slid my shorts off and stood with my jock on. My left hip and thigh were black and blue also. Becky had a pained look on her face.

"Jill, set up an ice bath. While you're doing that, I'll check to see if he has any other injuries."

She had me lie on my stomach, and then she started to prod my bruises to see if any of my ribs were broken. Then she moved up to my neck. Once she was satisfied that I wasn't about to die, she checked my hip. I'm not quite sure when it changed from checking for medical issues to playing with my butt, but when Jill came back in she cleared her throat loudly. Becky jerked her hands off my butt as if she had been shocked.

I couldn't see Becky's face, but Jill looked amused. So I figured now was a good time to tease her. Okay, I'm a dumbass. Never, ever tease your trainer. They can do evil things to you, and treatment was much better when they weren't mad at you.

"Oh, baby, why'd you quit? Please do the other side. It's feeling left out," I said, using my sexiest voice.

The crack when she smacked my butt sounded like a shot had gone off.

"Oh yeah! That's it. Smack my ass!" I moaned. "I think I'm in love!"

Jill was about to lose it. She grabbed my arm and dragged me off the table.

"Come on, Lover Boy, before you take on more than you can handle."

I turned around to leer at Becky, but when I saw her face, I figured I'd better let it go.

The ice bath was pure torture. They filled one of the whirlpool baths with water and then dumped bags of ice into it. When I noticed that my balls had decided to crawl inside me, I was determined to get out, but Becky pushed me back in. She only made me stay in for another ten minutes or so, but it felt like an eternity. When I crawled out, my skin was bright red.

At that point, I no longer cared. I pulled my jockstrap off because it was wet and freezing cold. The trainers didn't even flinch. Jill threw me a towel to dry off. They made me get onto the massage table and started to work on me, using an analgesic rub that both deadened the pain and warmed me. I felt a mix of pleasure and pain as they worked me over. When they were finished with my back, I was limp as a cooked noodle.

"Turn over," Jill said smacking my ass.

They started on my front. I definitely was going to have to get a tub of the cream they were putting on me. Both of them knew how to give a massage. I could feel them find a knotted muscle and work it until it felt like a spring as it released. Surprisingly, I wasn't turned on in the least. I think Mr. Happy was afraid they would dunk him back into the ice bath.

I fell asleep at some point. I slowly woke to find the entire training staff and Coach Lambert standing around me as they talked about me. Luckily, the girls had slid my shorts back on. Coach Lambert was pissed.

"Look at him. He looks like he was in a car wreck. Do we sit him this week?"

"Coach, he's one of the toughest players I've ever seen," Becky said. "He took shots last night that would have killed most players. He has a very high pain tolerance, which is bad because he keeps playing. As a training staff, we let this young man down. I'm embarrassed to say we let him back in the game after that first play," Becky said. She looked at me and gave me a concerned look. "Good, he's awake. David, roll over so I can show them your neck."

I did as I was told.

"Look at this bruise," Becky continued. "It was caused by the edge of his helmet pressing into his spinal cord. In college, I saw the exact same bruise. That player never walked again."

Jill had me roll on my side so they could see all my bruises.

"We rubbed him down with an analgesic to deaden the pain. The good news is we think that the damage isn't as bad as it looks."

"We'll work on him until Wednesday and see if we can get him ready," Becky said as she turned to Coach. "At the end of practice, we'll evaluate him. No physical activity until we clear him."

Mr. Hasting, the head trainer, weighed in.

"Coach, if I see him get blindsided in the next game I'm pulling him out, so you better fix your backside blocking or you won't have David playing. His future is not playing high school football, and we can't risk his health for a short-term gain. Eastside lost last night, so we're a game up and in control of our playoff destiny." He turned on me. "Next time Coach tries to pull you, let him. Good God, we were up four touchdowns."

I felt bad. There was no reason other than pure selfishness for staying in that game. I'm sure they thought I was showcasing my talent on TV. The real reason was almost as bad: I was pissed and wanted to crush them. Listening to the concern everyone showed made me feel irresponsible. The training staff went into Coach's office, so I got dressed and left.

✧✧✧

Luke called me when I got back to remind me that tonight was guys' night out and asked if I needed a ride. I still hadn't heard from Cindy or Suzanne, so I decided to make the best of a bad day and take him up on his offer. He picked me up, and we went to Monical's Pizza. He gave his brother Mike and Tim Foresee a ride also. We had a good time cutting up in the car. Monical's was packed with families as it always is on Saturdays. They're famous for giving you a lot of food for a reasonable price.

We saw many people we knew, and spent some time after we ordered to work our way through the restaurant, going from table to table. It turned out that only half of the guys showed up and none of the girls. The breakup of Beth and Gary really messed up attendance. I was happy to see that Jim Ball showed up. He still had a black eye, and was moving a little slowly.

We all finally sat down when our pizza was ready. Then it quickly became 'pick on David' time, and Magic was first at bat.

"So David, how was your hot threesome last night?"

"Dude! Totally uncool!" I said with a scowl. "First of all, Cindy and Suzanne are friends of ours. You know talking out of school will get all our balls cut off."

I saw everyone nodding because they all knew that those two could do it.

"Secondly, when have I ever talked out of school about a date?" I asked. "But because you guys won't be satisfied without some scoop, nothing even close to a threesome happened last night. And finally, I think you have all met Suzanne's brother, Jim."

Their heads snapped around when it dawned on them that they were talking about someone's sister. That was a serious breach of the bro code! Magic had a sheepish look on his face.

"Sorry, Jim. I was just giving David shit."

I smiled brightly.

"I did get a naked rub down and had my ass played with today, though."

That remark lightened the mood. Jim gave me a nod to acknowledge that I had headed off a potentially embarrassing situation for him. Luke, who seemed to live for my adventures, had to ask.

"There has got to be a great story behind that."

"Why, Luke, there is. First, I want to show you the results of not blocking for me."

I stood up and lifted my shirt. I could see the shock on all their faces. I heard a gasp behind me, and I felt a cold hand run up my side. Looking at me with concern was Gina. She almost had tears in her eyes. I was suddenly concerned for her.

"Hey, baby, it's okay. I might be out a week, but nothing's broken. This time."

It took a moment for that one to sink in.

"Shit! I might have to go back to quarterback," Magic scowled.

Kevin, our All State linebacker and defensive captain, looked even more pissed. Magic was switched to cornerback and was now our lockdown guy. Kevin could potentially lose his best cornerback. I winked at the guys and turned back to Gina.

"Hey, let's go somewhere for a little bit."

I could see the look in her eyes that told me she knew that I was playing with the guys. Then she shocked even me when she got on her tiptoes and kissed me. She had achieved her desired goal, because all of us had our mouths hanging open.

"I've wanted to do that since the first time I met you."

"Uh."

The gears in my mind were in a locked position. She grabbed my hand and guided me to her table. Sitting there was an older version of Gina. She looked to be in college. They both were exotically pretty. I knew from talking to Alan that they were of Indian descent. I sat down in their booth beside Gina and across from her sister.

"David, this is my sister, Emily. Emily, this is one of Alan's best friends."

Emily's eyes lit up. Emily was the oldest of the three sisters.

"Don't tell me you're the David that Gina talks about. I think if she wasn't dating Alan, she'd take a run at you. I can't say that I blame her."

Gina blushed, which made me laugh.

"What happened to the woman I know who's always in control? Looks like your sister can push your buttons."

Gina slugged my arm.

"Sorry, I forgot."

"Actually, it's the other side."

Somehow, that earned me another slug. I eyed their pizza because I could see the guys had devoured ours while I talked to Gina. Emily saw me, and she served me a couple of slices and filled a bowl of salad for me. Monical's special was called the 'Family Pleaser' and served family-style. Most everyone got that, which was a pizza, pitcher of soda, and a huge salad. The girls watched in fascination as I polished off their leftovers.

"I forgot how much teenage boys eat," Emily said as she shook her head.

"Thanks for last night. Once Alan loosened up, we had a lot of fun," Gina said to change the subject.

Emily gave me a look, so I filled her in.

"One of our friends was out on his first date last night. I guess the date wasn't going well. We explained to him he would remain dateless throughout high school if he didn't make a serious effort to show her a good time. He didn't seem to realize that girls talk. Alan and Gina were watching the car wreck happen. Alan got the hint that if he didn't show Gina a good time, he might be dateless also."

"Where were you when I was in high school?" she asked, and then turned to Gina. "You're right! He's perfect for Kara."

I perked up.

"Tell me about this goddess. I've only seen a picture. Please tell me that Gina isn't playing with me, and she Photoshopped it."

Gina pulled out her phone and showed Emily the picture.

"Actually, no. She didn't alter the picture. That's Kara." she laughed. Then she stage-whispered to Gina, "Should we give him the scoop, or should we let them both be surprised?"

"I was thinking that the surprise factor might be nice, but you know how full of herself Kara can be. It might help if he had some things to fight back with. Plus, I don't think he's helpless," Gina said.

"If half of what you told me is true, he'll be able to hold his own," Emily said, and gave me a leer that was so full of sexual heat that it shocked me. "I do have one question, David. Did you really take two girls to the Homecoming Dance?"

"It sounds worse than it was," I sighed. "They're actually best friends. The week before, I got dumped, and one of them won me in a bachelor auction. The other one didn't want some dork pawing her all night, so we all decided to go together."

"Forget Kara! I'm taking you home tonight to show you what a real woman's all about."

"No, no, no! Bad Emily! There's this thing called statutory rape," Gina said, waving her hands.

"Uh, I'm not telling," I said. "You'll have to drive because I don't have a license yet."

I knew that comment would get her to slow down. We could see the wheels turning as Emily tried to figure each angle. She'd periodically would give me a hungry look, and I could feel Gina stiffen next to me. I took Gina's hand under the table, and I felt her relax when she figured out I was messing with Emily. We finally saw her shoulders sag.

"Shoot."

"Tell you what, when I turn eighteen you can have your way with me."

"Kara isn't going to know what hit her," Emily said as she laughed.

I hung out with Gina and her sister for a while, until they had to leave for the movies. I wandered back to the guys, and Luke gave me shit about always finding a girl wherever I went. Luke was actually very sought-after, but for some unknown reason he seemed to think I had more success with the ladies.

After Monical's, we decided to go to the arcade. There was talk of miniature golf, but we decided it was too cold. Surprisingly, we pretty much had the place to ourselves. The guys had a good time goofing off. Magic took on all challengers to the dance game he'd commandeered. Once he'd beaten all of us, he made an announcement.

"Does anyone else want to take on the champ?"

"Do you mind if a girl tries?" Tomika asked, surprising us all as she came up behind us.

Magic spun around.

"Little girl, I don't know if you have the skills to keep up. Why don't you run along and save your quarters?"

We were playing challenger pays.

"Little girl, is it?" she said, putting her hands on her hips. She turned on us with a little heat in her voice. "Boys, do I look like a little girl to you?"

We all just took one step back. Magic got himself into this, and he could get himself out of it. Sometimes I wondered about my friends.

"Big talk for a little girl. Put up or shut up," Magic challenged.

She pumped quarters into the machine. They both started out seriously. We watched in amazement as they looked like they were in sync with the game. Then she gave Magic a hip check and her cute giggle lightened the mood. They started to just freestyle, the game be damned. Shortly after that, we lost Magic for the night. I didn't blame him. I would leave with Tomika if she asked.

I found Jim playing pinball by himself.

"How're you doing?"

He looked at me and he gave me the first genuine smile I could remember him having tonight. Most brothers aren't too fond of the guy who might be sleeping with their sister. To make things even more awkward, he went out with Tracy after she dumped me.

"Fine."

"How're the ribs?"

"They suck. I found out that I'm done with football this year."

"Ah man, that sucks," I said.

"Yeah, I'm looking forward to playing varsity next year."

"Jim, I'm hoping you play left tackle next year. I need someone to keep them off of me."

"No shit. You took a pounding. Those bruises look painful."

"Nah, they gave me some painkillers when I messed up my back before. I took a half of one before I came out tonight. Those things make me goofy if I take a full one."

He laughed.

"They do bring down some inhibitions. I'm lucky to be out tonight, given some of the things I said."

We spent the next thirty minutes just hanging out. I found he had a similar personality to his sister, so we got along great. Based on those similarities, I could also see something was bothering him. He sighed.

"You know I love my sister?"

"Yes, I think she's special, too."

He got a sad look on his face.

"I don't know any other way but to tell you: she and Cindy went to Cindy's lake cabin with their exes this weekend."

Whatever he saw in my face was not good.

"I'm so sorry. Suzanne made me promise not to tell you, but getting to know you tonight I realize you're too nice of a guy for them to take advantage of you like that."

I gathered my thoughts. My first instinct was to make excuses for them, but if I kept making the same mistake, I was a fool. The last thing I needed to do was vent to her brother.

"Jim, I'll always remember this. You're a true friend."

"The thing that sucks is that I know she likes you a lot. You have no idea how sick I am of hearing 'David this' and 'David that.' The only guy she would ever leave you for is her ex. She thought he was the one. He's a complete ass-hat. He always treated her like shit. Last night it was all I could do to not punch him out."

"Wow, how do you really feel?"

"Sorry, but you weren't around when he dumped her. When she started hanging out with you, it was as if she was back. I rather hated you because I didn't want to see her get hurt again, but I loved to see that spark again. The more I get to know you, the more I like you. I see what my sister sees in you, but she makes me so mad sometimes. For some reason she has a blind spot for this guy. Everyone around her knows he's a dick, but she won't listen."

"Thanks for telling me. I need a few minutes to collect my thoughts."

"I'm sorry, man."

I went outside the arcade and sucked in the crisp fall air. I thought about being a wimp and sending them a breakup text. I decided to man up and call Suzanne. When she answered, I could hear everyone laughing in the background.

"Hang on a moment," she said.

I heard the noise level go down. She obviously went to another room.

"How's your guys' night going?"

"It was going pretty well until a few minutes ago. After what you and Cindy went through, I never thought you would do it to me. I thought we were better friends than that. Now I know better. I don't want to have this conversation twice. Please let Cindy know we're through as friends."

I could hear Suzanne drop the phone and start crying. Cindy came on the line.

"David, it's not what you think."

I cut her off.

"Cindy, how would you know what I think? I'm told you're on a weekend with your exes, and that I'm not supposed to know. Sounds like you don't think much of me. At least I'm calling you to let you know we're through. In the past two weeks, I've taken too much crap from women I thought cared about me. I'm done. I hope this weekend was worth it for you."

"Oh, shit, David! I'm so sorry."

"A little late for that now," I said, and then punched the disconnect button and powered off my phone.

Ten minutes later, Jim found me sitting against the side of the arcade. He sat down next to me.

"Suzanne called me. They kicked both their exes out and are driving back. They want to see you."

"Are you kidding me?" He must have thought I was going to hit him for a moment because he flinched. "Sorry, this isn't your fault."

"Well, it is, in a way. I was the one who told you, but looking back, I know it was the right thing to do. They both feel bad. Will you agree to sit down and hear them out?"

I didn't need to think about it.

"Jim, I'm sorry, but they've broken our trust. That's the same issue I had with Tracy. Once doubt sets in, your relationship's doomed. To be honest, I'm not even sure I can remain friends with them. I guess the short answer is 'no.' Tell them not to bother."

"I was afraid of that. Let me call them, and then I'll give you a ride home. I don't think either one of us would enjoy the rest of the night."

Jim stepped away to call his sister. After a few minutes, things got heated.

"Sis, what did you expect? If he did this to you, would you give him a second chance?"

"Bullshit. You'd feed him his balls."

She must have made an impassioned plea. I could see he was about to explode, so I got up and took the phone from him.

"You little shit. You told him I was with Darryl to spite me. You've done some mean things, but this takes the cake."

"Suzanne, Jim told me because we're friends. It had nothing to do with spite. You put Jim in a no-win situation. Once you think about it, you won't be mad at him. At least I hope you won't," I said to defend my new friend.

She seemed to calm down.

"You're probably right. I'm just mad at myself. If Cindy and I promise not to act crazy, will you let us come see you and talk?"

I was resigned. I needed to get this over with.

"Okay, how long until you get here?"

I heard her ask and I heard a man's voice. I guess it was too much to ask that they drive up separately. Hearing his voice felt like a nail had been driven through my heart. Before she could get back to me, I ended the connection. I looked at Jim with a look of anguish. I handed him the phone and walked home.

✧✧✧

Chapter 26 – So We're Good?

Sunday October 20

From the arcade to my house is nearly eight miles. I made it a point to take a roundabout way to get home, which added nearly three miles to the trip. I didn't want to talk to anyone. It took me five and a half hours and it was close to 3:30 am when I walked up my driveway. I saw the light on in the kitchen. I knew Mom wouldn't go to bed until I got home, so I came in the back door.

Mom was seated at the kitchen table drinking coffee. When she saw me, she jumped up and came to me. She took one look at me and wrapped me in her arms. That was when the tears finally came. I felt her unconditional love for me, and it was as if the dam broke. I couldn't stop. At that time, in my mother's arms, I was able to grieve for the loss of my relationships with Tracy, Cindy, and Suzanne. She just stroked the back of my head.

"It'll be all right," she whispered over and over again.

I don't know how long I cried, but I eventually stopped. Once I stopped, I sat down at the kitchen table and Mom and I talked. I guess more accurately, I talked and she listened. I shared my time with Uncle John with her. How he'd helped me turn my life around. I explained how he helped me set my goals for my life and how I planned to work towards each of them. She was a little shaken when she realized how much I'd changed. She never judged or made a smart comment. She asked questions if she wasn't clear on something.

I then talked to her about my love of football. I think she was overwhelmed to see how far I'd progressed. I talked to her about my future goals for the game and explained how it would help me achieve my life goals. I could tell she finally accepted me playing. Her fear was always for my safety. I think it helped her to come to the game and see me play.

Then I floored her. I told her that I loved Tracy Dole. I'm not sure where it came from, but when I said it, I knew it to be true. If possible, I would marry her, even if we were too young. I explained how we were perfectly matched and how we were better together than apart. I told her that it wouldn't be anytime soon. We had to rebuild the trust in our relationship. She seemed skeptical, but at least she kept her thoughts to herself.

I told her about Cindy and Suzanne. I told Mom about my plans to put a hold on my love life. She actually laughed at me and wished me luck. By then it was eight in the morning and we had to go to church. I just washed my face and Mom changed. We went to early service.

For a moment, we considered not going. We were both dead tired. Mom got my dad up and made him drive us. We both felt like we needed church today. I couldn't tell you what the sermon was, but I felt better afterwards.

My relationship with my mother was forever changed that night. We both loved each other unconditionally, but now there was a much deeper understanding. My mom was firmly in my corner now. I found I could share my deepest thoughts with her with no reservations. Who would have thought that she kicked me out of the house just a few months ago? She became my anchor and sounding board. Right now, those were two things that I needed desperately.

When I got home, I turned on my cell and found thirty-eight messages. I sent Cindy and Suzanne a text telling them that I would meet them tonight and that they were not to call me because I was going to sleep. I turned my phone off and crawled into bed. As soon as my head hit the pillow, I was out.

✧✧✧

I finally crawled out of bed at 3:00 and hit the shower. I was starved, so I went to the kitchen and made myself a couple of sandwiches. Dad and Greg came in when they heard me getting something to eat.

"I'm making sandwiches. Do you guys want anything?" I asked.

Neither one of them did, but they sat down at the kitchen table and didn't say anything. It took me a few minutes, but I figured out Mom told them to give me some space. I started to chuckle.

"Let me guess: you both want to know what's going on, and Mom told you not to ask. Is that about the size of it?"

They both nodded. I gave them the shortened version of everything I talked to Mom about. When I got to the part about how Uncle John helped me and out of that, I set goals for my life, Greg wanted to know if Uncle John could help him. We made tentative plans to visit him at Christmas time.

I saved what happened with Suzanne and Cindy for last. I thought Greg might track them down and lynch them.

"I've known both of those girls since kindergarten. I thought we were friends. If they think for one minute they can treat my brother that way, they have another thing coming."

Dad was the voice of reason.

"Greg, let David deal with it. They're both young and are only thinking about themselves. I can tell you from personal experience, having an ex dump you, come back, and say they want to try again is hard to turn down, no matter how badly it ended. I know in my case it didn't take long for me to figure out there was a good reason they were an ex. David, I know you said you were meeting this afternoon. What are you planning on doing?"

"Well, for starters, Cindy is no longer my girlfriend. I don't want this to turn into a huge deal where friendships are hurt." I said, as I pointedly looked at my brother. "I think it's best if I bite the bullet and forgive them. What I can't do is forget. The only official contact I have with either of them is Suzanne as my tutor. I'll ask to either to be assigned someone new, or not have a tutor and use last period as study hall. After this afternoon, I'm going to take a step back from dating until after football season. Once football's done, I'll talk to each of them individually and we'll see if we can be friends. If I had to make that call right now, the answer would be no."

"Okay, Bro. I'll back off, but don't ask me to hang out with them."

"Greg, I can't pick your friends. All I ask is that you let us work it out."

"Fair enough. Do you want me to put the word out that you're focusing on football and not dating right now?"

"If you think it'll slow them down, then please."

"Some it might. Others, not so much. Are you planning on dating Beth?"

"I don't know. There's a hell of an attraction there, and our families have been friends forever. I think our moms planned for you and her to get together. I'm afraid if it goes south, it'll be a huge mess. Besides Tami, she's my best friend. I don't want to lose that friendship, too."

"We decided it was best to be friends. Now that Angie's in the picture, I don't think I'll ever date Beth."

"When's Angie coming home? Isn't the baby due?" Dad asked.

"She could have it at any time."

"Are you going to marry her?" I asked.

"I think so. We agreed to wait until I graduate from high school."

"Well, guys, I have to go prepare myself for seeing the girls. I need to talk to Tami first. I'll see you after I'm done."

"Good luck, man."

Dad just nodded.

✧✧✧

I went back to my apartment and sent a text to Tami. She was on the video chat before I turned on my tablet.

"So, I just want you to know that you're the talk of Wesleyan. Your little 'naked dance party' stunt has all the girls begging me to bring you over for a visit. I've had seven girls ask if they can come home with me for Thanksgiving."

"I hope you said no. I thought you and I were spending time together then. I miss the hell out of you."

She heard my voice tremble and instantly knew something was wrong. I caught her up on what happened.

"Tami, I do miss you. I'm afraid I'll go back to that dark place again."

"Snap out of it. You're not that scared little boy anymore. I never would've left if I thought you couldn't handle things. I love you too much. Don't make me regret leaving."

"Tami, I would never disappoint you on purpose."

"Okay, I'm going to tell you what to do so you can quit this brooding. First of all, you need to put some distance between yourself, Cindy, and Suzanne. End of football is too soon. You need to get past that and take some time to focus on what you want. Tell them you'll talk to them again after Christmas break. By then you'll know if you can be friends with them or not.

"I'm going to take over for Greg and manage your love life. I'll set up a date for you on Saturday night. This will be a casual, no-strings-attached, fun date. Your only responsibility is to show up and have a good time," Tami ordered me.

This was so like Tami. She was going to control my life from a hundred miles away. Right now that sounded good to me. I also knew that there was more to this. She would try to find me the right girl. I obviously didn't have the best track record in that regard. Tami was much more perceptive and knew me better than anyone else. I found I was actually looking forward to her meddling in my life.

I also knew that since the naked dance party night she was much happier at school. Being the only scholarship kid at an exclusive school was a recipe for disaster. Kids our age were cruel when someone was different. Tami would never admit it if they'd been mean to her. I could tell from our talks how much happier she seemed to be since I bared all.

"Since you're now in charge of my social calendar, why don't you bring one or two of your friends home over Thanksgiving? I'll take one of them out Friday and another out Saturday. On Thursday, you and your mom are invited to the Andersons' home as always. I'll tell Mrs. Anderson you're bringing a couple of friends.

"Next, let me know what the date of your Christmas dance is and I'll come up and be your date. That way I can meet all my admirers. If you can find a date for Luke, I can probably talk him into driving me," I suggested.

"Hell, if these girls knew you needed a ride to get here they'd hire a limo to bring you up. Let me think about Thanksgiving. I might want to be greedy and keep you all to myself."

"Just give me the word. So, since you aren't going to be here until Thanksgiving, who're you thinking would be a good match? Do you need a list of girls I think are cute?"

"No, I don't need a list, and no, I am not setting you up with Peggy. I can see your list now. It would have one name on it."

"Oh, you're no fun. Peggy has seen me naked and didn't run away screaming. That's a good sign, right?"

"Yes, that is a good sign, but you're not ready for Peggy."

"Shit, that's what Greg keeps telling me." Then I remembered a cute girl and started to do a little happy dance. "I have one for you that you don't even know."

"Really, let me guess."

"I bet you'll never guess."

"What's the bet?"

"Let's make it interesting. You win and you control my dating life for the rest of the year. If I win, you set me up with Peggy."

"Okay, you have a bet. Kara Tasman."

"You evil girl. How did you know about her?"

"'Stupid boy,' Gina and I are friends now that Alan's going out with her. We talk about you all the time. This is going to be so much fun. Hang on. I want you to tell my roommates what I won." She dragged her PC out to their common area.

"I have David on video chat!" Tami yelled.

The room quickly filled up, and I saw a girl I hadn't seen before looking at me on the screen.

"Oh, he *is* cute."

Tami came back in and took center stage.

"Okay, David, tell them what you agreed to."

"I lost a huge bet with Mistress Tami. She has complete access to my body from now until the end of the year, and only she decides whom I'm with. Did you need me to show them my body again, Mistress?"

The place erupted and Tami was beet red. Paybacks are a bitch. I started to take my shirt off.

"Stop!" Tami shouted.

"Yes, Mistress," I bowed my head. "Mistress Tami has told me that two of you will be accompanying her home over Thanksgiving. I'm supposed to take each one out on a date. I'm supposed to do *whatever* they want. Please let Mistress Tami know if you want to accompany her home."

I put on a little-boy grin.

"Did I please you, Mistress?"

Tami snatched the PC off the table and took it back into her room so she could talk to me alone. As soon as she closed the door, she broke out into a huge smile.

"Who do you love?" I asked her.

"You! This is going to be so much fun. If you can get Luke to drive you up, there might be an actual fistfight to see who gets to take him to the Christmas dance. See if Mike can come too. We'll have a good time. Just so you know, you've earned a reward for this Saturday. I'll make sure it's someone you can have a little fun with."

"Good call. Hey, I have to jump off here. It's almost time for Cindy and Suzanne to get here. Tami, thanks for being my friend. You lifted my spirits. We're going to have a good time with the Wesleyan girls. Make sure they know it's all just in fun. I don't want to get anyone's feelings hurt."

"I'm not worried about them. I am more worried about what they want to do to you."

She had a point. I'd sort of opened the door on that one.

✧✧✧

Cindy and Suzanne showed up a few minutes later. I was still in a good mood, and I think it surprised them to see me smile when they came through the door. We got comfortable in my living room. They sat on the couch, and I sat in my comfy side chair. They both sat quietly as they looked at me. I guess they were waiting on me to say something. The quiet stretched until it became uncomfortable. This was going to go badly if I didn't do something.

"You asked for this meeting. I assumed you wanted to tell me something." I tried to say it as nonthreateningly as possible.

They looked at each other, and I guess Cindy was elected as spokesperson.

"David, we're trying to figure out why you're mad at us. It's not like we're going out or anything. You're free to date who you want. Just as we are."

"Okay, I guess that's settled then. Thanks for stopping by." I stood up to usher them out.

They didn't seem to think things went the way they wanted. Neither of them got up.

"So you're not mad at us?" Suzanne asked.

"No, you're right. I have no say as to who you choose to date. All I care about is that you're happy."

"So we're good?" Suzanne realized that this was too easy.

"Absolutely."

She seemed to relax, but I could see the wheels turning. When she figured it out, she slumped into the couch.

"And you get to choose who you date," she figured out.

"You got it."

"And you choose not to date either of us."

"Correct. Now that we're all on the same page, I have better things to do."

Suzanne started to cry. Cindy also had tears in her eyes.

"Hold on, no crying. You guys got what you wanted. You can keep dating your ex-boyfriends, and I won't complain."

"That's not what we wanted!" Cindy blurted out.

"Do you two want to take a minute and figure out what you want to tell me?"

They nodded.

"Okay, I'll go into my bedroom. When you're ready, come and get me."

I went into my room and sent a text to Alice to see if she could chat. She wasn't free, but John was, so we jumped onto video chat.

"Hey Mr. All State, how's it going?"

"Not bad, Mr. Sixth-Best Freshman Quarterback in the Nation."

"What! Did someone get their list out?"

There were several recruiting sites. They tended to hold off on listing freshman rankings until later into the season.

"Yeppers, my favorite sister printed it off and put it in my Bible so I'd find it at church. Of course, I said a bad word when I read it, and Mom cracked me on the back of the head. Then Dad saw it and got the same treatment. We both got lectures on what can and can't be said in public."

"I love Alice. She's too frickin' funny. I bet the little angel didn't even crack a smile."

"Nope. You have to help me think of some way to get her back. With both of you working against me, I don't stand a chance. I'm not too proud to beg."

"You dork, all you have to do is ask. Alice can take it as well as she can give it out. I'll tell you a little secret: I'm bruised from head to toe after last week's game. The training staff says if I even get touched this week, they're benching me. My guess is I'll last about 3 plays at the most," I said to give him some scoop.

"We taped your Fox game and our coaching staff broke it down. I went in today and I learned a lot watching it again. I'll send you the report our assistant coach put together, but good God, you need a new left tackle. I'll admit, you're the toughest guy I know," John said.

I heard a soft knock on my door. I told them to come in.

"This is John Phillips. He was last year's All State Quarterback for the state of Kentucky, and it looks like he'll repeat this year. He was at the University of Kentucky when I made my visit. He was offered and verbally accepted that weekend. I met his family and we're good friends. They're actually coming to see my last game of the year."

John's eyes got big.

"What, I get to come and see you play?"

"Oops, sorry. That was supposed to be a surprise. Your game is Wednesday and ours is on Saturday afternoon. You're coming up Friday night and going to the game on Saturday."

"Alice is going to flip out when she finds out."

"Dude, who do you think put this together? Just play along. You can mess with her and tell her you have a big date that Friday."

"Good call."

"John, this is Cindy and Suzanne. They were my dates to Homecoming."

"I really feel like a dork now. I thought he was lying when he told me he was going with two of the most gorgeous and fun girls at your school. I can see why you like them so much. They're cute. Hang onto this one, girls, this is one of the greatest guys I know. Thanks for chatting. I'll let everyone know we talked, and thanks for the ideas. Alice'll never know what hit her."

I turned off my tablet. Both girls were looking at me in a strange way.

"What?"

"Do you really tell your friends that we're gorgeous and fun?" Cindy asked.

I popped my eyebrow, trying to figure out if I said something wrong.

"Yeah, I don't mean it in a bad way."

"I didn't take it in a bad way."

She made a big sigh.

"I'm such a self-centered bitch. I didn't even think of your feelings this weekend. I also realize that I said we were dating last Friday. Oh, man, I've messed this up good. I've hurt the nicest guy I know, all over an ex-boyfriend who thinks I should be his sex slave. I actually hope I never see him again. Now I'm afraid I'll never see you again."

Suzanne was looking paler than usual.

"Jim straightened me out last night when I got home. He said you and he became friends last night. Please don't hold what I did against him. He needs a friend."

"Okay, no more games. In the last two weeks I've been publicly humiliated by three women I thought I cared about me."

I could see them flinch when they put it together from my point of view.

"If I dwell on this, it's going to eat me up. I have responsibilities that affect this whole community. I can't have my personal life be a roller coaster and meet those obligations.

"A two-minute conversation could have avoided this whole thing. Instead, you chose to sneak off for a weekend with instructions that I didn't have a right to know. Well, you had it right earlier. I get to choose who I date, and it's not going to be either of you. I'm also not going to decide if we're friends or not right now. I need to take some time and not make a snap decision, because we've built a nice friendship that I'd hate to see ruined over something like this. I propose we get back together after Christmas break and decide then."

They both agreed. I had one last thing to say.

"If either of you catches any shit over this, you let me know. I still like you enough to care about both of you. I'll shut it down. If you think about it, Tracy was on her way to being lynched. No one bothered her because I put the word out that I wouldn't tolerate it. Suzanne, I'm Jim's friend. I'll also talk to him about getting on your case. If it doesn't stop, let me know, and he and I'll have a come-to-Jesus talk."

She giggled at that. I knew right then that Suzanne and I would be friends. The jury was still out on Cindy. For some reason, I felt her whole approach was calculated. Now that I knew the story about Angie being pregnant, and Cindy still using Greg for sexual relief, it was more than I wanted to know. I know if I got a girl pregnant, it would be game over. My playing-around days would end.

Suzanne had one last thing to say.

"I'm really sorry. There are just two things you and I need to clear up. Cindy, do you mind giving us a moment?"

Cindy got up and went into the living room, closing the door behind her.

"Sorry, what I have to ask you is personal and just between us. The first is would it be all right if I continue being your tutor?"

"If you had asked me that question fifteen minutes ago, the answer would have been 'no.' I think our friendship is going to last, so I don't have a problem with us working together."

"This one is a little more personal. I have certain needs and I really don't want to have them taken care of with someone I either don't like or trust. The only other guy I could ask this of is your brother, but he's in a serious relationship."

"Is what you're proposing a two-way deal? Can I come to you if I have needs?"

"Of course."

"This is the exact discussion I was going to have with you after Christmas break. I just decided this is what I was going to talk to you about. Are you going to talk to Cindy about this?"

"No, I think our friendship has been damaged more than yours and mine has been. It was her idea to try to reconnect with a weekend getaway. I knew it was a terrible idea, but I went along with it. She and I said some very hurtful things to each other. We didn't even drive over together tonight."

"Let me get rid of Cindy."

I went out into the living room. Cindy had already left. I went down and locked the door.

I came back into the bedroom, and after getting on the bed, I leaned back against the headboard, and she laid her head on my chest.

"I want to be up front with you: I see us being friends with benefits. I don't see us dating unless it's just to go out as friends. Well, hell, if we went on a date you might get lucky."

"David, that works for me. I'm still getting over what my brother refers to as 'that ass-hat.' He can be pretty funny and not even realize it."

"He's a great guy. Anyway, here's one of those things that only communication will help. I agreed today to allow Tami to manage my love life. I know it sounds strange, but she's my best friend and knows me better than I do. She's going to set me up on a series of dates. I suspect I'll have one-night stands. Just for full disclosure, Tami and I have been intimate.

"We plan on getting together over Thanksgiving. She's also bringing a couple of her classmates for dates over that weekend. I'll also be going over to Wesleyan for their Christmas Dance. I'm going to see if Luke will take me if I set him up on a date.

"I'm not telling you all this to rub salt in your wounds. I'm telling you this so if you're uncomfortable in any way, I can either alter my plans or you can back out," I said.

"Actually, your honesty is refreshing. I knew you wouldn't be pining away without us in your life. Cindy thought you didn't know you had options. She would shit if she knew Tami had girls lined up for you.

"Now it's time for me to be honest with you: I didn't even kiss my ex-boyfriend this weekend. That's one of the things Cindy was the maddest about. I'm not going to run her down, so don't ask. I don't plan on dating anyone other than friends," Suzanne told me.

"What I would really like is for us to not use condoms. But I think you would agree that if we do this, we need to get tested. Not that I don't trust you, but you're a little slut. We would also need to use condoms if either of us is with someone else," she proposed.

I would only do this with someone I trusted. So, did I trust Suzanne? The fifteen-year-old boy said hell yes, no condoms. Greg had told me that I needed to be responsible. He was the walking poster boy for the use of birth control. In the end, the fifteen-year-old boy won out.

"I'd agree to that as long as I know you're taking care of birth control and the same deal applies if you're with anyone else."

"David, I do care for you, and I promise not to hurt you if I can help it. That includes using a condom with someone else."

"I like you, too. Probably more than I should, but that's my issue. You'll never have to worry about me being a problem when it's time for you to either start a relationship or leave for school. If or when you come back for breaks, and we're both free, I'd love to get together with you."

She kissed me. It looked like we might just work our way past this.

✦✦✦

I think we were both exhausted, because Suzanne fell asleep and I joined her in a power nap. I woke up and heard my brother chuckle. My eyes snapped open and I saw him leaning against my bedroom door. Suzanne was softly snoring, and I found a wet spot on my chest where she had drooled.

"So, after Christmas break was the plan," he mocked.

"Yeah, I know. It didn't quite work out that way. Can you blame me?"

"Oh hell, no. I guessed you'd last a month, Dad gave you a week and Mom had you making it."

"At least Mom has faith in me."

"That she did. Speaking of which, she had me break in to drag you to Sunday dinner. Wake our Princess up and come down to eat. I'll tell Mom you'll be down in 15 minutes."

I woke Suzanne up and we went to the house. Greg, Dad, and I all were on edge as we waited for Mom to make some comment. She mystified us, as she was very pleasant with Suzanne. They actually seemed to hit it off. After dinner, Greg just shook his head in amazement. I hugged Mom and kissed her on the forehead as thanks. Who knew we could safely bring a girl to dinner?

✦✦✦

Tuesday October 22

Today I became an Uncle. Kyle Dawson weighed in at 8 pounds, 6 ounces and was healthy. Greg made the trek to see Angie in time for the birth. He sent us a ton of pictures. Now that the baby was here, Angie and Greg's lives were forever changed. Being in high school with a child was nothing new, but I knew I was much too young for that kind of responsibility.

✦✦✦

Friday October 25

The coaches decided not to let me even dress for the game. From the opening gun it was a defensive battle. Right before half, Luke broke a long run for a touchdown to put us up 7–0. Our lead held until late in the fourth quarter when they got lucky and blocked our punt. Their coach didn't want to go into overtime and decided to go for two. They punched it in and we ended up losing 8–7.

The loss dropped us into a three-way tie with Eastside and Mount Vernon with a 5–3 record. We needed to win our last two games to get into the playoffs, because it didn't look like any of us would have a chance at an at-large bid.

✧✧✧

Chapter 27 – Stranded

Saturday October 26

Tonight was my first date set up by Tami. I dressed in my Dockers, dark blue sports coat, and one of my fitted shirts with boat shoes. Of course, Tami picked the whole wardrobe, down to the silk boxers. I played fashion show, trying on several outfits, until I heard a giggle that wasn't Tami's. It turned out that she had half the dorm watching me on a big-screen TV in their lounge. I didn't let on that I knew what was going on. It was payback time.

"That one doesn't work. It doesn't bring the color of your eyes out. Show me the other one I picked out," Tami commented on my current shirt.

"How many more shirts do I need to try on?"

"Quit your whining. You want to look good for your date, don't you?"

"I really do. I've been looking forward to this. I had to beat off like five times so far today just to keep this guy down." I cupped my package. "God, I'm getting hard again."

"TMI, David." I saw her squirm in her seat.

"Man, I wish you were here. I get so hot thinking about the face you make when you orgasm."

I scrunched up my face, bit my lower lip, and rubbed my chest, moaning.

"SHUT UP! I've never made that face in my life!"

"Tami, you're making me hard again. You want to watch me jerk off and we can talk dirty to each other?"

"No! When did you figure it out?"

I gave her my perfect little angel face, which we both knew was a bunch of crap.

"What are you talking about?" I asked.

"Crap."

She knew I'd caught her and decided to fess up.

"Uhmmm. Okay, promise not to get mad?" she asked.

"No need, you set me up for a fashion show," I laughed. "If you'd given me a heads-up, the girls might have gotten a better show than listening to me whine. What do you want me to wear tonight?"

I'd dismissed her little prank. She knew it was game on, and our little video-chat war was just heating up.

"The second outfit. We all think your butt looks cute in those pants," she said as she gave me a sheepish grin.

"Nice. You only made me try on six other outfits until I caught on. Who's my date tonight and what are we doing?"

"Your date tonight is one Ms. Jennie Wesleyan," she said, and grinned when saw the look on my face. "Yes, that Wesleyan. I believe you met her uncle when you were at the University of Kentucky. She's picking you up at 4:30 p.m. It's an hour's drive to the country club. You'll be escorting Jennie to some family function."

"You're killing me. Please tell me it isn't some tweener with a crush on Double D who's having her thirteenth birthday party."

She cracked up. I'd told her about some of the weird requests I'd recently gotten. This sounded too much like a setup. Tami knew I would track her down if this whole thing were some sick fan's fantasy date.

"No, Jennie's older sister is introducing her most recent boyfriend, and she needs some serious eye candy. I also think you and Jennie will hit it off. She's a lot of fun, but is stuck here so she doesn't have a boyfriend. Apparently, her mom wanted to set her up with some twit."

"Does she have a sense of humor, or do I have to be on my best behavior?"

Tami shook her head.

"She would string us both up if you embarrass her. All you have to do is survive dinner, and then she has some plans afterward that sound fun."

"Alright, I trust you. I'll call you on Sunday and give you a report."

We logged off. I had three hours to get ready, so I kicked back and took a nap.

✧✧✧

When I got up from my nap, I was ready for whatever tonight might hold. I actually looked forward to going out with someone new. It felt good not to worry about a relationship. I planned to just take what came and have a good time, though there was some pressure, going out with a Wesleyan. I trusted Tami not to get me into something that might end up biting her in the butt if I messed up.

Right at 4:30, a black Lincoln Town Car pulled up and the driver got out.

"Mr. Dawson?"

"Yes."

"Ms. Wesleyan apologizes, but she will have to meet you at the Country Club."

He opened the back door for me to get in.

"How long is the drive?"

"An hour and fifteen minutes."

"Okay, I'm not riding in the back for that long. I'll make you a deal: when we get about five minutes out, we can stop and I'll ride in the back."

He just raised his eyebrows, but didn't object. When we hit the highway, I could see the driver had something to say. It turned out his son Mark was the quarterback for Eastside High. We talked football for the majority of the ride. When we got close, I asked him about my date.

"You seriously have never met Jennie?"

"No, this is a blind date."

He was the Wesleyan's driver so he was aware of most everything going on.

"She's been talking about you all week. Mark is jealous because he has a crush on her."

"So I take it she's cute."

"Cute, smart, and she has a wicked sense of humor. Let me give you a tip: if you fawn all over her, and I wouldn't blame you if you did, she'll take advantage of it. Don't let her boss you around. She likes strong guys. Don't be a jerk, though. She won't tolerate that."

"Sounds as if I'm going to have a good time tonight."

Mark's father smiled, but then his face clouded over.

"I almost forgot. There's a dance after dinner. Mark and some of his buddies are going to be there. If they try to dance with Jennie, let her handle it. She knows everyone, and they know her. She's dealt with this group all her life."

✧✧✧

When we got close, I jumped out, put on my sports jacket, and got in the back. We soon pulled up to the country club.

"Jennie's waiting for you. She's the blond," the driver said.

Damn. I could see why Mark had a crush on her. Jennie Wesleyan was a fox. She was tall, I would guess about five-ten, with long blond hair that was naturally curly. She had a slim figure and some impressive assets. She was wearing her school uniform, which was a short plaid skirt with a white button-up blouse and blue blazer. I saw her coming to the door to open it, so I pulled out a five and folded it in my palm.

When we came to a stop, she opened the door, and I stepped out. I handed her the tip and walked into the country club. Out of the corner of my eye, I saw her driver double over with laughter as she showed him the tip. She stormed into the Country Club and got into my face.

"Who do you think you are?"

I gave her the same look I gave Tami earlier. It didn't work with her either.

"Wasn't I supposed to tip you for getting the door?" I couldn't help myself, and I grinned. "Jennie, David Dawson, nice to meet you."

"You jerk."

Luckily, there was no heat in her words. I could see a twinkle in her eyes that made me wonder what kind of payback was in store for me.

"So, give me the lowdown on what you have planned for me tonight."

She took my arm and guided me through the country club. Wherever we went, all eyes were on her. She led me out to a patio. It was glassed in and there was a view of the golf course. A waiter brought us hot tea and finger sandwiches. She suddenly seemed shy.

"I was trying to impress you with tea. I can see now that it comes off a little snobbish. I mean seriously, who has tea anymore?"

I liked a girl who could make fun of herself.

"I'm all about experiencing new things. I've never had afternoon tea, so let's spend some time and get to know each other. Tell me what the family dinner's about so I don't embarrass you."

"Dang it, I owe Tami lunch. I bet her you would just talk to my chest, and I would have you wrapped around my finger in the first fifteen minutes. You looked me right in the eyes and have me so flustered that I feel like a naïve schoolgirl."

"Tami set you up. I have a superpower that only a handful of people are aware of. Can I trust you with my secret?"

"She did say you were a 'stupid boy.' I'll bite. What's your superpower?"

"Beautiful girls don't make me nervous."

"I call bullshit."

"No, it's true. My older brother is a legend at my school for dating the best-looking girls. He'd bring them home, and I'd talk to them while he went off and did whatever. If you don't believe me, ask your uncle to tell you about the time I met Lori Winnick."

"Okay, my uncle isn't going to be here tonight. Give me your phone. I'm definitely calling bullshit now."

I handed her my phone, and she called her uncle.

"Hey, it's Jennie." I couldn't hear what he was saying. "I'm sitting here with David Dawson. He told me you'd remember him meeting Lori Winnick."

She listened for a while and then gave me a shocked look.

"He did not!"

There was a pause as she listened.

"Did he really?"

Her uncle was clearly on a roll.

"He got all of them to accept?"

They said their goodbyes, and she gave me back my phone.

"Okay, so you have a superpower. My uncle also likes you. It's rare that someone impresses him, especially someone our age. Did you really get everyone to accept offers from Kentucky that weekend?"

"I guess I did. They all wanted to, but didn't know how to ask. So I gave them a little nudge."

"What's this story about condoms?"

"Tell you what, that's a story I only tell close friends. Let's see how the night goes, and I might tell you later."

"Can you hit on my sister tonight?"

Both my eyebrows went up on that one. This conversation had taken a sudden turn.

"What?"

"Sorry." She gathered her courage. "My sister's new boyfriend is a complete snob. He treats her badly, but I know her. She wants what she can't have. I need her to become interested in you, and you have to resist her. She'll dump the jerk."

"Your big plan for tonight is for me to be your date so your sister will hit on me and dump her boyfriend?"

"No! Well, okay, yes. I don't know. When you put it that way, it sounds kind of like a sucky plan."

"You're a frickin' nut! I think I'm going to like you."

She looked up with some hope.

"Really?"

"Yes, really. You keep me entertained with your half-baked plans for the rest of the night, and I'll tell you the condom story."

"Really?"

"You're a dork. Can we go do something before dinner besides have tea?"

"You can't call me a dork, dork. Dang it, why do you get me so flustered? That was the worst comeback ever." She got a serious look. "You tell anyone about tonight and you die."

I stood up and put my hand out to her.

"Come here. Your brain is just short-circuited. I know how to fix that."

I pulled her into my arms and kissed her. At first, she stood very still and barely kissed me back, but as I ramped up the kiss, she became a willing participant, and wow. Just wow! Jennie Wesleyan was no novice to kissing. I could hardly keep up with some of her moves. When we finally broke the kiss, she looked me in the eyes.

"That was your plan?"

"Ah, it was worth a shot. I actually just wanted to kiss you."

"Now I know why Tami calls you a 'stupid boy.'"

"Come on, let's go outside and let the cool air clear your mind. I need you coherent if I am going to seduce you and your sister at the same time."

She didn't even respond. She took my hand and led me outside. We walked the grounds and talked. She cornered me a couple of times and reminded me that she knew how to kiss. I think kissing is a great way to get to know someone.

✧✧✧

By the time we came back for our reservation, Jennie was herself again. When we got to the main dining room, we found that it was just going to be Jennie's sister Carol and her boyfriend Carlton. Carol was a freshman in college where she met Carlton. She could be Jennie's twin except her hips were a little bigger.

Carlton was a skinny boy who clearly had to be the center of everything. He was a junior studying prelaw. He took an instant dislike to me when he caught Carol eyeing me as we walked to our table. Jennie also caught the look, and we glanced at each other as if to say, 'game on.' When we sat down, Carlton tried to assert his dominance.

"Let's get a bottle of champagne and get the sampler appetizer. Then we'll get the cowboy rib eye with creamed spinach and garlic mashed potatoes."

The girls looked at him as if he was insane, but neither said anything. When the waiter came over, I had other plans.

"I think we'll be adventurous tonight. Tell the chef to plan a meal for the table. Let him know that Carol and Jennie Wesleyan always love his cooking and are looking for him to surprise us," I said.

Carlton's face went scarlet.

"But I thought we agreed."

Carol put her hand on his arm to get his attention.

"David has it right. That sounds like fun." She turned to the waiter. "Two of us are underage. Please get them some sparkling cider, and we'll have some champagne."

Carlton was sulking, so Jennie launched the next attack. Unfortunately, it was directed at me. She was just evil enough to turn me on.

"So David, my sister's a huge Kentucky fan. Tell her the story about your recruiting visit and the funny thing with the condoms."

I gave her a look for just a second. I could see her satisfaction in trapping me into telling her what she wanted to know. If she kept it up, I would have to punish her later. I wasn't sure who'd enjoy that more.

"Wait! Are you being recruited by Kentucky? What position do you play?" Carol asked, totally ignoring Carlton.

"I received an offer to play quarterback on my visit in September. I originally was there to do a workout for the University of Florida, but when Kentucky found out, they wanted to watch it also."

"What's your last name?" Carol asked.

"Dawson."

"Do you know who this is?" she asked, turning to Jennie.

Jennie gave her a blank look.

"What are you talking about?"

"This is Superman."

I shrugged when Jennie gave me a look.

"I told you I had superpowers. I even had your uncle confirm it. Yet you still doubt me."

I gave her a dramatic sigh. She gave me a look that would have me keeping my guard up all night.

"Bullshit. You're just a kid. There is no way Kentucky would waste a scholarship on the likes of you," Carlton said, getting his wind back.

I think it was about time he and I headed out to the parking lot. Instead, I decided to shut him up—without punching him. I pulled out my cell phone and opened my Dropbox app. I scrolled down until I found the scan of the offer letter and brought it up. I handed the phone to Carol.

"Carlton, you need to apologize to David."

She showed him the offer. He got up and stormed out. Jennie had a hard time containing her joy, but I gave her a look to cool it. Carol wasn't exactly happy that her date walked out on her.

"Here, give me the phone, and I'll show you what Carol's talking about."

I brought up the YouTube video and played it. Jennie's eyes were wide when it was done.

"I thought you played quarterback," she said.

"I do, but I started the season at fullback."

Carol snatched my phone out of my hand. She pulled up the quarterback rankings on 247Sports. Even with a week off, I was still the number nine freshman prospect.

"Look at this, Sis. Your date tonight could play in the NFL someday. Click on the link and look at who's recruiting him."

She read the list.

"Are you seriously considering Kentucky?"

"Look at the list and see who's actually offered," I told her.

"I see Kentucky and State, but are these other schools interested?"

"Yes, but I'm just a freshman. The big boys aren't about to take a flyer on me. Scholarships are usually too valuable to be handing out offers to freshmen, but Kentucky has actually made an offer. I want to play football at the next level, so I'm taking their offer very seriously. They were the ones that made the first offer. I have to respect them for that."

The waiter came to the table with our drinks. Carol explained that there would only be the three of us. The food was out of this world. For an appetizer, the chef did tuna three ways. The only tuna I'd ever had was out of a can. It melted in my mouth. For the main course, the chef prepared a rack of lamb with glazed baby carrots, roasted Brussels sprouts, and au gratin potatoes. For dessert, we had a hot vanilla soufflé that was amazing. It was the best meal I'd ever had, and the girls both loved it.

After dinner, we sat around and talked. People at the club came by and spent time talking to Carol and Jennie. You could tell people genuinely liked them. The girls enjoyed embarrassing me in front of the Kentucky fans who stopped by.

After dinner, we all went to the ballroom where a band was playing. They had a table reserved for their family. Carol saw some of her college friends and invited them to sit with us. I found myself sitting with seven girls. I was happy that Jennie laid claim to me, which kept Carol's friends at bay. A slow song came on, and I asked Jennie to dance.

I slid my hands under her jacket and rested them on her back right above her skirt. She put her hands around my neck.

"Thank you for tonight. I appreciate you being a gentleman."

"I was told that I had to be on my best behavior."

"I hope that wasn't on my account."

"No, I've gone through some girl-related issues over the last few weeks. Tami wants me to go out and have fun without the pressure of a relationship."

"Are you saying you're not interested in me?"

That one took me by surprise.

"To be honest, I hadn't thought about it." I could tell that was the wrong thing to say, so I tried to recover. "It's not you. That came out wrong and sounds horrible. Let's just tell it like it is. I am a 'stupid boy' at times and as such, I act like a jerk. Jennie, if I took two seconds to think about it, I would want to go out with you. As a matter of fact, I'd love to see you again."

"Nice save. I... well... shoot."

I felt someone tap me on the shoulder.

"Do you mind if I cut in?"

I turned to find Mr. California, Mark. I remembered his dad's advice and looked at Jennie. She gave me a slight nod, and I allowed Mark to take her in his arms. I walked back to the table and sat down. I tried to decide if I was pissed or not. I watched their body language, and Jennie didn't look comfortable. Mark tried to move closer a couple of times, and she moved back to keep her distance. She didn't say a word to him, and I could see that Mark was talking and glancing over at me.

It looked like Mark said something that pissed Jennie off. She stormed off the dance floor and went to the women's bathroom. After a while, I looked around and Mark was missing. At midnight, the band quit playing and everyone was leaving. It started to look like I'd been stood up. Carol and her friends had left earlier, so I didn't know anyone, and I was an hour from home. I walked out front to see if the driver was there. I was truly stranded. It was now 12:30.

I didn't have Jennie's cell number. I then called Tami, but she didn't pick up, so I left her a voice mail to let her know what was going on. Crap!

I finally gave up and called Greg. Of course he'd been drinking, and I could tell he was in no shape to come and get me. I talked to one of the valets, and he agreed to take me to a motel not far from the club. Luckily, I had enough cash to get a room for the night.

I went to sleep and vowed I would take a break from dating. I'd had a good time tonight until Jennie disappeared.

✧✧✧

Chapter 28 – Call Off the Dogs

Sunday October 27

Tami made the mistake of waking me up Sunday morning.

"David, I just got your message. Are you pulling my leg?"

"Bite me, Tami. Why would I lie about this?" I asked and then hung up.

Okay, it wasn't the smartest thing to do, but I was mad. I looked at the time, and it was 8:00 a.m. I called home and Mom answered.

"Hey, Mom, we may need to skip church today. I'm over an hour from home, and I need a ride."

"Do I even want to know?"

"It's not that bad. Tami set me up on a date, and the girl got pissed at someone else. She stormed out, leaving me to fend for myself. I called Greg last night, but he'd been drinking so I didn't even tell him I needed a ride. I got a motel room and waited until this morning to call you."

I saw that Tami was trying to call. I just ignored it. I gave Mom my address, and she said she and Dad would come get me. I hated that they were going to kill their Sunday morning by bailing me out. I couldn't wait until my sixteenth birthday when I'd be able to drive myself.

I cooled down and listened to Tami's voice mail. It asked me to call her. She knew me well enough to know that when I got mad I got over it quickly. So she learned to let me work through it and not to bother me. I dialed her number.

"Hey."

"David, I'm sorry. I thought you were joking around. I have a call into Jennie to find out what happened. So how did you get home?"

"Who said I was home?"

"Oh wow! Where'd you spend the night?"

"You know what, Tami? Can we drop it? The more I talk about it, the madder I get."

"Sorry."

"Look, it's not your fault. I think I learned my lesson last night. I've been treated like an afterthought by the last four girls I've gone out with. I'm done. Don't set me up on any more dates, and don't bother bringing anyone home for Thanksgiving."

It wasn't up to me to decide if she brought friends home.

"Well, you can bring friends home, but don't expect me to go on a date with them."

"I don't blame you. What do you want me to do about Jennie?"

"Nothing! Your scholarship is in place because of her uncle. I've seen how much her family's wealth influences people around here. I imagine it's ten times worse at Wesleyan. I don't want you to be hurt by any of this. If anyone asks, I had a great time."

"What should I tell everyone about you not dating? You do know that they're wanting to go out with you, many for the wrong reasons. I thought Jennie had it together and was self-confident enough to be a good match, but I need to tell them something."

"I figured. Tell them I'm slammed with football and need to focus on that right now. I know that not everyone is a self-centered bitch at your school, and I'd hate to ruin it for everyone else, but I can't handle this right now. Maybe by Christmas I'll be in a better frame of mind."

"David, I'm still shocked that Jennie stranded you. It's just not like her. I actually like her a lot. It's going to be hard for me not to say anything. But if you say I can't, I won't."

"Tami, I trust your judgment. I also don't want you losing a friend over this. I know you've worked hard to fit in. You know that I care for you and only want what's best for you. You decide."

"I'll make this up to you."

I could tell that Tami was shaken. She obviously liked and trusted Jennie.

"Hey, you know me better than that. No make-up is required. I know you didn't do this to be mean. I'm either having the worst run of luck with girls, or I have a 'kick me' sign on my back."

We spent the next few minutes talking, but she needed to go to breakfast with her suite-mates so we hung up. Thirty minutes later Mom and Dad showed up, and we hit a local diner for breakfast. When we took our seats, I noticed Jennie and Mark were at a table near the back. She saw me and looked confused. She got up and came to our table.

"Where did you go last night?"

What was she talking about? I just ignored her question.

"Jennie, I would like you to meet my mom and dad. They drove up to get me this morning after you left me stranded."

"Mark said …" she started, and then it dawned on her.

I saw her go from confused to beet red as she stormed over to their table. We could hear her as she screamed at him. I saw his dad come from the bathroom, and she screamed at him too. She put her hand out and Mark's dad gave her his keys.

"How are we supposed to get home?" Mark yelled.

"You didn't seem to mind stranding my date last night! You told me he'd left with that skank, Kelly! You can walk back to California, for all I care!"

My mom looked at me with a straight face.

"I think I like her."

"Careful, David, if your mom starts to approve of your girlfriends, something's wrong," Dad chuckled.

"Dad, Mom only has my best interest at heart."

Both of my parents laughed at that.

I saw all three of them head our way. Mark's dad was the first to speak.

"Mr. and Mrs. Dawson, I'm so sorry you had to come get your son this morning. David, may I ask where you stayed last night?"

"I got one of the valets to take me to a motel. Luckily I had enough cash on me to get a room."

I could see all three of them go stiff at the news. Mark looked like he was going to be sick. Mark's dad put his hand out, and Mark gave him his wallet. There was a wad of cash inside it. I never saw a high school kid with that much money.

His dad counted out stacks of money. Mark had about $500 on him.

"Okay, David, will a $100 cover the room cost?" his Dad asked.

I just nodded. It actually cost me $60, but I wasn't arguing.

"Mr. Dawson, you have gas, food and you and your wife's time. Here's $250."

He turned to his son.

"That leaves $150 for bus fare back to your mom's."

I could see tears forming in Mark's eyes. He ran out of the diner before he really started to cry. His dad followed him out. Jennie pulled up a seat and joined us. Our waitress hurried up and served us. She looked nervous, and I'm sure she was waiting on Jennie to erupt. She also had Jennie's tab, which she slid onto the table and then made herself scarce.

My mom wasn't fazed.

"So, Tami suckered you into going on a date with David."

My mother caught Jennie off guard, and she laughed. It was what we all needed. You could feel the tension leaving the diner.

"Actually, I think David was the one who got suckered. The first thing I asked him to do was to hit on my sister."

Mom arched her eyebrows.

"Really? I bet he did it, too."

"You would win that bet. He was smooth. He had her now ex-boyfriend so flustered he didn't even make it to the appetizers. Hell, he had me so flustered that when he told me that kissing him would clear my head, I believed him."

It was my dad's turn to laugh.

"Oh, God, he did not."

"Oh, yeah, he did. Then he said something like 'Well, it was worth a try.' When I see Tami, I'm going to have to tell her he's not a 'stupid boy.' He makes the girls around him stupid. I can't believe I fell for it."

"Quit your whining. I didn't hear any complaints," I said, needing to defend myself.

"I'm not complaining about the kissing. I'm kicking myself for falling for your charm."

"Your charm was always safe with me."

My mom smacked me.

"Quit hitting on her. I like this one. You will be nice, or you'll answer to me."

It was Jennie's turn to pop her eyebrows.

"I don't know if you realize what high praise you just received. I can't remember my mom ever saying she liked one of my or my brother's girlfriends. And just so you know, my brother's a slut, so we're talking a lot of girls," I smirked.

My dad nodded. Jennie took it in stride.

"So, you're not mad at me?"

I thought about what I'd learned about Mark and decided I wasn't mad at her, but that didn't mean I was dating for a while.

"No, but you did get me to swear off dating for now."

Both my mom and dad rolled their eyes. Jennie got pensive and we took a break in the conversation to eat.

"Would it be okay if I drove David home?" Jennie asked when we were done and ready to go.

My mom broke out in a huge smile.

"I was hoping you were going to offer. I didn't want to be around him while he pouted. He can be such a baby."

For whatever reason, Mom liked her. I stood up and took Jennie's hand in mine. We went to the cashier, and she paid her bill. Dad followed suit. When we got outside, Mark and his dad were sitting on a bench. I walked up to them.

"Come on. We'll give you a ride home," I offered.

Jennie looked like she wanted to object but deferred to my judgment. When we got into the car, I pulled my phone out.

"I better call Tami. I told her not to lynch you, but she doesn't always listen to me."

Jennie eyes got big.

"Thanks. She likes you a lot, and I'd be dead meat if she thought I'd hurt you."

I dialed and she picked up on the first ring.

"Hey, I'm with Jennie. You can call off the dogs."

"Why, what happened?"

"Her driver's son thought it would be a good idea to tell her that I'd gone off with another girl. He also thought it was perfectly fine to leave a fifteen-year-old boy to the elements in 40-degree weather."

"That's not true!" Mark yelled.

I turned on him.

"I didn't say a damn thing that wasn't true, you self-centered piece of shit! Everyone involved with this has been man or woman enough to admit his or her role in it but the kingpin of this debacle. Who, by the way, is sulking in the back seat, acting as if he were ten years old and got caught. Someday you'll learn to take responsibility for your actions."

Mark decided to go for broke and took a swing at me. I was ready and leaned back, which caused him to miss. His dad didn't. Mark had blood gushing out of his nose.

"You have embarrassed me for the last time."

We pulled up to the Wesleyan estate, and Jennie dropped them off at the back of the garage. Mark was glaring at everyone when he got out of the car. As soon as they were out, Jennie drove us out of town. I suddenly realized that Tami was still on the phone.

"Sorry about that."

"Oh, no, I've never heard you get that pissed. Did you hit him?"

"No, his dad did."

"Let me talk to Jennie."

"On speaker?"

"No, 'stupid boy,' I want to get the scoop."

I handed Jennie the phone.

"Yes. Uh huh. No, a perfect gentleman. He tricked me. Oh, yes." She looked at me and smiled. "Okay, I'll see you tonight."

She checked to make sure I wasn't mad.

"Okay, you're not yelling at me, so I'll take that as a good sign," I said.

"Can you tell me the condom story now, please?"

"I thought I did a pretty good job of not having to tell it last night."

"Yes, you were very slick at changing the subject, but I'm dying here. I was pretty pissed last night when I thought you went off with my sister's friend. I was actually mad I didn't get to hear the story. That's only part of it," she said as she looked sad. "I owe you an explanation. I've had a string of guys abandon me. I finally realized that the common element was Mark. He's been running them off. When I saw you this morning, I was sure you were just like the rest. I'd half-decided to give Mark a chance, even though I'm not attracted to him."

"Let's compare notes to see who's had it worse. My first date told me she wasn't allowed to go out until she was sixteen. My first girlfriend insisted that we weren't together. To prove her point, she dumped me in front of a couple hundred of my classmates. Then I went out with two seniors who thought it would be just fine to sneak around and spend the weekend with their ex-boyfriends. The capper was trying to get me to meet with them so they could explain why I was being unreasonable while the guys were in the car with them. Then finally, I got set up on a date over an hour from home, and my date walks out and leaves me to figure out how to get home on my own."

"Okay, you win. I just had them leave. I never had anyone go out of their way to hurt me."

"Man, I'm just feeling sorry for myself. I decided last night that I needed to take a break and figure out what there is about me that makes it okay to treat me like that. It's sad that I'm such a wimp that I've forgiven all of them. I'm starting to wonder if it's a character flaw. I don't know anyone else that would put up with that stuff and basically say everything's okay."

"David, I really am sorry. I should have gone back into the dance and confirmed you were gone. I feel bad asking you to forgive me."

"Don't worry about it. I can't seem to stay mad at anyone, so why should I start with you. Moreover, my mom likes you, and she's actually a very good judge of character. She even told me to break up with my first girlfriend. I was just too stubborn to listen."

"Since your mom likes me, I think it's time you told me the condom story."

"Okay, where to begin? Oh yes, my workout with Florida and Kentucky. I flew in on a corporate jet that was arranged by big Florida booster. The night before, our quarterback was knocked out of the game. Actually, it was the Eastside game."

Her eyes got big.

"I was at that game. Eastside had the game in the bag when your quarterback was hurt. Mark came over to make plans for after the game. He was laughing because your backup was a freshman. I remember his head snapping around when you threw that bomb on your first play.

"By the end of the game, I was actually rooting for you. I never put it together." Then she smacked herself in the head. "Damn it, you did it again. Now tell me to shut up and tell me the story."

"Out of courtesy to the Florida booster, the Florida coaching staff set up a workout to see what I could do. Kentucky had two quarterback prospects coming in for visits that same weekend, so it was arranged that I would work out with them. I got there a little early and started throwing to one of Kentucky's receivers. At the time I thought he was just an equipment manager, until I saw how fast he was.

"Florida's coaching staff got to the workout first, and when they saw me throw, they tried to move my workout to a private setting. Before we could leave, the Kentucky staff showed up and their receiver clued them in. After a little discussion, I was asked if I objected to Kentucky seeing my workout. I figured I wasn't that good, so I said sure.

"At the end of the workout, the receiver came up to me and told me that I was a real talent, but a raw talent. If I wanted to stand out, I needed to show leadership. I spent the rest of the weekend as Kentucky's guest. They put on the full recruiting blitz. I had a chaperone and everything. When I met the other recruits, I heard them all excited about going to a party where they'd been told they would probably get lucky.

"My brother taught me to use a condom. Heck, he's the poster boy, since he got his girlfriend pregnant. So, not trying to look like a wet blanket, I talked to them about the girls. I pointed out that if a group of high school boys could score with college girls, what had those same girls done the prior weekend when another batch of recruits was there?"

"I asked them if they wanted to take an STD back home to their sister."

Jennie whacked me.

"That's gross. That only happens at Tennessee. Remember that if they ever offer you a visit."

"Do you know that it took them almost two minutes to figure out I'd accused them of sleeping with their sisters?"

"Really?"

"You need to come up with a new line. People are going to make fun of you saying 'really' all the time."

"Shut up, 'stupid boy,' before I smack you again."

"I told them I brought my own condoms because I didn't want my manhood to fall off. We had a tour of the athletic facilities and to a man, they asked their chaperones where they could get condoms. The chaperones left us alone for dinner to go compare notes.

"I was the only one who had a female chaperone and, of course, the other recruits were quizzing me as to why I got a girl. I explained it was part of the questionnaire that I filled out. It asked if I preferred to have a girl give me head or a guy—or something as immature. By the time the chaperones came back in, they were having trouble understanding why everyone wanted to lynch me. I was pulled out of the meeting to go to the office.

"The head recruiter wanted to know what I said to make them all think that they needed condoms. I explained that if they got an STD and took it home, Kentucky would look bad. I also explained how handing those out in their welcome packet would make Kentucky seem cool in the eyes of high school guys. I also suggested that they give them a pack of six so the guys thought they were going to get laid a lot."

"I can see that."

"Long story short, Kentucky gave me an offer. They also went to their health clinic to get each guy a packet of six condoms. When I went back to dinner, one of the recruits asked me what I'd been up to. I showed him the offer and told him if he told his chaperone, the chaperone would take him to get an offer also. Somehow, word got around and I was left to eat by myself.

"When my chaperone came back with the condoms, I was chowing down on my third steak. I was pretty sure she was going to kill me until everyone came back with offer letter. Then the head guy announced that I'd arranged for them all to receive condoms. I think they were happier about getting the condoms than the offer."

"Did they really use all those condoms?"

"Get real. I probably used more that night then the rest of them combined. What college girl is going to sleep with a high school boy?"

"What do you mean, you used more? How many did you use?" she asked.

"Oops. Did I say that out loud?"

"You're a slut. Tami warned me that if I wasn't careful I'd be handing you my panties and begging you to defile me. Did you bang your chaperone?"

"I didn't put my wiener in her bun."

"You should go into politics. We eliminated you having intercourse with her, but that leaves a whole lot of other stuff that could have happened."

"And you, Missy, are too smart for your own good. So why don't we stop, and you can give me your panties?"

"Who said I was wearing any?"

"Touché. Game, Set and Match, you win. I'm going to wonder about that the rest of the way home."

"Rookie, stick with me, and I'll help you improve your game."

"Yes, Mistress. I'm yours to mold."

"Be good. This is only our first date. I have rules."

"To prove a rule, you need an exception. Why don't you make me your exception?"

"Call Tami and give me the phone."

I dialed Tami and handed it to Jennie.

"I need help. He has me so worked up that I want to, uh, let's just say very bad things. Here."

She handed me the phone.

"No, no, no, no! You're being a very bad boy right now!" Tami scolded me.

"But she told me that she wasn't wearing any panties."

"Give her the phone."

I handed the phone to Jennie.

"Yes, I might have said that. No way! What do you mean I'm on my own?" She hung up. "Dang it."

"So, want to pull over and find out how long my, uh, tongue is?" All I heard was a moan. "Is that a yes?"

"No. Oh God, you have me all flustered again."

"I know what'll fix that! Three or four quick orgasms."

"Uncle, I give up."

"Okay, I was just having some fun. I'm not the creepy guy that hits on you. I hope you didn't take it the wrong way."

"Dear God, if you were going to Wesleyan, you couldn't get rid of me."

"I feel the same way, Jennie. You're a lot of fun. If I thought you'd take me up on any of my offers today, I'd have been scared to death. You're a lot of woman, and I'm afraid I might not be man enough for you."

The rest of the ride was fun. We liked the same movies, books and music. She loved football. By the time we got to my house, we were friends. I didn't see us being more than that. She was from a vastly different socioeconomic background. She was upper crust, even by Wesleyan standards. 'Old money' was what they called it. Generations of being a part of the social elite made it almost impossible for an average guy like me. People like Jennie might have a fling with a regular guy, but she wouldn't bring me home to meet the family. We both knew that, regardless of the sexual and emotional chemistry, our backgrounds were just too different. It was a shame, because I really liked her.

I gave her a kiss goodbye just to remind myself that I was alive. If you don't feel alive kissing Jennie Wesleyan, then you've checked out. I might be aroused for weeks with just the memory of our kiss. It was a good thing that we had so much physical distance between us, or we may have done something stupid eventually. I could see why Mark made his desperate play for her.

Tami did well for a first date. She knew that my swearing off girls would be a temporary thing. That was why she didn't fight it. Heck, my parents even rolled their eyes when I proclaimed I was done dating. I would give it until Wednesday, and then call Tami to set me up.

I felt a little sad when Jennie drove away. I wouldn't turn down a fling with her. Maybe a weekend getaway was in the offing. She could bring her sister. It would almost be as good as doing twins. I would have to work on Tami to help make that happen.

✧✧✧

When I got to the garage apartment, I checked my emails. There was one from Kendal who wanted to meet this afternoon. I called her and set it up. I still had on my clothes from last night when she showed up. When she came in, she gave me a smirk.

"What's is the little smirk for?" I asked raising an eyebrow.

"Looks like someone did the walk of shame this morning."

"Laugh it up, Chuckles. If you're going to give me shit, I'm going to go change."

I went into my bedroom and changed into shorts and a t-shirt.

"Better?"

"You look fine. I wanted to talk to you about some interview requests. We've been putting them off, but they're starting to get insistent. Tracy said you'd probably tell them to take a hike. I wanted a chance to convince you that the right press is good for you."

This was something I wasn't comfortable doing. Too many guys messed up their careers by spouting off their opinions to the press. Tracy taught me scripts about teamwork and praising the other team that seemed to work. I know I sounded like the biggest hick doing it, but the fans want the All American boy-next-door being their sports hero. About the only thing I didn't do was thank God. Tim Tebow messed up any possibility of talking about your faith without being labeled a nut.

"Okay, give me your pitch."

"I've received three kinds of requests. The first group is fan-website reporters for the different colleges. These sites are run by rabid fans with huge egos. Most of these guys want to get some kind of scoop so they can look like they're insiders. It's funny to read the posts calling them out. I'd suggest that you avoid these guys unless it's a school you're interested in attending. There's normally a staff member at the college that monitors the sites. It's a way to raise their interest.

"The second group is area sports reporters. For the most part, they're fans as well, but at least these guys will play it straight and they actually do have access. This group you need to court. They are the ones you can go to when you need help setting the record straight.

"The final group is the national guys. This is the biggest risk and potential reward. Until you're established, I would avoid making any comments to them. They're normally jaded and just looking for a controversial angle.

Look at Johnny Football. He was the first freshman to win the Heisman. They loved him. One report of signing sports merchandise and making money, and they're all investigating him."

"What's your plan?" I asked.

"I would like to set up a weekly conference call where we can control access and content. I'd like to do this on Wednesdays at 12:15 for thirty minutes."

"Great, no lunch that day. Set it up."

"Quit your complaining. We'll make sure you're fed, you big baby."

"Hey, do you have any of the 'Double D' shirts left over?"

"We have a couple of boxes. How many do you need?"

"Could I get a dozen? I have some fans I want to give them to."

I was thinking of the Wesleyan girls and the Phillips family.

"No problem. I'll drop them off tomorrow."

"No hurry, I want them for the final regular season game when we travel south."

"I'll get it taken care of." She pulled out her tablet. "You're getting a lot of interest in this week's game. It's also the last home game. We're planning another band and cookout for the press, recruiters and fans. We have a local bank and car dealership sponsoring the event.

"The school is getting additional bleachers for the north end zone. We'll have to set up in the parking lot. The practice field will be used for overflow parking," Kendal added.

"Thanks for organizing all this. The last one was a huge hit. Are you planning anything for the seniors?"

"You know, we haven't, but that's a good idea. I'll talk to the girls," she said, and then caught herself. "Sorry, it's a bad habit. I'll talk to the team and see what we can come up with."

"Remember, this is almost a bigger deal for the parents. Make sure if they have any younger brothers or sisters to get them involved also."

"Alright. Good meeting." She pulled out a small shopping bag. "I hear you're an uncle. Tracy said you'd forget to get a gift. We had a 'Double D Fan' baby jumper made. We want to see pictures with Kyle in it."

That had to be the most thoughtful thing anyone had done for me in a long time, which got me a little choked up. Angie and Kyle were coming to dinner tonight. I couldn't wait to see the newest member of the family. Greg had sent me a ton of pictures over the last few days. I think I surprised Kendal when I hugged her.

"I don't know how to thank you."

"Seeing the look on your face was worth it."

Her whole demeanor shifted in the span of a few moments. She seemed really genuine, and I wished I were eight years older; I would make a serious play for Kendal.

She put her things away and we said our goodbyes. I was a lucky guy to have her help. If I ever made it big, I wanted her on my team. I would want someone I could trust, and she fit the bill. She made some mistakes, but I liked that she learned from them. You can tell a lot about a person when something goes wrong. If they point fingers and try to cover their ass, you don't need them. If they work to solve the problem, those are the ones you keep. Once Kendal recognized a problem, she came up with a solution. I admired her for that.

✧✧✧

Sunday dinner was a family affair. That meant two cooked and the other two cleaned up. Tonight, Mom and I cooked. Since we were having guests—my future sister-in-law and nephew—I knew Mom was going to put on a spread. I didn't expect her to want me to do the cooking. Not that my cooking was a terrible; I'd been doing it since I was eight or nine. If Mom and Dad ran late, Greg and I would switch off cooking.

Greg or I were never in charge of Sunday dinner. When Mom saw me come in, she cornered me.

"What are you cooking tonight?"

I was shocked. I went to the refrigerator and saw that we had a family pack of chicken thighs, leftover smoked ham, and Swiss cheese. I was thinking Chicken Cordon Bleu. From that, Mom and I could come up with a menu. When you were the head cook, you got to decide who did what. I put Mom in charge of deboning the chicken.

I noticed she was having some trouble and seemed to be in pain.

"Mom, are you okay?"

"I banged my arm getting out of the car, and it's a little stiff. I took some aspirin for the pain."

She had on a long-sleeve shirt, and I could see she was hurting. I'd had my share of bumps, so I was getting pretty good at treating them.

"Where did you bang it?"

She pointed to her bicep.

"Let me see. You know football and me. They taught me some tricks that might make it feel better," I said.

The sleeve on her blouse wouldn't go up far enough, so she had to unbutton it and slide it off her shoulder. My breath caught. Not only was her bicep deep purple, but there was evidence of prior bruising in several different areas.

"Wow, Mom, what's going on? You look like you play quarterback. Has Dad been beating you?"

"No, I've just been clumsy lately. I need to be more careful."

"Well, for now you're out of the kitchen."

I grabbed a bag of frozen peas.

"Go put this on your arm. When Greg gets here with Angie and Kyle, I'll come get you so you can 'Put them to the Question.'"

Mom loved to interrogate people. We were all wondering if Angie would move back home or not and a thousand other questions. I'm sure Greg was prepping Angie as to what to expect. We all still remembered Mom's infamous 'Well, if I never see you again…' parting shot to Greg's first girlfriend. I doubt she was going to go that hard on the mother of her grandson, but I'm sure Greg wouldn't take any chances.

When dinner was ready, everyone showed up. It was amazing how that happened. I'd met Angie only a couple of times when Greg had dated her in the spring. At the time, I was a pudgy little stoner, so it wasn't a surprise when she looked at me quizzically.

"David?" she asked.

"Hey, Angie, you're looking good."

Angie was still sporting some of her baby weight, but it did look good on her. She no longer looked like a girl, she looked like a woman. She held a small bundle in her arms.

"Is this my nephew?"

"Yes, this is Kyle."

He was sound asleep. Angie and Greg seemed so happy that I wanted to be happy for them. Dad pulled my old bassinet out of the attic and had it ready for Kyle. Angie was able to put him down while we all ate. From the early conversation, it became apparent that her parents weren't supportive of her keeping Kyle. I could tell from their body language that Greg and Angie weren't willing to put him up for adoption. Mom seemed to pick up on that also.

"If your parents don't want you to keep Kyle, are you welcome in their home?"

Mom always seemed to get right to the point. Angie for the first time today looked sad.

"If I keep Kyle, my parents aren't letting me come home. For now, I'm staying with my aunt and uncle. They've been very supportive, and I can stay with them as long as I need to."

Mom looked at Dad and he nodded slightly. She turned to me and I nodded also.

"Angie, if you'd like, you and Kyle can move in with us."

She looked at Greg, and he smiled at her.

"You can have David's old room. We can set it up as a nursery for Kyle," he said.

She still looked uncertain. Mom put that to rest.

"We love you and Kyle. Even if you decide not to marry Greg, you're welcome here. I know you don't have everything planned out yet, but at least this way you'll be close to your family and friends."

Angie jumped up from her seat, and she and Mom hugged.

"Thank you. My nights have been sleepless, worrying about what to do." Then the tears came. "I'm sorry. I don't mean to cry, but this is something that's been weighing on me. I never knew that having a baby would change my life so much. You don't know what this means to me."

After dinner, I got stuck cleaning up. I guess it was my day. Greg and Angie went to her aunt and uncle's and packed up all her and Kyle's things. Dad and I boxed up all my stuff. We went up into the attic and found a changing table and crib. We left the crib until Kyle was older. For now, the bassinet was large enough. Mom was in charge of cleaning. By the time everyone got back, Angie and Kyle's room were clean and ready.

Greg and I were in charge of bringing in all of Angie's belongings. Mom was in charge of Kyle. I could ask for anything at this moment and Mom would let me have it.

She was just so happy to be holding her first grandbaby. There was a special love reserved for grandchildren, and my mom had it bad.

By the end of the day, we'd added two new members to the family. I was surprised at how quickly Greg took to being a father. He'd taken off school since Tuesday, when Kyle was born. He seemed to be the happiest with them moving in. Now he'd be able to be a part of Kyle's life on a daily basis.

My biggest concern had always been Angie and Greg. We were brought up to take care of our responsibilities, so I never was concerned that Kyle wouldn't be supported by Greg and our family, but that didn't mean they would necessarily get married. To my relief, I could tell that they loved each other. It was all the little things—a sly glance, how they touched, a little smile. It made my heart hurt to see them so much in love. I understood what was missing in my life. I was also smart enough to know that I wasn't ready for that kind of love. For now, I would get my fix, so to speak, from my brother, Angie, and Kyle. It made me a little sad for Greg and Angie because they were so young, but my brother was very determined, and I knew he'd find a way to make this work. We had both been taught that God doesn't give us things unless we can handle them.

✧✧✧

Chapter 29 – You Need to Get Used to This

Wednesday October 30

I got a text message to meet Coach Harrington before school in his office instead of on the practice field. When I got there, Coach Lambert and Coach Engels were both there. I took a seat and Bo kicked off the meeting.

"David, I want to talk to you before you hear it from anyone else."

Oh, hell, this can't be good.

"After Friday's game, I'm no longer going to be able to help you. I have another assignment I have to take on. If I didn't have a long-term relationship with this other organization, I wouldn't be going."

I thought for a moment. Bo Harrington had helped me tremendously. I wasn't ready to lose him.

"Why exactly are you leaving?"

"The Houston Texans lost their starting quarterback to injury two weeks ago. Last week they lost to the Chiefs. This week is a bye week and then they play the Colts after that. I can't really go into detail, but they've asked me to come in and help out."

"Bo, what would it take to keep you?"

"Believe me when I tell you if it wasn't an emergency, I wouldn't be leaving," he said, and then chuckled. "You have the potential to be special. The biggest reason is how hard you work. I've only had a few guys work as hard to improve as you have. There are going to be players who can throw farther than you. There will be guys with more football savvy. There will even be quarterbacks who are better runners than you are. Not many guys have the combination of all three attributes, and that's what gives you such a high ceiling.

"I'm going to tell you some things that cannot leave this room. Can I have your word on that?" Bo asked.

"Of course."

"Coach Lambert also has some news."

"Thanks, Bo, for putting me on the spot," Coach Lambert said, looking uncomfortable. "I wanted to let you know I'll be leaving after the season."

He paused a moment for that to sink in. With all the attention that the program had received, now would be the perfect time for Coach Lambert to move into a better position.

"Someone's going to be lucky to have you, coach," I offered, as a smile broke out on my face.

I clearly surprised everyone.

"Thank you," Coach Lambert said.

"It looks like Coach Engels will also be moving on," Bo Harrington said.

This shocked me. I'd hoped he would take over for Coach Lambert.

"When I heard the news about Coach Lambert, I immediately thought of you as his replacement."

"I hate to disappoint you, David, but there's a requirement that our head football coach must have head coaching experience. For me to advance in coaching, I need to get that experience. I'll be moving on whether Coach Lambert goes or stays."

"Well that's just stupid. You guys are telling me that I get a new coaching staff next year?"

"You need to get used to this," Bo said. "In the next several years you'll have many new coaching staffs. It's rare that you'll have a team of coaches in place for more than a couple of years. If you're lucky, the ones you work with will be leaving for better opportunities. That'll mean you had a good year with them.

"This also means I need to have a conversation with you about your development. You're going to have to take over. If either of the two of your coaches were staying, I'd turn your development over to them. Since they're not, I'm giving the plan to you."

Bo pulled out four binders.

"This first binder is my evaluation of where you are as a player and what you need to work on in the future."

He picked up two binders.

"These two binders go together. This one has DVDs showing examples of skills and the drills needed to develop those skills. This binder is a detailed written description."

He picked up the fourth binder.

"This is the road map. Use this as your guide between now and college."

I could see the other two coaches eyeing the binders. Bo saw it too and got serious.

"David, you cannot share this with anyone." He looked at the other two, and they nodded. "This is my life's work, and I'm paid a ridiculous amount of money to do it."

"Bo, I'm honored by your trust. If I need advice, can I call you?"

"Absolutely. I'll help you get on a seven-on-seven team for the offseason, and I'll also get you slots in quarterback camps throughout the summer. Some of this isn't cheap, so either talk to your parents about it or get a part-time job. I might also be able to get you some waivers on fees if you agree to help by being a camp counselor."

"That sounds great. My parents make okay money, but there are some other priorities right now. I'll have to fund my own football-related activities."

Coach Lambert looked at his watch.

"It looks like school will start in a few minutes. Why don't you get going? We need to talk to Bo."

"I'll see you at practice," Bo said.

✧✧✧

I was deep in thought when I went to my locker. I was surprised when I found Tracy blocking it. Her mom sent me breakfast sandwiches each morning. I smiled when I saw her.

"Hey, Tracy, we met in the coaches' offices instead of having practice."

"No problem, I just thought I'd missed you."

She handed me the sandwich.

"I'm starved."

I wolfed it down, and Tracy just shook her head.

"Kendal will be here around 11:30 this morning to set up the conference call. Do you want me there?"

"What's going on?"

I'd assumed that Tracy would be at all my press events.

"Kendal."

That was all she had to say. Tracy was used to being in control, and she didn't want to answer to anyone.

"Can Kendal handle today?"

Tracy thought about it for a moment. The one thing I could count on was an honest response.

"I think she can."

"Tracy, either she can or she can't, which is it?"

"She can, but I would like to be there."

"Not a problem. Please call her and ask her. I don't want her to think you can come to me and override her decisions. Does that make sense to you?"

She didn't like my answer, but I could tell she understood. She just smiled.

"I'll see you at lunch. We're meeting in the coaches' conference room. Coach Lambert will be there too."

"Good, they can grill him instead of me."

She gave me a funny look that made me nervous.

"I hear you're single right now."

"Yes."

It's safer just to give one-word answers.

"Would you be my date to the Halloween Dance?"

"My first instinct is to say 'no.' Hang on, wait; it would be *Hell no!* Why aren't you going with Jim?"

Jim was the one she paid money for at the auction, after all.

"It seems that no guy's willing to take me out since I dumped you in such a public setting. The bunch of wimps is afraid I might do something similar."

I didn't expect to hear that. I really tried not to laugh, but I couldn't help it. She wasn't amused.

"David, it's not funny."

"I kinda think it is. Give me your pitch. Why should I risk going to the dance with you?"

"First off, we'd go just as friends." I nodded my agreement to that. "My doctor says I need to go out in a social situation, and she said you'd be a good choice."

Crud, she was using her mental health. I liked her and her family too much not to help. I found myself doing something I never thought I would do anytime soon.

"Okay, here's the deal: I'll be your date, but there are a couple of conditions."

"Anything."

"If you expect me to be in some kind of costume, you have to get it. Second, we're just friends. If I want to dance with someone, you can't get mad at me. I'll treat you right and dance with you, but if I meet someone, you have to act like my friend and not my girlfriend."

"Is that it?"

"Nope, we get to have dinner with your parents before the dance."

She smiled, knowing she'd won.

"Mom's been asking why you haven't been over. I'm sure that won't be a problem."

I shook my head.

"How did you talk me into this?"

"Easy, you love me."

"I can't argue with that," I sighed. "Will you do me a huge favor? Will you promise not to take advantage of my love for you?"

"I know I hurt you, and I'm sorry about that more than anything. At the time, I thought I had a good reason. I know now that you had nothing to do with the newspaper caption. I also know that the whole 'not together' thing was my doing. David, I'm still a little goofy, but I want us to work on being friends. I always enjoy being around you. I feel that when we're together, we're more somehow. I also miss the sex."

I didn't trust myself to say anything, so I ran.

"Tracy, I'll see you at noon."

I didn't even bother to get my books out of my locker. I know that I'm pathetic when it comes to standing up to girls I like. If I wasn't careful, I would do or say something to Tracy.

✧✧✧

After first period, I was able to make it back to my locker and get the right books. I was doing fine this morning until she mentioned the sex. My fear was that she would ask me to have sex with her. I knew for a fact that I couldn't resist that request.

By lunch, I was ready to face Tracy again. To my surprise, she wasn't there. I never asked Kendal because I assumed she didn't want her there. The interview went off without a hitch. There were four reporters on the line and, as I predicted, Coach Lambert answered most of the questions.

I'd pushed my luck even setting up the press conferences. Most coaches would never let a freshman hold them, but Coach Lambert couldn't say no to Tracy either. Now that they were started, both of us were stuck with the situation. I appreciate that he was with me on the calls. I needed to talk to Kendal to make sure we weren't causing any problems.

After the call, Kendal assured me that Coach Lambert appreciated my team organizing everything. It was one less thing he had to worry about. Kendal told me they had arranged the Senior Night event with the parents. She worked with Coach Lambert to do something special. I was happy with Kendal taking charge. The only thing that was lacking was lunch. She brought me a salad. What growing boy could just have a salad for lunch, especially one that burns through the number of calories I do?

✧✧✧

By last period, I was starved. I went to my tutoring session with Suzanne. When I walked in, my stomach growled.

"Sorry about that. I need to eat before practice. Do you mind skipping out before I drop from hunger?"

"You sound like Jim. I swear that growing boys eat enough for five normal people."

"This growing boy needs food now. I'm ditching with or without you."

"Okay, I get the message. Come on, and I'll take you home. Jim should be there. He's been excused from conditioning until his ribs get better, so he's just hanging out. You two can goof off while I feed you both."

We snuck out without being caught and were at Suzanne's house a few minutes later. Jim was in the kitchen. He'd made himself two peanut butter sandwiches. I snatched one off his plate. Jim was a little pissed.

"Dude, you don't take food from a hungry boy, especially one that outweighs you by at least fifty pounds."

"You do when I ask your sister to feed us some real food."

"Ah, that's different. Then my sandwich is your sandwich."

Suzanne was amused at us being dorks.

"Will pasta work?"

"Carbs are good before practice." I winked at Jim. "Your sister knows how to take care of her man."

She whacked me on the back of the head.

"No hitting on the sister when her little brother is present."

"Yeah, what she said."

"You two gang up on this man, and you both won't be taken out Saturday night."

Jim laughed.

"You're a kinky boy, asking a brother and sister out on a date."

"I was thinking Monical's and then a movie. Of course, one of you would have to drive."

"How about Tony's?" Suzanne asked. "They have great lasagna and unlimited bread sticks. You and Jim can see if you can eat so many they kick you out."

"I knew there was a reason why we keep your sister around. What do you think, lasagna instead of pizza?"

"Sounds good to me, though I only have one rule: I don't put out on the first date," Jim said with a straight face.

"I promise I'll not make a move on you. Just so you know, Suzanne gets to pick the movie. She, at least, might give me a kiss goodnight."

The pasta was done. She brought two huge plates out to Jim and me.

"Plus, she's a better cook than you."

"Actually, Jim's a much better cook than I am. It's a good thing I'm a better kisser," Suzanne laughed.

"Jim, is she right? Is Suzanne the better kisser?"

"Ah, David, bite me, I'm not kissing you or my sister to find out."

We all laughed. After we ate, Suzanne gave me a ride to practice. We had a very good practice. At the end, I was a little bummed when I realized that I only had two more days to work with Bo. I owed the man a lot.

✧✧✧

When I got home, I found Mom and Dad in the kitchen. They didn't look happy, so I sat down.

"What's wrong?"

Normally they would deflect my question. Ever since my talk with Mom, things had changed. She no longer treated me like a little kid.

"Your dad's hours got cut. Actually, everyone's hours got cut. They're making everyone part-time employees because of the new health-care law. Their CPA figured out it would be cheaper if everyone signed up for the government option. Your dad's boss is a dick."

The Park District had turned the operations over to a private firm a few years ago. Ever since they took over, Dad had said they were more worried about the bottom line than the parks or the employees. I think that if Dad didn't love his job and our town, he would have left when the change happened. The sad truth was that there weren't a lot of local jobs that Dad's skills fit.

"With Angie and Kyle moving in, we're worried that we may have to buy them insurance too. With your dad's reduced hours and the real estate market being slow, I'm nervous about money," Mom said.

"What are you thinking?"

I looked at Dad. Dad was the planner of the family. I was sure he'd considered all the options.

"We can take over the payments on the company insurance. It's not cheap. The government plan requires that we sign up this month and then we can shop plans come the first of the year. There'll be a gap in insurance for several months if we go that route.

"The state provides a child plan, so we could get you and Greg on that without much problem. I need to talk to Angie and see what she and Kyle are doing. The way things stand right now, with my reduced hours, we're looking at a shortfall each month of about $400. I can get another part-time job and try to make it up," Dad explained.

"How are we with savings?" I asked.

"We have some, but nothing we can go a long period using," Dad answered me.

"Okay, I was planning on talking to you about this after football, but now's a good time. I want to get a part-time job after the season. I'm sure Greg will get one also. If Greg and I contribute $200 each a month to the household budget, that should keep everything going until we can figure something out.

"Option two is my college fund. I'll be getting a scholarship," I offered.

Mom was the final decision maker.

"We'll talk to Angie tonight and come up with a strategy. Let's have a family meeting on Sunday."

"Great, now feed me."

Mom had a plate in the oven waiting for me. After I ate, I took my nephew back to my apartment. I told Angie I'd keep him for an hour or so. I could see that she was dragging. I was actually surprised when she loaded him up and the guys headed to the bachelor pad.

I, of course, wanted to show him off to my friends. I sent a text to Alice Phillips first, and we jumped onto video chat. She took one look at Kyle and yelled for her mom.

"You better come here. David's been up to no good and gotten himself in trouble."

With her mom there, it didn't take long before her dad and brother showed up.

"Hey, gang, I want to introduce my nephew Kyle to you."

We talked for a little bit and then I told them I had to show him off to some of my other friends. Tami and the Wesleyan girls loved Kyle. He was quite the little chick-magnet. To his credit, he didn't embarrass himself. We logged off when he fell asleep.

I took him back to the main house and found both Greg and Angie sound asleep in each other's arms. I didn't have the heart to wake them. I took Kyle to my mom and explained what was going on. She took him and promised to let everyone sleep. I went back to my place, and I was asleep as soon as my head hit the pillow.

✧✧✧

Chapter 30 – Superman

Thursday October 31

As a kid, Halloween had been my favorite holiday. I went as a farm boy every year because I wasn't creative enough to come up with a real costume. When I was ten, we had a dog named King. We went everywhere together, including with Greg trick-or-treating. He was great. He got dog treats at almost every home, and they seemed to pony up more candy than normal.

By the time we got home, we had two bags of candy that would last us a lifetime. Okay, until the end of the weekend when we would drop into a sugar coma, and Mom and Dad would steal the rest. Greg left his bag of goodies out, which was a very poor plan, in my estimation. Dad would raid it after we went to bed. Turns out it was a terrible plan. King ate all of Greg's candy. I felt bad for him, and King was sick, so he was sorry.

Turns out Mom made me sorry: she made me split my candy with Greg. I argued that his poor planning should not be the cause of my losing my haul of treats. She had the mistaken impression that was what brothers did for one another. We now laughed about it. At the time, I was devastated.

At the end of practice, Magic announced that there was a party at his house. I had no intention of going since we had a game tomorrow. All the seniors were going, and they invited all the starters. To their credit, they didn't push me. They all knew I didn't drink, and most of them knew the reason why.

Tracy picked me up after practice and took me to her house for dinner. I was happy to see Tom and Mary. I had time to show them some pictures of Kyle, and we ate quickly because Tracy said she needed some time to get our costumes together. She made me go take a shower and shave. When I came out, she had me go to her room and sit in just my boxers at her makeup table.

"I need to do your hair and makeup," she explained.

I decided to be a good sport.

"Do what you must."

Tracy got excited and called her mom.

"He said he'd do it. Come get him ready while I change."

Mary came up to Tracy's room and gave me a funny look.

"You're sure?"

"I trust you guys. Do your worst."

She just shrugged and started applying makeup. She gave me a cleft chin and more prominent cheekbones. She then styled my hair in a more conservative look. She went to the walk-in closet and came out with my outfit. Okay, they were both going to die. It was a Superman outfit.

Mary winked at me.

"Okay, Boy Wonder, lose the boxers and put on the suit."

"What!"

"This is spandex. It'll show your underwear lines."

She even said that one with a straight face.

"Oh dear God, is this really important to Tracy?"

Now she smirked.

"Yes. I thought she told you what your costume was."

"Okay, but if it's obscene, I'm not wearing it."

I grabbed the suit and went into the walk-in to put it on. I put on the blue tights first. As I expected, they molded to my manhood. They left nothing to the imagination. I pulled on the top and it felt like it was a size too small. You could see every muscle. It was a good thing I was in shape. Red underwear with a gold belt was worn outside the tights, and then red knee-high boots to finish. When I came out, Mary blushed.

I frowned.

"That bad?"

She shook her head. She had the red cape that completed the outfit. She came over, attached the cape, and steered me to a mirror. I was completely surprised. I looked the part. My only concern was the bulge in my tights was noticeable, and, if I got aroused at all, this could be an issue. I turned to Mary, and she was checking me out.

"You dirty girl. I take it I look okay."

"Yes, you look more than okay."

I heard Tracy whistle at me. She had on a Catwoman outfit that instantly tested the strength of my tights. Both Tracy and her mom burst out laughing.

"I can't help it. She looks so damn sexy in that outfit."

I turned around and adjusted things so it wasn't as obvious, but Tracy was the hottest Catwoman I'd ever seen. Halle Berry had nothing on Tracy. I grabbed the ticket for the dance out of my wallet. I didn't see any way I could bring a wallet in this outfit. When we got into Tracy's Mustang, she purred at me.

"Tracy, if you don't stop teasing me we're not going to make it to the dance."

She gave me an innocent smile.

"I just wanted to see if you were still interested."

"I'd have to be dead to not be interested in you. Now let's go have some fun."

We caused a little bit of a stir when we walked into the gym. It turned out that all the JV cheerleaders dressed as Catwoman. None of them were as hot as Tracy. She went off with them to harass the boys. I went to find my friends. As usual, Alan and Jeff found a table on the side of the dance.

Alan was dressed as a pimp. I hoped that Gina was dressed like a prostitute. Jeff was in an Aladdin-looking outfit. At least his date could be a princess.

"Who did you bring?" Alan asked.

"Tracy."

Jeff just shook his head.

"Did you bring a date?" I asked, as I looked at Jeff.

"I'm here with Gina's sister."

"Oh, Emily, I like her. She's funny."

Alan smirked, and he and Jeff looked at each other. Something was up. I looked towards the restrooms and saw Gina walking back with a vision. It was Kara. She was dressed as a princess from India, and I could feel my desire start in my toes and travel all the way to the hair on my head. My sexual attraction to Tracy was close to a ten. She pushed almost every button I had. Kara was off the charts.

My reaction was obvious because Alan and Jeff looked at me wide-eyed. Gina warned me that the attraction between us would be intense, but I just couldn't deal with something like this right now. I shook my head and looked at both of my best friends. I turned to Jeff.

"So, are you two…?" I asked.

"No, Gina asked me to be her date for tonight," Jeff said giving me a look. "Kara seems nice, but she isn't interested in me. This was just a setup so Kara could go to the dance. I think Gina's plan was for you to meet her."

"Are you cool with that?" I asked, because I didn't want to hurt my friend's feelings.

"We're good. Alan and I think you two will hit it off."

I just shook my head.

"No, not now. You have a good time tonight. Enjoy it. Every guy here'll be envious when they see you on the dance floor with her. I better take off before I start hitting on your date."

I spun around, making my cape billow. If you have a cape, you have to use it. I headed to the other side of the dance floor. I didn't dare look back at the exotic goddess that was Kara Tasman. I found Tracy and her band of Catwomen, and I stepped right into the middle of them. Tracy snorted when she saw my dazed look, and the lust level of her fellow cheerleaders ramped up. Before I knew it, I had hands running all over my body. I discovered that tights are just barely better than being nude. I looked at Tracy and my eyebrows went up, causing her to giggle. She waded in and started peeling them off me.

"Ladies, he's my date tonight."

Kim decided to be the spokeswoman for the group.

"You and David broke up. I do believe I was there when it happened. Rumor has it that he's single. The varsity cheerleaders got their shot. It's our turn now."

I was now in my element, teasing beautiful women.

"Okay, Kim's right, I'm a free man, and I have nothing against you girls. You're all very nice to look at, but I think you can all agree that there is only one of me and," I counted noses, "twelve of you. Do you mind if I narrow the field?"

Kim had a smug look on her face.

"No, please do."

All the other girls nodded.

"Okay, who currently has a boyfriend or is seeing someone?"

Kim glared at me because she knew that I knew who she was dating. Seven of the girls raised their hands, leaving five. One of the five was Tracy.

I motioned Kim, Mona, and Sammie over, and we got close so only they could hear.

"I don't know how to ask this without sounding like a pig. You know me, so don't kill me for asking. Which ones are virgins?"

All three of them gave me a look. I needed to clarify.

"If things progress, I don't want to be responsible for taking someone's virginity for casual sex. I think you all agree that the first time should be special."

It dawned on them, and they pointed out two who were moved to the side. That left Tracy and two other girls. I leaned in and asked my helpers.

"Okay, should I just pick Tracy?"

Sammie got in my face.

"If you pick Tracy, none of us will ever speak to you again. Carol and Reese both have big crushes on you. They're also a lot of fun, if you know what I mean."

"One at a time, or both at once?" I asked.

That got a chuckle.

"You better just do one at a time. You have a big game tomorrow, and we'd hate to see what happens if those two tag-team you." Mona said.

I nodded. That was a very good point.

"The winners of 'win a date with David Dawson' are Reese and Carol," I announced, and looked at the group.

They both came bounding up to me and wrapped themselves around me. Tracy just rolled her eyes.

"Okay, ladies, one of you gets me for the night. The other gets me Friday night."

They put their heads together, and Carol picked tonight. She dragged me onto the dance floor. When the song ended, one of the dance committee members made an announcement.

"Don't forget to vote for your favorite male and female costume. Right now we have a hot competition brewing, so every vote counts."

I took Carol over to the refreshment table to get her a soda.

"Carol, what year are you?"

"I'm a sophomore. Can I say something without making you mad?"

"Why not, everyone else seems to think it's okay."

She pondered her statement.

"Now that I think about it, I don't want to come across as a bitch."

"Carol, just say it."

"Why are you so stuck-up?"

Okay, I hadn't expecting that. I needed more information before I could decide if I was pissed or not. Right now, I was leaning towards pissed.

"You know, no one wants to come off as stuck-up. How could I change so I'm not stuck-up?"

"Well, for starters, you only hang out with upperclassmen. I've never seen you at one of the freshman or JV games. You never go to any of the parties. You're always in a hurry and never make time to speak to anyone in your classes. I don't know, you, you seem like a jerk."

Was it even worth defending myself? I hung out with upperclassmen because I played varsity football. I didn't go to the freshman and JV games because I practiced or worked out when they played. I didn't party because I didn't drink. I was in a hurry because I had a lot to do.

It wasn't worth it. I was attracted to older girls because of crap like this. There was no need to get mad. Not everyone would like me.

"Thanks for being honest with me. I'll work on that. Hey, I want to say hi to some of my friends. Are you opposed to meeting some upperclassmen?"

She didn't say anything, so I headed over to where Magic and Luke had a table. I noticed that Carol had followed me over. I guess I wasn't getting rid of her that easy.

"Oh my God! It's porn-star Superman!" Luke said, as he hit himself in the head.

"Did they run out of adult-size outfits?" Magic added, as he put his two cents in.

"I think he looks hot," Cindy said, coming to my rescue.

They all threw their napkins at her. I came up with an idea on how to get rid of my 'date.'

"Guys, this is Carol Wirth. She's a JV cheerleader. She had the misfortune of winning a date with me tonight. As you all know, I'm a stuck-up jerk," I said, and then turned to Carol.

Leave it to my friends to agree wholeheartedly with that statement. I looked around the table and saw Bill Callaway, who seemed to be the only single boy at the table. Bill was a good-looking guy and my wide receiver. Being a new starter, the girls hadn't found him yet. Carol would be a good fit for him.

"I brought her over here to see if maybe an upperclassman would show her a better time. Bill, would you be opposed to dancing with Carol?"

Bill got up and asked Carol to dance. I saw her smile at him. Maybe this would work out.

"You okay?" Luke asked.

"Thanks for asking, but I'm okay," I said and then I grinned. "You're not going to believe my last date."

Everyone gathered around.

"Tami sets me up," I began.

I told them about being stranded overnight.

"So that's why I'm off the market. No more girlfriends until at least after football."

"If I had your luck, I wouldn't date either," Magic said as he shook his head.

I glanced over at Cindy, and she wouldn't even meet my eyes.

"Are you coming to my party tonight? I know you don't drink, but maybe we could hook you up."

"I appreciate the offer, but I need to be ready for the game tomorrow."

"We know, but every party needs a stuck-up jerk, and you're our favorite one."

"I love you guys, too."

I was between tables when Gina caught me.

"Oh David, I have someone you need to meet."

"Dang it! I saw your sister, and she was better-looking in person. I need to focus on football right now. Can I meet her after the season?"

Gina gave me the look that Tami does when I'm being stupid.

"Come on. Meet my sister. You two are perfect for each other."

"Gina," I said, and then just sighed. "Okay, this is for you."

We walked over, and Kara took one look at me.

"Great, you make me meet all your loser friends, and now you bring over some pretty boy with a fake-muscle shirt and stuffed shorts."

I broke out in a huge grin and hugged Gina.

"Thank you. I'm no longer infatuated. Kara, it was nice to meet you."

I turned around and walked away. I heard Jeff and Alan burst out laughing.

This was turning into the worst dance I had ever attended. I might as well put another nail in the coffin. I tracked down Reese.

"Hey, I wanted to take a moment and talk to you."

She looked nervous. I might as well let her off the hook.

"Look, I know you accepted this date under less than ideal circumstances. Carol told me that I'm a stuck-up jerk. Another girl called me a fraud. If you want out, just let me know. The last thing I need right now is a pity date."

Hysterical laughter was not what I was expecting. That tore it! I was out of there. I felt my face get red. I was so done with women. I turned to leave and headed toward the door. I lost myself in the crowd as I walked to the door. I stopped myself. I needed to tell Tracy I was done with the dance. I found her talking to Mona.

"Hey, I'm leaving."

"What's wrong?" Tracy asked.

"I'm just not into this tonight," I said. I didn't want her tagging along. "Look, you stay and have fun with your friends. I'll walk home and see you tomorrow."

She looked concerned.

"Are you sure?"

"Yeah, have fun."

I made it to the front door and slammed the crash bar. It was a nice fall night. Maybe it was a little too cold to be running around in tights. At least now I could hear myself think. The music was starting to give me a headache. It was a good thing I wasn't going to Magic's party. I could have easily gotten drunk tonight. My mind went in circles. When I got home, I took a shower and went to bed.

✦✦✦

Friday November 1

When I got to practice, Bo and Coach Lambert were waiting for me. Coach Lambert had some bad news.

"David, did you go to Magic's party last night?"

"No, sir."

Both Bo and Coach seemed to relax.

"Last night the party was raided by the police. They arrested twenty-six football players for underage drinking. In one of the bedrooms, they found a girl who was half naked. That's why they arrested everyone. They're all getting DNA tests to see if they were involved. I've been on the phone with the athletic director and principal. We've decided to suspend all twenty-six players for tonight's game."

"Oh man." I was worried about Tracy. "Does one of you have a cell phone?"

Coach Lambert gave me his. I called Tracy's cell, and she answered.

"Thank God. Are you okay?"

"I'm fine, what's going on?"

"Did you go to Magic's party last night?"

"No, I'm not allowed to go to something like that."

"Good. The party got busted and we lost twenty-six players."

"That sucks."

"It gets worse. A girl was found in one of the bedrooms, and it looks like she might have been molested. Check on your girls and make sure they're all okay."

"What's going to happen?"

"I don't know. I'll see you at school." I needed her to take care of a couple of things. "Can you grab my stuff, and then call Kendal and let her know?"

"I'll take care of things. Focus on football."

"Tracy, you're the best. When the season's over, I want to work on building our friendship again."

"I love you, David. Don't worry about anything. Just get ready for the game."

✧✧✧

Coach Lambert was able to get both Kevin Goode and me excused from classes. It turned out Kevin and I were the only two starters that didn't go to the party. We met in the coaches' conference room. We were trying to put together a roster of scout team, JV, and freshman players. The biggest problem we had on offense was that the JV and freshman teams still ran the veer. There was a huge debate as to which offense we should run.

Bo Harrington slammed his hand on the desk to get everyone to shut up.

"Do you all remember why you switched offenses? Because this young man ran circles around your starting defense with scout-team players. You need five key players: a center that can get the ball back in the shotgun, a left tackle, and three guys that can actually catch a pass. If you find us that, we can at least be competitive."

Everyone was quiet for a minute. Then Coach Lambert took charge. By 4:00 that afternoon, the coaching staff had put together an offense and defense. They would have a limited number of plays, but it looked workable. It was decided that we would use the JV special teams because we didn't have time to work on those for kickoffs and punts.

We got some good news from the legal front. It turned out that the girl in question was with her boyfriend at the party. She'd passed out and Magic had moved her to a bedroom to sleep it off. The DA had dropped all the drinking charges. He didn't have the resources nor the will to prosecute all those cases. The desire to prosecute went down once the rape aspect was cleared up. He was also up for reelection and didn't want to be known as the guy that ended our football season. Coach Lambert was a different matter: he wouldn't allow them to play. He would let them dress in street clothes and participate in the Senior Night festivities. A decision on next week's game was up in the air.

Bo took me aside late in the afternoon.

"Watch yourself tonight. If they knock you out, this game is over."

"That's true of every game, but I'll be careful."

"I hate to put any more pressure on you, but you have to win tonight. Not just to get into the playoffs, but to make both Coach Lambert and Coach Engels viable candidates for jobs. If it looks like they lost control of this team, they may not even be back here. You have to win."

"Great. Any ideas?"

"Keep your head on a swivel. One of your strengths is your running. If in doubt, tuck it and run. Finally, take shots downfield. You need big plays to offset your weaknesses. Other than that, don't get killed."

"Let's hope that last one doesn't happen."

✦✦✦

At 4:30, our new team was in shorts and t-shirts, learning the offense. Most of the replacements were juniors who were on the scout team. There were a couple of exceptions. One was a behemoth of a left tackle. He was six-five, 250-pound freshman, Wolf Tams. Seeing him, I had dreams of Jim and Wolf anchoring the offensive line next year.

After seeing Wolf block in shorts, I was pissed he hadn't been given a shot at varsity. He was agile and had good hands. I could see him playing tight end at the next level. The basketball coach was excited that they thought they'd found a power forward.

The other player was a little five-two, 135-pound freshman tailback named Ed Pine. He was lightning quick with moves that made me wonder how anyone could touch him. The problem was that I needed someone to help pick up blitzes, and he didn't have the size. I talked to Coach Engels, and we decided to use two fullbacks or a fullback and a tight end. We moved Ed to a slot receiver where we could utilize his speed.

The problem with running around in shorts and t-shirts was that everyone looked good. I guess we would see how good we were when the game started.

I had a few minutes before the game, so I sent a text to Kendal to meet me. She was busy at the hospitality tent, so I went to her. When I walked in, I suddenly had a microphone and camera shoved in my face. The press was in a frenzy about the arrests, and the local TV stations wanted sound bites for their early news. I heard one of the producers say begin a countdown.

"We are live in 3, 2," he said a silent 'one.'

"Kim Bowman with Channel 3 News. We are live with David Dawson, Lincoln High's quarterback. David, do you have any comment on the arrest of most of your starting players for tonight's game?"

I smiled into the camera as Tracy had trained me.

"It's unfortunate that a little fun had such consequences." Tracy taught me to answer the question but then turn it to my central message. “The coaching staff has been challenged to come up with a plan to deal with our situation. What you’re going to see tonight is an outmanned team rise to the occasion. Coach Lambert and Coach Engels have me convinced that we will come away with a win tonight.”

The cameraman switched back to Kim who stood with her mouth open. She shook her head and turned to the camera.

“No one can say that David lacks confidence. I think we are in for something special tonight.”

"We’re out!” said the cameraman.

“Do you really think you have a chance?” Kim asked.

“Kim, I have faith in our coaching staff. I also know our players. Kevin Goode and I will not lie down. We will find a way to win this game.”

A big guy in Alabama gear, who I could only assume was a recruiter, stepped forward out of the crowd.

“Son, I love your attitude. Win or lose tonight, you’ll go far with an outlook like that. After watching you play two weeks ago and listening to you tonight, I’m a huge fan.”

He reached out and shook my hand. Kendal swooped in before I ‘bumped’ into any more recruiters or reporters. We stepped outside the tent and headed around back where we could be alone.

“Mayor Doxsee has just cancelled on us for the Senior Night presentation.”

“Coach Lambert can handle it. They’re his players. What did you get the seniors?”

“We got the players plaques with their football picture on it. For the moms, we have flowers. For the parents and siblings, we have t-shirts that say ‘Senior Pride’ and their son’s number on the back. They’ve been picking those up before the game. We got sponsors to pick up the tab on all this stuff.”

"Good job. Be sure to tell your team how happy I am. I've got to get ready."

Kendal surprised me when she gave me a hug and a kiss on the cheek. The glint in her eye made me nervous.

"Go get 'em."

✧✧✧

Kevin and I changed our normal pregame routines to walk around and talk to nervous players. By the time we walked out of the locker room, everyone was ready. We ran out onto the field to a packed house. Even the temporary bleachers in the north end zone were packed. The marching band found a bunch of cowbells, so they were adding to the noise.

I took in the scene and realized that for many of my teammates, this could be their last home game. I got a little emotional thinking about all the good times we'd had on this field. I couldn't imagine this being my last game at home. There was a special energy that was created when your fans were behind you. We would need them tonight if we hoped to win.

I scanned the stands to find my family and friends. I broke out laughing when I saw Alan and the gang all wearing Double D t-shirts, and they had them stuffed to look like they had huge boobs. I pointed at them, and they started chanting, 'Double D, Double D!' This got the crowd going, so I pumped my fist in time with their chant. The place was rocking.

Before the national anthem, they recognized the seniors. It was subdued seeing all but Kevin in street clothes. I'm sure they all wanted at least one playoff game at home so they could play one more time in front of our fans.

The visiting team won the toss and elected to take the ball. The JV team lined up to kick off and boomed it out of the end zone. The visitors had the ball at the 20 yard line.

The first play was a simple trap play that turned into disaster: Kevin slipped and fell, and that was all the back needed to rumble 80 yards for the score. The life was sucked out of the crowd until we saw the flag.

Our opponent was a .500 team because they made a lot of mistakes. They'd lined up in an illegal formation that just cost them a score. The ball was moved back five yards, and we repeated first down. The next two plays found them flagged for delay of game and one for them being offside. They were now on their 5 yard line. The next three plays worked them back to the original line of scrimmage at the 20 yard line. The defense had held and forced a punt.

We got the ball back on our 34 yard line. We huddled up, and I called the first play.

"Twins, Shotgun, Option Left on two. Ed, I want you back at tailback for this play."

"Down! Set. Hut, HUT!"

The snap was high, and I had to jump up to grab it. I didn't have time to put the ball into the fullback's belly, so I just went down the line to the left. Wolf brush-blocked the defensive end to slow him down and then released him. He saw me coming, and he was in no-man's-land: he needed to commit to either Ed or me. He chose me. I'd learned my lesson, and instead of running him over, I pitched the ball to Ed. I took the hit to slow down the defensive end's pursuit.

Ed cut up the field, and he was faced with a strong safety closing fast. Ed jab-stepped and spun, which left the safety to wonder where his jockstrap was. Ed did his best Barry Sanders imitation. The spin slowed his momentum, which allowed the defense to close, but Ed had another gear and burst free. No one would catch him as he scored.

From that point, the game turned into a contest of ineptitude. At halftime, I was 6 of 20 passing, with 10 dropped balls, 4 interceptions, and had been sacked four times. Two of the dropped balls should have been scores. We went into halftime with a 7–0 lead.

Ed was flattened on the second series and didn't come back into the game. At halftime, I found him.

"How are you feeling?"

"I got my bell rung. I'm okay for the second half."

"You know the freshman and JV players. Who can catch the damn ball?"

"Wolf can, and once he gets going, he's a load."

I grabbed Coach Engels and Wolf and we went out back of the locker room.

"Wolf, run a slant."

On the snap, he came off the ball better than I expected, and I threw a high fastball just to see if he could catch it. He reached up and snagged it out of the air.

Coach Engels eyes got big and I smiled.

"Go down ten yards and do a buttonhook," Coach said.

Wolf went down ten yards and before he turned, I sent a rope towards where I knew his chest would be. I expected the ball to bounce off him, but as he turned, he saw it coming and caught it. I did a fist pump.

"Yes!"

We went into the locker room and looked like cats that ate the canary. Coach Engels got Coach Lambert and Coach Harrington's attention. They were soon huddled up. Coach Lambert looked at me and motioned me over.

"Is this for real?"

"His hands are as good as Bill's. If we can get Ed back into the slot, I can use them to move the ball. We just have to be careful and not get Ed hurt."

"Okay, you go get ready for the second half."

When we went out for the second half, I was excited. Wolf was given a new number so he could play tight end. We got the ball to start the second half. Our kickoff-return team put us in the hole, and we started at our 6 yard line. The crowd got nervous, and you could feel them wanting to get excited about something. On the first play, we ran a quick slant for Wolf, and he caught the ball in traffic. It took three of them to pull him down for a seven-yard gain.

On the next play, Wolf got tied up at the line of scrimmage, which threw the timing off the play. I went through my reads and found the only open guys were the ones that couldn't catch. That was when I got blasted by the left defensive end. He planted his helmet in my lower back and slammed me to the ground. Somehow, I bounced back up. The ref threw his flag for the spearing penalty on the defensive end.

I had a shooting pain in my lower back, and I could feel it tighten up instantly. We needed to score quick and often before I couldn't walk. My new left tackle was almost in tears.

"David, I'm so sorry. Are you alright?"

"What do you think? That frickin' hurt!"

I looked at the entire offensive line.

"Look, if you have to tackle someone to keep me from getting killed, please do. We'll deal with a penalty, but I can't take too many more of those kinds of hits."

The next four plays we walked the ball down the field using Wolf on a variety of plays. I could see the defense start to cheat towards Wolf.

"Okay, everyone focus. This one puts the game away. We'll run the same play, but this time I want Ed to half-ass it. I'll pump-fake to Wolf, and then Ed, I'll hit you on a post."

What do they say about the best-laid plans? Wolf went out 10 yards and did his buttonhook, as planned. I pumped, and that's when I felt the big hand of the defensive end grab my facemask. I ducked my head to keep him from jerking my helmet off. I tucked the ball and stepped into the vacated hole the defensive end left. The outside linebacker had a bad angle on me. I lowered my shoulder, and you could hear the distinctive crack of pads that signaled a big hit. He slid off and I broke into their secondary. I was run out of bounds after a twenty-three yard gain.

We declined the penalty and ran the same play. This time they bit on the pump even harder. I lofted a long pass to Ed. The whole stadium held their breath as the ball sailed down the field. I was sure I had overthrown him, but he had more speed than I knew. He caught the ball in stride and walked into the end zone. With the extra point, our fans finally had something to cheer about.

At the end of the third quarter we scored on an interception return to put us up 21–0. Coach Lambert had the trainers hide my helmet and made me go in for treatment on my back. The seniors who'd been suspended snuck into the locker room right before the game ended and found me getting a massage. Luke cracked up.

"Dawson, you take the cake. Are you getting a manicure after this?"

When he got closer, he saw the huge red mark on my back that was starting to blacken. He got serious.

"Dude, are you okay?"

"No, but Becky knows what she's doing. She's fixed worse. If you ever get the chance to have Becky get her hands on you, I recommend it."

Crack. She smacked my ass. Luke cringed.

"Dumbass, never piss off a trainer, especially when they're working on you."

"You know me, I'm a slow learner. What's the score?"

"We're up 24–7 with less than a minute to go. You better get dressed before everyone sees what a lazy good-for-nothing you really are."

Becky had me sit up. She put an ice pack on my back, and then wrapped me with an ace bandage to hold it in place.

"Leave that on for 30 minutes and then come back."

The locker room exploded when the team came running in. The seniors gave everyone high fives and hugs.

Coach Lambert came in, and, when he saw me, he froze. I gave him thumbs up, and I could see him relax. Everyone had learned their lesson, so there were no parties tonight. The team planned to go to Monical's. I sought out Wolf and Ed to make sure they were going. They were all smiles when the seniors told them that they were buying tonight.

✧✧✧

I was one of the last ones out of the locker room. I found Reese waiting for me.

"You ready to go?"

"Excuse me?"

She looked confused.

"You said we had a date tonight."

"I think that was before you laughed in my face. Reese, I'm sure you're a nice person, but I think Carol put it best. I'm a stuck-up jerk. So feel free to let everyone know."

"Hang on. I thought you were kidding."

I just shrugged and walked out. When I got to the parking lot, everyone was gone. There were fans hanging out, but the football team was at Monical's. I saw the Alabama guy as he walked up to me.

"Looks like you need a ride."

I shook my head.

"Are you in anyway affiliated with the University of Alabama?"

"Good question. Yes, I am. I'm a major donor and as such, I shouldn't give you a ride. But my girlfriend isn't, and she can drive you."

His girlfriend was cute and in her mid-30s. She about talked my arm off about the virtues of Alabama's football program. When we got to Monical's, I jumped out as soon as she came to a stop. There was a line out the door to get in. I saw Gina's sister, Emily, with her boyfriend, waiting to get in. I snuck behind her and had to hush people in line because they recognized me. I slid my arms around her stomach and put my lips next to her ear so she could feel my hot breath as I talked.

"Hey, Baby, I thought you dumped this guy so we could go out."

She spun around and gave me a hug. Her boyfriend wasn't sure if he should be mad or not.

"David, this is my boyfriend, Alex. Alex, this is the quarterback that we went to see tonight."

Alex got a big grin.

"All I can say is, wow. I almost crawled out of the stands and strangled your receivers. How many balls did they drop?"

"They were just nervous. We turned it around in the second half."

"I wish I could go to the game Saturday, but it's too far."

"It is a long way. I think it's a two-hour ride. We should see if we could get some buses to take everyone."

I put that on my list of things to talk to Kendal about. I grabbed Emily's hand.

"Come on, I know some people, and we have some tables for the team. Unless you guys want to sit alone?"

Alex gestured.

"Lead on."

We walked to the front and the hostess recognized me and waved us in. Alex and Emily saw Alan, Jeff, Gina, and Kara, so they went to talk to them. Most of the parents were there, so I went around and talked to them. I love parents. They all had pizza for me. I was talking to Luke's parents when I saw him coming over out of the corner of my eye.

"It's too bad Luke missed tonight's game. Coach is going to start Ed."

Luke's dad shook his head.

"Luke seemed to be playing well."

"Dad, you have to stop hanging around pampered quarterbacks." Luke said and rolled his eyes at me. "We found him in the training room, getting a massage."

"Luke is just jealous he didn't think of it."

"Show Dad your back."

I pulled up my shirt.

"Just take it off, honey. Give an old lady a thrill," one of the moms said.

I laughed out loud and pulled it over my head. I looked across the room and Gina nudged Kara. Kara's mouth dropped, and I winked at her.

"Dawson, you're such a slut," Luke groaned.

I just grinned and put my shirt back on. People clapped, and I waved to my fans. Luke smacked me on the arm. I glanced over, and I could see that everyone at Kara's table was giving her a hard time about her comments last night. I continued to meet the parents until I'd met everyone that was there. It was nice to see them proud of their sons.

I made a dash to the bathroom. I was starting to stiffen up, so I wanted to head home and take a hot shower. As I came out of the bathroom, Kara was waiting on me. I smiled at her, said 'Hi,' and kept walking.

I said goodbye to everyone and made my way outside. I'd planned to jog home to clear my mind until I noticed Kara had followed me out. I smiled at her again.

"I think I owe you an apology."

"Sorry, do I know you?" I asked, with a blank look on my face.

It was all I could do to keep a straight face. Kara was used to everyone knowing who she was and fawning over her. Greg taught me not to chase pretty girls. If you did, you would always be in that role. If Kara and I were to ever have a relationship, it would be as equals.

She bit her lower lip as she struggled to decide how to proceed.

"I guess technically you don't know me. I'm Kara Tasman. You know my sister Gina."

"Nice to meet you, Kara. I'm David Dawson." I started to turn. "I'll see you around."

"Why are you making this so hard?"

"I'm sorry, was I supposed to do something?" I asked, and gave her my best confused look.

She started to get mad.

"Are you gay or something?"

I saw red. When were women going to stop treating me like shit?

"I think I'm lucky I don't know you. I don't get it. I've been nothing but polite to you, yet you feel the need to attack my sexuality. If I wanted this kind of abuse, I could just get a girlfriend. I don't have time for this crap. Go abuse some other guy."

"Sorry."

"Don't give me that bullshit 'sorry' line again. When you grow up and quit looking down on people, give me a call, and we might be able to be friends."

I hate it when I come off as some kind of preachy bastard. Kara's eyes filled up with tears, and then she cried. This was Superman's kryptonite, a woman's tears. I opened my arms and pulled her to me as she started to sob. Of course that was the moment Gina, Emily, and the gang walked out. The two sisters gave me an evil look as they wondered what I'd done to their sister.

"What did you say, 'stupid boy'?" Alan asked.

"Alan, Tami can get away with that, but I'll beat the cowboy shit out of you if you don't shut up."

Jeff grabbed Alan's arm and took him out of harm's way.

"Kara, Emily will give us a ride home," Gina said.

Kara just nodded against my chest. She stopped crying, but she held me in a death grip. Once they left, she grabbed my hand and led me to her car. I got in. She asked me where I lived, and she gave me a ride home. I got out of the car without saying a word. She just followed me into my apartment. She sat on the couch, deep in thought, so I went and took my shower. I let the hot water run until it started to cool off. I threw on a pair of shorts and walked out, drying my hair. She was checking me out.

"You ready to be friends?" I asked.

"Yes, I need a real friend right now."

I looked at her seriously, weighing what she said.

"Just so you know I don't need more than a friend right now."

"Agreed." She looked me in the eyes. "Everyone tells me you're the best guy they know. I really am sorry for acting like a spoiled brat. I've had to be that way for too long when working."

"What do you do?" I asked.

I sat down on the couch with her.

"I model, and I get hit on all the time. When you didn't chase me, I didn't know how to react. Both Gina and Emily told me that you wouldn't just fall at my feet."

"I can see that you're a beautiful woman, but you don't need me to tell you that." I thought for a moment. "Tell me the truth. Would you really respect me if I did fawn all over you?"

"No, I'd think you were just another drooling pretty boy."

"You think I'm pretty?"

She finally smiled.

"Are you digging for a compliment?"

"I guess I'm trying to figure out if you think I'm pretty-gay or pretty-studly."

"I'm thinking you're pretty dorky."

"Wow, I'm thinking you're pretty mean."

"Yes, I am. What did Alan call you, 'stupid boy'?"

"Oh hell no! You did not hear that."

She giggled. I started to like her and it scared me.

"Kara, I don't know if I can be your friend."

"What makes you say that?"

"I'm afraid I'll want to be more than friends. If we're going to do this, you have to know I'm crazy attracted to you. You'll have to be the strong one."

"Well, then, we're in trouble, because it's all I can do to keep my hands off you."

"This is bad. I think this is what Gina warned me about. Look, I've had a string of relationships that have gone up in flames in spectacular ways in the past few weeks. I'm more than a little gun-shy right now."

"Why don't you just give me a kiss to hold us over until you're ready?" Kara asked, and gave me her best little-girl pout.

"You're evil incarnate. I used almost that same line last Saturday."

"Did it work?"

"I'm ashamed to say, yes."

"Is it going to work today?"

I sighed and whispered, "Yes."

Our first kiss did it. It was far more intense than a first kiss should be. We broke away from each other as if we were scared virgins. The intensity sent a shiver through me. Kara was the aggressor. She pushed me back onto the couch and crawled up my body. This reminded me of my first time. She let her hair fall on my face to tickle me. Her eyes held mine to let me know that she intended to own me. She squirmed and rubbed her body against me. I about went insane with lust.

She straddled my waist and she found my arousal. I grabbed her hips to guide her movements. I felt that familiar buildup and worried it would all be over way too soon. I initiated a kiss, which stopped her grinding motion and saved me from embarrassing myself. She bit my lip. The sudden pain helped me focus for a moment. I sat up with her draped over me. I pulled my lips from hers and my emotions took over. I whimpered as tears welled up in my eyes, and I took a ragged breath to try not to cry.

She stroked my face.

"Baby, what's wrong? Why are you crying?"

"It's too much. I'm an emotional mess right now. I've been trying to hold down my feelings. Every girl I've been with in the past few weeks has hurt me in some way. I'm avoiding dealing with my emotions because I'm in the middle of football season. I'm scared if I break down, I'll fall into a deep depression. In the last few days, I've seen signs that I'm breaking."

"It sounds like you need something positive in your life right now. Let me help you. Let me into your life, David Dawson. From our first kiss, I knew you were the one I've been looking for. I want to smell you, taste you, touch you, hear you. I want you, I need you."

With her last words, she grasped me through my shorts. I stiffened and let my head fall back as my eyes closed. I caught my breath and then looked at the lust in her face.

"God, Kara, please stop. I don't trust myself right now. You have to be strong for both of us. Please," I begged.

She let me up, and I went to my bed and lay down facing the wall. I heard her go through my dresser. She made a quick call.

"Hey, I'm at David's," she said. "Yes, you were right; he is special. I'll see you in the morning."

The lights went out, and she crawled into bed with me. I felt her spoon me and wrap her arms around my middle. She lightly kissed the back of my neck. I drifted off to sleep as I felt her warm body pressed to mine.

✧✧✧

I woke with a start and just stared at the ceiling. Had I made a mistake in not going all the way with Kara? I didn't know any guys my age who would've turned her down.

Why had I? Was I really a ‘stupid boy’? There was such a thing as a one-night stand, and people seemed to be fine with them.

I looked over at her sleeping face and sighed. I’d made the right call. I wanted Kara to be more than just a meaningless tryst. I felt a real connection there and someday there might be more. I’d give up instant gratification to hopefully develop something more meaningful, even if it turned out we would just be friends.

Maybe that was a sign of growing up. The last few months had been interesting, and I felt I was starting to get my feet under me. I just hoped that the next few months would be even better. I looked at Kara and smiled. If someone like this was in my life, I knew it would be.

✧✧✧

More Books by G. Younger

Sell Anything On Craigslist!

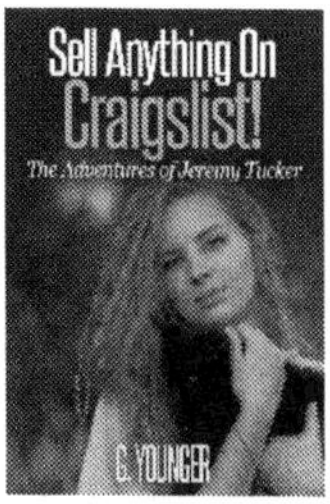

Jeremy Tucker thought he lived in the most boring town in the world. This town held its residents in the palm of its hand, and it knew everything about everyone that lived there—the good, the bad, every sin, every secret. This quiet little town was about to change, and all because he put an ad on craigslist. Some would say he was a genius, while others would accuse him of being the Devil himself. Read his story and you decide.

Excerpt:

I used to think our little town, tucked away in the mountains of West Virginia and buried in the backwoods, was the most boring spot on the planet. This was the place where nothing exciting happened and nothing was ever going to change. The place felt like it was a movie set from the 1950s. Each morning, as the sun began to peek over the ridge of the valley, you would hear the old milk truck shuddering down the back alley as he made his delivery just like it had been done for over 75 years. People liked tradition, and change was not easily welcomed.

As the sun would reach the crest of the ridge, people would be up and about, which was irritating for the teens in our town. My Grandma Tucker always said, '*Be thankful for another day, you never know when it might be your last, so don't miss a second of it*, which was usually followed with, *Get your butt out of bed!'* People were early risers, and by the time I was out of the house the old women would be sitting on their front porches, slowly rocking with a steaming cup of coffee clutched in their hands, watching everything that happened.

Our little town was great for kids, because we were allowed to run wild. No one worried about someone snatching a child like they did in the big cities. In our little town, everyone knew each other, and kept an eye out. While we were allowed our freedom, there was a price. If you did anything wrong, it beat you home, and there was a butt-whupping waiting for you. My granny was an *expert* with a hickory switch…

Our little town had a rhythm. Mondays were back to work or school; Tuesday was laundry day; Wednesday evening was church; Thursday was for doing the grocery shopping at the Shop 'N Save, the only grocery store in town; Friday was for football; Saturday you did your chores; and Sunday was for church and family.

This little town held us in the palm of its hand, and it knew everything about us; the good, the bad, every sin, every secret, and everything was known about each and every resident. Most people were from here. You could trace family trees back many generations to the Founders. Only a few ever left, and if they did, you never saw them again. My secret desire was to be one of the few. I wanted to be a writer, and to do that I needed to experience life outside our little town.

Our quiet little town was about to change, and all because I put an ad on Craigslist.

While normal folk cut their grass, or made out at the overpass, my imagination was taking flight. Some would say I was a genius, while others would accuse me of being the Devil himself. What they all agreed upon was that I was justified in what I'd done.

Notes from Author

Thank you for reading *Stupid Boy: The Beginning*. I hope you enjoyed this book. If you have a moment to post a review to let others know about the story, I would greatly appreciate it! I love hearing from fans.

Want to know when I release new books? Here are some ways to stay updated:

- Visit my website at: **www.GYounger.com**

Thank you again and I hope we meet again between the pages of another book.

Greg

80415650R00346

Made in the USA
San Bernardino, CA
27 June 2018